"Shut up, Collier. I'm serious."

Collier took her words and tone more as a challenge than a warning. "So, why not me, Mira, huh?"

"What are you talking about?"

"I've seen you leave Dave's with a guy now and again. You're not all that selective. Why not me?" He stood and took a step toward her.

She tensed, a predator ready for the kill. "Maybe you're not man enough for me." Her faced glowed in conquest. "Maybe I'm not interested in standing in for that ghost you won't let go."

Collier took another step. He stood inches from her, close enough to feel her icy tension. "What would you know about my ghosts?" He forced his words out though his throat tightened.

"I know you're freaking out because you have to go back to Nashville. You don't want to because there's some woman there who rejected you." She returned his glare. "You want to talk about waste of talent? I might get a little wild, but at least I feel!" She made a fist and pounded a spot over her heart. "I feel. I react. That's what humans do. You're frozen. You're frozen and you can't function because of some bitch who doesn't want you."

"Shut your mouth!" Collier leaned in, his arms braced on either side of her. He leaned closer, desire crackled and sparked between them. "You don't have any of the qualities she has."

Mira tipped her head to whisper directly into his ear. "I must have something, though, Collier, because you're here with me, not with her."

For a heartbeat, Collier locked his gaze with hers, a toxic mix of rage and desire coursing through him. "You've got nothing but bad attitude and tattoos, and you wear them both like some kind of armor." Collier grabbed her arm and shoved up the multiple sleeves. He stared at the exposed skin, stunned. Shooting a glance at her face, Collier saw the tears well up in her eyes, though her face remained frozen. "Mira, what the hell?"

1

A HERO'S SPARK

SPARK

by

SARAH J.

BRADLEY

This is a work of fiction. Names, characters, places, and incidents either are the product of the author's imagination or are used fictitiously, and any resemblance to actual persons living or dead, business establishments, events, or locales, is entirely coincidental.

A HERO'S SPARK

Cover art by Sarah J. Bradley

SJB Books/ Sarah J. Bradley
Twitter: @sarah_theauthor
Web: itcanonlyhappentosarah.blogspot.com
Facebook: www.facebook.com/sjbbooks

Published in the United States of America

For everyone who ever felt alone, useless or broken: Every day you get up and face the world, you are a hero to someone.

For Tom, Peter and Hannah: you are my heroes every day.

4

A hero is somebody who voluntarily walks into the unknown.

Tom Hanks.

COLLIER

"I swear if he makes us play that song one more time I'm going to stuff cheese fritters in my ears."

Startling from a doze, Collier James tried to sort out whether the speaker was Nate Stillman, or the older brother, Monroe. It didn't matter, since one or the other was always mad at him. Collier wasn't sure when he'd fallen asleep, but he was surprised to note it was night. Through the small window vents on the trailer he saw stars sparkling in the deep blue summer night sky. The window vents were just one source of dispute between him and his two band mates.

Everything has been a source of dispute between me and the guys for a long time…since we left Nashville on our summer tour.

Collier had known Monroe and Nate Stillman since they were kids growing up in the Nashville suburbs. They were neighbors, and the guys liked coming over when Collier's father was busy at the ice rink, coaching his Olympic hopefuls, which was pretty much all the time. After college, the friends started a trio. Collier's love of folk music melded nicely with the Stillman's blues grass harmonies.

6

The trio searched for a suitable venue for their expanding repertoire of folk music and sailing songs and found it at summer Renaissance Faires. They renamed the band the "Terrible Troubadours" and started touring. Everything was wonderful and successful.

Until Izzy. I was perfectly happy until Izzy showed back up in my life.

Collier blinked at the stars and wondered, not for the first time, if Izzy Marks, the love of his life and his father's favorite student, ever thought about him.

Doubtful, since she's married to the world's most heroic, handsome man, and they have a baby on the way.

He didn't envy Quinn Murray. Collier told himself that lie several times a day. It used to be true. Though he and Quinn had both lived in Nashville for several years, both famous in their own way, Collier had never envied the former hockey player turned sports radio color analyst. That is, until the day Izzy Marks fell in love with Quinn, and not Collier.

Collier had waited twenty years for Izzy to return to Nashville after running away with her skating partner. And, for twenty years and as many Renaissance Faires, Collier searched in vain for her face in the crowds. When she returned to Nashville, he thought he had a chance…until the moment she announced she carried Quinn Murray's child.

That was six months ago. He hadn't been home since.

Monroe and Nate took breaks from the road and headed home to see their parents and whatever women they happened to be dating, but Collier stayed away from Nashville, stayed in the trailer, and wrote songs. Most of the songs were pathetic, sad, and depressing dirges about his unrequited love. The Stillmans hated the songs.

The audiences loved them. Especially that one song.

After years of touring together, one song written with little thought threatened to tear the group apart.

Collier adjusted the window vents and stared at the brightest star. He was quite proud of that one song. He'd written it after a miserable gig in New York City at a Renaissance dinner theater. He was at the airport, eager to fly home to see Izzy. *I shouldn't have called her.*

It wouldn't have made one bit of difference.

And I got a song out of it.

While waiting for his plane, Collier called Izzy. Izzy told him she'd slept with Quinn for the first time. Collier's heart broke. From the pieces he gleaned the best song he'd ever written, a song he titled, "Thanks, No Thanks." Since then he made certain the Terrible Troubadours played it on every stage they crossed.

He breathed in the sticky night air and closed his eyes. The Stillmans, he knew, weren't angry because he liked having the window vents open. They weren't angry because he was writing a lot of songs.

No, they're angry because I insist on laying out my misery in front of every single person we play for, and the crowds love that one song more than any other. They're jealous because that song is a big reason we're doing so well this summer.

Collier ignored the discussion in the sitting area of the trailer. He was close enough to sleep to miss the point where it turned from a discussion to mutiny.

*

The Bristol Renaissance Faire grounds were miserable the next morning. The late summer Wisconsin heat continued to burn without mercy and the incessant wind only served to kick up the dust along the hard beaten paths. Collier, Monroe and Nate dragged their instruments to the tiny stage at the back of the park without much talk. Between the heat, the humidity, and the wind, Collier knew it was going to be a day heavy on exhaustion and light on tips.

He set his guitar case on the battered wooden stage and scanned the grounds. Few people came to the Fair Winds stage for the early show on a good weather day. *On a day like this, we'll be lucky to see a dozen people before noon.*

A few waited for the show, regulars he knew by name, people whose costumes were professionally made and who knew every word to every song The Terrible Troubadours wrote. Monroe and Nate greeted them while tuning their instruments. For Collier, the weather seemed to be a forewarning. Something was wrong but he couldn't put a finger on it.

"Hey, Col?"

Collier blinked and glanced at Monroe. "Yeah?"

"It's ten. You wanna start?"

Collier slung his guitar around his shoulder and nodded. "Good morning folks, thanks for coming out on a day like today. It sure is good to see some familiar faces." He paused for a smattering of applause. "So I'm thinking instead of playing a set, since we have just the very smartest people here this morning, why don't we take requests?"

Hands rose immediately, and the audience shouted song titles. Collier didn't hear them. He didn't need to. The guttural grunt from Monroe and the stony expression on Nate's face told him everything he needed to know. *Of course they're going to request my song. It's the only one that's even close to being fresh and new.*

He didn't play "Thanks, No Thanks," right away. He made the audience wait a bit. He told himself it was to keep from angering his band mates right away in the morning, but he knew, deep down, he held off singing his song until more people strolled toward the benches. His song, the one he wrote minutes after Izzy Marks broke his heart, was the song that brought in the tips, that sold the CD's, that kept the band fed when the crowds were slim.

When he finally did perform it, the benches in front of their little stage were packed. He stepped to center stage and strummed a few chords while Monroe and Nate, who had no part of the solo, stepped back and let Collier have his three minutes.

Collier focused, as he always did, on a woman in the back row. He had always pictured Izzy when he sang, but now her image was just too painful. He tried to erase her face from his mind's eye and replace it with another. This time, a young sandy-haired woman caught his attention and he sang to her.

There was something intriguing about her that went beyond her physical appearance. As Collier sang the woman did not, like so many, blush giggle and look away. She met his gaze and held it for the length of the song, as if daring him to convince her of something. Her eyes were green, the color green he'd only sung about in Irish folk songs. Something tugged at his frozen heart and for the first time in months he was able to see the woman in front of him without seeing a hint of Izzy.

He kept his gaze locked on hers the entire song, sensing he was suddenly speaking to her in a way he couldn't fully understand, but when the song was over, he didn't miss the tears welling in those beautiful green eyes. She stood, nodded to him, picked up an enormous shoulder bag and walked away. Only then, with the connection broken, did Collier hear the applause. He watched until she crested a hill. He wished he knew her story.

9

MIRA

Miranda Pierce, Mira to her friends, was furious with herself. She'd had every intention of sneaking out of the Renaissance Faire and escaping her sister, Madelyn's control once and for all. She was packed, she was ready to go. And Mira knew, if she didn't leave Madelyn's house, sooner or later, The Senator, Madelyn's husband, was going to knock on her door in the middle of the night. Again.

Living with Madelyn was lousy.

Waiting for The Senator to knock on her door was Mira's true nightmare.

Everything aligned as well as it could that morning for her to make her escape. And then she paused for a moment as a shred of music caught her attention. And now, because she stayed and listened to that hopelessly sad song, sung by a man who looked every bit as miserable as the song sounded, she was delayed enough that Madelyn, Dusty, and Carson, the family caretaker, found her.

"Aunt Mira, I thought you were getting me a bagel dog."

Mira looked at Dusty, marveling again how quickly he'd shed all hint of his babyhood. Recently turned twelve, he'd hit a growth spurt and stood nearly eye to eye with her. "I was, buddy, but then I heard this music and I just had to stop and listen for a minute."

Madelyn sniffed. Since childhood Mira recognized the sound of her sister's disapproval, though no one else likely heard the noise, or, if they did, put any weight on the common sound. A simple sniff carried with it years of disapproval and disappointment.

Well you should have done a better job of raising me instead of blaming me for our parents' deaths, and everything else that made you an unpleasant hag.

She shouldered her duffle, heavy with her belongings, her ever present sense of guilt, and now her fury with her own weakness. She ruffled Dusty's hair. "Come on. Let's get that bagel dog now."

"Mother, would you like one?" Dusty glanced over his shoulder at Madelyn.

"There is not one thing I'm eating here. Everything is so unsanitary."

"You'd eat a raw rat fast enough if there were cameras on you, and you know it." Mira spoke low enough so Dusty wouldn't hear.

"Well someone has to be aware of the image this family portrays. Not all of us can go around looking like homeless messes." Madelyn nodded to Mira's duffle. "Some of us have to behave and obey the rules."

Mira bit the inside of her lip, as she often did when tempted to shout at Madelyn. At twenty-eight, Mira was well beyond the age when most people live on their own. But Mira knew she not bear the idea of leaving Dusty alone with Madelyn, so her own perverse nature kept her ensconced in the house. Madelyn chafed every day seeing Mira. Mira reminded Madelyn of everything that could go wrong in her precariously balanced marriage to The Senator. The idea that she disturbed her sister's tightly controlled life gave Mira a little pleasure.

But now, Mira wanted to go and Madelyn wanted her gone. Unbidden, the singer, and the words of his sorrowful song, sprang to her mind. She knew how he felt, how hopeless he must have felt in writing and singing about longing to leave a hopeless situation and forget the pain that always came with leaving. She closed her eyes, recalling the singer, his gentle features, his steel grey eyes, the way he leaned over his guitar and sang, as if singing softly to a lover. She watched, in her mind's eye, how softly his strong, practiced hands touched each string. Mira glanced over her shoulder, hoping to catch a last look at him, but the crowd swarmed around the performers.

"Miranda, let's go." Madelyn's tone broke her focus.

Mira sighed and followed her sister and Dusty. *I can't leave yet. I have to stay for Dusty's sake. Dusty needs me.*

This was the mantra Mira kept in her heart for so long, and it was a hard one to break. As hard as she tried, as much as she ached to be free, it was going to take every ounce of concentration she had to leave Dusty. She was furious with herself for getting distracted from her goal. She was also furious with the singer.

Damn that man if his singing didn't keep me from my freedom.

COLLIER

"I'm tellin' you, Nate, I'm out. Either we stop playing that song or I'm walking."

Collier heaved himself off his bunk and left the air-conditioned comfort of the motor home. Monroe and Nate sat around a small fire, swatting mosquitoes and drinking beer. "Guys, is there a problem?"

"Yeah, there is." Monroe's antagonistic tone and the four beer cans at his feet put Collier on alert. "I'm sick to death of you getting all the glory while we're doing all the work."

Collier shot a glance at Nate, who seemed to be in the same state of inebriation, but a little less combative. "All the glory? We're a traveling minstrel band. Today we played four shows to maybe a hundred people. That's not what you'd call a ton of glory."

"Yeah, well you and your sappy sad song are getting everything."

Collier kicked some dust. "We split everything three ways, and you know it. That song does as much good for you as it does for me."

"Yeah, but your CD's outsell the band's and you get all of that. Everyone wants Collier's pretty song." Monroe crossed his arms.

Nate nodded. "And we're tired of getting shut out of our own shows."

Collier crossed his arms. "One song guys. One song. And it's been good for us all. Maybe instead of locking in on sailing songs and drinking songs we think about expanding our horizons a little and write more original material."

"See? I told you he'd say that. I told you he'd want to take control of everything." Monroe grumbled and Nate nodded.

"Look guys I don't want to take control of anything. I want us to be a great band."

"Well, we're not interested in changing. Except we want you out." Monroe drained a can and tossed it next to the others. "We want you out now."

"You can't be serious. Nate?"

Nate looked away, and belched.

12

"We've been together for a long time. We grew up together. Are you sure this is the way you want to go?"

Cold, stony silence from the Stillman brothers. Collier shrugged. "Fine. When we get back to Nashville after the Ohio Renaissance Faire, I'll clean my stuff out of the RV and go."

"No, you're out now."

"Monroe, be reasonable. Let me finish out the summer. We've got Ohio next weekend and then we're done."

"No, now. Tonight. Pack your stuff and leave."

Collier shrugged. *This will blow over when they sober up.* "Fine. I'll go and see if Sadie will let me sleep in the bakery tonight. That's where you'll find me if you change your minds."

"We won't."

Collier went back into the motor home and packed his duffle. He wasn't looking forward to sleeping above one of the faire shops. Many vendors did, in order to keep an eye overnight on their wares, but musicians camped in motor homes and tents outside the gates. Sadie, the woman who sold fresh baked cookies and deep fried dough treats on the hottest of days, was a friend to the band, but that didn't make her bakery floor any more comfortable. *One night and this will blow over.*

13

*

Collier woke to the hum of an engine. Sadie was loading the last of her equipment into her husband's panel van. "What time is it?"

"Almost noon."

Collier sat up quickly. "Noon?"

Sadie patted his shoulder. "You were exhausted. You needed the sleep. I didn't have the heart to wake you."

"Did Nate or Monroe come by yet?"

"No, but there was a lot of commotion out there last night. You know, last night together for the whole gang. Lots of stories and tall tales swapped one last time until we all get together next summer. I don't imagine any of those boys will stir until later."

Collier stood, body stiff, and picked up his duffle. "Well, thanks Sadie. You're very sweet to let me stay last night."

Sadie climbed into the van. "See ya next year, Col!"

He waved at the departing van, until the dust got to be too much. He walked slowly back to the RV lot. *By now they've slept it off and it'll all be okay.*

He reached their lot. The remnants of a campfire still smoldered, but the RV was gone. Collier scanned the nearly empty field, wondering if he'd gone to the wrong lot. *They wouldn't have just left me here, would they?*

"Collier! Man, what are you doing here?"

Collier squinted into the hot sunlight at the speaker. It the bass player from another group. "I slept over at Sadie's last night. The guys and I had artistic differences."

The other man frowned. "It was that song, right?"

"Yes! Yes, it was that song. Everything is because of that song!"

"Whoa, buddy, calm down. Everyone knew Nate and Monroe were worn out with that song. I personally wished I could write something half that awesome, I mean, it's a complete booty call. I bet you got a pile of tips, didn't you?"

Tips! Collier's heart sank. He'd been so confident the Stillmans were just kidding, he hadn't bothered to get any cash out of the safe. *So my ride is gone…and I have no cash.*

14

"Hey, man, can I give you a lift someplace?"

Collier closed his eyes. He had few friends and even fewer family members. He thought of his friends in Nashville, any one of whom would gladly wire him more than enough money to get home. *But I'm not ready to be more pathetic in Izzy's eyes. I couldn't take that.* "Where are you headed?"

"I'm goin' up to see my sister in Milwaukee. There's always some kind of festival goin' on at the lakefront there and she'll let me hang out there as long as I want. You could stay with me if you wanted."

Collier pondered the offer for a moment. "No, I can't impose like that. But I've got an uncle in Milwaukee. I can probably crash at his place for a day or two."

"Hop on in!"

Collier got into the car and leaned back in the cracked faux leather seat. He pretended to sleep for the hour-long drive. He didn't feel like making small talk while humiliation overwhelmed him.

*

It only took an hour to drive from the faire to the bus depot in Milwaukee, but Collier wandered up and down Milwaukee's lakefront for a long time, unable to gather the courage to call his uncle. Finally, with the last hint of sunshine fading behind the horizon, Collier dialed a cab company. Within minutes, a cab pulled to the curb and Collier crawled in and slouched in the back seat.

Once in front of his uncle's apartment building, Collier set down his duffle bag and scanned the classic architecture of the building. *This is the place I let myself get to. I'm standing outside this building, getting ready to beg from a family member I haven't seen in ages.*

I'm a complete cliché. I'm the broken hearted-musician with no place to go.

Collier shook his head and opened the door to the foyer of the building. It didn't take him long to find his uncle's nameplate and, swallowing his pride, Collier pushed the buzzer.

"Good evening?"

The formal greeting matched the formal building, but did not surprise Collier. "Hello Uncle Archie. It's me, Collier. Can I come up?"

15

MIRA

Mira slammed her bedroom door and kicked it for extra emphasis. She knew Madelyn heard her, Madelyn heard everything. She didn't care. It was over, it was done. She had to leave. This wasn't about Dusty. She needed to save herself.

The ride home from the Renaissance Faire the day before had been an icy affair. The sisters had long ago promised to never fight in front of Dusty and with him sitting between them, the long drive from Bristol at the Wisconsin/Illinois border through Milwaukee and up to Madison forced them into a cold truce. Once home, however, Dusty ran to his room and Madelyn attacked.

"I don't know what you think you're doing, but you're going to stop."

Mira dropped her duffle on the marble floor of the foyer and glared at her sister. "I have no idea what you're talking about."

"Honestly, Miranda. Anyone looking at you would think you were a homeless junky."

Mira bit the inside of her cheek and waited. This wasn't the first shot fired in the war between the sisters, it was merely the opening salvo of something far bigger, and she knew it.

"You're twenty-eight. You act like a child. You walk around this house, a college drop-out, a complete waste of time and money. You do nothing."

"That's not entirely true, sister dear. I pose for family pictures endlessly so that the entire state of Wisconsin can praise you for raising your poor, orphaned, possibly mentally defective, sister. I let the whole world believe that Dusty is yours." Mira knew well the only reason she hadn't been thrown out years ago was because of this one secret. Madelyn Pierce Anderson, if she feared anything, feared the world would find out Dusty was not her son, but Mira's, conceived when Mira was not quite sixteen.

"We are not discussing that."

"I think we should. I think it's time I get on my own, I completely agree with you. Dusty and I should pack up, right now, and leave."

"You won't be taking Dustin."

Madelyn's words bespoke no fear. It was a simple statement of fact, and Mira knew it. "I'm pretty sure I should. Dusty is my son, not your photo op. You and The Senator can go find another kid to pose with."

Madelyn slapped her, and not for the first time. Growing up, Mira was forced to make adult decisions and raise a child before she was out of her teens, Madelyn relied on violence to control her. "You are more than welcome to leave, but you are not taking Dustin. Do you think I would let you take him, when you have no where you can go and no way to support him?"

"I've got a job and a house waiting for me in Rock Harbor, and you know it."

Madelyn laughed. "Oh, yes, waiting tables in that horrible bar and doing your little songs on stage…yes, that's quite the job. But it's not a lifestyle I'm going to let you force on Dustin when he has everything here, everything a child needs."

"Oh, yeah, I remember my own privileged childhood at your hands, Madelyn." Mira rubbed her jaw for emphasis. "Look how I turned out."

"You think you have the tools to raise a child, when you can barely take care of yourself without our help?"

17

Mira mentally shut away The Senator's image. She was able to battle with Madelyn. That was almost a level field. But the mere mention of The Senator and Mira's fears overwhelmed her. "In Rock Harbor I can take care of both of us. I will live in the old house. I've got a job and friends up there."

Madelyn's eyes glowed with a cold maniacal hate. "You are free to leave. Go live with all our old neighbors. See if they want to have anything to do with the person you've become."

Mira said nothing, waiting for the second attack.

Madelyn took a step closer to Mira, her eyes coal black and glittering with rage. "But I promise you this, Miranda. If you so much as think you're taking Dustin with you, or if I find out you've told anyone you're his mother, I will start proceedings to sever any parental rights you think you have."

"I have parental rights, Madelyn. I'm his mother."

"You gave him to me before he was even born. Do you think Dustin is going to love you if he knew that?" Madelyn's face glowed in triumph. "So go ahead, leave. Dustin will be sad for awhile, but better he be sad now than he realizes as he grows up that his 'Aunt Mira' is nothing and will never be anything more than nothing."

Paralyzed with rage, Mira waited for Madelyn to leave. Furious, she stormed to her room and slammed the door. She was leaving, and she was leaving immediately.

She lay on her bed and stared at the ceiling. Instinctively, she reached between the mattress and box spring. The small velvet box was still there. She pulled it out and opened the clam shell lid, revealing a neat row of flat, shiny razor blades.

She hadn't cut herself in a long time. Closing her eyes, Mira remembered her first time. She was fourteen, Madelyn was newly married, and Mira had developed a crush on The Senator. A crush The Senator didn't seem to mind at all. In fact, he seemed to reward her starry-eyed adoration with tender attentions. A touch of the hand here, a hug that lasted a beat too long there, it was the first kindness Mira had received in a long time. She reveled in a fantasy that he would leave Madelyn and marry her.

Behind her teen dream, though, was a dark layer of guilt.

It was the day after they put new carpet in the Rock Harbor house that Mira stepped on a razor blade left behind by a careless workman. The cut, though not deep, felt like a release. Even now, fourteen years later, Mira remembered clearly the momentary beat of relief. She kept the razor blade hidden, making small cuts in her arms or legs only on rare occasions when the stress of living with Madelyn was too much.

When she was fifteen, the night The Senator first visited her in her room, Mira began cutting herself every day. The cuts on her arms and legs stopped healing and thin raised scars lined her limbs. She stopped wearing shorts and short sleeved shirts.

She hadn't cut herself since the day Dusty was born. She couldn't separate herself from Madelyn for Dusty's sake, but she knew she also had to stop any behavior Madelyn might consider destructive.

She slid a blade out of the box and held it against the pale, soft skin on the inside of her arm. With one quick unconscious motion she flicked the blade and opened a small wound.

The relief was immediate and short lived. A tear rolled down her cheek. She wiped the blade free of blood and slipped it back into the box. Then she tossed the box into her duffle bag.

COLLIER

Fresh from a shower his uncle demanded he take, and swathed in a robe that felt like a comforting hug, Collier sank into the sofa and accepted the cup of tea Uncle Archie offered him.

Few called Archibald James "Archie," and with good reason. Though he looked like a gentle old man, Collier knew his uncle was a hardnosed business lawyer who'd fought countless legal battles for Milwaukee's business elite for the past forty years. Still, sitting across a coffee table, watching him sip tea in the middle of the night, it was difficult for Collier to think of his uncle as anything more than what he remembered: his father's far sweeter tempered older brother who always had hard candy in his pockets.

"It's lovely to see you, Collier. It's been a long time."

"Since Pop's funeral."

"Has it really been that long?" Archibald shook his head. "I suppose your grief was quite deep."

"He was all I had. I wasn't old enough to remember Mom when she died." Collier tried not to let his uncle's words stir a deeper guilt in him. "I wasn't in a good place, then, after Dad." He set the empty tea cup on the coffee table. "And I'm not in a good place now."

"Tell me how I can help."

Collier told his uncle everything in an unbroken stream, starting with the day when, at eighteen, he left home after learning Izzy had slept with her skating partner. He finished with his most recent flight from home six months ago when Izzy once again chose a different man over him. Archibald said nothing, listening to each chapter carefully, tapping his index finger against his temple as if committing the story to memory via Morse code. Finally, exhausted, Collier finished. "It's stupid. I'm too old for this, but I really have no place else to go."

Archibald remained quiet for a moment. "Collier, I don't think there's an age where heartbreak no longer touches us and makes us do things we wouldn't do if we were in control of our full faculties. It seems to me that you are at a crossroads. You don't want to go home, but you're not travelling with your band."

"Can't say I blame the Stillmans. I've been a black cloud for months."

"It's not an easy thing to overcome, losing a dream you've had for so long. I know."

Collier looked around the exceptionally tidy apartment and absently wondered if Archibald had ever been in love. "In my brain I know I have to move on, and I know this is not her fault or mine, it just is what it is. I just can't seem to function since she and Quinn married. Now they're having a baby. I can't go back. I can't move forward and I can't stay where I am."

Archibald looked thoughtful for a moment. "It's too late tonight to solve anything. Let's sleep on it and see if the morning doesn't bring us a solution."

"I doubt it will." Collier stretched out on the sofa and covered himself with the afghan that was draped over the back.

Archibald picked up the teacups and turned out the light. "I find looking at things in the morning gives me a new perspective."

Guess we'll see. Collier pulled the afghan up to his chin and closed his eyes.

20

MIRA

The Rock Harbor bus had a flat tire, so there was a layover in Green Bay. Mira paced the grungy depot floor. She was less than an hour from Rock Harbor and it was nearly dawn. She was restless, thinking about starting a new life in her old home town. She wanted to do something that showed the world she was no longer going to be her sister's pawn. Unable to settle, unable to quiet her mind, she scanned several websites on her cell, hoping something would spark an idea that would make a visible statement to the surge of independence she felt. The search bored her quickly.

The drugstore across the street from the depot opened early, and, knowing she still had at least an hour before she had to get back on the bus, Mira strode up and down the aisles like a restless predator until she came to the shelves of hair coloring products. Resolution washed over her. She touched each box, imaging her face framed by the pictures. The last one she touched was the one she wanted. It was not a wildly drastic change, but it would be enough. She bought two boxes and some bath towels.

21

Checking her watch as she crossed back to the depot, she realized she still had time enough to color her hair before her bus to Rock Harbor pulled out. She wasted no time mixing and applying the harsh smelling hair color. The allotted wait time was torture, because she was anxious to see the results. Rinsing the colorant from her hair in the small sink was awkward. She dried her hair under the hand drier on the wall and had only a few seconds to check the look in a mirror. Pleased, she jammed the towels in the garbage can and joined the rest of the passengers on the bus, none of whom seemed to notice or care that the solitary woman now had jet black hair.

COLLIER

Sleep, as it had for months, came uneasily. As comfortable as his uncle's sofa was, especially after months of sleeping in the RV, Collier tossed and turned much of the night. Images of Izzy twisted through his mind with images of the Stillmans, all underscored by wisps of sorrowful music. As dawn broke over Lake Michigan, Collier gave up all attempts at rest and followed the smell of fresh coffee into the kitchen.

"Good morning, Collier. I hope you slept well?" Archibald handed him a mug of black coffee before pouring himself a cup and sitting across the table from Collier.

"I didn't, but that's not your fault. I never sleep that well. I didn't expect to see you up, though."

"Oh, I'm busy, and I find that the morning is when I am most focused."

"I thought you were retired."

Archibald dropped two sugar cubes into his coffee. "Generally, yes, I am. Oh I keep track of business trends in the state and I do enjoy following politics, but those are my hobbies. I do have one client who keeps me quite busy. She keeps fairly odd hours, and we've found that we meet in the middle in the early mornings."

"Oh, what sort of business is she in? Or can't you tell me that?"

"Actually, I was going to tell you about her because I think she's the solution to your quandary."

Collier set down his mug and studied his uncle. "You're not going to try and fix me up with her, are you?"

Archibald laughed a light, musical sound. "Not at all. She's quite happily married."

"Let me guess, she's amazing, and he's her hero."

Archibald stilled, though his eyes still twinkled. "Yes, I'm afraid so. But this is not about your romantic woes. Only you can fix that. No, I'm thinking the two of you should meet for strictly business reasons. She's a bit of a music genius. Has a real ear for producing, that sort of thing. She has her own recording studio in a little town north of here, Rock Harbor. North of Green Bay."

Collier swirled his coffee and stared at it. "I don't know. I'm not sure I'm really ready to record anything. I mean, I just have the one song, I don't have an album or anything. Not unless you count the stuff I did with Nate and Monroe, but that was really for the Ren Faire circuit."

Archibald waved a dismissive hand at him. "What I'm suggesting isn't a few days up north, my boy. I'm suggesting you take a good long break. Work on an album with her. Really find your voice. See where it takes you. Work through your heartbreak by writing. Shara will be more than happy to work with you for as long as it takes."

Collier frowned. "Shara?"

"Yes, Shara Brandt. Shara Jacobs now, I always forget. You've hear of the band 'Teachers' Pets'?"

Collier set his mug on the table and laughed. "Heard of them? I saw them at the Ryman the last time I was home. Killer show. She owns 'Orphans and Runaways Recordings' right?"

Archibald nodded. "The very same. I don't imagine she was with them in Nashville. She doesn't tour as much with the band, now that she has the children. But she is the driving force behind their original music. You're familiar with her studio?"

23

"By reputation." For the first time in months, Collier felt a shadow of interest. "You can really get me time in that studio?"

"My boy, if you're willing to put in the work, you'll have all the time there you want. Miss Shara believes in taking time to develop talent, but only if she and her team think there's talent there. I'll call the studio and tell them to expect you. I'm sure you'll be able to stay at the studio, at least for a while, so you don't have to worry about housing. Shara has a loft above her barn. Many of her protégés stay there while they're working with her."

Collier leaned back in his chair. "I'll need to get a car." He closed his eyes and tried to imagine getting anything productive done in his Nashville apartment. "It's not like I have any plants or pets that need tending back home. I could probably take a couple weeks and sort things out."

His uncle smiled as he dialed his phone. "You can take one of my cars, and take all the time you need. Who knows? You may be able to solve more than one problem while you're there."

MIRA

The Pierce Place, as everyone in Rock Harbor called Mira and Madelyn's home, was dark and cold when Mira dragged her duffle and her guitar case up the front walk. She fumbled with the keys and finally was able to open the door to the cavernous house.

The Pierce Place was the biggest house in Rock Harbor, and therefore, Mira remembered, always a point of interest for the simple farmers and store owners in the area. Her parents were the wealthiest people in town, as her father's family had been before them, and therefore, also a topic of town conversation and gossip.

Everyone liked Lester Pierce, a jovial man who loved Rock Harbor and never flaunted his wealth. He was at ease with the simple dairy and cherry farmers in the area. Mira remembered him fondly. She had no memories of her mother, though she was well aware that Ellen Pierce had a reputation as a social climber who loathed everything about Rock Harbor.

24

Her parents, however, had never been the molding force in Mira's life. Madelyn had been the one to raise Mira in the big, cold house. First as a single mother to Mira as a toddler, then later, as a woman married to a man whose political ambitions would lead him to the State Senate.

Mira put a hand on the banister and shuddered. She could almost hear The Senator's footsteps on the stairs.

I need to do something. I can't think about this right now.

Mira dropped her duffle on the floor of the foyer and set her guitar case down with a bit more care. "Home sweet home," she muttered as she felt along the wall for the light switch.

She shivered. While late summer heat still simmered in Madison, the Door County autumn was settling in, and the night air was cold.

She glanced around the empty room with its ghostly furniture and realized she did not want to stay here tonight. She pulled her cell out of her pocket and dialed. "Hey there, Chanel. It's Mira. I'm home for good. When can I start work?"

*

An hour later, she was sitting at the far end of the bar at Dirty Dog Dave's. Her friend Chanel, was a long time waitress and some time paramour of Dave, the owner. Mira found Dave's improbable Southern accent and an unabashed love of cash, rather charming. Right now Chanel stood far away at the opposite end of the bar, tapping her long red nails.

Dirty Dog Dave's had at one time been a dairy barn. A farmer sold to a developer decades earlier, but the developer ran out of money or interest in the project and the building sat empty for years until Dave bought it. Putting as little cash into renovations as possible, Dave set up a kitchen, and office, a bar and a stage. The rest of the massive building was filled with an odd assortment of mismatched furniture: tables and chairs gleaned from rummage sales and estate auctions; couches found at the side of the road, pieces too large for garbage trucks to remove; even a few rows of theater seats retrieved when an ancient theater in Green Bay closed. Easily half the building was dedicated to the largest dance floor in the state. The stage, situated perpendicular to the bar was the focal point. The stage had been unused for years until Shara Brandt came to work for Dave eight years earlier. It was Shara who insisted Dave allow Teachers' Pets to play. And since then, Dirty Dog Dave's was the place for any band starting out.

Mira loved the place. More a central gathering place for the people of Rock Harbor than a nightclub, she'd all but grown up within the dimly lit confines of the bar, spending many fine evenings sitting at her father's arm while he conducted business with the farmers and merchants in town. After his death, before Madelyn moved them to Madison, Mira often came on her own, enjoying the sense of community and welcome she got from the place, something she didn't have at home.

"Dave will be out in a minute, Mira. Are you sure about this?"

"I've played here before, Chanel, what's the big deal?"

"Well, are you working with Shara yet?"

"I've got a call in to her, yeah. She told me to call her when I was back in town. So I guess we could say yeah, I'm working with her again."

Chanel nodded. "That's good. You know how Dave's always been tight with her, that stage is pretty much hers to book."

"I'm aware." Mira's cell hummed in her pocket. "Hang on. Oh, it's Kelly Fuller."

"Oh, right. I heard Shara's busy tonight, so Kelly's handling her calls."

Mira nodded. Kelly Fuller was Shara Brandt Jacobs' right hand man and one of the founding members of Teachers' Pets. She knew if Kelly gave her the green light, she'd be able to work with Shara. "Hello Kelly."

"Hi Mira. So you're in town?"

"I am, and I'm ready to work."

"Well, that is good news. Where are you now?"

"I'm at Dave's. I'm waiting to see if Dave'll give me some stage time. And a waitress job."

"Tell you what, Shara's busy tonight, but I can come down and listen if Dave gives you time."

"Great, I'll tell him. Thanks Kelly!" She ended the call. "Kelly said he'd come down if Dave lets me play tonight."

"And why should I let you play, Dahlin'?"

Mira glanced over her shoulder at Dirty Dog Dave's bulky owner. "I need a job…and a gig."

Dave eyed her up and down. "My girls are curvier."

Mira shrugged. "So I'll tend bar. Dave, you know I'll work hard for you. Just give me a shot, I won't disappoint you."

Dave grinned. "You won't have a chance to disappoint, Darlin'. You can wait tables, starting tomorrow night. One of the bands dropped out tonight, so you can play for a couple hours. You got enough material?"

Mira nodded. "I've got enough new stuff and covers for a couple hours."

Dave squinted, a look Mira recognized. He was calculating how much money he would make with her on stage. "Less original stuff, more covers tonight, understand?"

Because people will always like a song they know more than a new song. Mira nodded. "I understand."

"And y'all work for straight tips like all the other girls"

Mira nodded again. Dave only paid his bar tenders and cooks. Everyone else in the place worked for tips, including the music acts.

"We open at five. You go on at nine. Don't be late."

"I won't be." Mira grinned. "Thanks, Dave." She hugged Chanel. "Thanks, Chanel, I owe you."

She left the bar ready for a new chapter to begin.

COLLIER

The rain north of Green Bay fell mercilessly. By the time Collier reached the city limits of Rock Harbor, he was exhausted and unable to find the county highway address Archibald gave him. Collier eased the Mercedes into a muddy parking lot outside a bar called "Dirty Dog Dave's." He parked as close to the door of the hulking building as he could, and ran inside.

The inside of Dirty Dog Dave's was cavernous. The place seemed deserted, though the lights were on. Collier took a seat at the bar and tapped his fingers. "Hello?"

The only answer to his single word was the click of a handgun safety releasing. Collier stopped tapping his fingers, his blood frozen.

"Put yer hands on the bar where Ah can see them."

Collier squinted to the darkened end of the room, searching for the face to match the low, guttural voice and the completely fake Southern accent. He splayed his hands out on the dented bar, trying hard not to recoil at the sticky feel of the scarred wooden surface. "I'm not here to cause trouble. I just need directions."

"Ah'll just bet y'all do."

Despite the apparent danger he was in, Collier struggled not to smile. The hidden man's accent was simply too funny. "No, really. I'm trying to find Shara Jacobs' place."

As if his words were some sort of incendiary device, the man with the gun leaped from around the corner, and grabbed Collier by the collar. The man was enormous, and holding an even more impressive handgun. "Just what would y'all be wantin' with Miss Shara?"

"Oh, for the love of all that's holy, Dave, put that man down!"

Collier held his breath as Dave's grip on his collar tightened. He heard woman's quick foot steps behind him and in a beat a tall, beautiful woman the color of a perfect cup of mocha stood next to him.

"Chanel, now this doesn't concern y'all."

"It does when you're pointing a gun at a customer. Put that thing away and give the man dinner or something."

Dave didn't loosen his grip on Collier. "Chanel, this man is driving Mr. James' Mercedes. But look at him, he's no driver for Mr. James. So either he stole the car...or he stole the car. Plus, he's lookin' for Miss Shara."

Chanel turned her focus on Collier. "Did you steal Mr. James' car?"

"No." Collier tried to swallow, but Dave's enormous knuckle was in the way. "No, I'm his nephew."

"Ah don't buy it."

"You don't buy anything." Chanel frowned at Dave. "Look, Mister. Dave here just got his concealed carry permit and he's itching to use that beastly thing. If I were you, I'd say something a bit more convincing."

"My uncle, Archibald James, sent me here. I'm a..." Collier struggled for air.

"Oh, for heaven's sakes, Dave, put him down and let him talk."

Reluctantly, Dave released Collier. "Now talk...and Ah'd best like what you say."

"I'm a musician. I'm a singer, and my uncle thought I should work with Shara Jacobs. Said she's a client of his. He's letting me use his car because mine is back home."

"Where's that?"

Collier cleared his throat and turned a baleful eye on Dave. "Nashville. Tennessee. Where people have real accents."

Chanel burst out laughing. "Dave, you have to give this man free burgers for life or he may just blow your cover!"

Collier allowed himself a weak smile. "I don't want to blow anyone's cover or anything. I just...I'm looking for this address." He held up the piece of paper. "I can't find it in the rain."

"Of course you can't, Sugar." Chanel strolled behind the bar and filled a glass with beer. "Here you go." She slid the glass to Collier.

"Now just a minute! Since when do we give free beer to strangers?"

"Oh, about the same time we started pulling guns on people who show up looking for directions." Chanel grinned at Collier. "Dave, you say one more word to this boy and I'm going to let him tell everyone that you've never been further south than

Kenosha." Chanel turned back to Collier, her voice easing into a warm tone reminiscent of thick hot cocoa. "Now, go ahead and finish what you were saying."

Collier took a swallow of beer. "I'm a sort of traveling musician, but my band...broke up. So my uncle sent me here to do some recording work with Shara Jacobs. He said I could stay at her place."

"Probably means the loft."

Collier didn't miss the softening of Dave's features. "You know Shara Brandt Jacobs?"

Dave chuckled. "Know her? I discovered her."

Chanel clicked her tongue against her teeth. "You did not discover her, Dave. She had to beg you for months to let 'Teachers' Pets' play here, and you know it. Now, what's your name honey?"

"Collier. Collier James."

"Okay, Collier James, I'm about to open this place up for the evening, but I promise you, if you don't mind sitting here a bit and having the best burger you're ever going to eat, I'll see to it that someone gets you out to the Jacobs' place tonight." Chanel patted him on the shoulder.

30

"We're giving him food, too? What, you're trying to bankrupt me?"

"No, Dave," Chanel rounded the bar and stood in the kitchen doorway, "I'm trying to keep him from suing us."

Collier was amused by the couple. His initial fear of Dave melted. The smell of grilled meat emanating from the kitchen made Collier's stomach growl. "Ok, I guess I wouldn't mind a burger at all."

*

Time in Dave's was a relative thing. It seemed like hours before the first customer crossed the dank threshold and yet when he looked at his watch at the height of late night revelry, Collier was astonished to see that several hours had passed. Dirty Dog Dave's transformed from a dark cave to the epicenter of sound and music and joy. It reminded him of Second Chance's in Nashville, and Collier felt a rare pang of homesickness.

"Collier James, I'd like you to meet a good friend of mine," Chanel took a break from waiting tables to talk to him. Next to Chanel stood a beautiful, older woman, the kind of woman, Collier sensed, became more attractive as she aged. Though she was, Collier assessed, probably in her fifties, she retained a youthful glow and smoothness of features most would envy. "This is Molly Hunter."

"Miz Hunter, pleased to make your acquaintance," Collier extended his hand.

"Shara told me to expect you." Molly shook his hand with a firm grip. "Pleased to meet you. You're Mr. James' nephew?"

"Yes ma'am."

Molly smiled. "You have his wonderful manners, too."

"Collier, Molly is a good friend of Shara's. I told her you needed some help finding the place."

Collier nodded his thanks to Chanel, who faded back to the welling throng of people.

"So what does Mr. James want you to do with Shara and Bryan?"

Collier shrugged. "I'm a musician. I guess he thinks I should work with Shara."

Molly nodded. "He's a wise man. Come on, I'll lead you up there."

"You're sure it's okay?"

"Absolutely. If Mr. James sent you, you have every right to stay there."

Collier pushed his glass away and turned to leave the bar when the singer on stage caught his eye. She was striking with long raven colored hair that flowed to the middle of her back. As she settled herself onto the stool and shifted her guitar to a comfortable place on her lap, Collier could not help feeling he'd seen her before.

"Who is that?"

Molly glanced over her shoulder. "You've got an eye for talent. That's Miranda Pierce. She's a local girl."

"She's got a decent voice." Collier studied her with a critical eye. "And she's pretty."

"She is. I liked her better before, though."

"Why's that?"

Molly opened the door and stepped into the rain soaked night. "I think she looked better with her natural hair color. It was a really pretty sandy brown. She dyed it black recently."

Collier glanced over his shoulder and trying to picture the woman on stage with lighter hair, and realized why she seemed familiar. *She's the woman from the Renaissance Faire, the one with the green eyes.*

Molly was already in her car, starting the engine. Not wanting to get lost again, Collier let the bar door close and headed for his uncle's Mercedes.

*
—

Collier followed Molly's car closely on the shiny, rain-slicked roads. They drove through what felt like endless miles of dark farmland until Molly turned up a narrow drive. Collier eased the Mercedes up the drive and past a garage to a flat area on the back side of the barn. Getting out of the car, he followed Molly back up the drive to the yard, a large space between a small cabin and the barn where, he surmised, would be the loft.

"Sorry about the hike. Since the studio's become so popular and busy, Bryan flattened this space behind the barn for people to park. He got tired of always having to move people's cars to get his out of the garage every morning."

"People stay that late a lot?"

"People who are serious about working with Shara work as much as they can. She's set up some beds in the upstairs of the studio." Molly nodded over her shoulder to a shadowy building behind the garage. "But the loft is far more comfortable."

"Well I appreciate you opening it for me."

Molly flashed a smile. Collier was again surprised at how beautiful the older woman was. "Anything for Mr. James."

"Did my uncle build a bridge or something? You. Dave. It's like Uncle Archie's a superhero or something."

"He didn't tell you?"Molly blinked raindrops from her lashes and smiled. "That's like him. Let's just say your uncle helped save Shara from a pretty miserable life. He's a bit of a hero to that family."

Collier shook his head. "We haven't been that close."

"Well, ask him to tell you sometime." Molly slid open the barn door and turned on a row of dim overheard lights. The soft whicker of horses greeted them. "Shhh, Pepper, shhh girls." Molly patted the horses in each of the four stalls. "You'll be up those stairs in the loft. It's really more of a small apartment. There's a bathroom. It's not glamorous, but it'll suit I'm sure. Light switch for the barn is at the top of the stairs, so you can turn it out when you get there. I'll close this door. You'll find everything you need in the loft. Shara serves breakfast at seven. Don't be late for that."

"I can get my own…I mean, she doesn't have to make breakfast for me."

Molly smiled. "She won't be. Your uncle called her, told her what you needed, and she wants to meet with you first thing. It's a business meeting, so be on your toes."

"Thank you, Miz Hunter."

Molly waved a dismissive hand. "I know you're Southern, but plain old Molly is good enough for me."

"Okay, Molly it is. So when will the Jacobs' be home?"

"Oh, they'll be back soon enough. They're just over at the Shepaski house for dinner. I think Shara said something about a Scrabble game. Those do tend to go on for a while. But Bryan and the kids have school in the morning, so they won't stay out terribly late."

Collier raised an eyebrow. "Not exactly big recording mogul stuff."

33

"No, but Shara isn't a typical big recording mogul. She and Bryan could have both been big shots with huge fortunes. They both turned it down, and it's a good thing, too."

"How would turning down a fortune be a good thing?"

Molly smiled and leaned against a stall door. "They would never have met each other if either of them had stayed in their family's business."

"Uncle Archie said they had a romance for the ages." The words tasted bitter on Collier's tongue.

"He wasn't wrong. And they have two precious children to show for it. You'll meet them in the morning."

"I'm not sure I'm up for a happy romantic couple," Collier kicked a bit of sawdust.

"Sounds like you've got secrets of your own."

"Not secrets. Just stuff I don't want to talk about."

"Well, good luck trying to keep anything quiet around here." Molly stepped out of the barn and pushed the rolling door halfway. "You'll find most folks have some sort of secret they want to keep hidden, but everyone knows it because," she smiled, "you can't keep a secret in a town this small. The winters are long and cable TV service is uneven at best. Discussing everyone's lives is our biggest form of entertainment."

"I'll keep that in mind. Thanks."

Molly patted his arm. "You're going to fit in well here. I can feel it."

Collier reached the top of the stairs as Molly rolled the barn door closed. He opened the loft door, snapped off the barn light and turned on the loft light. The room was small, but as cozy as any he'd ever seen. He set his duffle bag next to the Bentwood rocker and flopped onto the firm mattress that took up most of the floor space. Rolling onto his side, he gazed out the window down at the cabin. In the distance he was better able to see the two story structure that was the recording studio. Recalling the conversation with Uncle Archibald, Collier knew the building was formerly a burned out shell of a farmhouse that Bryan had converted to a studio as a wedding gift for Shara.

Another perfect romance, another perfect hero for his woman, and I'm stuck in the middle of it all again.

Collier closed his eyes and fought back images of Izzy as he drifted into sleep.

34

MIRA

Mira played her set with as much focus as she could, but seeing the singer from the Renaissance Faire startled her. There was no question, even though he wasn't in costume, the dusty haired, grey eyed man talking to Molly Hunter was definitely the singer from the faire.

What on earth is he doing here?

Before she had a chance to take a break, he was gone. With some effort, Mira pushed the thought of him out her head as she sang cover songs to the rowdy patrons. Eventually, the last beer-soused customer put on his coat and the cook turned off the kitchen lights.

She sat at the bar, sipping a beer, waiting for Dave to hand her the night's tips. All the musicians who played at Dirty Dog Dave's were paid strictly in tips. The musicians' tip jar was kept on the bar under Dave's watchful eye. No one questioned whether or not Dave skimmed money from the jar. While it always felt like something illegal was going down at Dave's, everyone knew Dave actually ran a very clean business and loathed anyone who stole.

"Here ya are, darlin'."

Mira thumbed through the wad of bills. "That's it?"

"That's all of it."

"I expected more." She counted the bills again. "This is only fifty bucks. I was expecting more than double that."

Dave shrugged. "Play better next time. A busy night like tonight, you should be rollin' in it, but you were distracted. My customers know when they aren't seein' a full effort."

"Are you sure you aren't maybe taking a cut?"

Dave's expression melted into barely contained fury and Mira instantly wanted to bite back her words. "Dave, I'm sorry. I'm sorry." She put her hand on his beefy arm. "I'm sorry. It's been a rough week for me. I just got back into town and I'm not feeling good. I know you don't skim."

"You better, gal." Dave squinted his eyes and lowered his voice to a heavy growl. "You want to work in this town? You want to play in this place, you better know Ah don't tolerate none of that noise."

"I know, I know. I'm sorry. I'm just…" She shook her head. "I'm sorry, Dave. I'll play better next time."

Dave's dark look lightened to a smile. "That's my girl. Now, you goin' home tonight?"

Mira swirled the beer in her glass and sighed. The idea of going back to the big house in the middle of a dark, rainy night did not appeal to her at all. "No," she said slowly, "I'm gonna talk to Kelly Fuller for a bit and then I'm headed to the loft."

"You are? But Ah thought…" Dave frowned. "Well, Ah must've been wrong." He shrugged. "Okay, well, Ah've got an opening on Monday for the early part of the evening. 'Teachers' Pets' is playing late, so it's a solid gig for ya. Interested?"

Mira nodded. "That would be great, Dave, thanks!" She finished her beer. "If 'Teachers' Pets' is playing, will Shara Brandt be playing with them?"

"Ah never know that. You're stayin' at her place, just ask her over the weekend." Dave picked up a couple empty beer glasses and headed for the kitchen.

"There you are, Mira." Kelly Fuller, a lanky man with a young face and ginger hair, strode up to them. "I was looking for you back stage."

"Hey Kelly. So, what did you think?"

"Not bad. You gotta shake a bit of rust off, but you know you've always had great pipes."

"Not my best night, I'm afraid." Mira patted her purse.

"You did look a little distracted, but hey, it's your first night back in a long time."

"Thanks Kelly. You've always been a great cheerleader."

Kelly shrugged. "It's my nature. But tomorrow you'll see Shara, I'm sure, and you'd best not be distracted then."

"I won't be, I promise."

"Because the last time you played for her…"

Mira closed her eyes. "You don't have to remind me."

Her last time in Shara Brandt Jacobs' studio had been nothing short of a train wreck, and Mira knew it was her fault. She'd been up for days, writing and working frantically to produce something Shara would love. But the sleepless days took their toll and when her audition day finally arrived, she'd overslept.

No, I didn't oversleep. I crashed. And I missed my shot.

She showed up, late, haggard, and unable to focus on her performance. The end result was not unexpected. Shara told her to keep working, keep writing, but get a grip on things and be more dependable. Above all things, Shara Brandt Jacobs demanded professional dependability.

This time I'm not going to screw it up. I'm going to be completely focused and dependable.

"You need a ride someplace?"

Mira opened her eyes, realizing Kelly was still looking at her. "No, I'm driving that old Civic Madelyn used in high school."

Kelly whistled. "That thing was a beater when she had it thirty years ago."

"Not quite thirty, but yeah, it's old. I'm hoping to get something newer soon."

"You better. I don't see that thing making it through the winter." Kelly checked his watch. "I gotta hit it. We have rehearsal tomorrow early. Shara's getting everything ready for that tour in December. You staying out at the old house?"

"Of course." It was a lie, but she couldn't tell Kelly the truth. The house was just too cold and lonely right now. Her plan was to sneak into Shara's loft and sleep there for a few nights, just until she was ready to get the house into livable shape.

She followed Kelly out of the bar and zipped up her coat. Mira shivered as the first cold drops of rain splattered onto her hair and rolled down her neck. She didn't like starting her new life out with a lie, but every corner in the big house was crowded with dark memories, and she wasn't ready to face those memories yet.

COLLIER

What woke him, Collier didn't know, but even in the haze of deep sleep, he knew he wasn't alone in the loft. Someone latched the door quietly and stepped closer to the bed before turning on the overhead light.

"Who's there?" he called out as the light flashed on, momentarily blinding him. A woman's scream pierced through the shock of light and he squinted in her general direction. He recognized the black hair immediately. Surprise mingled with confusion. "What are you doing here?"

"I could ask you the same thing." She held her bulky shoulder bag in front of her like a shield. "Who are you?"

Collier shifted to sit up. She froze. "Don't move. I've got mace in here."

"Calm down. I'm not going to move, since I'm pretty much naked here." Collier grinned. "But you and I both know you don't have mace."

The angry light in her eyes quavered, giving way to uncertainty. "How would you know what I have in my bag?"

"Well," he kept his voice calm, sensing she was more afraid than dangerous, "because if you had mace in there, you would have started spraying it the minute you realized there was a man in the room. That's what I hear from most women, anyway."

She blinked away the uncertainty, her face settled into a mask of defensiveness. "Oh, and you know most women, do you?"

"No, Miss, I don't. But I'm pretty sure most women wouldn't ask any questions before mentioning they have mace. So relax, put the bag down and tell me what you're doing here."

"I've stayed here before. I've worked with Shara."

"You're trying to be mysterious. Why do I feel like you're lying to me?"

"Okay, well, I've lived here almost my whole life, and you're a stranger. That's enough mystery for me to call the cops. Give me one reason why I shouldn't."

"My uncle said I could stay here and Molly Hunter brought me here."

She seemed less likely to want to kill him, but her countenance remained stony. "Who's your uncle?"

"Archibald James."

"The lawyer?"

"You know him?"

"Everyone knows about Archibald James." She relaxed. "Okay, maybe you're not a mass rapist." She sat in the rocker. "But still, you can't stay here."

"Why not?"

"Because, I'm staying here."

Collier chuckled. "I was here first. And, I'm not wearing pants."

"I'll close my eyes. Get dressed, and get out." Her tone was clipped, cold. Collier again sensed she was covering fear.

"Why should I get out? I got here first. I was sound asleep, and you woke me up." He gave her a small smile, hoping to soften the deep furrows in her brow.

She shrugged. "Not my problem. You can't stay here."

"It is your problem. I'm not leaving." He grinned. "We could both stay here. It's a big enough bed." He patted the spot next to him.

She tucked a strand of hair behind her ear. "Of course that's what you want." Her eyes flashed hot and angry.

"It's not what I want, Ma'am. I want to go to sleep. But if you have other ideas, well, I am from the South. We believe in accommodating women whenever we can."

She stared at him, and Collier doubted his humor was warming her attitude. Clearly, some sort of battle waged behind her emerald eyes.

Her face slacked into exhaustion. "I need to stay here."

Collier's curiosity made him push the point further. "Well, I'm from out of town and have no place else to go. From what I hear, Miranda Pierce, you live in Rock Harbor which means you do have someplace else to go."

"Don't call me that."

"Isn't it your name?"

"Call me Mira." A shadow crossed her face. "I'm not going to that house tonight. You can't make me." her voice held the echoes of a willful child. "And how do you know my name…oh, wait…"

"Molly Hunter."

Mira nodded. "She knows everyone and everything in this town. Steer clear of her if you want to keep anything private."

"She didn't strike me as a person who spread gossip."

"She doesn't. She just knows everything. The potential is always there."

An interesting read on the lovely Miss Molly. "So the two of you aren't grand friends then?"

She leaned back in the rocker. "I try not to make attachments. It's easier to leave if there aren't any attachments."

"Sounds like someone who wants to run away."

"I've always wanted to run away. I feel like I'm running away from something every day of my life."

Collier wanted to be annoyed by her cryptic statement, but watching her face, he sensed it was probably the one completely truthful thing she'd said. Collier tried to assess her age. "You're what, thirty? You're old enough to go out on your own. What's stopping you?"

"I'm twenty-eight, thank you."

"Oh, that's a huge difference." Collier nearly laughed aloud at the wounded expression on Mira's face.

"I can't leave because it's complicated. But I can't go home tonight."

The glimmer of true fear returned in her eyes. Collier relented. "Fine. Just go…go in the bathroom for a minute, let me get my crap together and I'll go sleep on the hay downstairs."

"You want a blanket or something?"

Her friendly tone annoyed him. "What, now that you've won the bed, you're worried about me?"

The softness melted from her face and her jaw line hardened. "Not really. I couldn't care less about you having a blanket, so long as you're not in here."

"Suits me fine. I'd rather sleep with horses than up here with you. Less shit to deal with."

"Oh, very nice. They teach you that language in the South where men are supposed to be so mannerly?" She glared at him as she stomped into the small bathroom and slammed the door.

"No!" Collier yelled as he pulled on his jeans. "I learned manners just fine, because where I come from the women aren't complete bitches!" He stuffed a few things into his duffle bag and slammed the door behind him, startling the horses in the stalls below.

There was a blanket hung from a hook near a stack of hay bales. Collier spread the blanket over the bales and stretched out on the hay, thankful his years on the road in the Renaissance Faire circuit had toughened him. Staring at the ceiling, he watched the light that glowed from between small cracks in the loft floor. When the light switched off, he closed his eyes. *Still, she is pretty.*

Pretty bitchy.

41

MIRA

Mira waited for Collier to settle in downstairs. Within a few minutes, everything was still and quiet. She sat on the edge of the bed and pulled off her boots, letting them drop to the wooden floor with a loud thud. Collier's muttered curse made her smile. She wasn't sure why annoying him gave her pleasure.

She stretched out on the bed, still warm with his body heat. She pushed her face into the pillow and inhaled his scent. It wasn't unpleasant.

Closing her eyes, Mira saw him again, sitting in the bed, shirtless, the sheet and blanket pooled at his waist.

Also not unpleasant.

She shook her head. *Now is not the time to be thinking about a guy. No matter how good he might smell.*

She picked up her boot and tossed it in the air, this time giving it more velocity so that when it hit the wooden floor it sounded like a thunder clap. The sound of the horses below whinnying and rustling in their stalls didn't cover Collier's curses, this time spoken at volume she knew was meant to reach her ears.

Mira smiled, closed her eyes, and went to sleep.

42

COLLIER

Collier opened his eyes when he felt the toe of a boot in his side. Sunlight filled the barn and he squinted, just able to make out the form of a tall man. "Well at least you're not holding a gun. Good morning."

Laughing, the man moved aside and let Collier sit up. "Good morning. I'd like to say that finding a strange man in my barn is a rarity, but I'd be lying. Are you one of Molly's strays or Shara's projects?"

Collier rubbed the sleep out of his eyes and focused on the man leaning comfortably against the stall wall. "Bryan Jacobs?" The man nodded. "I'm Collier James, my uncle Archie James sent me here." Collier stood and extended his hand. Bryan shook his hand. "I guess I'm one of Miss Shara's projects although Miss Molly brought me here."

Bryan raised an eyebrow. "You're not from around here, are you?"

"Tennessee. But I've spent the last several years traveling. It's the accent, isn't it? Is that going to be a problem with people around here?"

"Only because the only Southern accent most people around here have heard has been Dave's over at Dirty Dog Dave's." Bryan grinned.

"Yeah, we've met."

"I figured. I'm guessing he brought his new gun out, right?"

Collier nodded. "I had to all but give him my birth certificate proving I was related to Archie before he'd give it up. You got that much crime around here?"

"Not even a little. Dave's very…protective of his friends. Mr. James is sort of a hero up here. That's good news for you. You're Archibald James' nephew, so you're family." Bryan strode around the end of the stall and stroked the neck of the big bay stallion. "And as for your accent, the women around here will love it."

Collier shook his head. "I don't much care what the women think about my accent, or me." He regretted his tone of voice immediately when Bryan's friendly expression turned intense. "That didn't sound right."

"I realized a long time ago that the women around here run things, no matter what we men think. So you may want to at least listen to what they have to say." Bryan patted the neck of the bay again and strode to the barn door. "If you're hungry, Shara's got breakfast on." He paused and shook his head. "I suppose you know, you're not the only house guest."

Collier glanced at the ceiling. "I've met your other guest."

Bryan laughed and shook his head. "You slept on the hay. Being able to have a disagreement with Mira Pierce, and come out without scars, you'll do just fine here. Come on to the house. You can use the bathroom there, get yourself presentable and then have some breakfast with us."

*

"So you're Mr. James' nephew?" Shara Brandt Jacobs shoveled pancakes onto Collier's plate. "And you're a musician?"

The pancakes smelled heavenly and looked even better. Collier didn't realize how hungry he was until manners dictated he answer a lady's question before eating. "Yes, ma'am. I've been a traveling musician for a long time."

"Collier, you don't have to call me ma'am. Just call me Shara like everyone else does."

"Yes, ma'am...yes Miss Shara." He couldn't ignore Bryan's grin. "I'm sorry. It's how I was raised."

"You'll have to get over it. The only person allowed to call me 'Miss Shara' is your uncle, and that's only because he's been calling me that since I was little. So you've got some songs you want to record?"

"I suppose. I have one, anyway. My uncle suggested maybe you could help me find more direction."

"Oh, she'll do that for sure." Bryan spoke through a mouthful of pancakes.

"Bryan, I'm working here. Don't you have to be at school?"

Her words were sharp, but Collier couldn't mistake the adoration in her eyes when she spoke to Bryan. *And if Izzy hadn't handed her heart to that hockey meathead, that's how she'd look at me, maybe.*

Collier glanced at Bryan and the image of Quinn Murray sprang to mind. Both men were tall, dark, and ridiculously good looking, even in Collier's harsh opinion. *They both look like heroes.*

I look like a vagabond who slept in someone's barn last night. Which might be a romantic notion if it weren't the truth.

"Kids! It's time to go to school with your father!"

Two children raced down the hall to the kitchen table. The boy, dark haired like his father, but with his mother's enormous dark eyes, studied Collier for a moment. "Are you working with my mom on a record?"

"Yes, sir, I am."

"You talk funny, like Uncle Dave at the bar."

"Hunter Andrew Jacobs! Manners!" With a deft motion, Shara tapped her son on the shoulder with her spatula.

"Sorry, Mister."

"It's okay kid. I do talk funny like Uncle Dave. That's because I'm from Tennessee."

"We're learning about Nashville, Tennessee in school." The girl, a perfect miniature image of her mother, down to the white blond hair, never took her dark eyes off him. "Aunt Molly teaches us that. She is our teacher sometimes when Ms. Allen is sick or something. Do you know Aunt Molly?"

45

"I believe I've met her, missy."

"Everyone knows Aunt Molly, 'cuz she's the school nurse. I'm Katie, but when my mom's mad at me, she calls me Katherine Joanna."

Collier shook the girl's outstretched hand and smiled. "Glad to meet you, Miss Katie. And you, Mr. Hunter." He extended his hand to the boy, who shook it.

"Hey! Mira's here!" Katie leapt toward the door.

"Oh, yeah, I forgot to tell you, Shara, Mira stayed the night in the loft."

Shara arched an eyebrow at Bryan. "So where did our expected guest stay then?"

"He slept on the hay bales in the barn."

"Oh, for heaven's sakes." Shara's fair skin turned pink.

Instinctively, Collier wanted to put her at ease. "No, it's fine, Miss Shara. We, I mean, Mira and I, decided she should have the bed. I've slept on more than my share of hay bales believe me. A couple decades on the Renaissance Faire circuit, you get used to sleeping on whatever might be handy."

"Yes, well, I'll deal with her and you'll have a bed to sleep in tonight, Collier." Shara watched as her children hugged Mira in the doorway. "Hi, Mira. I didn't realize you stayed over."

"Good morning, Miss Miranda." Collier knew calling her by her full name would annoy her and he wasn't disappointed by her reaction.

Mira seemed surprised, but her eyes met with Collier and her friendly expression melted to a cold glare. "Just call me, Mira, like everyone else, okay? And Shara, yeah, I finished up at Dave's late and didn't feel like driving all the way home."

Shara stepped back and let Mira walk to the table but Collier noted her expression changed subtly, though the smile never left Shara's face. *Mira must be lying, and Shara seems to know it, but won't call her on it.* Collier was surprised at how intrigued he was.

"So, Collier," Shara sat and passed him a heaping plate of pancakes, "your uncle's opinion is highly respected here. He tells me you're a singer, and you want to move away from the Renaissance circuit and into something a bit bigger."

"Oh, gawd!" Mira's words burst like a storm cloud over the table. "You're another damn project?"

A marked hush fell over the table. Even the children, Collier noted, froze.

"Miranda Pierce, you will not use that language in my home, do you understand?"

Mira blinked as if shocked by her own outburst. "I'm sorry, Shara, I really am. But this guy? This guy is a new project? I thought you and I were going to work together this fall."

Shara's warm, open face closed into a steely expression. It was a look Collier had only ever seen his father wear when a figure skater he coached had not performed to expectations. "Mira, we've talked about this. You know what you have to do."

Mira glared at Shara, then pushed away from the table. "I guess I'm not that hungry anymore. Clearly, I've got work to do."

"I guess you do." Shara focused her gaze on the pancakes she cut for Katie.

Mira left without another word, but the chill hovered in the room.

Bryan nudged Collier with his elbow. "She's kind of a hard ass, my wife, isn't she?"

"Bryan!" Shara's exasperation burst for a moment, then faded to a warm smile. "The children."

"Daddy said ass!" The twins giggled until their faces turned bright red.

"Okay, and with that, it's time for your father to take you to school. You're Ms. Allen's problems now." Shara handed each child a colorful lunchbox as they headed out the screen door. She handed Bryan a brown paper bag, their hands brushing in the exchange.

Collier tried not to stare, but what sparked between the two of them could not be ignored. It was a lightening bright flash of love and passion. His stomach churned, as he recalled the same current flowing between Izzy and Quinn. He stared at his sticky, syrupy plate and cursed himself for ever letting his uncle send him here.

The screen door slapped shut behind Bryan and the kitchen was very quiet. Shara sat across the table and looked at him. "Well, that was a lot to take in for one morning, wasn't it?"

"I guess."

"Collier," she put a hand on his arm, "I want you to know you're completely welcome here. Mira, that's a whole drama you don't need to worry about. You're here. You're my focus, at least until you give me a reason to not focus on you."

Collier didn't miss the serious tone in her voice. "Should I be nervous?"

She stood and started clearing the table. "Not at all. I'll work with anyone so long as they have talent, material, or the will to work hard. Having all three sort of assures you a place here."

A shiver of doubt ran through Collier. "Look, I don't know what Uncle Archie told you..."

She smiled and he suddenly felt at ease. "Let's not worry about things until we have to. If you want to get warmed up, you should probably go down to the studio now. Your audition is in half an hour."

Collier put his fork down and stared at her. She wasn't kidding.

*

"Orphans and Runaways Records" was located in the lower level of the old two-story farmhouse in front of Bryan and Shara's cabin. There was a beaten earth path from the cabin around to the front of the property, where the old farmhouse stood. Collier paused at the door, his heart beating harder than he expected.

He wanted to laugh at himself. "I've been to Graceland a million times, and this little place is overwhelming me?"

"Yeah, well, Graceland is a museum. 'Orphans and Runaways' is a place that can make or break you."

Collier startled at the male voice behind him. "I'm sorry. I didn't realize I'd said that out loud." He studied the black leather clad man in front of him. "Wait…you're Jake Winter. From 'Teacher's Pets'."

Jake nodded as he opened the door to the studio. "Honored you've heard of us."

"Are you kidding? I've been trying to get the guys in my band to listen to your stuff for the last five years."

"Which would be cool to know, man, except we've been headlining stuff for the last eight years."

Collier's cheeks warmed, but he saw the Jake's grin and realized the man was teasing him.

"So you got a band?"

Collier shook his head as he stepped into the studio. "Not anymore."

"Yeah, most people can't keep up with my awesome talent either." Jake grinned and turned on the lights. "You're auditioning for Shara today?"

"I guess."

"You're the nephew, right? Mr. James' nephew?"

Collier was surprised until he thought about Molly Hunter's words. "News gets around quickly."

Jake nodded. "You can't keep a secret around here long, man. This isn't Nashville, which by the way, we're hitting on our

48

holiday tour. No pressure, but if you're any good, Shara might let you open for us."

Collier's breakfast threatened to make an appearance. "Really?"

"Oh, yeah. See, Shara's always looking for someone local she can work with who will work with us, you know, fit musically. So yeah, man, no pressure, but this audition you're doing could lead to something serious…or be a complete crap out." Jake grinned.

"Thanks for that."

"Don't mention it. You play piano? Guitar?'

"Both."

"Any good?"

"I think so." *Although now I'm not so sure about anything.*

"We'll see what Shara thinks." Jake set a guitar stand next to the piano. "You've got a few minutes, go in there and warm up. I've gotta run upstairs for some music stands. Don't be nervous, we're not that tough. All you have to do is be awesome."

Collier swallowed hard. "Thanks." He stepped into the studio and watched as Jake closed the door and sat in a chair in the recording booth. Collier looked around, taking the studio in, trying to get his brain to engage and absorb where he was. He sat at the piano and closed his eyes. *No pressure. This is just another thing you're doing. And if this doesn't pan out…*

Then what? I go back to Nashville and play in front of drunk college kids at Second Chances until I'm too old to hold a guitar?

Unbidden, Izzy's face came to mind. Her smile warmed him like it always did when he felt stressed. Even when they were kids together, her smile could ease any of his uncertainties. He wished, not for the first time in a day, that she were there sitting next to him, smiling. *Everything would be the way it's supposed to be if she'd just love me the way I love her.*

He rubbed his eyes. There was no use thinking that way. Izzy was married, pregnant, hopelessly in love with the super human Quinn Murray. And he, Collier, was sitting in a studio in Northern Wisconsin, readying himself for what would likely be a last long shot at success.

49

Hold it together. Try not to crap yourself.

"Ok, Collier, let's see what you've got for us."

Startled, and unaware of any time passing, Collier stared at the group assembled in front of him, and then at the piano. He felt ridiculous. After performing on the road for more than twenty years, he had no reason to be nervous in front of five strangers. Still, he couldn't get past the fact that 'Teacher's Pets' was a successful band and Shara Brandt Jacobs was the engine behind that success.

For the first time in his life, Collier James felt underprepared.

"Let me do the introductions," Shara pointed to Jake at the far end of the piano. "Jake Winter, lead guitar and vocals. Kelly Fuller, vocals, sax, and he's pretty much our writing and arranging guy."

Kelly shook Collier's hand.

"Over there we have Tony Jones, bass and Dan Jones, our drummer."

Collier nodded to the other two musicians. "I'm sorry. I guess when my uncle set this meeting up..." he stopped. Even to his ears, his tone sounded whiny, though not as whiny as his words. "I guess I didn't expect to be performing for...all of you."

"Buddy, that's rock and roll. You have to buck up. You have to answer the call of the music."

Everyone else groaned at Jake's words.

"Collier," Shara's voice was calm, soothing, and motherly. "These guys are some of the finest musicians I know."

"Some?" Tony, the bass player, gave her a surprised look. "Wow, eight years together, you'd think we'd get a little more credit than that."

"Tony, dude, you know Tom Petty was here that one day. Petty, man. Petty. No way are we better than Petty." Jake crossed his arms, as if that argument was over for good. "But that's pretty much the only guy better than us."

Shara waited for the din of debate between the men to subside. Collier thought she looked more like a mother controlling unruly boys than a genius music producer and musician, but he realized, listening to the members of ''Teacher's Pets'' argue and mock each other, much of her genius was just this: calming the noise so the talent and art could shine through.

Collier knew the story well. She'd taken 'Teacher's Pets' from a cover band playing in a few bars in Northeastern Wisconsin to a headliner and indie rock favorite. They were famous for their short and rare tours. While they played at their old haunts in the area quite often, it was a rare thing for them to leave the close knit Rock Harbor community for more than a couple weeks.

Shara's devotion to family was legendary, but Collier knew the stories about the band members, too, how they kept their day jobs in spite of their success. Kelly was the town cop. Jake helped run his family's dairy farm. The Jones Brothers were a big part of the volunteer fire department when they weren't operating the biggest orchard and cherry farm in Door County.

Quiet settled over the studio and Shara spoke. "Collier, I've played with these gentlemen for the better part of a decade. I trust their opinions, and I think you should, too. You come highly recommended by someone we all respect, but this is a business. If you want me to help you make that next step, you have to play for my guys."

"I understand." Collier cleared his throat and sat at the piano. He stroked a key to get a feel for the instrument. The keys were cool, smooth, still very new compared to most of the pianos Collier had played on before.

"Oh, I should say one more thing."

"Yes, Miss Shara?"

She grinned, her dark eyes snapping with mischief. "This is a business, but it's also a family. A really loud, rude family with no edit buttons. If they don't like what you play, these guys will not be shy about their opinions. Don't take it personally, but if they think you're terrible, they will tell you."

The ice broke as Collier returned Shara's smile. "Okay, no pressure, and I should be prepared for some seriously harsh comments. Thanks for that."

"But, by the same token, if you are any good, they'll do everything they can to boost your career." She patted his shoulder then moved away from the keyboard.

With five faces circling the piano, Collier tried to focus. He took a deep breath and played the first few chords of "Thanks, But No Thanks," the song he wrote the day after Izzy slept with Quinn for the first time, shattering Collier's hope that she'd ever love him. The notes, so often played, still held a cool echo of the original sorrow, because it was a feeling he'd never been able to let go. His voice trembled slightly with the opening phrase, but he lost himself, as he did so often, in the song, and Izzy's image rolled past his mind's eye with shocking clarity.

The image was a knife in his heart. This was why he didn't play the song on the piano all that often. It was simply too similar to the morning he'd written it in a New York hotel bar. He'd been suffering a brutal hangover in addition to his heartbreak, and all he wanted was to put his pain into a form he could touch and understand and control.

Playing on a guitar, on some dusty stage, while wearing period costumes, that was fine. There was a layer of separation between the pain that birthed the song and the performance.

This time, sitting at a piano, the memories were almost too much. He had little awareness of his voice, or if he even played the right notes. He was less performing a song than doing battle with his memories.

He finished, and the final chord echoed lightly in the air above them all. He let his hands drop to his lap, and waited for someone to say something, praying no one noticed the newly opened wound in his heart.

No one said much of anything for a few beats. Collier looked up, and saw five still faces.

"You must have loved her very much." Shara's voice was softer but soothing.

"There was so much in that song." Kelly nodded to Shara.

Tony and Dan mumbled something Collier couldn't understand, but chose to take as a compliment.

Jake glared at them all. "You've got to be kidding. That was a giant pile of suck."

Defensive, Collier fixed his glare on Jake.

"What are you talking about, Jake? That was a beautiful song," Shara scolded.

"A beautiful pile of suck, then."

Jake's words lit a fire under everyone and sparked several minutes of argument. Collier was not asked to speak, nor did he. He studied each face as someone spoke either in favor of, or against the song, his playing, his voice, and his overall talent level. While the argument raged he noticed movement behind everyone, in the mixing booth. He stared at the shadowy figure until she opened the door. It was Mira. How long she'd been in there, he didn't know, and he couldn't read anything on her face in the brief second her features were visible. She closed the door. The mixing booth went dark.

He didn't know why, but he wondered what she thought of him in that moment.

"Oh, I'm sorry, I thought we were here to listen to a musician, not some love sick wet mop." Jake's loud comment cut through Collier's reverie.

"Did you just call me a wet mop?"

It was the first sound he'd made since singing, and apparently everyone had forgotten about him, since they all looked at him with unmistakable surprise.

"Shara, the new guy is talking. Why is the new guy talking?"

Shara waved her hand at the group. "I'm well aware of that, Tony, but did anyone tell Collier he couldn't talk? I mean, this song is clearly born of some really deep emotions, and that's good."

"But the song blows. It blows big greasy chunks."

Kelly shook his head. "Thank you, Jake, for that polite, delicate opinion."

Collier stood up and placed his hands on top of the piano. "I'm sorry. I'm not understanding the problem. You asked me to play my best song, something I'd written, and I think that's it. So, Jake, why does it blow, as you say, big, greasy chunks?"

"Dude, it's a break up song, right?"

"I suppose. I wrote it after a break up of sorts."

"There's your problem. That song is all about the boo-hoo and she left me and now I'm miserable. It sucks, man."

Kelly shook his head. "Jake does not speak for all of us."

"I thought it was lovely. It's certainly something we could record." Shara's words were a balm on Collier's gaping emotions.

Jake stood and leaned on the piano, opposite Collier. "Sure, we can record it. But it's not a hit. You came here to move your career out of the weeds and away from sailing songs and limericks about ales, right?"

Jake's charade was gone. Collier was shocked but pleased that a real musician lay beneath the head-banger veneer. "Yes, yes that would be true."

"And I'm guessing, when you wrote this, you weren't thinking about singing it to middle-aged women in sweaty corsets. Hell, you probably weren't even thinking about the woman that made you so freakin' miserable. If you are really, really honest with yourself, you wrote this song because you felt like complete crap and you wanted to do a little whining."

"Jake!" Shara's tone was sharp.

"No, no." Collier waved a hand at Shara. "He's not...completely...wrong." Collier shook his head and sat on the piano bench. He started to play a few soft chords, a habit he'd had since he was a child just discovering the joys of stringing notes together. Over the soft notes, he continued. "I was shattered when I wrote that song. A woman I'd been in love with my entire life, had just told me she'd...well she'd chosen someone else. She told me by phone. I was sitting in an airport bar in New York. It was a complete cliché, right down to this strange woman coming up and talking to me. Suddenly, I was attractive to a woman where five minutes earlier I felt like a disease. Fueled by that attention and the copious amount of whiskey I'd consumed, I asked her back to my hotel room. We went there and...after...it didn't help. Instead,I felt like I'd betrayed Izzy. Except, she'd betrayed me first. So I went down to the hotel bar. There was a piano there. I just, I just started putting words together in my head."

54

Jake sat in his chair, crossed his arms, and looked very pleased with himself. "That's the problem with this song. It isn't about love lost or a break up. This song is about feeling like crap because life sucks. There's no shame in that, and if you embrace that then hey, the song is a freakin' marvel of modern music."

"You really are an idiot," Kelly grumbled.

"What you need, Collier, is passion. Not just emotion. I get that a song like that can get you laid. I mean, I'll bet you did real well on the bustier circuit with that song. Women weeping over your broken heart, your sad eyes, and they want to be the one to fix you, make you happy. I get it. But...if you are going to have a hit...if you are going to get people to sit up and take notice you need to put some passion in your music. You need to put some rage in your music. You need a primal scream of a song that says, 'this woman done me wrong!' And then, people will listen to anything else you have to say because you've already said something they completely understand in a way they respect."

Collier looked for Shara's reaction. She smiled quietly and nodded. "As you said, Collier, he's not completely wrong."

"What do we do next?"

Kelly pulled out a notebook and started writing. "What sort of time frame are you working with?"

Collier closed his eyes and tried to think of one single reason to return to Nashville. He had no band, no job, and no family to go back to. The only important thing in Nashville, as far as he was concerned, was Izzy, and she was busy having Quinn's baby and being blissfully happy. Collier pushed the ever-present image of Izzy's face out of his mind for a moment. "I have nothing pressing on my schedule. I can stay here and work as long as you'll have me."

Shara clapped her hands. "Good." She frowned. "The first thing is to sort out your living situation."

"I don't want to ruffle feathers."

"You're not the one ruffling anything." Shara tapped her lips with a pen. "You're not allergic to cats, are you?"

"No, ma'am."

"I'm sure Molly won't mind putting you up until we can get the loft situation cleared up. I'd let you just sleep upstairs, but it's getting to be winter and those rooms aren't comfortable."

"I appreciate you working with me."

"You may not, in a month. This won't be a picnic for you. The studio is open for the next several weeks, until we get serious about rehearsal for the tour. I want you here, working. Work with the guys, when they aren't playing a gig. Maybe travel with them. Listen to music. Listen to a lot of music. Upstairs you'll find a wildly comprehensive collection of recordings. Every genre, all kinds of artists, new, independent and well known. The goal here is to get you to find your voice, your sound and get you writing several songs we can compile into an album by spring." She looked him up and down. "You'll need a haircut and a shave. That long hair doesn't work."

Collier gripped his shoulder length hair in a makeshift ponytail. "Really?"

"You're not on the Ren Faire circuit now. Kelly?" Shara glanced at Kelly who was writing frantic notes.

"On it. I'll make sure he gets a haircut and a shave."

"Good." Shara returned her gaze to Collier. She smiled.

Collier got the feeling she was laughing at him. "What's so funny?"

"You're from the South. Winter comes early and lasts long here. You're going to need some mittens and snow boots, and a coat, soon. Kelly?"

"Coat and boots." Kelly wrote more notes.

Collier realized none of this seemed unusual to anyone else in the room. But there were issues no one had brought up. "Shara, I appreciate all that, but I need a job, you know, to pay the bills."

"Don't worry about rent and meals as long as you stay here. As for a job, I'm sure Dirty Dog Dave will have something you can do at his place. You'll probably be working…"

"For tips!" the four men yelled in unison.

Shara shook her head. "Then again, I think Dave might actually pay you."

"Why would that be?" Kelly looked surprised. "Dave doesn't pay anyone. Everyone at Triple D's works for tips."

Shara's dark eyes danced with mirth. "Because Collier, unlike our friend Dave, has a real Southern accent. He may pay Collier for elocution lessons."

Collier joined in the laughter with the others, but stilled when the mixing booth door opened again. This time he watched as Mira walked out.

She's been here the whole time but she wanted me to think she'd left.

What is up with this girl?

56

MIRA

Mira wiped one angry tear from her cheek as she stormed up the stairs to the loft. She slammed the door behind her and started stuffing her few belongings into her duffle bag. *Shara's promised him the loft. Now I have no choice but to go back to that house.*

She slapped away another tear and took a deep breath. Loneliness engulfed her. Even with the uneasy relationship she had with Shara, the loft was a much happier place than the house.

She thought about the fall and how Madelyn liked to come up some weekends to enjoy the solitude.

And she'll probably bring The Senator with her.

Fear and shame shuddered through her.

She struggled to stuff a pair of jeans into the already over-stuffed bag when suddenly Collier tapped her shoulder. She startled and glared at him. "What the hell do you want?" She regretted her sharp tone for a moment. Then she remembered he was the one kicking her out of the loft.

"I'm sorry. I did knock. You must have...not heard me."   57

"Whatever."

"You're leaving?"

She yanked unsuccessfully at the duffle zipper. "Yes, I'm leaving. You're the new project, so I'm out and you get to live here while Shara and her band of misfits make you the next rising star."

"You heard everything, then." He didn't seem surprised. He had a calm, old soul way of speaking.

Right now his voice annoyed her. "Of course I heard everything. I knew the minute I saw you lying in that bed last night what was going on. I can't blame Shara, she's been great to me, but...dammit." She swiped her hand across her eyes and inhaled. "I'll be stuck in this stupid town forever playing for tips at Dave's." A new thought, and a new anger flooded her. "And you've managed to screw that up for me, too."

"What are you talking about?"

She liked the worry in his eyes. "You distracted me last night. I didn't get half the tips I normally do. I figure I was short eighty bucks."

"Oh, you figure that, do you?" His steel gray eyes cooled and his posture stiffened. "So if I hand you eighty bucks, you'll somehow turn into a sweatheart?"

"Guess we'll have to see what happens. I mean, it would be the gentlemanly thing to do. That and, of course, not forcing me to go home."

"Oh, home? Home? So you do have someplace to go?"

There was no point in lying. "I do. I have a place, a house. My parents' house."

"And you'd rather stay here why?"

She bit her lip. "Look, none of this is any of your business so just get out and let me finish packing and then I'll be out of your way."

"Did I do something to piss you off that I'm not aware, or is this just how Wisconsin girls treat men?" His voice was soft, there was no trace of combativeness.

"I can't expect you to understand, and I'm not in the mood to explain." She raised stinging eyes to him and noticed his face held no trace of malice. *Damn...he's good looking. He's actually got kind eyes. And he seems to be a decent guy.* "Is there any chance you can just give me some time here?"

58

Collier closed his eyes and let out a deep breath. "Shara says I can stay with Molly Hunter. I'll stay there a couple days and you can, you know, make a more easy transition."

"Fine. Whatever." Force of habit, she swallowed down the flood of gratitude and responded with a cold tone she regretted. "Thanks." She blinked trying to keep as much loathing from her expression as possible.

His eyes clouded for a moment, and he shrugged. "Anything for a...lady."

He left as quietly as he came. She sat on the bed and glared at the door, annoyed by the sarcasm in his final words. *He has nice eyes. He's a selfish pig with nice eyes.*

She ignored the niggling feeling that she was being unfair to him.

COLLIER

Collier set his cup down and patted his stomach. "Miss Molly, that was the finest dinner I've had in a long time."

Molly Hunter set their plates in the sink and sat across from him. "I'm glad you enjoyed it. I don't get a chance to cook all that often. There isn't much point to it, when you're cooking for one."

"Well, you do know your way around a pork chop. I don't believe I've had a finer one."

Molly gave him a scolding look. "You were raised in the South, you should know better than to praise anyone's cooking other than your mother's."

Collier smiled. He liked Molly. Sitting here, at her table in her tidy little house, he felt at home. Molly Hunter was older than he was, but Collier couldn't tell how much older. She had a warm, ageless quality about her. Bryan Jacobs told him every man in Rock Harbor had been in love with Molly at one time or another, but that no man would ever measure up to her deceased husband, Robert. "Well. ma'am, I don't remember my mother that clearly. She passed when I was very small. And my father was hardly a cook. He passed a couple years ago."

"I'm sorry to hear that."

Collier poured more coffee into the dainty china cup in front of him. "I guess I'm just an orphan. A thirty-eight-year-old orphan." He smiled, his tone light.

"Well, your parents clearly raised you right, no matter how long you had them. What did your father do?"

Collier stirred a teaspoon of sugar into his coffee and stared at the dark brew, watching the white crystals meld into blackness. He didn't like to think about his father too often because his father was forever linked with Izzy in his memory. "He was a figure skating coach."

"Oh, he taught skating lessons?"

"It was more than that. He coached high-caliber talent. Sometimes they made it to the Nationals or the Olympics, sometimes they didn't, but he always got them to that high a level."

Molly looked impressed. "My, that is interesting. For as much ice as we get around here in the winter, I doubt we have anyone with any sort of skating talent."

"How bad are the winters?" Eager to change the subject from anything touching on Izzy, Collier turned to mundane conversation on the weather.

Molly laughed. "You really want to talk about the weather, Collier? Are you sure you aren't trying to steer me away from something?"

"How are you so good at reading minds?"

Molly shrugged. "I've always said the only people who wind up in Rock Harbor are orphans or runaways. Archibald James sent you here, and I doubt it's because you're a thirty-eight-year-old orphan."

"Orphans and runaways...that would explain the name of Shara's recording studio."

Molly nodded. "Bryan and your uncle named it. The studio was a wedding present from Bryan to Shara."

"Wow. That guy is a real hero, isn't he?"

"He wouldn't say so, and he sure doesn't want anyone else thinking like that. And stop changing the subject."

"I'm sorry. I'm not comfortable talking about myself."

"Okay."

"What's Mira's story?" The question surprised him.

"You won't talk about yourself, but you are eager to get the dirt on someone else?"

"No, not like that. We met in a fairly unpleasant way and she struck me as someone who has something going on."

Molly stood and set the coffee pot on the counter. "What makes you think that?"

"She'd rather sleep in that loft than go home. Doesn't she live with a sister and some senator or something?"

Molly nodded with a look of approval on her face. "You got a finger in local gossip already. Yes, she lives with Madelyn and The Senator down in Madison on and off. Mostly she stays at her parent's house. It's one of the houses closest to Bryan and Shara's place. Nice big spread, lots of room, and very cushy. But I don't get the feeling she likes being there."

"She doesn't like living in Madison with her sister?"

Molly shook her head. "She and Madelyn aren't what you'd call comfortable with each other. Mira went to UW Madison for a couple years, but dropped out. That's when things really started getting strained between her and Madelyn. Madelyn's raised her since their parents died when Miranda was four, so she's been more of a mother than a sister, and I think Mira's rebellious spirit annoys Madelyn." Molly pulled a tall stool to the middle of the kitchen. "Come on, let's take care of that hair."

Collier gripped his hair protectively. "Now?"

"Now's as good a time as any. Sit on this stool." She grinned at him. "Don't worry. I won't ruin your head. And if you're good, I might discuss Miss Miranda Pierce."

Obediently, Collier sat on the stool. Molly wrapped a white sheet around his neck and spread it out to cover him.

"Most of this happened before I moved to Rock Harbor, so all I know is what they've said for years." She started combing and cutting. "Madelyn is sixteen years older than Mira, give or take. Ellen and Lester Pierce had lived in Rock Harbor for years. Lester inherited the place from his father, and they moved in, Madelyn was just a baby. We were all so surprised when Ellen turned up pregnant at forty-four. I mean, sure, they'd wanted more children than just Madelyn, but it didn't seem like it was meant to be. So it was very near a miracle when she told everyone at church the news. Then they vanished for two years."

"Vanished?"

"Went on a long vacation I guess. When they came back, Miranda was already walking. Ellen was dead and buried."

"How did she die?"

"They say it was a boating accident."

The story intrigued Collier. "And no one thought anything of the Pierces just taking off for two years?"

"People thought plenty, but the Pierces had money. An extended trip like that wasn't out of the question, especially the way Ellen was. She was never comfortable here. Folks did ask questions when they came back and it was just Lester and the girls. Poor things. Lester died two years later. They say it was a heart attack, but most around here figure he just couldn't live without Ellen. As odd a couple as they were, he loved her."

Molly moved around him, cutting hair and letting it fall to the floor.

"Miss Molly, I can't help but feel there's more to the story than that." Collier tried to ignore the long locks fluttering around him.

"Well, everything beyond Lester's death is just local rumors and guesses on my part." Molly stopped moving around him and brushed loose hair from his neck. "Like I always say. Everyone has a secret. And, in a town like this, everyone knows what it is long before you actually tell anyone. We just don't choose to talk about it out loud, especially with each other. Secrets come out, I've found, all on their own, and soon enough."

She removed the sheet. Collier sensed that the subject was closed for the moment. He ran a tentative hand through his hair. Molly handed him a mirror so he could check his reflection. "This is going to take some getting used to." He let Molly think he was referring to his new look as opposed to his growing interest in the thorny woman living in the loft.

62

MIRA

The crowd was a rowdy one, for a Monday night, exactly the mood Mira wanted. Opening for ''Teacher's Pets'' was a big deal, because it was more than likely Shara would be in the audience. *If I bring down the house, she'll have to let me stay in the loft, and I won't have to go back to the house. There won't be any chance for Madelyn to just drop in on me. I'll be free.*

Her first several songs were covers, crowd pleasers she'd played many times before. Scanning the crowd, she didn't see any sign of Shara, though she caught Kelly Fuller's eye. Taking a short break, she waved him to the stage.

"So, is Shara coming tonight to hear me?"

Kelly looked confused. "Was she supposed to?"

Disappointment flooded her. "No, I guess I just thought…you guys are playing tonight, and Dave asked me to open for you."

"Oh, I see." Kelly patted her arm. "No, the group we booked a month ago dropped out. Dave didn't want any dead time on stage."

"So, Shara is not going to be here."

"Doubtful. One of the kids has a really bad cold and Bryan has a teacher's meeting late. But hey, don't worry about it. You're totally warming this place up for us, which is great."

Mira scanned the crowd again. Collier James was sitting at the bar, talking to Dave. She watched as they shook hands and Dave poured Collier a beer, for which, Mira noted, Collier did not pay.

Now he's working here? Furious, she picked up her guitar. *He took my space at Shara's, he's going to get the loft and now he works where I work.*

Damn that man.

Well Dave, you want focus, just watch me now.

She played for the next forty minutes with a wild abandon that first thrilled the crowd, then stilled them into fearful muttering. She ended her last song, a vulgarity laced rant she'd written about Madelyn, and glared at the crowd. Without a word she stormed off the stage to a smattering of confused applause.

63

COLLIER

Collier watched her angry exit with the same shocked feeling everyone else seemed to have. *What is up with her?*

"Chanel! What the devil is wrong with that girl? She's done here!"

Collier looked over his shoulder at Dave and Chanel, who were clearly arguing about what everyone had just witnessed. Chanel spoke quietly and after a few minutes of discussion, Collier sensed Mira wouldn't be fired from waiting tables, but she wouldn't be playing on Dave's stage for a very long time.

She has some real talent. No discipline, no control, but talent. She's got a real spark.

Collier finished his beer and watched as 'Teachers' Pets' took the stage, excited to finally see them live. Unfortunately, his focus was divided between what was happening on the stage and what was happening at the bar in front of him.

Mira, still clearly fuming about something, appeared as if out of nowhere and settled on a stool. She started chatting up the bartender. Collier couldn't hear anything that passed between them, but her body language was entirely too obvious. In the course of half an hour she threw back several shots and said something to the bartender that made the man remove his apron immediately and grab his coat. Without a look at Dave, who, Collier noted, looked less than pleased at the departure of one of his bartenders, the man followed Mira outside.

64

"You really shouldn't stare." Chanel pushed another beer in front of him.

"What was that about?"

"What do you think?"

"He leaves, just like that? Dave allows that?"

Chanel smiled. "Why do you think he hired you so easily? That guy was on his way out. Tonight was his last night. He's headed to UW Milwaukee at the end of the week."

"Did Mira...did she know that?"

"Doubtful she cared if she did."

"She's done this before?"

Chanel studied him. "You got feelings for her?"

Collier laughed. "Hell, no. She hates me because I'm getting the loft at the end of the week. Every time we're near each other, we're arguing."

"Good. I love the girl, but she is pure poison when it comes to relationships. Almost makes me wonder sometimes…"

A shadow passed over Chanel's face. Collier didn't miss it. "Makes you wonder what?"

"Makes me wonder about the men she goes with. This is a small town. You'd think her reputation would stop at least one once in a while."

"Speaking as a man, most of us don't tend to turn down something that's offered." Collier shook his head. "So that's her deal, then? She sings like she's on fire and then she goes home with some guy?"

"Not all the time." Chanel shook her head. "She's been like a little sis to me, you know? But there's only so much a girl like that will listen to before she goes on her own."

"She gonna be okay?"

"Oh, yeah, she'll be fine. I mean, she's sort of like an alley cat, nine lives, you know?" Chanel shrugged. "Dave won't fire her, so tomorrow morning she'll still have a job. And she'll have plenty of regret, I'm sure."

Collier nodded and Chanel walked away to help a customer. Glancing at the door, Collier realized he was very concerned about Mira.

That surprised him.

MIRA

Mira cast a final glance around the loft before slamming the door behind her. She was angry, and she wanted to be angry at Collier, but, deep in a remote corner of her brain, she knew that wasn't fair. It wasn't Collier James' fault her life was beyond a mess. She stomped down the stairs and through the barn, ignoring Bryan's quizzical glance.

She yanked open the hatchback of her aging Honda Civic, dumped her duffle bag and guitar case in and slammed the hatch closed. All she wanted to do was run away from Rock Harbor, from Madelyn, from everything. *A fresh start some place would be so easy.*

Except it wasn't. Not for her. There was no way she could turn her back on Dusty. She was tied to this place, this life, because she was tied to him.

"Mira!"

Mira paused, her hand on the car door handle. Shara waved her up to the porch. "Yeah?"

"You have to understand this has nothing to do with the talent I know you have." Shara placed a hand on her shoulder. "Take some time, go at your own pace. Get your stuff together. I see that spark in you, and I'll be happy to work with you any time you want."

Mira stifled the urge to slap Shara's hand. Only a couple years separated them, yet Shara acted so much older, so much more together. Mira knew the stories about Shara's childhood, about her evil grandmother and her more horrible fiancé. Mira knew Shara wasn't putting on an act. She respected Shara for everything she'd survived.

But Shara knew nothing about her and what she'd survived, and what she battled every day.

"Yeah, I'll be fine." She shrugged, less to shake away Shara's hand than to give herself an air of nonchalance. "I get it, I do. I just like it here, you know? I hate how empty that house is."

"Stop by any time for dinner. You know the kids love you. Bryan and I do, too."

Mira's lips twisted into a sneer. "Bryan tolerates me because of you, and you know it." She respected that Shara didn't

66

protest. "Look, I'll be okay. I just…" she shivered, thinking about where she was headed.

"I know. It's lonely on your own. But hey, at the end of the month the kids all have a long weekend for teachers' conference. Madelyn could bring Dusty up with her?"

Not an improvement. "Well, I guess we'll see. Madelyn, you know, she doesn't approve of me. I don't fit the mold for her husband's plans. I'm not exactly great in photo ops these days."

"So he's going to run, then? For governor?"

Mira nodded. The Senator, as everyone called Madelyn's husband, had no intentions of coming back to Rock Harbor when he ran for governor. Mira knew it was the only reason she moved back to her childhood home. The idea of running into him in the hallway or sitting across the table from him was more than she wanted to consider. "Yeah, they've got all kinds of meetings and stupid stuff. Madelyn's crazy busy."

"Well maybe they'll send Dusty up here on his own."

That would be as close to heaven as I'll ever get.

"He can hang out with his Aunt Mira and have a wonderful break."

Right. His aunt. I'm his aunt. Mira blinked back a stinging tear. "Anyway, hey, good luck with your new project." She couldn't completely bite back all the sarcasm in her words.

67

"Thanks. I think Collier will be okay, with some work."

"With a lot of work." Mira didn't know why the idea of Collier James rubbed her so raw, other than she was losing a cozy, safe place to live now that he was moving in. Mira ignored the quizzical look Shara gave her as she got into her Civic and backed down the drive.

Only when she was on the road, alone, did Mira allow the tears to roll down her face.

*

The house phone was ringing as she opened the door. "Carson!" Mira called for the property caretaker, her voice echoing in the hollow hall. Getting no response, she dropped her bags and ran to the phone. "Hello?"

"Oh, you are home, then, we were beginning to wonder."

Mira's skin prickled at the sound of Madelyn's voice. "What do you want, Madelyn? Where is Carson?"

"Where have you been? I've tried calling you several times."

Didn't bother dialing my cell..."I was working."

"I know that. I called that horrible bar, they told me you'd been doing your little act on stage. I mean, where have you been sleeping?"

"It's not a little act, Madelyn. I'm a singer and a song writer." Mira hated her defensive tone.

"I know you like to think that, and I don't have the time or the interest to debate the value of what you do with your private life. So long as you keep it private."

"Right, we wouldn't want anything to damage The Senator's chances at being The Governor, would we, Sis?"

"No, we wouldn't. But you haven't answered my question. Where have you been sleeping?"

"Don't you mean, 'who have I been sleeping with? And don't bother correcting my grammar. You're not my mother and you're not my English teacher."

There was a pause on the other end of the line. Mira could almost hear Madelyn's brain trying to formulate a sharp comeback.

"You still haven't answered my question."

It was useless to lie, Mira knew too well, especially when Madelyn took that cold, clipped tone. Madelyn knew everything. She had people on payroll to keep tabs on everything that might affect The Senator's political progress. Mira knew she was one of those things. "Not that it's really any business of yours, but I was staying at the Jacobs' place. Shara and I were working on some new music, and she let me stay in the loft. Now, answer my questions: where is Carson?" Mira strolled through the front room to the kitchen, noting there was not one sign that Carson, the long time family assistant, had been anywhere near the house.

"I had Carson come back here. He's far more use to us than he is rattling around an empty house up there. But now that I know you're back in the house I'll send him."

"No need. I can manage by myself."

Madelyn's laughter was as irritating as her voice. "You can't heat a can of beans."

Mira gripped the receiver tightly, trying to get hold of her temper. Madelyn had raised her, but had always treated her like she was mentally incapable of anything. "Why would I want to heat a can of beans, Madelyn, when I can cook a perfectly good dinner for myself?"

"Don't be ridiculous. I'll send Carson tomorrow."

"How about if you send Dusty instead?" Mira hated how she sounded. Like she was begging.

Madelyn was silent for a beat. "No, I don't think that would be a good idea. He has school."

"They have a break in a few weeks, at the end of October. Just send him up here then. We'll do Halloween together. He'll have fun, I promise. Plus, you can keep Carson, so you won't be inconvenienced."

"Not possible, Miranda. You know The Senator is starting his campaign the end of October. We need Dusty here."

"Madelyn, he's not a photo op, he's a child and he needs some fun." Mira bit back the words she ached to say. *And I need to see him.*

"Be that as it may, if he comes, he comes with Carson. I'm certainly not sending my twelve-year-old across the state alone."

"I'm sorry, your twelve-year-old son?" Mira couldn't stop herself. Madelyn knew too well how to raise her dander with one simple phrase. And though she knew she'd just opened up their oldest and ugliest argument, Mira didn't care. She was angry, she was hungry, she was tired.

She was lonely.

"Yes, Miranda. My twelve-year-old son. Which is what he's been every day of his life since he entered this world and which you'd better not forget or I won't allow you any time alone with him."

Mira rubbed her stomach, as if remembering the feel of pregnancy. She cursed her weakness, the day she found out she was pregnant. She was a child, fifteen, and scared to death. Madelyn's offer to raise Dusty as her own seemed like a godsend back then. The agreement, Madelyn's terms, were that no one, not Dusty, not anyone, was to know Dusty was hers until Dusty turned twenty-five, or until the Senator retired from public life, whichever came last. Madelyn's motives were, always, political, and a baby meant big poll numbers and popularity for The Senator. Mira's only request, before agreeing to Madelyn's

69

terms, was that Madelyn never ask her the identity of Dusty's father. *That part of the secret is mine to deal with.*

It had been easy, at first. Madelyn announced she was pregnant, and was going to move back to the privacy of Rock Harbor, away from the hustle and bustle of Madison, and she was taking her younger sister to finish school in the calm confines of her old home town. The lie played well to the Madison elite and Madelyn knew few in Rock Harbor paid enough attention to point out the Pierce girls never arrived back home.

The sisters traveled to a remote town Canada where Madelyn and Mira owned a cabin inherited from their father. No one knew about the cabin, not even The Senator who stayed in Madison pursuing his political career. Mira stayed at the cabin her entire pregnancy, cared for by Carson. Madelyn traveled, though Mira never knew where she went.

Seven months later they returned to Wisconsin. Madelyn, at thirty-one, was the picture of a happy first time mother. Holding a baby made her look ten years younger, something Mira knew Madelyn loved. Mira, though she regretted the arrangement almost immediately, was content enough to be a favorite aunt. Somehow, though, life lost all taste and interest for her. Mira finished high school. She went to college, floundered, dropped out, and spent most of her time playing music for tips in one coffee shop or another.

Now, at twenty-eight, Mira was confident of few things. But she knew, deep in her heart, she'd be a better mother to Dusty than the cold, inattentive Madelyn. She ached to tell her son the truth, now that he was older, but to break the agreement would be to lose Dusty forever, because while there was no signed agreement between the sisters, only Dusty's birth certificate, a slim piece of paper hidden in a safe only Madelyn knew about, testified the truth. Mira knew Madelyn never made threats lightly. The small amount of time Mira had with Dusty was the slim thread that kept her tethered to Madelyn.

"Fine, whatever Madelyn. You know I won't say anything." *I'm very good at keeping our secrets…all of them.*

"Good. While I'm on the phone, have you talked about The Senator's campaign? What's the feeling in Rock Harbor?"

"I'm not your pollster, Madelyn. I'm not on your payroll."

"You think not? So I guess having money for college, a roof over your head your entire life, music lessons, not to mention a loving home for you and for Dustin…"

"That's enough!" Mira wanted to throw her phone across the cavernous front room. "Fine. No. I haven't taken a poll of my friends. Most of the people I hang out with aren't exactly what you'd call <u>voters</u>."

"Then you should 'hang out' with a better class of friends. It would be a terrible shame if the Senator didn't carry our hometown, after all. He would be very disappointed in you."

Madelyn didn't wait for Mira to respond before hanging up. Mira tossed her phone on the hall table and dashed a tear from her face. "I've spent too much time being weepy today." Her growl echoed in the vast room. "I need to get on track and write something worth singing."

She squared her shoulders and crossed the front room. She reverently removed the dust cover from the pristine grand piano. Since her earliest days, the piano was her very favorite place in the house. In part of a memory, too faint to be trusted, she recalled hiding beneath the piano while heated arguments raged around her between Madelyn and her father, in the early days before her father died. In her teen years playing the piano was an escape from Madelyn's constant criticism, and from The Senator's constant, uncomfortable attention.

Mira opened the piano lid, sat down, and stroked a few keys gently. *Perfectly tuned. Carson knows to keep it tuned.*

Carson was the closest thing to an ally Mira had. He was the one person Madelyn approved of, though she didn't fully understand or appreciate Carson's staunch defense of her younger sister. Madelyn didn't approve of anything touching Mira's life, while Carson, in his quiet, stodgy way, treated her like a favorite child. It infuriated Madelyn, but she'd never fire Carson. He'd been with Madelyn since the day she'd married The Senator, and Mira often sensed Madelyn feared what Carson might say if she let him go.

Her phone rang. Mira stopped playing, and checked the grandfather clock in the corner of the room. She didn't need to see her phone's display to know who called. It was after four in the afternoon. Otis would be on the other end of the line.

Mira ignored the guilty twinge of conscience. Madelyn had every right to disapprove of Otis, who made his living as a small time drug pusher, selling weed to high school kids and assorted prescription pills to anyone who answered his phone calls. But Mira's gnawing loneliness was too much to bear. Otis was a warm body in a cold house. She answered the phone. "Hey, Otis."

"Mira, baby! I have been trying to reach you for days."

Shara Brandt, also, did not approve of Otis. Mira knew this and when she stayed at the loft, she stayed away from him.

"I've been around. Just got into town a week ago. Been staying out at the Jacobs' place."

"Dude, Mr. Jacobs…that was one cool teacher. Do you remember that time you and I smoked some cigs behind his barn and he chased us away with a pitchfork? Classic."

Mira rubbed her temples. Otis was the eternal high school kid, and sometimes, like now, talking to him could be exhausting. Still, she was alone and painfully lonely. "Otis, I really don't want to talk about Bryan Jacobs. How about if you just come on over? We could hang out and watch a movie or something."

Otis hooted and ended the call. Mira built a fire in the fireplace. He wasn't much company, but at least she wouldn't have to be home alone in this house.

She carried her duffle upstairs to her old bedroom and set it on the bed. Unzipping it, she pulled out a pair of sweats. The black velvet box fell on the floor. She picked it up and held it for a heartbeat. *One quick, little cut. It really won't make a difference. Just one.*

Her hands trembled as she dropped the box. It hit the hardwood floor and bounced under the bed. She sat on the bed, stripped off her jeans and slid into the comfort of her sweatpants.

It took conscious effort on her part not to look under the bed as she turned out the light and closed the door.

COLLIER

Sun streamed through the window and across Collier's bed. The loft was warm, but he could see frost on the awning just outside his window. Absently he wondered if he could sit on the overhang and take in some of the morning sun without sliding off and hitting the drive below. He decided he could. Reaching for a shirt and a pair of jeans, he shivered as his bare skin met with the cooler air in the loft. Once dressed, he took his guitar out of his case. *Might as well try and work on something…in case any inspiration hits.*

As he crawled through the window, Collier doubted the view would help. In the month since he'd moved into the loft the only original thing he'd come up with was a bawdy drinking song about a dark haired harlot. While he had no doubt the Stillman brothers would have enjoyed it, he didn't want to think what the reaction at the studio would be.

Collier also didn't care to analyze why everything he felt like writing lately always featured an unpleasant brunette.

"You wanna go for a ride?"

Collier looked down at Bryan from his perch on the overhang. "You mean on a horse?"

"Sure, unless there's some other farm animal you'd like to ride. I think Marva Blakely has some goats, if that's more your speed."

Collier grinned. As much as Collier didn't want to admit it, he enjoyed spending time with Bryan. In the short time he'd lived in the loft, he and Bryan had developed a friendship. "I can't remember the last time I rode a horse."

Bryan chuckled. "It'll be fun for me, then."

Collier slipped through the window and laid his guitar on the bed before heading down the stairs where Bryan saddled the mare, Lucy. "She's not going to throw me is she?"

"Not if she likes you." Bryan hoisted a saddle across Lucy's broad back.

"Then I'm in trouble. Not many women like me."

Bryan laughed. "There was a time I would have envied you that." He handed the reigns to Collier. "Hold her while I saddle Pepper." He didn't say anything as he lead the big stallion

73

out of the stall and cross tied him before lifting the saddle to the horse's back. Bryan finished his task and then nodded to Collier, who surprised himself by getting into the saddle without aid. Bryan made a few adjustments to the mare's cinch before swinging onto Pepper.

Once in the open field Bryan spoke companionably. "I gotta ask: How is it possible women don't like you?"

"Not a weird question coming from you at all, Bryan."

"No, I mean, you're a musician. You're not…horrible looking…and you seem like you'd actually like some female attention now and again." Bryan shrugged. "And yes, that did sound weird coming out of my mouth just now. Like suddenly Shara or Molly are speaking through me."

Collier laughed. "You want the truth?"

"Why not?"

"Women like guys like you, tall, dark, mysterious…guys like Quinn Murray. I don't fit that mold."

"The hockey player? You know Quinn Murray?" Bryan looked surprised and interested.

"Yes," Collier expelled the word from his lungs like a dreary cloud. "I know Quinn Murray."

Bryan studied him. "You don't much like him, though, do you?"

Collier shrugged. "What's not to like? He's a great guy. He's everything to everyone. He's Captain Freaking America."

Bryan laughed, startling both horses. "Well, since I already regret bringing up the subject, I might as well ask: I'm guessing Quinn Murray stole your girl?"

She never really was my girl.

Collier tried to swallow the bitter thought. "It's not just that…" Protest was pointless. "Okay, yeah. He did. She was the love of my life, since we were kids. And I finally thought I had a real shot with her; then he swoops in and it's over."

"It might not be over. You could get her back. Love conquers all and all that crap."

"They got married."

"Oh, yeah, married is pretty serious."

"And they're having a kid. Or they had it. I don't know."

"You need to start looking elsewhere."

"I would…if I felt like it." Collier leaned forward in the saddle a bit. "But what's the point? Women are looking for heroes. I mean, look at you and Shara. I hear from just about everyone in town that you saved her life a couple times. When guys like you are around, what hope do us mortals have?"

"I do appreciate how you're not turning into some whiny brat about this." Bryan grinned and slowed Pepper to a walk. "I need to stop asking people things. It never ends well. You'd do better having this conversation with a woman. Talk to Shara."

"I can't talk to Shara about something like this."

"Why not?"

"She's my boss. I am not talking to my boss about my big heartbreak and how much I hate the guy she married. Do you really want me to ask your wife how to make me a hero just like you?"

"A valid point. So go talk to Molly. She seems to like you and she's a woman."

Lucy shied from some weeds, and Collier lost his footing in a stirrup. He righted himself and shook his head. "Molly's great, everyone around here is great. But…"

"But Molly is one of the people who told you the great love story of Bryan and Shara." Bryan chuckled. "Bonus, her husband was cut from some pretty heroic cloth. She's been a widow for ages, and not a man in this town has caught her eye."

"She's a wonderful woman." Collier blushed at his candid comment. "The best way I can describe her is a very fine wine."

"I think she'd like that. But I get it. You're working under some delusion that you can't get a woman because of all the heroes floating around." Bryan cleared his throat. "I'm not entirely equipped to give you advice."

Collier nodded. "Look, Bryan, you're a really great guy. I don't want to make you uncomfortable…"

"Too late."

"I sound miserable, but dammit, I am." Collier blinked, surprised he said the words out loud.

"So what, you want some pointers on how to be an awesome, heroic guy women can't keep their hands off?"

"Geez, when you put it like that…okay, yeah."

Bryan halted Pepper; Lucy followed suit. He pointed to a creek bank that sloped down in front of them. "I think we need to sit down. I'm going to just have to set you right about a few things."

They dismounted and tied the horses to a nearby tree. Sitting in the shade, Bryan nodded toward the water. "Shara fell in that creek and nearly froze to death once."

"Was that where you found her when she first got to Rock Harbor?"

Bryan arched and eyebrow. "Oh, right, you stayed with Molly for a while. She would fill you in on everything." He paused. "No, this was later."

"You saved her from almost drowning twice? Geez man, what else?"

"You know about the barn fire?"

"Yeah."

"And my maniac of an ex-wife who tried to kill her?" Bryan's eyes snapped with mischief.

"Yeah."

Bryan grinned. "I'm pretty sure that's it."

"Oh, is that all? What a relief. I thought I'd have way more to live up to."

76

"Just shut up, okay? I've never told this story to anyone else, so only Shara and I know this even happened. It was early spring, she'd just moved into the loft. She was supposed to be my housekeeper, but Molly and Joanna, Jo's married to Drew, the principal at the school, anyway, Molly and Jo thought it was a good idea to have someone keep an eye on me, make sure I ate my vegetables and didn't try to drink myself to death."

Though Bryan spoke with a light, even tone, Collier was surprised. "Was that a possibility?"

"Every day for almost three years. My marriage failed in a spectacular manner and I spiraled. Turned myself into a hermit. A drunken hermit. Every woman in town thought I was this wonderful, dramatic, wounded guy who just needed a good woman to bring him back from the brink…and every woman in town tried her darndest to be that woman. But I wanted to stop hurting, and the best way I found worked was mass quantities of liquor." Bryan shook his head, a shadow passing over his face as he spoke. "I doubt anyone knows just how close I was to ending everything. Not even Drew, who is the best friend any guy can have. I walled myself in and sentenced myself to a slow death."

"What happened?"

"Shara happened. The day she turned up in Rock Harbor, suddenly there was this other person who didn't know my whole story and had zero sympathy for me." Bryan tossed a pebble into the creek. "I hated her. I accused her of being the heiress wanted for the murder of her grandmother."

"You weren't wrong."

"Nope I sure wasn't. By the time I found that out it didn't matter. I was hopelessly in love with her. But at first I hated her, and I did everything I could to make her miserable."

"Gee, Bryan, that's not how heroes act." Collier laughed at his own sarcasm.

"Which is what I'm trying to tell you. We weren't this mythical romance. I didn't trust her and I gave her every reason to hate me. At first."

"So what changed?"

Bryan leaned back against the tree. "We got to know each other. It took a while, but by the time Jo and Molly convinced me to let her live in the loft, Shara and I were sort of friends. We both had secrets we didn't feel like sharing and I think that was something that bonded us together. And then, sometime after she moved here, she and I went for a ride. Her horse startled and ran away, heading for this creek. I had no idea whether or not Shara knew how to ride a horse, and I was afraid she'd get thrown. But she knew what she was doing. She rode that crazy beast right into the deepest part of the creek. That slowed the horse without any injury."

"But Shara?"

"Shara thought she would grab the reigns and walk that horse up the creek bank and everything would be fine. But it was the spring thaw and this innocent little creek was twice as deep as it is now and rushing fast. She was in the water for a few minutes, but it was enough for hypothermia to set in."

Even though Bryan spoke softly, Collier saw the scene as if it played out in front of him. "It's a pretty long ride from here to your place."

"Scariest ride of my life. I held on to her the entire way back, and got her in a tub of warm water."

"So, you saved her life."

"That was not what I was thinking at the time," Bryan grinned. "I realized that night I was very, very aware that she was wearing a pink bra. I hadn't given her under things any thought to that point."

Collier laughed out loud, startling the horses. "But how is this supposed to apply to me? I can't very well go around scaring horses hoping one of them will dump a lady in the creek."

"No, see, I'm telling you this, Collier, because until that moment, until that second I realized I might lose her, I had no idea how much Shara meant to me. Oh, believe me, after that we went through several layers of dramatic hell, but that's the stuff everyone knows. That night, on this spot, that's when I realized I wanted to be some kind of hero, if I could, at least for her. Before that, I'd fought the notion like it was a plague."

"Yeah, but anyone would've pulled her out of the creek."

"Which is why when people talk, I laugh because I never think I did anything all that heroic. Collier, it's not what you do that makes you a hero to a woman. It's what you want to do."

Collier frowned. "I'm not sure I follow you."

"Think about it this way," Bryan stood and brushed dry grass from his jeans. "All those love songs, all those romantic movies women like. What's the sentiment every hero blurts out?"

78

"I don't know."

"You're a song writer, Col, this shouldn't be this hard."

"Okay, okay. They all talk about wanting to die for the person they love."

"There you go. And have you ever felt like that for anyone?"

"Well, no. That's not a real emotion. No one would truly die for anyone. What would the point be, if you want to be with that person?" Collier mounted his horse and stared at Bryan.

"It's very real, my friend," Bryan swung his leg over Pepper and looked back at Collier. "There will come a moment when you realize that you will do anything, but not just for any woman, this one specific woman. You will move heaven and earth, you will give up anything, everything that's important to you, to make sure she's safe and cared for because you know you'll never be able to survive this world without her in it. The moment you feel that way for even just a heartbeat, that's the spark that turns you into a hero.

<u>MIRA</u>

"Aunt Mira!"

Mira looked up from the keyboard. "Dusty!" She leaped up and caught the boy in her arms. "I can't believe you're here!" She held the boy close to her, inhaling the smell of him.

"Cool hair! Black looks awesome!"

"Thanks buddy." She hugged him tighter. "I'm just so happy you're here!"

"I'm off of school for a couple days and Mother said we could come up."

Mira froze. "Mother?"

"Hello, Miranda." Madelyn strode in, followed by two assistants who carried her bags. "It's good to see you."

Mira loosened her grip on Dusty. "You didn't need to come up, Madelyn. You could have just sent Carson with him."

"The Senator needs Carson this weekend. Besides, I thought it would be nice to come back…home…for a weekend. Dusty can, as you suggested, go trick or treating with the Jacobs and the Shepaskis. You and I can catch up on a few things."

"Dusty, why don't you go on up to your room and get unpacked." Mira released her son from her grip and frowned at her sister. She waited until Dusty was out of the room until she spoke. "I don't know what you want, but there was no need for you to make the trip up here."

"There is every need for me to be here. <u>My son</u> is here."

Mira let the barb slide. "I'm perfectly capable of taking care of Dusty for a weekend."

Madelyn perched herself stiffly on one of the wing back chairs. "I don't think you are, Miranda."

What did I do this time? "Madelyn, what in the world are you talking about?"

"You've been in contact with Otis Drumm."

Mira stared at Madelyn. "What, you've got my cell tapped now?"

Madelyn pursed her perfectly lined lips. "No need. It's not like you're discreet Miranda. You know how I feel about drugs and drug dealers."

"He's a friend from high school. I didn't buy a thing from him. He came over and we watched a movie."

"I'm sure."

Mira felt the rage rising inside her. Her skin burned like it always did when Madelyn was around. "Test me if you want, Madelyn, I'm clean, just like every other time. I don't know what you think you're going to find, other than the occasional trace of alcohol."

"I'm glad you agree." Madelyn waved to her assistant. "Lisa will take your sample."

"You've got to be kidding." While it used to be a regular thing, Madelyn hadn't tested Mira for drugs in years.

"I assure you, Miranda, I am not. If you insist on consorting with known drug dealers, then you need to accept the fact that I don't trust you to keep yourself clean."

Mira glared at her, but knew she wouldn't win. She never did, with Madelyn, and fighting only made it harder for her to have any time with Dusty. "Fine," she snarled. "Do you want blood or urine this time?" She prayed it would urine. There were new wounds on her arm.

"Urine will be fine."

Mira snapped the sample cup out of Lisa's hands and stormed off to the bathroom. Filling the cup quickly, she screwed the cap on and stared at it. *This is what I'm reduced to just because I committed the cardinal sin of having the child Madelyn couldn't or wouldn't.*

A secret smile played around her lips. *Madelyn can test me all she wants. There is one thing she doesn't know and someday I will crush her with it.*

She washed her hands and made her way back to the sitting room, never bothering to hide her smile.

Madelyn looked up from her papers as Mira returned. "What's so funny?"

"Nothing. So, what do you want to do now, sister dear?"

"I have some things to attend to, things I should be dealing with back in Madison, but since Dustin got wind of you wanting him up here for his school break, I was forced to bring him here."

"I doubt anyone ever forced you to do something that didn't serve your purposes."

Madelyn raised an eyebrow. "You might be right about that, Miranda."

"Hey, score one for me."

Madelyn studied her. "I have to say, I was surprised to see you staying here. I certainly would think you'd be at Shara Jacobs' loft."

Mira's clenched her jaw. "Oh, yes, well, I felt I could get more work done here, you know, the piano is right here and it's way more quiet. The studio's been packed lately. It just made more sense."

"She kicked you out."

Madelyn's tone was even, unsurprised. *That's what you would expect wouldn't you, from your screwed up sister?* Mira bit her lip. "As a matter of fact, no. I did move out on my own. I had the option to stay. I decided to work here."

Madelyn shook her head and turned her attention back to the papers in front of her. "She found someone more talented, which probably wasn't that hard, and she kicked you out."

"You haven't heard a word I said." Mira kept her voice as low as possible, but couldn't keep the waver of rage out of her words.

Madelyn glanced up. "Miranda, many things have passed between you and me over the years. The truth has never been one of those things."

Well you got that right, anyway.

Mira balled her fists at her side, and stared at her sister until Madelyn returned to her papers. Rage choking her, Mira stomped out of the house to her car. Jabbing the key into the ignition, she roared the vehicle up the drive and hit the road at a high speed, trying to put as much distance between herself and Madelyn as possible.

*

She pulled into Dave's parking lot, her car speed lower, but her rage still heating her body. She slammed her car door, the feel of the force calming her a little. By the time she was inside, much of her anger had cooled. "Hey, Chanel."

"Hey, Mira. You're not waiting tables tonight, are you?"

Mira wanted to laugh at the concerned expression on her friend's face. "No, I'm not. And you don't have to candy coat it. I know Dave's pissed at me for my last performance. Hell, everyone around here is pissed at me for one thing or another."

"You're just in a rough spot, that's all, girl."

"I know. I know. But I've got something. I think I really have something, I just need to work on it. I was hoping I could use the backstage piano?"

Chanel looked around and shrugged. "It's quiet tonight. Go ahead. I'm sure it'll be fine."

"Dave won't mind?"

Chanel grinned. "If he does, I'll take care of him, don't you worry. You just go write something brilliant so you can get back on track."

"Thanks Chanel. I knew I could count on you!"

She wasted no time heading to the dark back stage area. A battered old piano was parked directly beneath the lone light bulb in the space. She opened the cover and sat on the bench. She set her music folder on the music rack, and pulled out the sheets she'd covered with notes and lyrics. Taking a deep breath, she touched the scarred keys lightly, listening to the echo in the wide room. Softly, almost in a whisper, she sang as she played, stopping only to write a note here or there on the music.

Time stopped when she worked. With each note she played she knew this was a good song. She liked the overall feeling, but today, after her encounter with Madelyn, a second, darker verse popped into her head and she really liked how the lyrics paired with the music. It was definitely a song to be proud of, and it was all hers.

She stopped playing for a moment and wrote a few more notes on the music. As she jotted, she sensed someone behind her. Looking over her shoulder, squinting at the shadows, she saw him. "You. Can't you ever not be where I am?"

Collier stepped into the dim ring of light. "Sorry. I was in the back, putting away dishes and I heard you playing."

"Yeah, well, you can go back to putting away dishes. I've got work to do."

"You've got a good song there."

"Not that I need your opinion."

"I'm just sayin'. It's good."

She hated that his approval gave her a sense of calm. "Whatever. I'm playing it for Shara tomorrow."

"Oh, well, that's good, right?"

She grit her teeth. "Yes, Ren Faire Boy. It's great. It's freakin' awesome that she was able to take some time out of her busy day of praising you to listen to what I have to offer. It's super amazing that I have to beg and scrape for time now that you're the golden boy at the studio."

"Hey, look. I'm not the one who can't play when the tiniest distraction shows up. I'm not the one who had a freak out on stage the other night."

"No, you just always seem to be there when I screw up."

"Why is that, I wonder. Are you threatened by me?"

She didn't miss the glimmer of humor in his steel gray eyes. "I'm not threatened by you. And I have more talent in my left hand than you'll ever have in your entire life."

"That might be true. But talent isn't always going to be the thing that gets you what you want in your career."

She wanted to punch him in the throat. "No, what gets you where you want to be in your career is being the spoiled nephew of Shara's lawyer."

"That has nothing to do with it."

"The hell it doesn't. If it weren't for your uncle, you'd be begging your guys from your pirate band to take you back."

His expression registered a minimal amount of surprise and just a touch of hurt. "So that story's gotten around I see."

"It doesn't take much in this town. But don't try to deny it. If you didn't have a connection, you wouldn't be here."

"You don't have to be bitter."

"Oh, you're right. I don't have anything to be bitter about. No, I've lived in this town forever and I've worked my butt off to get a chance at working with Shara and then you swoop in, you second rate cover singer, and you get my spot."

"I might be a second rate cover singer, but you're unstable. And that will always get in the way of your talent."

She hated how calm he was. She hated how little her barbs seemed to affect him. Mostly, she hated how much he was probably right. "Get the hell out of here Collier James. I have work to do."

"Fine. I'm going. I'm going. I just wanted you to know…that's a good song you've got there."

As he left, she shook her head, trying to dislodge any sense of pleasure she got from his compliment.

SARAH J. BRADLEY   *A HERO'S SPARK*

COLLIER

The next morning, Collier got up and helped Bryan with the chores. He liked the way physical labor made him feel, like he'd actually accomplished something once the task was done. He appreciated that Bryan didn't feel the need to fill every moment with talk. They could work together, cleaning stalls, moving hay bales, filling the water tank, without much chatter. It was calming for Collier who'd spent so long trying to make as much noise as possible to shut out thoughts of Izzy. Now, in the morning stillness of the barn, he realized he hadn't thought about her in a couple days.

After chores, Collier shared a companionable pot of coffee with Bryan before heading to the studio. As he got close to the building, he didn't have to open the door to hear the argument raging inside. He stepped into the building with caution, surprised to hear Shara Jacobs' voice involved in anything quite so heated.

What didn't surprise him was Mira, once again voicing an opinion opposite Shara's and the other members of 'Teachers' Pets'. Collier eased open the booth door and sat in the shadows, his curiosity rising by the second.

"I'm not doing a duet!" Mira stood in front of them all, her back turned to the booth window, her fists balled at her sides. "This is a song I wrote and I want to sing it. Alone."

"Well that's just fine because the one thing 'Teacher's Pets' doesn't do is country." Jake did nothing to hide his acrimony, his arms crossed and his eyes blazing.

"It's not country." Mira chewed the inside of her cheek.

"Really? Because all I hear is twang, twang, twang."

Mira was about to retort something when Shara put her hand up. "Enough. Mira, this is a good, solid song. But I'm with Kelly and Jake on this one. This is definitely a duet, and I'd like to package it as such."

Collier watched as the room settled into an unsteady truce.

"That said, it does skew a bit country and Jake's right, 'Teacher's Pets' is definitely not a country band."

"Told you!"

Collier stifled a laugh. Jake looked like a four year old, and Collier suspected Mira was struggling to keep from sticking her tongue at him.

"Although there was a time when this band didn't allow 'chicks' in either, if I recall correctly." Shara shot a glare at Jake, who settled down immediately. "Guys, I think it would be really appropriate for us to at least think about performing this song when we do the holiday tour. We'll be in the heart of country music and wouldn't it be nice to stretch our fan base just a little?"

"Shara, okay, fine. But it's a duet, like you said. So who do we get to sing it? I'm no country singer. Kelly's no country singer. Tony and Dan," Jake grinned, "They're not singers at all."

There was a general shout of protest from the guys in the band. Collier could see Mira's confidence crumbling little by little. For all the fight and snarl she had in her, Collier realized her music might be the one thing Mira had that wasn't protected by her thorny outer shell. It was the one place where she was completely honest.

"I'll do it."

Everyone turned to squint at the glass. Collier whipped his finger off the speaker button, shocked as anyone that he'd spoken.

"You haven't even heard the song. You might not like it."

Collier stepped into the studio and ignored Mira's icy glare. "I heard part of it last night, Tony, and I liked it. Besides, if Miss Shara says it's good enough, it's good enough. If you guys aren't sure about it, I've got a connection in Nashville where she and I," he nodded at the still fuming Mira, "could try it out on stage. I know a few musicians there who could back us up, so you wouldn't have to do anything but listen. You guys can gauge the crowd reaction. That way we can perform far, far away from 'Teachers' Pets', but we can still sort of do some promotion for you guys. It's a win all the way around, if you think about it." He grit his teeth, hoping they bought the idea because he doubted he could suggest performing at Second Chances again. There were too many memories in that old place.

"I like the idea, but I think you two should work on this a bit before you sign anything. Starting now. Guys?" Shara held open the studio door for the others to leave.

Collier sat at the piano and looked at Mira, who hadn't moved a muscle in the time he'd been there. "So let's hear it from the top."

"Like I really want to share this song with you."

Collier shrugged and got up. "Suit yourself. I've got my own stuff to work on. 'Teachers' Pets' want me to come with them for the holiday tour as the opening act." He put his hand on the doorknob.

"You really got a connection in Nashville? A good one, not some dive?"

Collier grinned and turned around. "Well, 'Second Chances is not as glamorous as Dirty Dog Dave's, but it's a great place to work out new material. Mostly a college crowd, very music savvy. I used to try out new material there all the time. The food is sort of horrible, but the wine list is decent."

He looked at Mira closely. There was definitely something different about her.

Mira ran a hand through her hair. Collier frowned. She looked pale and thin. He hadn't noticed it last night, but she'd lost some weight recently. "Hey, are you okay?"

"I'll be fine." Mira sat down and shook her head. "When I'm writing, I forget to eat, that's all."

Collier wasn't quite convinced, but he wasn't going to push. "Okay, so show me what you've got and let's see if we can't put a little country into 'Teacher's Pets.' Then I'll get you a burger over at Dave's."

"I'll play it for you, but I'm really not working this weekend. My..nephew is in town." Mira handed him some sheet music. "It's a song about not getting anything handed to you. How some people have to work for everything they get while others just get everything." She bit her lip, then gave him a defiant look, daring him to cut down the song.

Collier read the lyrics and was surprised by how good it was. "I can definitely get behind this one. I'll give you the weekend off, but then, Monday, we work."

*

In the weeks that followed, Collier and Mira developed an uneasy working relationship. Collier respected the way Mira devoted all her energy and focus while they were working. Their shared goals forced them to keep their adversarial relationship under control. Mira's focus forced Collier to play up to her level, a level of talent and work that seemed to grow every day. Most days they worked late into the evening, stopping only when Collier couldn't keep his eyes open. Her energy astounded him.

Working long hours in the studio with Mira, Collier was able to do two things: he put together a short set of songs he was really proud of. Second, he was able to push the dread of his return to Nashville from his mind. The closer the tour date came, the more he tried to ignore it. The idea of seeing Izzy again, knowing she'd had Quinn's baby and was blissfully happy, made Collier's stomach turn to ash.

Collier called Chance and booked the date of the performance. He hoped one phone call would be the last contact with anyone there until he actually had to face everyone, but it was soon obvious Chance hadn't wasted much time calling his buddy, Quinn, and announcing Collier's homecoming.

Collier's cell, which had been mostly silent for several weeks, now filled every day with text messages from his friends. Not a one from Izzy, however.

She knows I'm coming home. She can't manage a text? Would I read it, if she did?

"What is your deal?" Mira stopped playing and stared at him. "You are really off beat today and not in a good way."

"Yeah, well, I sound like you look." Collier wanted to bite back the words immediately. It was clear Mira had lost more weight in spite of their nightly trips to Dave's for burgers and cheese fries. While she'd always been thin, she'd always seemed vibrant, like some internal furnace burned hot. Today, Collier noticed, she shivered even though she was wrapped in a turtleneck, a sweatshirt, and a heavy cardigan sweater. There were dark rings under her eyes.

"My one bad hair day is not going to ruin this chance for me. But, your weak excuse for talent will, so either use whatever drama you've got rolling in your head to finish this song, or push it out of the way."

Her argumentative tone irritated him. "You'd be the one who knows about drama. You create plenty for yourself."

She put her guitar in the case. "And now we're done."

Collier shook his head, weeks of pent animosity bubbling to the surface. "Sure, go ahead. Run away like you always do. You pretend to be grown up, but then you run away any time anyone confronts you."

Mira closed the guitar case and hoisted it off the floor. The effort, Collier noted, was a mighty one, as if the guitar weighed more than she did. "I don't have to listen to this from someone who's never had to live in the real world."

"Like you know anything about me."

Mira's laugh was short, and mocking. "Please. You weren't in Rock Harbor ten days before everyone knew everything about you. And now here you are, playing the part of a struggling musician, cooking for Dave a couple nights a week, looking all artsy and sad."

"And what's wrong with any of that?"

"It's crap. It's not true." She leaned against the piano.

"How would you figure that?"

"Really? We're going to do this now?" She gave him an exaggerated sigh. "Fine. You've got a sob story about how your world fell in on you," her eyes flashed with fury, "and it's all bull because reality is you have a rich uncle who is tight with Shara. Your life is a golden ticket and you're too busy wallowing in some misery you made up to acknowledge what a freaking gift your life is compared to most people."

88

Collier slammed the piano cover closed and swung a leg over the bench to face her. "Oh, really? You're one to talk. You grew up in the biggest house in town, and then you moved to a state senator's house. Next I hear you'll be riding your sister's checkbook to the governor's mansion. I'm pretending? You're a twenty-eight-year old spoiled brat pretending you have so much to overcome when what you've managed to do every time someone challenges you to be better is beat them over the head with your silver spoon."

"You don't get to judge me." Mira's eyes narrowed as she set her jaw. "You don't know a damn thing about me."

"Oh, no, Princess, you started this, we're going to finish it." He ran a hand through his hair. "Yeah, I have a rich uncle. He's been nothing more than a Christmas card for the last ten years. The only reason I went to him this summer is because I was left flat broke a thousand miles from home and I needed a place to crash." He took a breath and waited for her to respond. Mira's face remained stony still but her eyes flared.

Collier couldn't stop himself. "Beyond that I've worked my whole life and lived on what I earn. Meanwhile, you could be really great, but prefer moping around, acting the part of the angry, misunderstood Goth chick. You've got talent, but you'd rather assault your audience because they aren't cool enough to 'get' you. You pick up guys in some pathetic attempt to give yourself a bad girl image."

"Shut up, Collier. I'm serious."

Collier took her words and tone more as a challenge than a warning. "So, why not me, Mira, huh?"

"What are you talking about?"

"I've seen you leave Dave's with a guy now and again. You're not all that selective. Why not me?" He stood and took a step toward her.

She tensed, a predator ready for the kill. "Maybe you're not man enough for me." Her faced glowed in conquest. "Maybe I'm not interested in standing in for that ghost you won't let go."

Collier took another step. He stood inches from her, close enough to feel her icy tension. "What would you know about my ghosts?" He forced his words out though his throat tightened.

"I know you're freaking out because you have to go back to Nashville. You don't want to because there's some woman there who rejected you." She returned his glare. "You want to talk about waste of talent? I might get a little wild, but at least I feel!" She made a fist and pounded a spot over her heart. "I feel. I react. That's what humans do. You're frozen. You're frozen and you can't function because of some bitch who doesn't want you."

"Shut your mouth!" Collier leaned in, his arms braced on either side of her. He leaned closer, desire crackled and sparked between them. "You don't have any of the qualities she has."

Mira tipped her head to whisper directly into his ear. "I must have something, though, Collier, because you're here with me, not with her."

For a heartbeat, Collier locked his gaze with hers, a toxic mix of rage and desire coursing through him. "You've got nothing but bad attitude and tattoos, and you wear them both like some kind of armor." Collier grabbed her arm and shoved up the multiple sleeves. He stared at the exposed skin, stunned. Shooting a glance at her face, Collier saw the tears well up in her eyes, though her face remained frozen. "Mira, what the hell?"

She yanked her arm away and jerked her sleeves down. "You have no idea what real problems are. You think you're so wonderful because you survived a break up. And it wasn't even a real break up it was a break up all in your head. How about if you just live your little romantic drama and leave real life to people who have real shit going on?"

With that, she shoved past him and grabbed her guitar case. She stormed out of the studio, slamming the door behind her. Collier stared at the space she had just occupied, as if she were still standing there.

Just how much weight had she lost? Collier couldn't shut out the image of her arm, her skin almost translucent, her veins obvious, giving her tightly stretched skin a bluish quality. Her hands, always slender and delicate, had a glass-like quality to them. Her whole arm seemed thin enough to snap with very little force.

And then there were the scars. Like blank measures on a sheet of music, thin red lines in varying degrees of healing circled her pale skin. It was clear to him she hadn't eaten or slept well in a long time, and now, he was faced with the evidence she was also hurting herself.

Anger faded to concern for a moment and he wondered if he should follow her. Then Mira's words about his feelings for Izzy echoed and his anger returned. *She can go wallow in her own problems all by herself.*

He closed his eyes and took a deep breath. The anger left completely, leaving him weak and remorseful. He put on his coat and headed for the door.

MIRA

She struggled with the weight of her guitar case, but her pride was far stronger than her body's need to collapse. *I'm not going to fail when I'm so close to getting everything I want. I'm not going to let Collier get in my way, either.*

Mira hoisted the guitar into her car and slammed the door. *Collier thinks he knows about suffering and working. He's clueless.*

She dug her keys out of her bag. Her hand trembled as she fought to insert the key into the ignition. Unable to keep a grip on the key, she dropped it. "Oh, damn it all, anyway."

Mira leaned forward to pick up the keys and bumped her head on the steering wheel. She let out a string of oaths as she finally managed to get the key in the ignition and get the car started. Looking over the steering wheel, she saw Collier standing in front of the car, his face a picture of concern.

Ignoring him and her own internal cries for help, Mira snapped the car into reverse and roared down the drive.

The drive to the house was short and vulgarity laden. She spun off the road into the drive and roared the car to a sudden stop in front of the house, the back end of the vehicle fishtailing in the snow and hitting the porch stairs.

Scrambling out of the car, Mira slammed the door behind her and ignored the possibility of any damage. Storming into the house, she dropped layers of clothing, starting with her coat and mittens and working down until she was in nothing but a pair of leggings and a thin T-shirt. Shivering, she built a roaring fire in the fireplace, stoking it until the flames shot up the chimney. Satisfied with her work, Mira sat at the piano and stared at the keys for a moment. Then she looked up at the table next to the piano. Next to her black velvet box there was a glass of water, and the pills Otis gave her to help her focus.

She picked up the bottle and studied the white pills, bouncing them a little in the plastic bottle, watching them tumble on themselves. She counted them. "Four, five, six, seven."

Seven.

Seven should be enough, now that the songs are done. Seven should get me at least through Nashville, and hey, I won't need anything once Shara sees I'm ready to tour with them.

Seven will be more than enough.

Her cell jangled. She glanced at the display, recognizing Otis' number. "Hey Otis."

"So, you were going to call me today and put in an order."

She shook the bottle again. "I think I'm good."

The line was quiet for a beat. "Are you sure, Mira? Don't you want some kind of insurance?"

"No, no I'm good with what I have. I mean, the whole reason I got these was to get some focus on my writing, and that's done. I've got a few to get me through the first concert, but by the time I run out it won't matter. Shara will give me a spot."

Another pause. "Mira, man, I've been selling these things a while and you can't just take as many as you have lately and not have a couple just in case. You don't know what's gonna come up on that tour."

"I'll be fine, Otis. I need a couple to help me put the finishing touches on some songs, and by this time next week I'll be on the bus to Nashville and everything is going to be perfect."

"Mira, ya know, ya sound shaky. I could come over and we could smoke a little…just to even things out."

"Oh, for god's sakes, Otis!" Mira regretted her sharp tone immediately. "You know I don't smoke."

"Right. You don't use drugs. You're way above all that, right Mira?"

Mira sighed. *Why can't everyone just get off my case and get with the program today?* "Otis, I need these pills right now to help me focus. Once I get on the tour, I'm not going to need them. And you know very well I've never done any of the other…stuff."

"Yeah, okay. I'm just sayin' you sound shaky. If you don't know what you're doin' with those, you might wig out or something."

"I'm not going to wig out, Otis. I've got a lot on my mind, that's all."

"Okay, well, good luck then, Mira."

Otis ended the call. Mira stared at the display, surprised, briefly, at his concern for her.

A log tumbled in the fire and the popping sound snapped her to attention. *I still have plenty of work to do here before I can relax.*

She opened the bottle, tossed a pill in her mouth, and washed it down with the water.

Time to focus. She closed her eyes, letting the water roll down her throat. The image of Collier leaning over her, his body taut and humming with electricity filled her senses. Even the shadowy memory of his heat warmed and aroused her.

She shuddered and opened her eyes. *No. Not him. Music. Time to focus on music.*

93

COLLIER

It snowed hard the day they loaded the tour bus. Collier struggled to keep up with the pace the others set rolling instrument and speaker cases through the icy slush as wind sharpened snow stung his face. The teasing was good natured, however, and Collier felt more comfortable than he ever thought possible with this collection of talented musicians.

The material he'd written for his opening sets had been thoroughly approved by Shara and most of band, although Jake still bemoaned the fact that there was no 'kick ass' song. Collier doubted he'd ever be able to produce the kind of thunderous music Jake wanted. In spite of the brief flash of it the last time he'd seen Mira, Collier doubted he had anything approaching what Jake called 'inner rage.' The only emotion Collier felt, as he loaded luggage into the bottom storage cubby of the bus, was nervousness. Everything about this trip had him tied in knots. The one thing at the top of the list, the one thing he couldn't share with anyone on the bus, was the unavoidable reunion with Izzy in all her domestic glory and happiness.

His stomach turned over again, for about the sixth time in an hour.

"Hey, Col, your girlfriend showed up!" Jake pointed up the snow covered drive.

Collier squinted into the blowing snowflakes, just able to see Mira's face buried beneath several scarves. After their argument in the studio, he hadn't seen her, and he, along with everyone else, had been quite certain she was bailing on the tour. As furious as Mira made him most of the time, Collier was relieved. Somehow, the idea of playing Second Chances seemed less scary with her there.

"You guys look like you were about to leave without me." Mira set her guitar case next to the bus.

Collier noted she looked even more exhausted, thinner, than the last time he'd seen her. "Are you…are you okay?" He spoke in as low a voice as possible.

She laughed, a shaky, loud burst of sound that seemed to fall out of her and catch her by surprise. "I'm fine. Just wait until you listen to some of great changes I've made to the arrangements. You are going to crap yourself."

"You got everything you need, Mira?" Kelly, the self-appointed road manager, shouted from the door of the studio. "I'm locking up, so if you need anything…"

"No, Kelly, thanks. I'm good." She pointed to her small rolling suitcase. "I've got everything I need in this case."

"Well, I do like a girl who travels light." Jake picked up her case and slung it into the bottom compartment of the bus. He used the same amount of enthusiasm chucking his own duffle behind it. "Come on y'all!" he shouted with a horrible accent. "Let's go tour the hell out of the South!"

"Jake!" Shara shouted, pointed at the twins who stared at Jake with wide eyes and mischievous smiles.

"Oh, I'm sorry guys. Yes, everyone, shall we now get on the bus so that we may depart and perform musical events for the residents of the American South?"

"Not better!" Kelly shouted from the bus steps.

Good humor settled over everyone as they got out of the snow and into their seats. Collier glanced out the window just in time to see Shara exchange a passionate kiss with Bryan before getting aboard. Collier closed his eyes. Knowing his luck, the first thing he'd see getting off the bus would be Izzy giving the same kind of kiss to Quinn.

And won't that be fun for me?

Mira settled next to him in the wide seat. "You don't look all that happy to be going home."

"You look worse." Collier wanted to bite back his words. *It's not her fault I'm in a foul mood because we're going back to Nashville.* "I'm sorry, that came out wrong. You just look tired. Have you been eating?"

Mira shrugged off her coat and turned it around to make a blanket. "I was working. Here," she waved her MP3 player at him, "listen to this. I did a rough recording of a couple songs. It's just me on the piano, but I think you can get the general gist of it. I figured we could add them to the set at that Second Chance place. You know, if you can figure out where you would fit your voice in behind my brilliance."

He was glad her sharp sense of humor was at least intact. "Do I have to listen to it now?"

"Well, no. I suppose we could just wait until we get on stage and then you can just wing it. Would that suit you?"

Collier frowned at her. "Look, if all we're going to do is argue…"

Mira shook her head. "I'm sorry. I wanted to come in and just start fresh. Can we do that? I know the other day was…intense. And I'm sorry about what I said about…her. That's none of my business."

He studied her face and realized she was being genuine. "I said some pretty awful things, too. Sorry."

"So, truce?" She held out her hand.

He shook it. "Truce."

"Good. Now you have to listen to this!"

Collier rubbed his temples and unplugged his own MP3 player from his ear buds. "Fine, hand it over."

"Awesome. And what do you have on your player?" She grabbed his player out of his hand and scrolled through some songs. "Dude…what is it with you and Toto? I mean, okay, 'Africa' is a pretty cool jam, but seriously, who still listens to Toto?"

Toto was Izzy's favorite music. She skated to it. His stomach churned at the memory of the last time he saw her skate. Closing his eyes, Collier pictured Izzy's rapturous smile as she landed the double toe loop Quinn had thrown her into. All set to the music of Toto.

He hated and loved the band's music. And he was physically unable to remove the songs from his MP3 player. "Just give it back."

"Oh, no, I'm going to try and develop and appreciation for Toto." She gave him an almost flirtatious smile. "You go on, you have some lyrics to learn."

"Whatever." Collier stuck the ear buds in and turned up the volume. Within seconds, Mira's song wrapped itself around his thoughts, pushing out everything else. As he listened he made mental notes, feeling where an instrument or a line of harmony would be added. He lost himself completely in the music and ignored everything around him, except for the feel of Mira leaning against him, sleeping.

MIRA

Hours later they arrived in Nashville. Night had fallen and the city lights sparkled, gems against a black canvas. "Wow. It's beautiful," she breathed against the window.

"Yeah, it is." Collier leaned over her to look out the window.

"You left this? On purpose?" She couldn't take her eyes off the neon beauty.

Collier settled back against his seat. "I had my reasons."

Mira blinked. "You know," she didn't look at him as she spoke, "I know I give you crap about your whole break up thing, but I shouldn't. How you feel is how you feel, right?"

He didn't answer. Mira glanced over her shoulder and saw a tear shining in his eye. She turned her attention back to the city scene. "Anyway, I'm sorry for giving you crap."

"Thanks."

His voice was still, calm, like always. But in the single word, Mira knew she heard the echo of heartbreak.

*
—

They unloaded and checked into the hotel near the downtown music district. Mira knew Collier planned to stay at his own apartment, but as they watched the bus drive out of the lot to a bigger parking space, she sensed he was trying to delay his return to his home.

"It looks like the guys and Shara are gonna chill in their rooms tonight. I'm too wired from the drive to sit in my room and stare at the television."

Collier nodded. "I know that feeling."

"I could really use a cup of coffee, if you know a place."

Collier checked his watch. "I know the perfect place, and they're probably still open. Let's go get my car and we can get a cup of coffee and the best cinnamon roll you've ever eaten."

They walked a few blocks to his apartment building. Collier said nothing and Mira, not wanting to disturb whatever thoughts he was mulling over, remained quiet. The parking garage was darker than the street, but the warm neon glow still filled the concrete structure.

His car was parked four levels up, in a row facing the Columbia River. He leaned against the railing and stared out over the water. "I've lived in and around Nashville most of my life. I've seen that river almost every day."

"It's a beautiful view."

"One of the reasons I got this parking spot when I moved into the building." He pulled a car key out of his pocket. "Now, let's see if the car still knows how to run." He unlocked the doors and, ever the gentleman, strode around the back of the vehicle and opened the door for her.

She climbed into the seat, admiring the leather interior. "This is a pretty upper class car for a traveling minstrel."

"Don't start." He didn't look at her as he turned the key in the ignition. "My father bought it when I was in high school. He loved rebuilding cars when he had spare time, which wasn't often. This one was trashed in an accident. The frame was intact, but that was about it. A body shop buddy of my father's thought he might like a project. It took us three years, but we finished it and he gave it to me for graduation. It was pretty much the only thing we did together." Collier eased the car out of the space and curled around the tight turns of the parking garage easily.

"You miss him."

Collier checked traffic and pulled out onto the street. "I miss the years I wasted. When I was young I knew I wasn't going to be a figure skater. I had the talent, but…" he stopped at a light and sighed.

"You don't have to talk about any of this if you don't want to." Mira touched his shoulder, hoping to break him out of the fog of memories that seemed to cover him.

"No, we're going over to Cat's, you probably should know some of the back story. I was supposed to be paired up with this girl, Isabella. Izzy. She was a really strong talent and her parents insisted she skate pairs. My father thought she'd be a good singles skater, but they insisted, so he paired her with me."

"What happened?"

Collier's face melted to a faraway smile. "Those were the best days. I was fourteen, just figuring out the whole girl thing, and here was this wonder, this twelve year old wonder of a girl. I fell in love. I didn't even know what the word meant, but every

98

time we were together, no matter what we were doing, I was the happiest I knew I would ever be."

"So how long did you skate together?"

"Not that long." Collier made a right turn. "I was way too aware of her, as a girl, to want to be her skating partner."

Mira looked at him. "What does that mean, exactly?"

Collier shook his head. "Never mind."

"Hey, you're the one bringing up back stories. I just wanted a cup of coffee."

"Okay, fine. Let's just say every time I had to touch her I felt awkward. And then, when we started having to do lifts, I had to put my hand…" Collier broke off and laughed. "I was not comfortable with putting my hands…there, in front of my father and judges."

"Still, I mean, you had the talent, you couldn't push through it? Everyone's awkward at that age."

"I didn't like skating all that much, I just did it to be close to her. So, I quite skating and was her best friend. And I kept loving her right up until…" he stopped.

Mira sat back against the leather seat. *So this is the mystery woman? His skating partner when he was a kid?*

"I hated her for getting pregnant with her skating partner. I left home the minute I turned eighteen. I couldn't bear the idea of her being with another guy. I stayed away for a couple years. Then I took up with the Stillman brothers and we were on the road for months at a time. I missed a lot of time with my father. Looking back, if I'd stayed as a figure skater, we would have had so much more time together." He relaxed a little, driving with his left hand. His right hand rested on his thigh.

"Yes, but you wouldn't have become a musician. You wouldn't have written that amazing song." Mira wrapped her hand around his. "We wouldn't have met."

Collier glanced at her, surprise crossing his face quickly.

"Don't look at me like that, Collier James. I can be nice sometimes. And when something's good, I say it. That sad song of yours is wonderful and haunting, no matter what Jake thinks. It's something you can be proud of."

She saw no change in his expression, but she felt a thrill as he squeezed her hand lightly.

COLLIER

"Here we are." Collier drove the car to the parking lot behind Silver Screen Coffee.

"Are you sure this is a coffee place? It looks like an old house."

"It is." Collier got out, rounded the car, and opened her door. "It was anyway. My friend, Cat, owns the place. I got my start here, singing in this coffee shop."

"Why is it called 'Silver Screen'?"

Collier grinned. "Cat's a huge movie buff. There's a giant TV in there and she's generally got some movie or another running. She holds movie festivals all the time."

"That's cool."

"Yeah, you're going to like Cat." It surprised Collier, as he said it, that he also hoped very much Cat would like Mira.

"It's late, though, isn't it? Are they still open?"

Collier guided Mira gently over the uneven ground of the parking lot. "If the lights are on, they're open. Cat doesn't keep really strict hours. If the lights are on, someone's still up." He eased the squeaky back door open. They walked up the short hall to the kitchen. "Hello?"

100

"Collier!"

Collier braced himself for Cat's leaping hug, but wasn't prepared for the force of her pregnant bulk, and nearly tumbled to the floor. "Whoa! What is going on here?" He patted her stomach. "And here?" He pointed to her normally wildly colored hair. "What is up with this...hair?"

She brushed a loose strand of hair from her face "I know, isn't it boring? Hair coloring isn't good for the baby, so, until this little critter is out of me, I have to go natural."

"Or just serve a lot of the blonde roast." Collier recalled fondly how Cat's hair color changed with the featured flavor coffee of the week. His favorite had always been "Blue Pirate."

"No one wants nine months of blonde roast."

Collier sat at the counter and smiled. "So you and Benny are gonna be parents."

"Yeah, and Benny is totally over the moon. Who knew that weird sex monkey would be so jazzed about parenthood?" She waddled around the counter and leaned across from him.

"Any plans to make it all legal?"

Cat laughed. "We were planning it, but we didn't want to take any thunder away from Quinn and Izzy…" her voice drifted off. "We're planning for something after the baby is born."

"I must have missed the invitation."

"It's not like you've been around. I did send you a text." She snapped a bar rag at him.

Collier dodged the snapping towel. "You're right. And maybe it's for the best. I'm not a big one for romance right now."

"Well, that answers about fifty questions, so that saves time for me." Cat gave him a knowing look. "And here ends the maudlin part of the conversation. You want a cinnamon roll?"

Collier cleared his throat, and tried to clear his head. "I thought you'd never ask!"

"How about one for your friend?"

In the haze of reminiscence, Collier had almost forgotten Mira, standing next to him. "Um, yeah, Mira, you hungry?"

"I could eat. The rolls smell amazing." She looked around. "But I could use a ladies' room."

"'Round the corner there. You can't miss it." Cat nodded to the left. Mira vanished around the corner.

"Has she been sick?" Cat lowered her voice. "She doesn't look like she's had a proper meal in a good long time."

Collier, unable to erase the image of Mira's translucent, skeletal arm, shook his head. "She doesn't eat much when she's working. It's been a long couple months getting ready for this tour."

"You creative types. How anyone can forget to eat is well beyond me." Cat set two plates on the counter and slid two hot, gooey rolls onto the plates. "We'll introduce her to Southern food and see if we can't improve her outlook."

Collier smiled, content to warm himself in Cat's optimism as Mira returned and sat next to him. "Now, let me give proper introductions. Cat Countryman, I'd like you to meet my singing partner, Mira Pierce. Mira, Cat's an old friend of mine."

"Yes, Col, that's exactly what a pregnant woman wants to hear, that she's not only fat, she's also old. Mira, pleased to meet you. Is Mira short for something?"

"It's short for Miranda."

"Yeah, I'd shorten it, too. Did your parents hate you, or just have terrible taste in baby names?"

"Um, I guess they had bad taste?" Mira smiled weakly and shook Cat's hand. "Good to meet you."

"Who's that ugly man bothering my woman?"

All eyes turned to the boisterous voice at the door. Collier grinned as he spotted the husky figure of Benny Jensen, Cat's fiancé and the stereotype of a jolly round man. "Hey Benny, how are you?"

"Boy, you sound like a proper Yankee." Benny shook his hand. "You've been away far too long."

Mira frowned at Benny. "You're kidding, right?"

Benny, a man who loved women like some loved fine art, eyed Mira with an appreciation Collier knew was ingrained in his DNA. Even as a soon to be family man, Benny had no way of squelching his delight in meeting and talking to women. "I don't believe we've been introduced."

"Benny Jensen, this is my singing partner, Miranda Pierce. Behave."

"Collier you do not need to tell me how to behave around a lady." Benny shook her outstretched hand gently, as if sensing she was something delicate. "Miss Miranda, I'm very pleased to meet you."

"You can call me Mira, if you don't mind." She smiled. "But there's no way Collier sounds like a Yankee. We can't understand him half the time back home with that accent."

"Well I'm in the same boat, Miss Mira, because I haven't a clue what he's saying." Benny punched Collier's shoulder playfully.

Collier set down his coffee cup and folded his napkin before looking at Benny. "You are lucky Cat likes you because if she didn't, I'd take great pleasure in pouring something hot and sticky all over your head."

Benny roared with laughter. "See, now all I heard was, blah, blah, blah."

Collier grimaced and retorted. The conversation got louder as Cat draped her arm across Mira's shoulders. "They might go on like this for a while."

"They don't like each other, do they?"

Cat grinned. "Benny's always been a little jealous that I had a thing for Collier years ago. And Collier finds Benny exhausting sometimes. But I guess we all do."

Mira pondered this for a moment. "Funny, Benny isn't at all what I expected."

"How do you mean?"

"Well," she shrugged. "It's not like Collier talks a lot about himself. He's mentioned a few people from here."

Cat nodded. "I imagine."

"I figured Benny would be...taller." Mira shrugged. "Collier said he'd been a hockey player."

"Oh, I think you're mistaken." Cat giggled. "Benny was never a hockey player. You must be thinking of Quinn Murray."

Mira frowned. "But aren't you...?" She nodded at Cat's stomach.

"Oh, wait..." Cat shook her head. "I see the confusion. You're definitely thinking of someone else. No, honey, I'm not the one Collier's pined after his whole life. No, that would be Izzy. And she's not pregnant anymore. Just had that baby last month, which Collier might have known if he ever listened to his voice mail." Cat smiled. "You'll probably meet them tomorrow. They're real domestic now that they've got the baby."

Collier turned his attention to Cat, "So, boy or girl?"

"We are having a troll, thank you for asking." Cat grinned.

"I wasn't..." Collier shook his head.

"I know that. She had a girl. Pretty little peach of a girl."

"What can you expect, with that gene pool?" Benny sat next to Mira. "Next to her, our baby is going to look like some science lab mishap."

Mira laughed with Benny, but stayed generally quiet, a fact that did not escape Collier. After half an hour of cheerful chatter, he finished his coffee and nodded to Mira. "We've got a long day tomorrow. I should get you back to the hotel."

"You're not staying at your place?"

Collier shot a look at Benny and realized his friend had made a couple assumptions. "I am. Mira has her own space."

Benny and Cat exchanged quizzical looks, and Collier hoped Mira missed the entire exchange. He was too tired to explain anything, and too on edge from the coffee to sit still. "Okay, Mira, let's go."

Mira finished her coffee. "Very nice meeting you both." She shook hands with Cat and Benny again.

"We'll see you tomorrow. Breakfast. Early." Cat shot a stern look at Collier. He knew he had no hope of disobeying her.

"We'll be here."

He ushered Mira out into the darkness again. They were silent as he drove past partiers and noisy bars back to the parking garage. He opened the door for Mira again and they both leaned against the railing and stared at the river.

"They're nice people, Cat and Benny."

"Good friends."

Collier scanned the river walk, spotting the bench where he'd first professed his life-long love to Izzy.

Suddenly, the idea of going to his apartment alone made him sick. "Hey, look. I've got a lot of..." he stopped. *How can I put this into words that don't make me sound like some sort of creeper?* "Mira." He couldn't get beyond that.

"What?"

"You don't...I mean, hotel rooms are so..."

Mira tipped her head and looked at him, a faint smile playing on her lips. "Collier James, are you trying to ask me something?"

Oh geez. All I want it to not sit in that apartment alone. "No, I mean, yeah. Fine. Here it is: Coming back here is a lot. Going to breakfast tomorrow is going to be even more. I'd like to maybe not sit in my apartment alone." He took a deep breath. "Does that make me creepy?"

"You got a couch?"

Collier nodded, grateful for her matter of fact tone. "I can't promise much in the way of anything, else, but I do have a pretty comfortable couch."

She nudged his shoulder. "Come on. Let's go get some sleep. Things will be less weird in the morning. Probably." She tucked herself under his shoulder and he draped his arm around her. A perfect fit.

His apartment was dark but, as he turned on the lights, not nearly as filthy as he'd imagined it. "Someone's been in to clean the place," he commented. "Cat, probably."

104

"You weren't kidding about a couch." Mira crossed the living room to the large, comfortable sectional. Stretching out, she leaned against the back of the couch and looked out the picture window. "You've got a stellar view from here. If this was the view from my window, I'd never be able to leave."

Collier paused as he locked the door and looked across the room at the window. *Well, you don't have the memories I do.* He shook his head. "You want a beer or something?"

She didn't look away from the window. "Sure."

He put his keys on the kitchen table and opened the refrigerator door. A horrible, dead smell hit him. "Holy mother…" he stopped his curse mid-sentence as he gagged into the sink.

"What's going on?" Mira crossed the room as he dry heaved into the sink. "What is that smell?"

The stench of rot filled Collier's senses. He could taste it. "The fridge…" he gagged, "close the door!"

Mira leaned over the open door and peered into the fridge before closing it. "Well, it smells like someone committed murder in there and left the body to rot. But I think your fridge shorted out or died or something. Whatever meat and dairy you have in there went really, really bad."

"Close the damn door!" Collier gagged again. He took a breath, but was unable to stand up. A sharp, sheering pain in his churning gut kept him locked in a bent position.

"Okay, come on." Mira guided Collier away from the sink to his bedroom. "I'll take care of the smell, and then I'll make you some tea. Just lie here and stay still. You got any bleach?"

"Under the sink," he murmured, the tightening in his stomach easing a little.

"Okay. Stay put. I'll fix this in a minute."

He nodded, unable to speak for fear the foul cloud, which was starting to ease away from him, would come back.

MIRA

Mira hummed softly while she emptied the fridge and freezer shelves and wiped everything down with bleach. *For a guy who was on the road most of the summer, he had a lot of perishables.*

She sat back on her heels and looked at the two garbage bags full of rotting food. *Then again, maybe he wasn't planning on being gone for long stretches at a time.*

She tried to picture Izzy, and remembered she'd see the woman in the morning. *It'll be interesting to meet the woman that made him want to leave his home.*

It was nearly one in the morning when she finally finished the clean up. Looking around, she was satisfied that the stench was gone. She went to the bedroom and peered in to find Collier still awake. "Well, I've got good news and bad news."

"Okay."

She sat on the edge of the bed. "The good news is that the smell is gone and you don't look like you're in need of an exorcism anymore."

His wan smile was his only response.

"The bad news is you're not getting a new fridge. Somehow the thing got unplugged. And that's why, since you've been gone for so long, everything in there didn't just get moldy, it outright decayed. I'm surprised your neighbors didn't call the super, and have someone make sure you weren't dead."

Collier's smile widened a tiny bit.

"So you won't have to call your super tomorrow. Right now I think we should call it a night."

She rose to leave the room. He put a hand on her arm. "Thank you."

His touch, undemanding and grateful, warmed her skin the way nothing else had in a long time. She turned and smiled. "Get some sleep. We have to be rock stars tomorrow."

COLLIER

Collier checked his watch again. "I can't believe we overslept."

"It'll be okay. We'll get a quick cup of coffee and then get over to Second Chances for a sound check. We just can't stay at the coffee shop for as long a visit as you wanted."

Mira's words, though logical, annoyed him. He wanted to slap her down with a snarky retort, but he knew he shouldn't. *She doesn't know that my plans include staring at Izzy for at least an hour while silently wishing Quinn would evaporate.*

Yeah, a shorter stop there might be healthier.

He pulled the car into the parking lot. Mira, more sure of herself and eager for a cup of coffee, led the way to the door.

"Hey all!" Collier called.

"I was expecting you guys earlier." Cat gave them a stern frown as they sat at the counter. "What happened?"

"Apparently Collier is incapable of tolerating bad smells." Mira picked up her coffee mug and drank. "He opened his fridge last night and was unable to continue life as we know it."

"Why?"

"Something clearly died in the fridge. Somehow the fridge got unplugged a while ago. I opened it, and it was like opening a casket on a hot day." Collier defended himself weakly.

"When the body hasn't been embalmed." Mira grinned at Collier who shook his head.

"Wait, are you telling me that there was still something in that fridge?" Cat looked surprised.

"Two garbage bags full of what used to be meat and veggies and cheese." Mira nodded to Cat's offer of more coffee. "I cleaned it out myself."

"Ah ha. Yes. Well…" Cat moved around the corner to the back hall. "Benny!"

"I don't like where this is going." Collier murmured.

"Why?"

"I bet Benny was supposed to do something he didn't."

"Is that my beloved's dulcet voice I hear whispering on the breeze?" Benny walked up behind Collier.

"Run, man."

Benny looked confused. "Why?"

"Were you supposed to empty my fridge?"

"Oh, crap…"

"Benny Jensen!" Cat returned to the counter. "You told me you were over at Collier's apartment cleaning out his fridge. You told me you had to go back a couple times because you were out of bleach."

"There was a big bottle of bleach under the sink." Mira grinned over the rim of her coffee cup. "It was new. I had to break the seal."

"Your girl is pretty, but cruel," Benny mumbled to Collier.

The bell over the front door jangled and Benny looked relived. "She can't kill me in front of guests, can she?"

Collier shook his head. "She's pregnant. She can do whatever she wants and get away with it."

Benny looked over his shoulder. "I lose again. It's just Quinn and Izzy. Cat would love to kill me in front of them. They wouldn't defend my honor."

"You have no honor." Collier tried to sound nonchalant, but knowing Izzy was in the building, feet away from him, he was unable to keep the quaver of nerves out of his voice.

"Hey, Mira," Cat leaned on the counter.

"Yeah?"

"Look over your right shoulder. That right there…that's Quinn Murray."

Mira looked toward the door and watched as a couple with a baby stroller entered the room. "Oh, my."

"That is pretty much the reaction every woman has," Cat nodded. "Like something off a romance novel cover, right?"

Mira couldn't take her eyes off the tall, fit man. "I never saw anyone like that in real life. Is he moving in slow motion…or is it me?"

Cat laughed out loud. "Oh, I like you! Come on, let's go get some coffee cups from the back. And you may want to wipe your mouth. You're drooling."

Mira closed her mouth and blushed. Following Cat into the kitchen, she shared a laugh with her new friend.

Collier didn't miss Mira's reaction to Quinn. He found it impossible to absorb his own reaction to seeing Izzy for the first time in so many months. He knew she'd just had the baby, but in his eyes, she was as beautiful than he remembered.

Mira's phone jangled next to him, breaking his concentration, and attracting everyone's attention. Mira trotted out of the kitchen, checked the display, murmured a few words, and stepped out the back door. Collier was barely conscious of her movements. He was absorbing the smile Izzy flashed him.

"Collier." Izzy handed her jacket to Quinn and wrapped Collier in a tight embrace. "I thought we'd never see you again!"

Collier closed his eyes, and wrapped his arms around her. He'd lived and relived this moment in his mind, but nothing compared to the feel of Izzy's body pressed against his.

"Collier," Quinn extended a hand. Collier reached only far enough to shake his hand and then returned fully to Izzy's embrace, "Good to see you."

Izzy loosened her grip on him. Collier suddenly felt cold. "When Chance told us you were coming to town we just couldn't believe it. Where have you been?"

"He's been to the north woods of Wisconsin." Cat returned from the kitchen, several coffee mugs in hand.

"Wisconsin! What on earth were you doing up there?" Izzy put her hand on his arm.

Collier braced himself for the surge of electricity he always felt when Izzy touched him.

There was none.

Confused by his reaction, or lack thereof, Collier pretended to be interested in his coffee. "You heard the Stillmans and I broke up, right?" Everyone nodded. "Well, my uncle is a lawyer in Milwaukee. He's got just one client, this woman named Shara Brandt Jacobs. She's sort of a musical genius. She specializes in indie musicians who want to, you know, move forward. So I've been working with her and her band for the last few months."

"Wait," Benny finished chewing a mouthful of cinnamon roll. "Are you talking about 'Teacher's Pets'?"

"You know them?"

"Know them? Their concert at the Bridgestone Center has been sold out for weeks. Everyone between the ages of eight and eighty is crazy to see them. And you've been working with them?"

Collier grinned. "I'm their opening act."

The general cheering uproar reminded him of the many conversations and debates they'd had over the counter at Silver Screen. Benny, Cat, Izzy, Izzy's daughter Jenna, and even Quinn, they'd all spent so many nights sitting, drinking coffee, and solving one problem or another. He didn't realize how much he missed that.

"Col, that's so awesome!"

Collier smiled at Izzy, who now held her baby, the child he'd not yet met. "No, it's a job." He nodded toward the infant. "What you've got there, that's awesome."

"Well, then you should be introduced." She held up the sleeping bundle, a perfectly pink baby girl. "Col, this is Catherine Colleen. We call her C.C."

"Catherine Colleen?"

Cat patted his arm. "Yeah, after her two godparents. Me and you. Of course, I get top billing because I was actually at the christening."

Izzy handed C.C. to Collier and he studied the baby. "Iz, she's so beautiful."

"Yeah, she won the gene pool lottery." Benny laughed. "Meanwhile, our bundle of joy is going to look like a troll. He'll be one of those naked troll doll things with the weird furry hair."

Collier snuggled the baby close to him, close to his heart. He watched Izzy lean against Quinn's shoulder, her eyes fluttering closed. *Just like Mira did to me on the bus.*

He was suddenly very aware that Mira wasn't in the room. He looked around, slowly, not wanting to startle the baby. "Hey, Cat, where's Mira?"

Cat nodded toward the back door. "She got a call and went out back. She was yelling pretty good for a bit there, but now she's quiet."

"Who's Mira?" Quinn draped an arm around Izzy's shoulders, and she snuggled deeper against him.

Collier stretched to look out the kitchen window and saw Mira pacing, her phone still close to her ear. "Mira is my singing partner. At least tomorrow night she will be and then we'll see."

"What do you mean by that?"

Collier handed C.C. to Quinn. "She's sort of auditioning, like I am. See, 'Teachers' Pets', and Shara Jacobs especially, like to nurture new talent. But there has to be a lot of talent. So, for the last several months I've been working on new material, which Shara and the band have decided is good enough for me to be their opening act. At least while we're in Nashville."

"So they're playing the hometown boy as the opening act angle?"

Collier nodded at Cat. "Now, tomorrow, Mira and I are going to be doing material that she wrote. The band hasn't heard it yet. They want to see what other people think of it before they take a chance on her."

"She's a bit of a question mark, isn't she?" Cat refilled everyone's coffee mugs.

Collier sipped the dark roast, enjoying the bitter bite. "She is. Crazy talented, but from what I've seen, she gets in her own way a lot. And her work habits are a little uneven."

"That's a problem for a rock band?"

"'Teachers' Pets' isn't one of those entitled, wild, rock bands. All the guys have day jobs that aren't related to music. So they have to run a very tight schedule when they do have time to play. And Mira is more of a…" Collier paused, unable to find the right word to define her. "I guess you'd call her a free spirit. Schedules don't work as well for her, unless she's in a zone, and then she's the most focused person I've met. So it's a bit uneven working with her, and that makes the guys and Shara a little wary."

"Yeah, but she's smokin' hot, which makes her worth tolerating the crazy, right Col?" Benny took a big bite of a cinnamon roll and grinned.

Collier looked from face to face and shook his head. "It's not like that, you guys. We're not…" he stopped, his gaze resting on Izzy who had taken the baby from Quinn and was snuggling with her while gazing adoringly at her husband. "We're not like that." *And we'll doubtfully ever be…like that.*

A faint sense of disappointment filled Collier. That surprised him. He looked back at Izzy and Quinn, who were clearly wrapped up in each other. The happy domestic image stung less than Collier thought it might.

That surprised him more.

Mira walked back into the building, her face gray.

"Everything okay, honey?"

Mira glanced at Cat and gave her a shadow of a smile. "Just my older sister. Family stuff…you know."

"Well, take a load off, pretty lady, and I'll get you a cup of coffee." Benny patted the seat next to his. "Just don't tell my woman, she's very possessive."

"And the pregnancy hormones make her crazy. No telling what she'll do…or put in your coffee." Cat hoisted herself onto a stool.

Mira sat down next to Benny and glanced at everyone around the table. "Oh, hi. I'm sorry, we haven't met." She extended her hand to Quinn.

Benny let out an exaggerated sigh. "It's not even a fair playing field when you're in the building, Quinn, you know that, right?"

Quinn reddened and shook Mira's hand. "Pleased to meet you. I'm Quinn Murray and this is…"

"Izzy." Mira interrupted him and stared at Izzy. "You're Izzy Marks, aren't you?"

"Izzy Murray." Izzy looked slightly surprised. "Yes."

"Collier's mentioned you."

"We go way back." Izzy's cheeks colored lightly.

Collier studied Izzy's face, then Mira's. The gentle volley between the two women was interesting, and it had little to do with anything Izzy was saying. For reasons he couldn't fathom, Mira, and what she said, was holding his attention.

Mira smiled. "I mean, Collier's mentioned all of you. He talks about this place all the time, don't you, Col?"

There was a new note in her voice, a warmer tone. Collier hadn't heard it from Mira before, but he recognized it as a tone women used when flirting or teasing a man. He'd heard it many times when on tour with the Stillmans. *Why is she trying to flirt with me here, now?*

"Oh, yeah, he talks about the great coffee, and the cinnamon rolls and all that. All the time. So it's so great to meet you all. But you know, Col, sweetie? We have to go. We have to do a sound check."

"No, you don't have to leave, really." Benny mocked pleaded with her.

"Yes, Benny, they do have to go. They have work to do. And you and I have a conversation we have to have."

"Geez, Cat you sound serious. What did Benny do this time?" Quinn arched an eyebrow.

"You used to work with him, Quinn, you know what a loss of brain cells he can be." Cat fixed a faux grumpy expression on her face.

Collier grinned at Quinn. "It's what he didn't do. Apparently he was supposed to empty my fridge…and he didn't. And the fridge died. And then I about died from the stench."

"Look I meant to clean it out, but come on…I get there and you've got killer satellite TV, Collier. I got distracted. Cat's…"

"Cat's what?" Cat put her hands on her hips.

"Well I'm just going to tell it like it is. I mean, with Cat being so…so huge and pregnant, hey a man's got needs ya know. I need a place where I can go to be alone with my…thoughts."

Amid the laughter at the table, Collier realized he had forgotten how raunchy Benny could be. Everyone else, including Mira, laughed. Collier stared at her and wonder what had changed and why she was trying to act like they were a couple.

"Well with all the fun from last night, we didn't get to do any…unpacking. And I need to…unpack right now in the worst way." Mira arched an eyebrow to emphasize her double entendre.

113

Collier ignored his friends' continued laughter because he was too busy feeling confused. "Okay, Mira, yeah, let's go. I have to stop at the apartment to pick up something."

Mira giggled, which others may have thought normal, but which was a fake, wildly foreign sound to Collier. "Oh, listen to him. 'Pick up something.' Baby, these are your friends. You don't have to use euphemisms with them."

Collier picked up his jacket and slid it on, never taking his eyes off Mira as she hugged everyone, even Izzy, with enthusiasm.

"I should have known. 'Not like that between you two.' Hah! You are a dog, man! A dog!" Benny shouted, slapping Collier on the back.

Collier barely acknowledged the contact. Mira's odd behavior bothered him. It bothered him so much, he followed Mira out of Silver Screen without saying good-bye to anyone…including Izzy.

MIRA

Once in the car, Mira was too furious to say anything. Madelyn's call could not have come at a worse time.

That's Madelyn's skill, isn't it? She knows the exact time to swoop in and shatter me most. She always knew how to hurt me with a single sentence.

Because Mira left the state without informing her, Madelyn was proceeding with papers to sever Mira's parental rights to Dusty. And Mira, if she wanted to have any contact with Dusty ever again, was just going to have to live with it, so Madclyn told her.

The cruel exchange played through Mira's head.

"If you breathe one word to Dustin about any of this, you know what will happen. I'll cut you off immediately."

"I haven't taken a dime from you in years."

Madelyn's voice always got sweeter, like sugary syrup, when she was delivering her most deadly words. "Oh, my dear girl, this has nothing to do with money. Oh no. I'll cut you off from ever seeing Dustin."

It was a threat Madelyn uttered frequently, but this time there was a note of resolution in Madelyn's voice and it chilled Mira. "How can you do this to me? I am your sister, and I am Dusty' mother! Does The Senator know what you're doing?"

Madelyn was silent for a moment, and in that heartbeat Mira hoped she'd changed her sister's mind, at least a little. "I do not know how I can make this any clearer to you, Miranda. The Senator is not your ally. And he prefers to never again think about how you behaved around him, so if you have any sense, you won't speak of him to me again."

"How can he not think about it, about what he did to me?" Mira closed her eyes, trying to calm her beating heart. She knew, she'd always known, that it would come to this. In spite of his many promises to her, there had never been anything between The Senator and Mira, other than her childish crush on him and the nights he exploited those feelings for his own pleasure.

"Mira, no one cares about your stories. As far as I'm concerned, and as far as anyone is concerned, Dustin is my son. He is living with me, under my roof. And, as you know, possession is nine tenths of the law. So when you come back from your little road trip, the papers will be here ready for your signature."

Mira had bitten her lip so hard when Madelyn hung up, she could still taste blood even now. She was thankful Collier wasn't in a chatty mood. Between the phone call from Madelyn and the fact that she was definitely on the down side of one of her last pills, Mira doubted her ability to hold it together. *And I have to get through a sound check and a performance yet?*

And what was that flirty crap I was trying to pull at the coffee shop? What was that all about? She closed her eyes and tried to steady her breathing. *I can't fall apart now. Not now.*

COLLIER

The ride to his apartment was uncomfortably silent. Once behind a firmly closed door, Collier could hold his angry curiosity no longer. He glared at Mira. "What the <u>hell</u> was that back there?"

Mira settled onto the sofa. "What was what?"

"That whole flirty thing…you let them think we're together? Why?"

"I was trying to do you a favor."

"I'm sorry, I'm not getting how lying to my friends about whether or not we are a couple was helping me. Especially since I'd just told them we were not a couple."

"No, you wouldn't get that, would you? Because you were turning into a pile of wet suck in front of that Izzy person, who by the way is not anything near the way you droned on about her, and I was trying to make you seem less pathetic."

"I was pathetic? You're the one arguing with your sister in public."

"Well, Skippy, first of all I was not in public, I was in a parking lot, far away from Scooby and the gang. Second, what goes on between my sister and me is my business because it's just a little too real for your happy -slappy world. And finally…shut up!"

She hopped up from the sofa and started pacing

"Mira, what is going on with you?"

She stopped pacing only long enough to stare at him with dark, wild eyes. "Nothing is going on with me. This is just the biggest shot I've got and, just like every other thing in my life, I have to work for it twice as hard as anyone else. So you'll have to excuse me if I don't have all the time in the world to let you, the person who I have to depend on to get this right, play sad sack over a woman who clearly has married the perfect guy."

"He's not the perfect guy for her."

"Are you blind? He's the perfect guy for anyone! Screaming hot <u>and</u> he can keep his mouth shut? So much better than you, Mr. Judgmental."

Collier stormed to the refrigerator and whipped it open. It was still empty. He slammed the door. "You met him for one minute. You have no idea what you're talking about."

116

"And there you go, yap, yap, yap."

Collier checked his watch. "Okay, so now we have to go to Chance's. Do you think you can act like a non-crazy person for an hour while we go over things for tomorrow night? Do you think you can do that? I mean, this is, after all, <u>your shot</u>."

"It's your shot, too," she snarled, her mood darkening.

"Last time I checked, I'm on the tour."

"Yeah, in Nashville. You're the hometown boy. You said it yourself. But if you think Shara and her band of music snobs are going to let you stay beyond this point, you are more stupid than you look."

Collier stilled. He didn't want to believe what she told him, yet he knew there was truth to her words. He knew Teachers' Pets used local bands for their opening acts as a way to draw in crowds. He knew, even though they liked his music, he would have to be beyond excellent to stay with them. Everything, he knew, was riding on his performance tomorrow night and then how he handled himself on Saturday at the Bridgestone Center in front of a massive crowd.

And I'm saddled with an unstable mess. "Look, just promise me you'll be polite and not do…whatever it is you're doing right now. Maybe try not to be an over-sexed flake or a screaming bitch, at least for the next hour, okay?"

"I guess that all depends on whether or not you're going to be a human person or some sort of 'woe is me' whiner guy."

Collier yanked the door open and she swept through it. He slammed it, giving the only voice to his anger his manners would allow. "Just in case you're missing it, I'm not a fan of this new attitude of yours."

"I don't like you very much right now either," she snarled as she stomped down the stairs. She didn't wait for him to open her car door, and he didn't make a move to do it. They drove downtown to Chance's in heated silence.

Second Chances was just as he remembered it: Huge, dark, and, when not filled with screaming college co-eds, creepy. Collier led Mira to the second level where the bar, and Chance, were ready for business.

"Collier James, it's been a long time." Chance, a man whose avarice was as legendary as his ear for talent, reached across the bar and shook Collier's hand. "Who is this?"

"Mira Pierce, my…"

"I'm his partner." She nudged Collier away from the bar and hopped onto a stool.

"I see. And have you and Collier been partners long?"

"Chance, she's not…"

"Oh, awhile, I guess," she flashed a sensuous smile at Chance, a smile Collier had never seen before.

"How does a stiff like Collier land a lovely like you?"

"Mix me a martini, Chance, you'll find out for yourself."

Chance grinned and turned his back. Collier grabbed Mira's arm and swung her around. "Would you stop this?"

"Okay, ouch. And what is your problem?"

"Why are you acting like you're acting?"

Her eyes darkened to a black he knew well. "How am I acting Collier? I'm friendly. I thought that was what this whole Southern thing was, being friendly. You know, unlike us cold, heartless folk up north." She clenched her jaw and glared at him.

Collier released her arm and stepped back. "So, Chance, I have a playlist." He unfolded a sheet of paper and smoothed it out on the bar.

Chance handed Mira her drink and kept his eyes locked with hers. "You gonna do anything anyone else has ever done?"

"No, it's all going to be new material. Mira wrote everything and we arranged it together. There's a duet in here that we really want to focus on."

"How about that soapy song you played the last time you were here. Women love that song."

Collier shook his head. "It's not on the playlist, Chance."

"Hey, Mira, sweetie, tell your man there to play that song so Chance here can get his lady friend in the right mood."

Collier turned just in time to watch Mira fling her drink in his face. "That song is a gigantic wad of snot and there is no way I'm sharing the stage with anyone who sings that song!" her words dripped with unexpected venom.

"Mira!" Collier grabbed her arm and set her in a booth. "Chance, I'm so sorry. I have no idea…"

"No problem, Col. Hey, I like my women spicy, you know that." Chance dabbed his wide face with a bar rag. "But is she going to be that much of a pistol tomorrow night?"

Collier stared at Mira, who glared at him from the dark depths of the booth. "Chance, I gotta be honest with you, I have no idea."

Chance let out a hearty laugh. "Good! Then it will be an adventure for us all!" He put a hand on Collier's arm. "I wasn't kidding, though, when I said I wanted you to play that song. If you double check the contract we signed, the house gets some say in the playlist. I'm the house."

"Chance, we didn't sign a contract. I called you and asked if you I could work out some new material. I didn't think I needed a contract. You and I have never had one before."

"You never brought an insane woman to me before."

Fair enough, I guess. Collier glared at Mira, who still looked like a caged wildcat, ready to pounce.

"I've have insane people on this stage, don't get me wrong, Col, but you know, you're a known quantity in these parts. Your name is going to draw a certain kind of customer, people who know your name and have an idea what to expect from you. I'm all for letting the little missus here work out her as yet undefined mental issues on my stage, but not with your name on the playbill. There's got to be some of just you in the set tomorrow or it's a dead deal."

Either way it'll be a dead deal. Chance won't let me play without that song and 'Teachers' Pets' doesn't want to hear that song again.

Collier closed his eyes and thought for a moment. "Okay, fine. We will do the song."

"I'm sorry…we? I don't recall that song being a 'we' thing the last time you performed it here."

Collier shook his head. "For better or worse, Chance, I'm doing the performance with her. My name's on the playbill, but so's hers, so it'll have to be a duet."

"I don't see how that will work."

I don't either. "Let me worry about that, okay?"

Chance chuckled. "You've got plenty to worry about, don't you?" He nodded toward the stairs. Mira was leaving.

"Dammit!" Collier nearly tripped over a bar stool as he chased after her. He halted just outside the door and watched as she began a heated telephone conversation.

MIRA

"Otis, you gotta get me something!" Mira stomped heavy, raging steps along the street to the Cumberland River path that strung along behind Second Chances.

"Mira, sweetie, I can't do a thing. I'm in Wisconsin, in the middle of the biggest snowstorm since snow was invented. You are in Nashville. I told you, you should have stocked up. You should have taken the extra along with you, but did you listen to me? Of course not. I always say if you don't accept what you are and what you need, you're just going to be miserable and there you go. You didn't want to take along extra just in case."

"Otis, I'm not messing around here, I'm losing my mind and this is the biggest shot of my life and I need you to get me something or put me in touch with a contact here or something."

Otis' laugh made her skin crawl. "What world are you living in? I'm not some kind of prescription drug kingpin. I am, as your sister likes to tell you all the time, a two bit nothing. I don't have contacts in Nashville. I've got about a dozen fifth grade boys in the Greater Rock Harbor area who are willing to risk detention twice a week so they can sell me their Ritalin for five bucks a pop. I turn around and sell it to college kids who need to stay up and study or creative types like you who want to stay on a project for a couple days in a row. Someday, if I'm lucky, I might find myself helping a fashion model, but that's a far off dream because, well, I live in Wisconsin, and we are not known for our fashion model business."

120

Mira rubbed her arms and fought the urge to fling her phone into the river. "Otis, I am down to one pill, and I'm going insane right now. I just threw a drink in a man's face because he said we should play a song that wasn't on our playlist."

"Well that's just rock and roll!"

"Otis!"

"Look, I don't know what you want me to tell you. Try getting some antihistamines from the drug store. They still sell the good stuff behind the pharmacy counter, but they look at I.D. and they are very skittish about selling to someone who is in the middle of a rage, so try and use your best manners. And you may want to try…" he stopped.

"Try what, Otis? Try what?"

"Well, they say, some of my better customers do, when they can't get a full dose, they take a handful of stomach antacids and that sort of boosts the high, you know?"

She stopped pacing and stared blindly at the river. "You're telling me some Tums will help me get my focus back?"

"That's what they say."

"But you don't know for sure."

"No, but I have it on the best authority. So, 'please' and 'thank you' are the magic words."

Mira balled her left hand into a tight fist. "You are useless!"

"See, this is why I told you weed would be better for you. Helps with the creativity just the same, but mellows you out instead of makes you a Type A bitch."

"What am I supposed to do?"

"Hell if I know, sweetheart. Next time, plan ahead."

Mira listened to dead air as Otis ended the call. She paced back and forth on the sidewalk, ignoring the few curious joggers and couples passing her. Her head pounded. She jammed her phone deep into her jacket pocket. Everything felt so out of control, like all of her movements wound up being so much more forceful than she wanted them to be.

I threw a drink in that man's face.

All I wanted was to have the energy to finish those songs and maybe not be a complete bitch on this tour. And look at me. I'm a skeleton, I'm losing my mind, and I have no idea what is going to come out of my mouth next.

I'm going to blow my big shot.

I'm going to blow this shot for Collier, too.

She wasn't sure, at the moment, which bothered her more.

She heard footsteps behind her. Turning, she saw Collier running to catch her. He didn't look angry. He looked worried.

"Hey, Mira." He stopped next to her, and caught his breath. "What was that all about? Are you having some kind of breakdown? Because we are partners on this tour and if you're having a breakdown, I'm pretty sure you should tell me."

She forced a smile and hoped she didn't look insane. "No, no, I'm fine. I'm okay. Just…family stuff. You know. Big sister doesn't approve of my attempt at a rock and roll lifestyle."

He didn't look convinced. "Are you sure?" He put his hands on her shoulders.

The weight of his touch seemed to ease her frenetic energy and ground her a little. "Yeah, yeah. You know I just have butterflies or something. You...you don't have any Tums or antacids do you?"

Collier shook his head. "Who knows what I have back at the apartment? We'll stop at a drug store on the way back."

"You don't want to drop me at the hotel?"

"Nah." He smiled, his grey eyes warming. "You can crash at my place tonight if you want. Your stuff is there anyway, no point in moving everything now. Clearly I need to keep an eye on you. Besides, you know I have a really comfy couch."

"You do, which is good. I won't feel guilty about you while I'm sleeping in your bed." She bit her lip, hoping he understood what she said to be a joke.

Collier laughed easily, a sound she hadn't heard from him ever. She stared at him. "I didn't think you knew how to laugh."

"You've never said anything funny before." He draped his arm around her shoulders companionably as they strolled back to the car. "Tell you what, maybe later tonight, after dinner, I'll show you some more fascinating Nashville sights, you know, other than my bed."

His light tone was not lost on her. She returned his laughter, happy, for a moment, to have a solution to her problem. *I will get through tonight...and tomorrow night...and I'll figure it out from there.*

122

COLLIER

"Hey, do you feel up to an outing before dinner?" Collier buckled his seatbelt. He watched Mira open the plastic bottle of antacid tablets and shake out four tablets.

"I suppose it would take my mind off the show." She popped the tablets in her mouth. "What do you have in mind?"

"Well, I have to go touch base with the skating rink, see how things are going out there."

"I'm sorry, did you say 'skating rink?' Like where they have all skates and preteens hold hands and everyone wears sweaty old skates crawling with foot grunge? No thanks."

"No, it's not a roller skating rink. It's an ice rink. My father, he coached there until he passed. I'm still part owner."

"Part owner, huh? Who else owns it?"

Collier hesitated, though he wasn't sure why. "Well, Izzy and Quinn own the majority of it."

"Izzy and Quinn? And you. You three are business partners?" Mira's face was a study in confusion. "I thought you hated Quinn."

Collier shrugged. The history of his father's skating rink, and how Izzy and Quinn refurbished it after Collier let it sink into disrepair, was a lot for even him to understand. How could he possibly explain any of it to Mira? "Come on. We'll go, we'll be social, we'll come back. It won't take long."

"You're feeling claustrophobic?" She looked surprised. "I've never seen you nervous."

"I'm not nervous." Collier rubbed his forehead. "We don't go on until really late tomorrow, and there's a ton of time to kill between now and then. We could spend that time rehearsing, or we could do something that'll take our minds off how tomorrow night might be the biggest night of our lives."

She smiled. He hadn't realized before that he liked her smile. "Okay, Collier. Let's go check out your skating rink. Besides," her smile turned into a mischievous grin, "I could stand looking at Quinn for an hour or two."

He must have made a face he wasn't aware of, because she laughed.

He decided he liked her laugh as well.

MIRA

"Collier, I don't think this outing is doing much for your nerves. You look more jumpy than you did at the drug store."

Collier hadn't said much on the drive to the skating rink. Mira had grown accustomed to his quiet nature, but today it chafed her. She felt jittery and unstable herself.

"Why would you think I'm nervous?"

"Because you haven't said a word since we got in the car and you haven't looked at me once, and while I'm sort of used to both those things, it's kind of annoying right at the moment."

"Oh." He glanced at her, then fixed his eyes on the road. "Sorry."

"So, okay, how on earth did you sell part ownership to Izzy and Quinn? There's a story there."

Collier sighed. "Okay. I suppose. I asked you out here, I should really give you some of the history. Izzy and Quinn bought their part of the skating rink from the people I sold to after Pop died. When he died, I had no use for the place."

"Lost your skating skills? Didn't want a reminder of your former days of glory?" She nudged his shoulder, hoping to jostle him into better humor.

"I'm still a very good skater."

She was happy to get a rise out of him. "So you say."

"I was Izzy's first skating partner. We won a junior championship. It's not like I'm a beginner."

For a moment Mira was sorry she asked. Knowing this piece of the Collier/Izzy history didn't make her happy. She brushed the thought and a strand of hair away quickly. "Fine. You're a magnificent skater. You gave it up for love of music."

"Close enough."

Mira chose not to push the issue. "You sold a chunk of the property to someone else?"

"Yeah. They turned it into a place where kids had their birthdays. It went downhill really fast. My Pop coached Olympic and world talent in that place. It was state of the art. They put in a snack bar, a pizza oven, and a disco ball."

"Ooh, yikes."

124

"When Izzy came back to Nashville, she started skating there again. It was a charity event Quinn hosted. He's a big charity guy around here."

"All goes with his Captain America image."

"Yeah, it does. Most people didn't realize he was trying to redeem his soul back then."

"Why do I think you're not going to tell me that part of the story?" Mira shifted in her seat to face him.

Collier ignored her question. "When Izzy got her insurance money from her husband's death, she and Quinn bought the half I'd sold and they fixed the place up and now they teach skating lessons and Quinn coaches a high school hockey team. There it is."

"I get the feeling that was the abridged edition of the story."

Collier got out of the car, rounded the front, and opened her door. "You'd be right. But it's not a story I feel like getting into. Come on. I'll give you the tour."

Inside, the large, open building was cooler than outside. No sunlight warmed the place. They walked in at the top row of seats and then walked down several stairs to get to the rink itself. Mira was no judge, she knew, but everything seemed clean. She checked the ceiling. No disco ball.

Quinn was on the ice with a group of boys, working on some sort of hockey moves, and Mira couldn't deny he was the most handsome thing she'd ever seen. She didn't realize she was staring until Collier tapped her shoulder.

"Would you like a napkin to wipe your drool, Miss Pierce?"

Mira looked at him, surprised at the sharp, almost jealous tone in Collier's voice. "Not drooling, just appreciating fine art."

"Whatever. Come on. I'll show you Pop's office."

He led her down a long hallway. The number of framed photos of Izzy was dizzying. "Wow, so she was really a big deal, huh?"

"Pop said she was the most natural talent he'd ever seen." Collier paused in front of one picture, a reverent expression on his face. "Pop always wanted her to skate as a single. Her parents didn't believe in her, so she wound up skating pairs…and she wound up with Jason." He pointed to another picture where a young Izzy stood next to an obviously older man.

Mira wanted to ask more, but the dark look on Collier's face stopped her. Instead, she studied each picture until she found one that made her laugh. "Is this you?"

Collier looked at it. "Yeah, that's when Izzy and I won our first junior regional championship."

"Col, are you wearing a spandex unitard?"

"I am wearing the prescribed costume for that routine." He grinned. "Yes, a spandex unitard…in lime green."

"Oh, this is the best. Look how cute you are!" She nudged her shoulder into his.

"Shut up." His words were sharp, but she heard the laughter in his voice.

"I mean, hey, it's no Captain America, but I can see in this picture that you were going to turn out pretty good looking…and sure enough," she cocked her head so they were face to face, "you are."

Collier blushed. She liked that. He cleared his throat. "Come on, I've got some papers in the office I have to sign and then maybe you and I can take a spin around the ice."

Mira smiled. She hadn't skated in years, but she liked that Collier thought enough of her to think she could.

His paperwork was done quickly. Once back at the rink, Mira saw that Quinn and his team were off in a corner. Izzy was working with a young girl. Though Izzy wore simple black leggings a long sweatshirt and gloves, there was no way to ignore her presence on the ice. Even in the small motions she taught the girl, Mira saw Izzy's grace and poise.

She envied her that.

"That's enough for today, guys. Hit the showers." Quinn ushered his team off the ice, then skated to them. "Col, Miss Miranda, good to see you again."

Mira put her hand in Quinn's extended one, half expecting him to kiss her fingers. He shook it gently. She was a little disappointed. "Uh, just call me Mira, okay?"

"Sure, Mira." His smile made Mira aware of two things: Quinn Murray had a beautiful smile and Collier was watching her. She liked the idea of both.

"Collier tells me you guys own this place together."

"Well, it's mostly Col's. We keep the lights on." Music started and Quinn let go of her hand. "Take a look at this student Izzy's working with, Col. Doesn't she remind you of someone?"

As Quinn and Collier watched Izzy and the girl, Mira watched Collier. She'd never thought of it, but he really was a good-looking guy, with a gentleness about him that she liked. Briefly, she wondered what it would be like to kiss him.

"She takes that double toe loop just like Izzy did."

"Yeah, but this kid is eleven."

Mira had no interest in what was happening on the ice. She couldn't take her eyes off Collier, and she realized, she didn't just wonder what it would be like to kiss him. She very much wanted to kiss him.

The thought surprised and annoyed her.

"Quinn, can you start the music from the beginning please?" Izzy waved to them. "Hey guys, good to see you." Izzy skated to the railing while Quinn cued the music. The opening bars of a Toto song flooded the arena.

Mira blinked, understanding in a flash Collier's obsession with the 80's band. *Izzy must have skated to Toto. He's so into her, he can't even delete those songs from his MP3 player.*

She shook her head and pushed away any thought of kissing him.

"That's quite the talent you've got there," Collier nodded to the girl. "Think she'll go far?"

"Maybe, if she'd get her timing right. She executes all the moves like a champ, but she has no sense of rhythm."

Collier nodded. "Mira, Izzy here had the best feel for music my pop had ever seen in a skater."

"I'm sure." Mira was quiet for a moment, focusing as much as she could on the young skater in front of them. The girl was having trouble getting her jumps timed with the music. Izzy had Quinn cue the music and she skated the routine for her student. In that moment, Mira wanted to hate Izzy for her grace and beauty, because Izzy was the woman Collier loved.

Damn, she's amazing. "She's really something, isn't she?" Mira didn't recognize her own voice.

"She is."

"I mean, she's really…really talented and…beautiful."
Mira hated every word as it dropped from her lips. *Just shut up!
Just shut up now!*

She turned to look at Collier and was surprised to meet
his gaze. His clear grey eyes held something of a promise. There
was a directness about his gaze that sent a shiver up her spine.
"What?"

"I hope that didn't hurt too much," he murmured, draping
an arm around her shoulders. "I know you're not a big one for
saying nice things about other women."

She wanted to fire back a snarky comment, but the weight
of his arm around her softened her temper, gave her a sense of
calm. She held very still, afraid if she moved at all, he'd take his
arm away. The fact that Collier was hopelessly and forever in
love with someone else didn't matter so long as he had his arm
around her.

"Are you hungry? I was thinking we'd hit Waffle House
for dinner."

She nodded, almost afraid to speak.

"Hey, guys!" Collier called to Quinn and Izzy. "We're
taking off."

Whether they said anything or not, Mira didn't hear. She
was too caught up in the fact that, even as they climbed the stairs
to the door, Collier kept his arm around her.

COLLIER

Collier closed the bedroom door softly and sat on the sofa. Mira had fallen asleep almost immediately after returning from dinner at the Waffle House.

The truth of it was, he was worried about her. Not about the tour, not about performing, he was worried about her. Something was definitely going on, and she wasn't sharing.

He knew her relationship with her sister was rocky, but there was something mysterious about the phone call she made right after running out of Chance's, Collier had a nagging suspicion that had nothing to with Madelyn. When Mira talked to Madelyn she tended to keep things tightly wound, in control. The conversation at the river sounded furious, almost at the edge of panic.

The memory of her scarred skin opened in his mind's eye. He wondered if the person on the other end of the phone had anything to do with her cuts.

He stood, stretched, and unrolled the sleeping bag on his sofa. His apartment was chilly, but Collier didn't mind. Sliding into the sleeping bag and staring out the window onto the streetlights below, he felt at home for the first time in a lifetime. Being back in the coffee shop, seeing everyone, even Izzy, had been a far easier homecoming than he anticipated. Even going to the rink hadn't been as horrible as he'd thought. Catching up with his Nashville life had been a pleasant distraction from focusing on the importance of their performance at Chance's.

He chose not to analyze that feeling and instead concentrate on what might be going on with Mira. She exhibited none of the strange behavior at the rink or at dinner that she had at Chance's. *Maybe throwing a drink in Chance's face was sort of a cathartic moment for her. God knows Chance deserves more than one drink thrown at him.*

Comfortable with the thought, Collier settled back against the soft sofa cushions. He plugged his ear buds in and turned his MP3 player to 'shuffle.' He fell asleep as he did often; with the band Toto playing in his ear.

Only now, as he drifted to sleep, he didn't picture Izzy skating on a perfect sheet of ice.

129

*
—

They were scheduled to start playing at ten that night, but the crowd on the other side of the curtain was a rowdy wave of chaos after the first band, a local college foursome of skateboarders who preferred shrieking into the microphones rather than producing actual music, left the stage. The second group, a female country duo, shot Collier looks of panic before taking the stage.

"Leave it to Chance to have zero clue about the bands he's lined up for the night." Collier pushed the heavy, smoky curtain aside just enough to glance up at the second floor where Chance looked every bit like a ringmaster at a very loud, not well controlled circus.

"Hopefully we won't have to mop vomit off the stage before we go on. Those girls look terrified." Mira sidled up behind him.

There was a nervous energy rolling off her like a wave of heat. Collier turned to look at Mira and could not help notice, now that she wore a short-sleeved shirt. Though the scars seemed to have faded, her arms looked even more skeletal than they had weeks earlier. She was tight, like an electric guitar string, as if she'd start shaking at the slightest touch.

"It'll be fine. You forget, I've played here before. I've done new material in the building many times. It'll be fine."

"And you forget," her voice was low, almost a growl, "that this is my audition. It's my material, not yours."

The underlying current of anger was obvious in her tone. "Geez, sorry. I didn't mean to offend." *Her bad mood is back.* Collier's stomach rolled.

"Just remember this. This is my night. You're already on the bill for tomorrow night. Shara likes you. It's hugs and tea and air kisses all around for you and 'Teachers' Pets'. Meanwhile, I'm killing myself just to get someone to hear anything I have to put out there and I'm stuck having to perform my best song as a duet with you." She threw two more antacid tablets into her mouth and chewed with a furious energy. "Hell, you could go out there and play some weak-assed Toto song and everyone would love you." Her smile was wide and cold. "And you still wouldn't be happy because there's one person out there who wouldn't care."

She never raised her voice during this outburst, but there was no denying that Mira was trying to pick a fight with him. Collier glared at her. The crowd noise on the other side of the curtain only added to the jumbled emotions that threatened to overwhelm him and the last thing he needed was for his partner to fall apart. He knew not only Shara, but the rest of 'Teachers' Pets', sat on the other side of that curtain.

Izzy was there, too.

Mira's words about Toto songs hurt, but not the way he expected. It was as if Mira had somehow worked her way past his defenses and found his tender spot, one he wasn't completely aware existed, and she stuck a thorn into it. "You know what, Mira? You can be a bitch all you want to be, but the minute that curtain goes up, you get yourself into some kind of professional frame of mind. If you're even capable of something like that."

Mira responded with something he couldn't hear. *Probably for the best.* Collier didn't need to hear the words to understand her intent.

The country duo left the stage in tears and the stage manager came out to introduce Collier and Mira.

Collier heard none of the introduction. His stomach lurched. Izzy was out there, along with all his Nashville friends. He wanted to prove to them, to her, that he was going places, he was talented, and his months of exile in Wisconsin had a purpose. There was no room tonight for Mira to ruin this.

"Now's the time to get it together!" he growled at her as the curtain inched up. "Cut the crap and let's go do a show."

Mira didn't say anything, but her eyes spoke volumes. They held a cold focus that gave him the feeling she had far more strength, far more resolve than what he saw in her thin, pale face and in the dark circles under her eyes. She nodded slightly as the hot stage lights briefly blinded them. She took her spot next to the piano. Collier sat, his hands hovered over the keys, and waited for her signal.

"Hello Nashville!" She shouted in a voice stronger than he'd heard from her in weeks. "How the hell are ya?"

The music set was, beyond that moment, a blur of sound and color for Collier. Mira was clearly the star of the show, creating a pace to the set that left both Collier and the audience breathless. Her material hit the mark with the crowd which roared and danced. Second Chances was a hot party and Mira was at the center of it all. She glowed with energy and joy. Collier was as mesmerized by her, as was the audience. He could not take his eyes off her as she blossomed under the hot white lights.

There was a pause as she introduced "Thanks But No, Thanks" to the audience. Collier poised his fingers over the keys, waiting for her cue, more nervous than he'd ever felt performing ever. This would be the first time he'd sung the song in front of Izzy. He shot a quick glance to the balcony where Izzy stood at the railing cheering. He lost himself for a moment, looking at her. Their past rolled through his mind as Mira calmed the crowd.

They'd decided to make the song the last of the set, but to kick the tempo up a bit so that they didn't end on a quiet note. Collier, as he waited for Mira to end her intro, realized he didn't mind rearranging the song to suit her voice more than his. Singing this song in front of Izzy, he doubted his ability to control his voice. Absently he wondered if Jake would still think it was a giant pile of suck.

He needn't have worried. Mira carried out the changes perfectly and the set ended in a whirl of noise and cheers. Collier stood next to Mira, took her hand, and they bowed to the crowd. He looked up to the balcony and caught Shara's eye. She was clearly pleased.

Izzy and Quinn were near Shara, a few feet down the railing. In the middle of his triumph, with the whole place cheering for more of his music, Collier watched as Izzy snuggled under Quinn's arm and shared some little private conversation.

In a flash, he finally realized Izzy was lost to him forever. As far as Izzy was concerned, Quinn was the only man she loved and it didn't matter if Collier played the most beautiful music in the world. She would be happy for Collier, he knew that. But Quinn would always be the center of her world.

Izzy would never be his.

Collier wanted to laugh at himself. *Well, duh. What did I think was going to happen? I was going to win her back by having a good set?*

He expected to feel sad, finally coming to terms with this truth. But he felt a lightness instead, like he'd just set a heavy case on the floor and would never have to pick it up again. He realized he still held Mira's hand. He smiled at her, and squeezed it gently.

She returned the smile. She looked, he thought, almost happy. Her color was better than he'd seen in a long time and her smile was genuine.

The curtain lowered slowly, amidst loud protests from the crowd.

"Do you want to do the encore?" He shouted at Mira over the din.

She nodded and Collier let go of her hand and signaled the band to prepare for the song they planned as an encore.

He turned to see the curtain rising and Mira slumping to the stage.

MIRA

Mira felt herself crumple, but it didn't seem real. It was more as if she watched herself from someone else's brain, observing how a foreign body behaved. She was very aware of the lights, the noise, the crowd, and the feel of the greasy wood on the stage against her cheek, and yet, though she heard Collier shouting "Drop the curtain! Mira! Mira! Are you okay?" she didn't feel as if any of it was happening to her.

From her out of body view above everything, Mira watched Collier. He lifted her head from the floor and cradled it in his lap. He said her name over and over, like a chant, as if saying her name would somehow bring her back. She thought it strange that she didn't feel anything for the woman at the center of the attention. That woman didn't look like her, didn't feel like her. Mira was merely observing the frantic activity like a half-interested bystander.

"Someone call an ambulance!"

Collier's command forced Mira's brain to work inside her body again and now she was aware of the fact that she, her whole self, lay on the floor *This is serious. This is happening to me. I have to get up.*

She tried to move, to get up, but she slipped into a further state of weightlessness. Her body was not working. *I have to get up. I have to get up! GET UP NOW!*

This time she opened her eyes and propped herself on her elbows. She didn't ask what happened. "Collier." She smiled and put a hand on his arm.

"Geez, Mira, what was that?"

"I fainted, no big deal. The crowd, the lights, it got to my head. I don't think I ate lunch today."

Collier frowned, and she watched as concern darkened his steel gray eyes. "We're taking you to the hospital."

She sat all the way up and waved her hand at him. "No, I'm fine, really. I just got overwhelmed. You know this was a huge deal. My brain just…" she couldn't find the right words, so shrugged at him. "I don't need an ambulance."

"Yes, you do." Collier nodded to the EMTs who rolled a gurney onto the stage. "We're going to the hospital."

134

Having no strength to protest, Mira allowed the EMTs to poke at her a bit. She answered their questions, and let them strap her to the gurney. As they rolled her off the stage to the back door of Second Chances Saloon, Mira realized Collier was in complete control of the situation. He was going to make sure she was safe.

It was a new feeling for her, having someone actually, taking care of her.

She managed a weak smile before drifting back into unconsciousness.

COLLIER

Collier couldn't sit still in the emergency room waiting area. He paced, his thoughts loud and jumbled. He checked the wall clock repeatedly, at once amazed and yet not surprised by the passage of time. His cell buzzed several times, calls from his friends who witnessed Mira's faint. He ignored all of them. He'd get to them, as soon as he knew anything. There was no point to making calls in the wee hours of the morning before he had any information. The first person he'd have to call would be Shara.

He didn't like to think about how that phone call would go.

"Collier James?"

Collier focused on the nurse standing in the hall. "Yes?"

"If you'd like to have a seat in the conference room there," she pointed to a tiny, dimly lit room, "the doctor will be in with you in a few moments."

He sat on one of the well-worn chairs and tried to relax. *Impossible.*

"Mr. James?"

Collier stood as the doctor, a tall, icy blond woman in a lab coat walked in. "Yes, ma'am?"

"I'm Doctor Blanche Passavant. You brought Miranda Pierce in?"

"I did." Collier shrugged. "Mira and I work together. She lives out of state."

"Miss Pierce has given me permission to talk to you. I can't tell you specific details, mostly because I don't know many. She has been drifting in and out of consciousness. I'm hoping you can help me. Please sit down." She pointed to a chair.

"What happened to her?"

"I was actually going to ask you the same question. What can you tell me?"

Collier sat and tried to find a comfortable position before speaking. He failed. "I don't know. I mean, I knew she wasn't feeling great lately, but I sort of chalked it up to how hard we've been working."

"Are you from around here?"

"Yes, ma'am, Nashville born and bred."

"But you've been away for some time."

136

Collier gave her a weak grin. "A few months, in Wisconsin. My accent is that different?"

"It's not pure Nashville anymore." The doctor smiled. "Anyway, you've been working with Miss Pierce in Wisconsin?"

"Yes. Since the end of October, on and off, I guess."

"What do you do?"

"We…"he stopped. *How do I explain this to a doctor?* "We're musicians. We played at 'Second Chances' tonight."

"Musicians. I see."

Collier frowned, sensing what she was thinking. "No, Doctor, I don't know that you do."

"Mr. James, I have in my exam room a young woman who is dehydrated, desperately malnourished, and coming down from having taken something. Not to mention the evidence of long term self-harm on both her arms and legs. You tell me you're musicians. I've been a doctor a long time and one thing I've learned is that the most obvious answer is probably the right one. If you can't tell me what she's taken, we'll have to wait for the tox screen, but that could take a while."

Collier lowered his head and his voice. "Ma'am, I'm telling you, I'm not aware that Mira is using any kind of drugs. She and I have been working in a studio for hours on end, every day. I know she's lost a lot of weight in the last few weeks…"

The doctor looked up. "She hasn't always been this thin?"

"Not like that. She told me when she's writing she forgets to eat. I've worked with all kinds of musicians. I've never seen anyone who focuses like she does. She's a machine."

The doctor studied him thoughtfully then made a few notes on her pad. "Would you say she's super focused?"

"Yeah."

The doctor tapped her pen against her lips. "Tell me, have you noticed mood swings?"

Collier let out a mirthless laugh. "Mira is a very…well they call her 'thorny'. She's had it tough. She's got a pretty thick shell so she seems grouchy most of the time."

"But lately, have you noted different moods, quickly shifting moods? "

He closed his eyes and pictured the scene at Chances the day before. "I guess. Recently. One minute she was really flirty with people she didn't even know and then next she was throwing a drink in someone's face. It was bizarre, even for her. She's been sort of a powder keg since I met her."

"Flirty…that's not normal for her?"

"There is not one person back home who would think of her as flirty." Collier paused, realizing he'd just referred to Rock Harbor as 'home.' "People who have known her longer than I have would think she was acting strange."

"Mood swings and rapid weight loss fall into a pattern."

"What is it?"

Doctor Passavant put her pen back in her coat pocket. "I'm sorry, Mr. James. I know this is frustrating, but I can't go into specifics with you. I do think, however, once we've got enough fluids into her, we'll be able to let her go without admitting her. I do have to go over her tests and then maybe you and I will speak further. If you have someplace you want to go for the next few hours, get some rest, that's fine. Just leave your phone number with admitting."

She left without another word. Collier mulled over a thousand possible things that could be wrong with Mira.

And not one of them made him feel any better.

He walked out of the conference room and was about to begin his pacing again when he heard a familiar voice behind him. "You know, you could have at least told us which hospital she was going to."

138

Collier looked down the long entry and saw Shara and the rest of 'Teacher' Pets' coming toward him. "Guys? I can't believe you all came."

"It took a little time because someone's not picking up his phone." Shara gave him a hug. "How is she?"

"I just talked to her doctor. They don't know much."

"Sit down before you fall down, Col." She sat down and patted the seat next to her. "Guys, see if you can find some coffee or something."

Kelly and the rest of them obeyed Shara, patting Collier on the shoulder as they passed him.

Once they were out of ear shot, Shara's face set in firm lines. "Is she on something?"

Doubt crowded Collier's mind. *If everyone thinks the same thing, how can I be so wrong?* "I don't know. They seem to think so. I never saw her take anything."

"I never did either, but I had a suspicion. I've worked with enough musicians to see all kinds of things."

"They say she's dehydrated and malnourished."

Shara nodded. "Are they going to admit her?"

"The doctor said maybe not. They were going to get more fluids in her and then release her."

"Shara, there isn't any coffee in this place." Jake led the band members back to the waiting room.

"That's not true, Jake, there was a coffee station in that hall." Tony pointed in the general direction where they'd been.

"Tony, I don't know where you were raised, but where I'm from coffee is black and doesn't smell like chemicals. I'm not drinking anything that came out of that coffee station."

"Guys, guys, listen. It might be a few hours yet, and there's no point in you guys hanging around here." Collier nodded toward Kelly, who looked exhausted. "Why don't you go back and get some sleep. I'll keep you posted."

There was a general murmur of agreement. Collier ushered them out of the hospital into the crisp night air. He followed them to the van and assured each of them he'd call if anything changed with Mira.

Shara waited until the others were in the van. "Col, you and I need to go over a few things. Where we can meet later?"

"There's this place called "Silver Screen Coffee." It's a great little coffee shop and bakery." Collier typed the address into his phone and sent it as a text to Shara's phone.

"Got it. Meet there around nine?" Shara checked her watch. "That's about five hours from now. Are you going to want to get some sleep before that?"

Collier waved a dismissive hand. "I won't be sleeping any time soon."

She climbed into the van. "If you can't make it…if there's something else with Mira, just text me."

Collier waved to the van as it pulled out of the lot before he returned to the waiting room. Settling into a chair, he wondered what he would do next.

Then he realized, he already knew.

MIRA

"Miranda? Miranda?"

Mira opened her eyes and immediately squinted out the bright overhead lights. "Just call me 'Mira,' okay?"

"Mira, my name is Doctor Passavant. I need to ask you a few questions."

Mira's mouth felt stale, dry. "Can I have a drink of water? I'll answer whatever you want."

A nurse handed her a cup with a straw in it. She tried to reach for it with her right hand, but that, she discovered, was attached to an IV bag hanging over her head. Holding the cup in her left hand she turned her attention to the doctor. "Fire away."

"What have you taken in the last forty eight hours?"

"Geez Doc, you don't make with niceties before asking the big questions, do you?"

"I don't have that kind of luxury when I'm trying to make sick people well."

Mira closed her eyes. "I haven't taken anything today."

"That doesn't answer my whole question."

"You don't have to be a cold bitch about it." Mira wanted to bite back the words. *This woman is just trying to help me. Why am I being so completely nasty to her?*

"I'm going to assume you're still experiencing mood swings because you're coming down from whatever it is you're on. If you tell me, I could help speed the process along for you."

Mira nodded. "Fine. I took the last one tonight…and then I took a bunch of those chewable antacids, you know, Tums?"

"What did you take?"

She couldn't concentrate. Her focus was gone. She was cold, tired, and her mouth was still dry. She took another sip of water and cleared her throat. "Ritalin. I took Ritalin."

"How much?"

Mira shook her head. "I don't know. Otis got them for me. They help me focus on writing." She took a deep breath.

"I assume then you have no prescription?"

"I had to have focus. Everything was riding on this tour, this performance."

"How long have you been taking them?"

140

"Couple months. Since October. It was just so I could really write some good songs. I have to make this work. I have to get my kid back." The enormity of it all made her tremble. "You have no idea."

Dr. Passavant smiled for the first time and the smile calmed Mira. "I might have some idea." She made some notes in her chart. "You are a very fortunate young woman. You have a very good friend waiting for you outside."

"Collier?"

Dr. Passvant nodded. "He'll be happy to know you're going to be okay."

Relief washed over Mira. "Are you sure?"

"Yes, I am." Dr. Passavant put a hand on her shoulder. "You're very lucky. Some of what you've experienced has been severe, and could have been very severe. Once we get you back to good hydration levels, all you will need is rest and a few good meals and you'll be just fine. Physically anyway."

Mira smiled and relaxed against the pillows. "And I'll able to perform tomorrow night?"

Dr. Passavant frowned. "I think I may not have been clear. Mira, you are going to need complete rest. Not from the effects of the Ritalin, I'm confident that will pass soon without too much trouble. But you have effectively starved and dehydrated your body for weeks. You're extremely susceptible to a hundred different things. I want you to rest. I'd like you to get drug counseling, but I understand you're not from around here, so when you get home I'd like you to find a therapist. Maybe one," the doctor paused, "who can help you with your other issues."

Mira blinked. *What other issues?* She took a sip of water and glimpsed her inner arm. *Oh, right.*

" Time away from the spotlight is mandatory, at least for the very near future." The doctor patted her shoulder. "I'll let Collier come in to see you."

Numb, as the doctor's words hit her, Mira nodded. "Just give me a few minutes, okay?"

Doctor and nurse both walked out of the room, leaving Mira to weep in private. *No performance tomorrow night? She wants me to get mental therapy when I get home?*

Madelyn'll have all the ammo she needs to keep Dusty.

With this uneasy thought, she drifted into a restless sleep.

*

She woke, she had no idea how much later, and realized a nurse was removing her IV. She squinted at the bright light until her eyes adjusted. "You're a different nurse."

" I'm the one with good news. You get to go home."

"Home?" She struggled to form the word, in part because her mouth still felt sticky, but also because she had no idea where 'home' was at the moment.

"Well, not home, maybe, but your boyfriend is out in the waiting room just waiting for you. And sugar, he is a fine looking man. You keep hold of that one."

"Boyfriend? Oh. Collier."

The nurse finished her task and smiled at her. "Now you just settle a bit. I'll be along to give you your walking papers."

It wasn't long before the nurse returned, pushing a wheel chair. She helped Mira into it and started toward the door.

Dr. Passavant stopped them. "Miss Pierce, I have a couple pamphlets I'd like you to take," she handed Mira three or four brightly colored fliers, and knelt in front of Mira. "Believe me when I say, the last thing in the world I want is to see you back here. I'd much rather see you performing on stage. Understand?"

142

Mira brushed away a tear and nodded. "Thanks, Doctor."

Dr. Passavant patted her shoulder and the nurse rolled her out the door to the waiting room. Collier was there, sitting in a far corner, dozing.

"There he is, honey. Now that's what I call devoted."

Mira was annoyed by the tears streaking down her face. She tried to ignore the wave of relief that washed over her knowing someone cared enough to pick her up.

The nurse rolled her to where Collier sat. He opened his eyes. "Oh, hey, you're out?"

He gave her a sleepy half smile that warmed Mira's heart. "Yeah. Um, thanks for, you know, being here."

"Well I'll leave you two." The nurse paused. "You can park the chair in the entry right here."

They said nothing as they watched the nurse cross the waiting room and disappear behind the emergency room doors. Mira turned her attention to Collier, who seemed to be studying her closely. "What?"

"Are you okay?"

She shrugged. "Who knows? I must be, they cut me loose." She forced herself to sound cavalier.

"Stop it."

She'd never heard this tone from Collier before. He'd always been one who spoke softly, but now there was a firm, undeniable inflection in his voice. "Stop what?" She didn't recognize her own voice. She meant to sound authoritative, in control. She sounded more like a child. She felt like a child, aching to be cared for.

He didn't answer her question. He rolled her to the door.

"Where are we going?"

"Are you hungry?"

The question surprised her, but she realized she was. She was hungrier than she remembered ever being. "If you're hungry, I could eat, I guess."

"Stop being evasive or cute. Say what you mean."

Mira twisted in her chair to look at his face, but saw nothing other than a sense of calm. It was an expression she'd seen a thousand times. "Where are we going?"

"First, we'll hit a Waffle House. Then I'm going to get you settled at my place."

"Your place? I thought Shara was shipping me home."

"You're going to stay with me for a while." He held out his hand to help her stand.

She took his hand, and the warmth of his touch flowed through her fingers up her arms. She allowed him to guide her out the door into the rosy first light of the morning.

She was happy to let Collier take charge of her.

143

COLLIER

Nine on the dot, Collier watched Shara enter Silver Screen. He nodded to Cat, who brought two cinnamon rolls to his table. Shara settled across from him, and watched as Cat poured coffee in her cup. "This place is great!"

"Thanks. It's been my favorite place in town for a long time. Cat's an old friend." Collier smiled at Cat, who disappeared around a corner.

"I love Rock Harbor, but I have to say, it's always nice moving around the country and checking out places like this. Dirty Dog Dave's is great, but I can only eat so many cheeseburgers. Now I can add Waffle House and this place to my list of favorite places."

Collier smiled and toyed with a sugar packet.

"Okay, I guess enough of the small talk. What's going on with Mira?"

"They released her an hour after you guys left."

"Where is she now?"

"At my place." He toyed with the sugar packet again. He'd spent the last hour practicing what he would say, but was still nervous. "I didn't think she should be on her own in a hotel room." He knew Shara's expression. She guessed much of what he wasn't saying.

"We all make mistakes, not always for wrong reasons." Shara drank more coffee. "I suppose she won't be able to perform tonight?"

Collier shook his head. "No. The doctors said she needs complete rest and a decent diet for a while." He paused, not sure he should continue. "They also said she should get addiction counseling. Maybe see a psychologist when she gets home."

Shara nodded, her expression revealing no surprise. "Sounds like a sensible plan. When is she leaving for home?"

Collier sat up and looked directly at Shara and suddenly pictured Bryan, and heard Bryan's words again. His nervousness faded and resolve filled him. *It's only my future.* "She's not. She's going to stay here for awhile…with me."

Leaning back in her chair, Shara studied him. "That's a very generous thing you're doing, Col."

"She's got no place else she can go."

144

Shara studied him. "This is a big decision for you."

Collier nodded. "I've thought it over. I just don't feel good about shipping her someplace alone. It wouldn't be right."

"You can't send her back to Madelyn?"

Collier tried to shut out the things Mira shared with him on the ride back to his place. "That's not an option, at least not in my mind. It's too messed up."

Shara's smile held a shadow of irony. "So you're going to be the one to save her?"

"I…" He looked at Shara, clearly, and he understood what Bryan had tried to tell him. Collier knew, beyond words, that he was willing to do whatever it took to keep Mira safe. He knew it and he had no regrets. "I am."

"You're not traveling with us for the rest of the tour."

Collier shook his head. "I hope you're not…angry."

"Angry?" She looked surprised, as if the thought had not occurred to her. "Collier, family always, always comes first, and your band mates are family, even if it seems crazy at times. If you had said you were putting her on a bus I might have been disappointed in you." She cocked her head, her dark eyes dancing with mirth. "There is going to be a place for you…and Mira…at 'Orphans and Runaways.' Get her well. The album will wait."

She stood to leave, but paused, and looked down at him. "You want to ask me something?"

"So last night…it went well? We were good enough?"

Shara laughed and patted his shoulder. "Collier, I knew you two were going to be spectacular, I knew that first morning when you both showed up for breakfast. I knew she had talent, and I immediately saw the chemistry between you."

"So…I'm confused. What was last night about if we weren't auditioning for you?"

"Last night was about the two of you realizing you belonged together on stage. You were auditioning for each other."

He was eight years older than Shara, but in that moment he felt a child-like joy surge through him. He leapt up and hugged her. "Thank you!"

She returned his hug. "I do have one regret."

He stepped back, his enthusiasm cooled. "What's that?"

"I'm definitely bummed you two won't be opening for us tonight. Because the next time you and Mira hit the road, you'll be way too big to be our opening act. Jake's not going to like it when I ask ''Teacher's Pets'' to open for you."

She gave him a quick hug, picked up her bag, and left. Collier felt like dancing, or something. His relief and joy needed an outlet.

"Oh, my lord!" Cat waddled out from behind the counter. "I can't believe it! You are going to be so big time!" She took his hands and they started jumping up and down, cheering.

Benny walked in, and stared at them. "Okay, couple things. First of all, what's with all the cheering and joyfulness? I thought you were Mr. Depressed? Also, I don't think you should be making the pregnant woman jump up and down so much. I do not want that troll baby out a minute earlier than he has to be."

Cat punched Benny in the arm. "Quit calling the baby a troll. Collier just got the best news ever. So we're happy dancing a little bit."

"Happy dance away. You and that Mira girl kicked serious ass last night. So, what's the good news?"

Collier drained his coffee in a single swallow and checked the clock. "Cat's gonna have to catch you up. I gotta go."

"Gotta get a nap before hitting the big stage tonight?"

Collier shook his head. "Nope, I'm not playing tonight."

"What? But…"

"Benny. He has something more important he has to take care of."

"Dude, what is more important than taking the stage in front of twenty thousand women screaming your name?"

Collier paused at the door. "One woman. One sick, damaged woman, who really just needs me right now."

He left before Benny could argue.

SARAH J. BRADLEY A HERO'S SPARK

MIRA

"I'm going out. Do you need or want anything?"

Mira looked up from the newspaper. "How about we go shopping? I feel the need for a new dress. And then tonight we could hit the town!" She forced a smile on her face. She knew what Collier's answer would be.

Collier shook his head. "You know that's not going to happen. It's only been a couple days. You need rest."

"It's been two weeks and I'm bored. Can't we at least go to Chance's so I can stand on a stage and pretend?"

"Nope. You're resting."

"I'm rusting."

Collier gave her a faint smile. "I'll see if I can't bring back some movies maybe we haven't seen. Or a board game."

"Did I suddenly turn eighty? Is this a retirement home?" She lowered her voice, "am I dying and you're afraid to tell me, so you're going to bore me to the point where I won't care?"

Collier laughed. "I'll be back in maybe a couple hours. I'm headed over to the ice rink to sign some papers."

"And see Izzy."

Mira wanted to bite back the words but the damage had already been done. The spark of good humor faded from Collier's eyes. "Col, I'm sorry...I didn't ..."

"I'll be back in a couple hours." He walked out and closed the door a bit more loudly than he probably needed to.

I'm such an idiot. Mira settled onto the couch and sighed. Two weeks since her collapse and she felt like a new woman. Collier was a very strict caretaker and other than tiring quickly most of the time, Mira felt healthier than she had in ages. Collier treated her better than anyone ever had.

Mira couldn't remember a moment in her life where anyone cared for her as gently as Collier. There was no need he didn't seem to anticipate, no discomfort he didn't work to eliminate. Mira smiled. He'd moved her into the bedroom and slept on the couch. He treated her kindly.

And very much like I'm some sort of delicate china that might break. So he has to put me on a shelf, away from everything and everyone.

Mira chafed under the doctor's orders, and Collier's religious adherence to them. She'd gone to a drug support group a couple times, but the sessions served more as a warning to her than any sort of self realization. She looked around the room and saw hardened drug users, people who stole money from their children to get high. She didn't think of her life being a parallel to theirs, but rather the early stage. She had no intention of getting to the point many of the people in the group were, so the sessions, after the first couple, seemed like overkill to her.

But at least the meetings get me out of the apartment.

As nice as the view from Collier's window was, it was just a view. She saw lights of Nashville, she sensed the city's pulse, but she couldn't reach out, touch it, be part of it. With the exception of the group and the occasional quick visit to Silver Screen, Mira's world was Collier James' one-bedroom apartment. She felt caged.

Worse, she felt like she was keeping Collier caged.

He never complained. He spent nearly every moment either in the apartment with her or taking her to the doctor or to the group. He never expressed any desire to go out at night, or really to do anything other than sit companionably with her and watch movies.

148

But there were times when he'd have to run an errand without her, or he'd go to Silver Screen to pick up coffee and rolls for them both.

Or when he just seems very far away.

It was Izzy, it had to be. Mira knew there was little she could do about it. He never said anything, not to Mira, but she couldn't escape the feeling that he was doing a very good acting job for her benefit.

The very thought stung. She longed to get all of her strength back so that she could go back to Rock Harbor and let everyone get back to their lives. As kind as Collier had been, as kind as his friends had been to her, Mira felt like a burden. She knew well what he'd given up to tend to her. This knowledge only added to her sense of guilt.

And then there was the Izzy factor. It saddened Mira every time Collier came up with some reason to leave the apartment so he could, she assumed, go to the rink to watch Izzy. It broke her heart.

In her most honest moments, Mira didn't deny the frequent twinge of jealously, but she dismissed the feeling quickly. *He'll never get over Izzy, so he'll never really be available to anyone...else.*

She got off the couch and looked around the apartment. The one thing Collier wasn't was tidy. She felt guilty for her snarky comment about Izzy, so she started cleaning up the dishes and socks and sheets of music paper Collier dropped everywhere. She filled the dishwasher and ran it. Then she took the garbage from all the garbage cans to the hall incinerator chute. She wiped down all the kitchen surfaces with bleach spray.

Exhausted from the exertion she sat again on the sofa where he'd recently slept. She remembered the first time she'd seen Collier up close, the night in Shara's loft. She didn't know why she always went back to that image, whether it was the spirited argument she liked to recall or his defined chest muscles. Even now, as she sat on the sofa and warmed in the sun, she didn't allow her thoughts to trail too far down that path.

No point wasting on something that is never going to happen.

The door buzzer sounded. She got up and pushed the button to unlock the building door. "Come on up!" She didn't ask who was coming up. Anyone who came to Collier's door, she'd found, was a friend. He was a man with no enemies and many good-hearted friends who liked to check in on her and bring them food. Mira discovered quickly Collier was the worst of cooks. His friends, knowing this, made sure Mira didn't starve.

Usually it was Cat, with or without Benny, but today, Mira opened the door and there stood Izzy.

"Oh, hey there, Izzy, come on in." She knew she couldn't hide the surprise in her voice. Mira wanted to hate Izzy mostly because she didn't want to admit she was finding it harder and harder to ignore certain thoughts she had about Collier. But Izzy was unfailingly sweet and genuine. Mira couldn't help liking her.

Izzy carried in a crock pot full of something that smelled amazing. "How are you feeling?"

"Better every day. Have a seat. You want anything to drink?"

Izzy handed her the crock pot and sat at on a kitchen chair. "I'm fine, thanks. Cat asked me to bring this up, said the

149

baby decided to wedge his foot between two of her ribs and she can't move without her lung getting crushed."

"I remember just hating those last months when I was pregnant."

"I didn't know you had kids."

Izzy's response was conversational, but Mira felt dizzy for a moment, realizing what she'd just said. "I…" She crossed the room and knelt in front of Izzy. "You cannot say anything to Collier."

"What, that you were pregnant?" Izzy looked confused. "Collier doesn't know that?"

"No. He thinks Dusty is my nephew. Everyone thinks Dusty is my nephew." She tried to keep the panic out of her voice. "I can't talk about this. He can't know."

"Calm down. It's okay. I won't say a word." Izzy put a hand on her shoulder. "You want to talk about it?"

Izzy's manner calmed her. Mira sat down across the table from Izzy and folded her hands. "It's the one thing I promised I would never tell anyone."

"Your secret is safe with me." Izzy reached over and patted her hands. "I might know a little of what you've gone through."

"How would you know anything like that?" Mira bit her lip, hating that her thorny nature leaked out.

"Did Collier ever tell you why I quit figure skating?"

Mira shook her head. "No. Collier has a way of saying your name and then sort of drifting off someplace in his head." Her words echoed the jealously she felt sitting across from Izzy who was so perfect, while Mira was desperately trying to cover up the hot mess that was her life.

If Izzy noticed Mira's bitter tone, she did not acknowledge it. "When I was sixteen, I got pregnant." She held up a hand to stop Mira from commenting. "He was much older than I was, and he was my skating partner. He said we had to leave Nashville. So we did. For almost two decades I was a loving wife and mother. And then, one day, he died, my husband did. He died in an accident."

"Oh, wow, Izzy, I'm sorry."

Izzy shook her head. "Don't be. I realized after the funeral that I never really loved him. I am passionate about our daughter, but I never loved him. And, we discovered, he didn't care for me or for Jenna. Before he died, he drained our bank accounts. We lost out house. Jenna was going to Vandy on scholarship, thank heavens. We had nothing, but there was nothing holding me there, so I moved back here with her."

"And you met Quinn."

"I met Quinn." She smiled. "It wasn't exactly love at first sight. It was more like two people adrift in the world sort of bumped into each other. We both had baggage, tons of it. Turns out, his was a little more dramatic." Izzy paused. "Collier really hasn't told you this?"

Mira sighed. "Collier does like to talk about Quinn. But I don't think I can repeat much of what he's said."

Izzy laughed. "Yeah, they didn't like each other, at all." Izzy paused. "Someone else is raising your son?"

Mira nodded. "My older sister and her husband."

"Passing him off as their child?"

"Not that hard to do. The Senator is Dusty's father."

The words sat between the two women like a heavy curtain. Mira stared at Izzy, shocked that she'd actually spoken the words out loud. "Izzy…really, no one, not even my sister, no one knows that."

Izzy shook her head. "Mira, I'm the last person who is going to judge you or share your secret."

Relief washed over Mira. "It's such a mess. I was like you, I was really young. I thought I was in love, but what the hell did I know? He…he was kind to me, at least for a while. I thought he loved me. Now Madelyn gets to raise my boy, and I'm here, trying to make something of myself." Mira rubbed her face with both hands. "I'm a hopeless mess."

"You're not. You have baggage, just like everyone else." Izzy's voice was soft, calming.

Mira sniffled and wiped a tear from her eye. "I can see why Collier…why he likes you. You're a good person."

Izzy smiled. "I don't know about that. I just know what it feels like to be young and pregnant and afraid. You wind up doing things you probably felt were your only option. I moved to Wisconsin and married someone I didn't love. You let your sister raise your son." She paused and looked at her cell as it buzzed. "That's Cat. She needs me to pick up more antacids. Her heartburn is the worst." She stood and put a hand on the door. "Are you gonna be okay?"

Mira wiped her eyes again. "Oh, yeah…yeah. I'm fine. And thanks for the…well, for whatever is in that crock pot."

"Cat says it's an old family recipe. It smells good, so it can't be too horrible." Izzy grinned and opened the door. "Mira?"

"Yeah?"

"This is probably none of my business, and you can tell me to shut up if you want. But I have to say it."

"Go ahead."

"After Jason died, I wasted a lot of months trying to prove something by being on my own. I pushed Quinn away, and I almost lost him because of it."

"What, he was going to leave you for someone else?"

"No. His ex tried to kill him."

"Oh,." Mira couldn't grasp the idea of anyone wanting to kill the stunning Quinn Murray. "I have no response for that."

"Few do." Izzy smiled softly. "But I'm telling you this because I sense you feel you have something to prove. Don't try to be so strong you wind up pushing away someone who wants to help."

152

Collier's face sprang to Mira's mind. "I might know what you mean."

"I thought you might. So listen: being independent is fine, but way overrated when there's someone out there you could team up with. Having someone who really cares, letting that person in…it's just so much better than being alone."

"I'll keep that in mind." Mira watched as Izzy left the apartment and closed the door.

COLLIER

Collier signed the last paper with a flourish. "There you go. I think we're done here."

Quinn picked up the papers and thumbed through them. "Col, are you sure about this? Izzy and I are fine with the way things are right now."

Collier sat back in the desk chair and looked around the memorabilia-filled office, most of it highlighting Izzy's skating career. "This place isn't part of my life anymore, Quinn. It's not fair to you and Izzy to wait for me to sign something so you can change a light bulb or whatever." His gaze landed on one of the oldest pictures in the office, the only picture of Izzy and him as skating partners. "This place, you and Izzy are doing great things with it, and I know Pop would be proud of the two of you."

Quinn slid the papers into a folder. "Are you sure you don't want cash? I mean, it feels wrong to just take this without giving you anything for it."

Collier shook his head. "Keep your money. You're going to need it next year when the roof finally caves in on the place."

The two men stood and shook hands. "You're really going to move up north?"

153

Collier nodded. "I'll keep the apartment here."

"Benny will appreciate that," Quinn grinned.

Collier chuckled. "I bet. I'll keep the place here, for when I come to visit. But my life, my career, it's all up there now."

They walked to the door of the rink. Quinn held it open for Collier, but put a hand on his shoulder to stop him from leaving. "Izzy is going to have a few things to say about this, you know. You are a very big part of her life."

"I know it kills you to have to admit that." Collier grinned at his old rival.

Quinn shook his head. "I can't lie. But you know she'll hate the idea of you moving away permanently. We all will."

Collier arched and eyebrow. "All of you, really?"

Quinn shrugged. "What can I say? You're not a completely horrible person to have around."

Collier shook hands with him again. "Well, take care of the old place. And Izzy."

"I will, don't worry. And don't be a stranger."

Collier waved as he walked down the stairs to the parking lot. Getting into the car, he gave the rink one last look in his rearview mirror.

Then he drove back to the apartment and Mira.

*

She must've fallen asleep reading a book on the bed. Collier noticed the cleaning she'd done. *Over-did it and wore herself out.*

He pulled a blanket over her slim form and closed the door. She'd kept the crock pot turned on low. He dished himself a plate of Cat's stew and sat on the sofa. Staring at the lights of Nashville, Collier felt as if he'd made all the right decisions for the first time in his life.

<u>MIRA</u>

Mira woke with a start. It was dark, but moonlight streamed across the bed casting everything in a silvery glow. She didn't remember falling asleep, but now awake, she sat up, sensing there was something she had to do.

She pushed back the blanket and shivered slightly, her thin t-shirt and shorts doing little to ward off the chill in the room. Her eyes adjusted to the minimal light as she crossed to the door. Mira put her hand on the knob, her skin chilling at contact with the cool brass. She opened the door slowly, not wanting to disturb Collier if he was asleep, but feeling too restless to stay in the bedroom.

Collier sat on the sofa, his head resting in the crook of his arm. He could have been looking out the window, or asleep, Mira wasn't sure. The air in the living room was chilly. Mira shivered again as she noticed the blanket Collier used lying on the floor. Moving carefully, she picked up the blanket and covered him.

The moonlight created a silver halo around him. His face was smooth, unlined. Earlier in the day he'd been quiet and distant, as if he had something on his mind. Now, relaxed and still, he seemed at peace. Without conscious thought, she stroked his cheek lightly with her fingertips. His skin was warm.

155

"Izzy?"

She startled at his sleepy voice. "No," she whispered, "it's me, Mira."

"You okay?"

"Yeah, yeah. I'm fine. Everything's okay."

"Okay. Good." His eyelashes fluttered, then stilled.

She knew she should leave him, but she couldn't take her eyes off him. He was the one person who had been truly kind to her, who had given up everything to make sure she was taken care of. Gratitude welled in her. She brushed a wisp of hair away from his face and kissed his forehead. His clean, soapy scent warmed her.

She sat on the edge of the couch, and stroked his hair which shimmered like new honey. She closed her eyes and imagined his embrace, strong, protective, gentle. Tears welled in her eyes. She let them overflow and roll down her cheeks unchecked. Leaning forward, she brushed her lips across his.

He stirred, and she retreated, wishing to fade into the shadows if he woke, but unable to leave his side. He stilled and she leaned forward and touched her lips to his again. This time he returned the kiss, so subtly she was not positive he'd moved at all. She rested her head on his shoulder and closed her eyes.

His touch was light as his hand trailed up her arm to her shoulder. She turned her face to meet his and he held her gently as he kissed her eyelids, then captured her lips in the softest of kisses. She met him halfway, her restlessness eased as if this was exactly what she needed to do.

Collier shifted and wrapped his arms around her, warming her, comforting her, making her ache for something she hadn't known she wanted. She pressed herself closer to him. He embraced her, claiming her lips again in a kiss that warmed her like red wine.

They broke apart as softly as they'd come together and Mira studied him in the pale white streetlight. "It's okay if you want to pretend."

Collier's eyes darkened and clouded. "Pretend what?" He sounded confused.

She stood, and felt the cold of the room again. "It's okay, you know, if you want to pretend I'm…" She bit her lip, unable to say the name. She realized, standing there, inches away from his embrace, from his warmth, that she loved him. Knowing only added to the cold ache in her heart because he was in love with Izzy.

He sat up and reached for her. "What are you talking about?"

She stayed just out of reach, realizing that it did matter, that she couldn't bear the idea of being a stand in for Izzy. "No. No. I can't. I'm sorry. I can't do this." She shook her head and escaped back to the bedroom where she closed the door and buried herself beneath the blankets.

She tried to smother the sobs when she heard the door open. He was there, at her side, wiping a tear from her cheek.

"I'm not in love with Izzy anymore."

His words were not everything she longed to hear, but it was enough. Without another word, she dropped her defenses. He kissed her again, this time wrapping her in a protective embrace. She floated, her senses filling and her skin waking as he caressed

156

her gently. The cold ache deep within her melted away beneath his hands. He leaned forward and laid her against the pillows, his body shielding her from the outside world.

There was no break, no pause in his touch, even as Mira heard him open the nightstand drawer and retrieve a condom. Gone was darkness, worry, panic, anger, distrust. In Collier's arms she was light and warm. She was ready to give herself completely to him.

He removed her shorts gently and dropped them to the floor. He rolled the bottom of her tank top up to her shoulders and she raised her arms. He lifted the thin shirt over her head and dropped that to the floor as well. She lay bare beneath him, and he kissed the base of her throat, her collarbone, each of her breasts with a reverent tenderness.

Then he was there, above her, his grey eyes locked with hers. She saw new light in his eyes, a spark of something commanding, something powerful, something she'd never seen in Collier James before. He blinked, and the spark was dimmed, more respectful.

"Are you sure?" he whispered. "This is what you want?"

Unable to speak, unwilling to mar the moment with more words, she nodded and arched her body to meet him. Wrapped in each other's arms, their bodies joined, Mira felt complete, and safe, and loved, for the first time in her life. She laced her fingers in his hair and kissed him. He breathed her name against her skin as he rocked her with a gentle rhythm she was able to match until they moved together perfectly, one heartbeat between them at the final crescendo of release.

Collier held her as they separated and the heat between them cooled. The sound of his even breathing soothed Mira and she drifted to sleep just as the first light of dawn crept into the room.

*

She woke to the sound of her cell buzzing. Loathe to leave the warmth of Collier's embrace, she stretched and dragged the phone to the edge of the nightstand. She held it close and squinted at the text message.

It was from Carson.

157

"Miranda, Dustin broke his arm sledding last night and had to have surgery to repair the break. Mrs. Anderson was not going to tell you. I thought you should know."

Fear gripped her. *Of course Madelyn would use my absence as a chance to make Dusty think I don't love him. Anything to put more distance between us.*

I have to go back. I have to be with Dusty.

She crawled out of bed, pulled on the first clothes she found, and collected her things quietly. She knew if Collier woke, she wouldn't have the strength to leave him, but she had to go back, she couldn't lose what little contact she had with her son.

Checking her purse, Mira frowned. Eight dollars was not going to get her to the bus station, much less to Wisconsin. Collier's wallet was on the end table in the living room. She bit her lip. *I have to. It's for Dusty.* She opened the wallet, pulled out eighty dollars, and set the wallet back on the table.

She pondered leaving Collier a note, some kind of explanation. *What could I possibly say that would make him understand?*

There's no way I can tell him the truth.

In the end, she wrote, "I'll pay you back as soon as I can," on an old envelop and left it on the kitchen table.

With a final, sorrowful glance at Collier, who remained asleep, she left the apartment and flagged a cab.

COLLIER

Cat set a cup of coffee in front of him. "So she just left like that…no word, no note?"

Collier rubbed his face and stared at the coffee, numb. "She left a note about owing me money. I didn't realize that meant she cleaned out my wallet until I had to pay the cab for getting me here. So thanks for covering that."

"Don't mention it." Cat grinned. "Where's your car again?"

Collier shrugged. "I took it to the shop yesterday for a tune up. I figured if I was going to drive it back to Wisconsin, I should."

"You're going back to Wisconsin? You're not going to spend Christmas with us?" Cat pouted.

Collier drank some coffee before answering. "Ya know, 'Blue Pirate' just doesn't taste the same without your hair being blue."

"Stop dodging my questions."

"Fine. I planned on driving back so Mira could spend Christmas with her family. It was going to be a surprise for her."

"I didn't get the impression she had a lot of tight family connections."

Collier set his cup down. "She's got this nephew she's devoted to and she's never missed a Christmas with the kid. She hates her sister, but she loves this kid."

"Hm."

"What does that mean?"

Cat looked at him, wide eyed and innocent. "What?"

"You said, 'hm.' That means something."

"Col, I'm pregnant, that could just have been a belch." She shook her head. "But in this case it's not."

"What does that mean?"

"Ok, this is just me talking, right? And I don't know Mira except what I've seen these last few weeks which, you have to admit, probably haven't been her best."

"Agreed."

"Okay. But…okay, I love C.C. with all my heart."

"Not seeing your point."

"Let me get to the end of a thought. I love C.C. with all my heart. But C.C. is not my child. I'm spending Christmas with Benny because Benny is my family. If C.C. lived five hundred miles away, I would still be spending Christmas with Benny."

Collier frowned. "You love your fiancé and you love your godchild. And you choose to spend the holidays with your fiancé. Congrats, Cat. You've just stated an incredibly obvious thing, and, one that has nothing to do with Mira just up and leaving this morning."

Cat snapped him with a dishtowel. "Geez, for a songwriter you are so stupid about women!"

"Yes, but I'm not going to learn anything if you get violent with me." He stirred two heaping teaspoons of sugar into his coffee. "She probably just wanted to see the kid."

"Without telling you? Plus she took all your cash when you would have driven her there in a minute."

Collier rubbed his temples. "Cat, how about if you treat me like I'm an idiot…maybe like I'm Benny. Just say what you mean to say and stop playing the guessing game with me."

"Where were you when she left this morning?"

"I was asleep."

"On the couch?"

Collier suddenly found the blowing snow outside very interesting. "Not exactly."

"Right. And tell me, Collier, before you slept in your bed, were you and Mira entwined in the sacred dance of love?"

Collier stared at Cat for a full minute, then burst out laughing. "Oh, my lord woman! No more romance novels for you! 'The sacred dance of love?' What does that even mean?"

"You know full well what I'm talking about Collier. Stop being so stupid and think! Was this your first time, you two?"

"Yes."

"And suddenly she's up and gone. So I'm thinking either she's hiding something from you or…and you know I love you. Is it possible you…did something…that scared her?"

"What?" Collier stared at her again. "What in the world is going on in that head of yours, Cat? Seriously, get that baby out of you, because it's messing with your brain!"

"What's messing with my woman's brain?"

160

Collier looked over his shoulder and frowned. *Oh good…Benny.* "Don't you have a job?"

"I do. And I've done it." Benny nodded toward the clock. "Quinn filled in today, so the show actually ran long. Screening the calls from all those women who just love him, it's rough. Some of them have such sexy voices it's hard to stop talking to them, you know?"

"Benny, I'm standing right here, with your troll baby in me." Cat hit him with the towel.

"Ow!"

"She got me, too." Collier grinned.

"What, or who, are we talking about?"

"Well, as it turns out, Collier and Mira…you know."

Benny grinned. "Did they entwine themselves in the sacred dance of love?"

"Oh, for the love of God!" Collier slammed his empty cup on the counter. "Yes! Mira and I…"

"See, it's not that easy to say. I mean, if you want to sound all mushy, you can say, 'we made love.' If you want to be clinical about it you can say, 'we had sex.' Or if you're Benny…"

"If you're Benny, you say, 'I satisfied that woman in ways she won't begin to realize until tomorrow.'" Benny laughed as Cat smacked him with the towel.

"Benny, you're a pig. But yes, Mira and I made love."

Benny turned to Cat. "He writes loves songs for a living, doesn't he? You'd think those words wouldn't sound weird coming out of his mouth."

"Benny, he's right there. He can hear you. And besides, the problem is not that they slept together. The problem is that Mira took off and she cleaned out his wallet."

Benny whistled. "What did you do that scared her off? It must have been freaky because Mira strikes me as a semi-freak in her own way, you know? So, come on, what did you do? Because someday this baby is going to be born and I'm going to have sex with this woman again and I need some new moves!"

"I didn't do anything to scare her!" Collier was exasperated with the whole conversation. "Everything went very well, I thought."

"And she left."

"Yes."

"Maybe she's just a criminal?"

"Benny!" This time Cat snapped Benny's cheek with her towel. "She is not a criminal!" She turned to Collier. "Right?"

"No. She's not. She's a lot of things, but criminal isn't one of them." Collier rubbed his temples.

"Tell us more about this sister. Don't leave out any juicy details. Is she hot, like Mira? Could they be twins?"

Collier frowned at Benny, then held his cup for a refill. "She's much older than Mira. Raised Mira after their parents died. Married a state senator and they've got this kid, Dusty. He's twelve. They live in Madison, but come up to the old family place in Rock Harbor for vacations. The sisters don't like each other much."

"That's it?"

"That's all I know."

"Mira told you this?"

"No." Collier shook his head. "A nice lady named Molly told me this stuff."

"Molly's reliable?"

"She's lived in Rock Harbor for a long time and she knows everyone and everything."

162

"Big gossip?"

Collier smiled, remembering how Molly changed the subject when they started talking about Mira. "No, but she's a good cook and she does wonders with a haircut. What's with the twenty questions, Cat?"

"Mira doesn't seem like the kind of girl who gives it up easily. I know she seems tough. She might have done some stuff to sort of build up a bad girl rep, but I think that's a cover. The two of you, you have something, a vibe together. You were awesome on stage. You've been living in close quarters, taking care of her for weeks. Maybe she has feelings for you, something real. Since we've decided you didn't do anything freaky to her last night, it stands to reason that, under normal circumstances, she'd want to be with you. I bet she went to her sister's."

"But why?"

"I told you, she loves Dusty."

"Yeah, yeah." Collier turned to Benny. "Benny, you've got nieces and nephews…"

"I hate those little bastards!" Benny yelled through a mouthful of cinnamon roll.

"Mira isn't Benny."

"Thank God."

"Right. I have no interest in any kind of moves Col here might have for me. Even the freaky ones."

"Not now, Benny," Cat frowned at her fiancé. "It's weird she left without a word. Especially right after you two spent the night together. What's she hiding?"

"Cat, why would she be hiding anything?"

"Benny, care to address this one?"

Benny took another bite of cinnamon roll before answering. "Oh, yeah, that chick's hiding something."

Cat put her hand on Collier's shoulder. "Benny knows nothing about manners, but he knows about women. You find out what she's hiding, you find out why she left."

Collier finished his coffee and pushed the cup away. "I guess I've got something to think about."

"You want a lift to the shop?"

"Nah, they can hold on to the car." He checked his cell. "I can catch a ride back with band. They were going to come through Nashville today. Shara asked if we needed a ride."

Cat reached for her coat. "Well let's get you back to your apartment and packed so you can go after your woman!"

MIRA

Mira dragged herself to the bus depot and slumped into a cold chair. She'd sent several texts to Carson and to Madelyn saying she was on her way and would be there soon, but there was no response from either. Somewhere, on the endless trip from Nashville to Madison, her phone died. For the last five hours, she'd been without any contact at all.

Once at the bus depot, she checked her wallet. There wasn't much left of what she'd taken from Collier. She'd spent most of it on a Christmas present for Dusty, a Nashville skyline snow globe. She thought it was beautiful. It looked like the view from Collier's apartment window.

Collier.

She hugged her knees to her chest and tried to push away the memory of the feel of his skin against hers.

I can't think about that right now. I have to get to Dusty and prove to him that I love him before Madelyn turns me into some kind of monster in his eyes.

I won't let her make me be the monster in this story. Not a chance.

164

She pulled some change from her pocket and slid it into the filthy payphone. She punched in Carson's number, praying he would come and get her.

COLLIER

Sitting on the tour bus, Collier didn't have the heart to leave yet another message on Mira's phone. For whatever reason, she was simply not picking up, and after a couple dozen tries, he was tired. He rubbed his eyes, glad Shara was able to pick him up. The idea of driving back to Wisconsin had seemed adventurous, even a little romantic.

When Mira was going to ride with me.

Now, late December snowstorms threatened darker and darker with every state line they crossed. Snowflakes first fluttered gently around the bus but, by the time they crossed into Illinois, visibility was nearly nonexistent.

He stared out the window without actually seeing the snow. *Why did she leave?*

It was a question he asked himself every time he checked his cell for some response from Mira. He turned the question around and around until he was asking himself the words in reverse order, but still no answer came.

Exhausted from the tour, most of the guys in the band left him alone, unable to muster enough energy to break through the cloud that hung around him. Shara, first, then Kelly approached him but gave up after several miles of weary silence. It wasn't that Collier didn't want to talk. He simply didn't want to start a conversation and somehow lose the answer to the question he was thinking about so completely.

"Col, you're bummin' everyone out."

Collier stared at Jake. "I'm sorry?"

"You look like death warmed over in a microwave, man. Go get into my bunk and get some sleep. It's like two in the morning and all you've done is stare out the window. You're freakin' me out and ruining my creative flow. Kelly and I are trying to write."

Collier rubbed his face, and looked out the window, this time focusing. *When did it get dark?* "Don't you need your bunk?"

"Nope. When we're on the road, I'm an 'up all night, sleep all day' kind of guy. And," he lowered his voice, "snowstorms are awesome. I love being out in them."

Collier grinned and got out of his seat. "You are sort of a freak, my friend, you know that, right?"

"It's all rock and roll, brother." Jake slapped his shoulder. "Sleep well."

"Thanks." Collier climbed up the narrow ladder into Jake's upper bunk. He settled into the dark compartment and pulled the curtain, feeling very much like he was in a cocoon. There was a small fan that circulated cool, fresh air around the otherwise warm space. He turned the fan to its highest setting, giving the space a bit of a chill, just how he liked to sleep. He kicked off his shoes, and shoved them to the floor, not regretting the thump they made when they landed. He pulled the sheet and blanket over him and closed his eyes. *I'll never be able to actually sleep.*

It was his last conscious thought before he drifted into a black, dreamless sleep.

<u>MIRA</u>

"Dusty? Dusty?" Mira ran through the hospital hallway, peering into every door.

"Miranda, honestly! Must you be so loud?" Madelyn stuck her head out of a room and frowned.

"Is he in there, Madelyn?"

"Yes, but he's sleeping." Madelyn blocked the entrance to the room. "And you smell horrible."

"Of course I smell horrible. I took a bus from Nashville the minute Carson sent me a text about Dusty's accident. I've been on that bus for almost twenty hours so I could get here to be with my…with Dusty."

Madelyn's face settled into deep lines. "That's all well and good. He's had the surgery and they say he's going home today."

"What happened, Madelyn…and why did Carson have to text me? Why didn't you call me?"

"He was sledding with some friends. Silly boys, they built a ramp of snow to do jumps or some such, and his went wrong. His sled spun and he crashed into a small tree." Madelyn continued to block her way into the room. "As for why Carson contacted you, it's simple. I did not know how to reach you."

"Bullshit."

"Miranda! Language."

"Madelyn, you know my number. You understand how cell phones work. Stop trying to cover for the fact that you never thought I'd make it back in time to be here for Dusty."

Madelyn sighed as if bored. "Miranda, I was here for Dustin. I was the one who signed all the forms and made sure he has health care in the first place. And I'm the one who is going to be here when he wakes up, not you. You are his aunt. Your place is back at the house, in the guest room, where you will stay after…" she sniffed, "you've cleaned yourself. You smell like a public restroom."

Mira was about to argue further, until she looked down the hall at a handful of people approaching the room. "Madelyn…are those photographers?"

Madelyn feigned surprise. "Oh, I just can't seem to go anyplace without them following me."

"Madelyn for God's sakes…you're turning this into a photo op?"

"No," Madelyn smiled and fluffed her hair. "I'm taking this opportunity to comment on just how great Wisconsin medical care is, especially here at the UW hospital."

Mira glared at her sister. "How can you be this callous? Dusty is, as you always remind me, your son. He just had surgery. You're holding a press conference outside his hospital room? Don't you have any consideration for him?"

Madelyn turned cold, black eyes on her. "I do have quite a bit of consideration for him, Miranda. That is exactly why I'm not letting you visit him here. Seeing you here, especially looking and smelling the way you do, would confuse him."

"Confuse him how?"

"Oh, that's simple." Madelyn pushed Mira aside so that the press could see her clearly. "He might think you love him more than I do. That you would sacrifice more for him than I would. We cannot have him thinking that."

Madelyn's expression left no room for argument as the reporters and cameramen filled the area outside Dustin's room. Impotent rage pumped through Mira as she grabbed her duffle bag and stormed away from the mêlée.

COLLIER

Collier opened his eyes and realized that the bunk mattress was on top of him and he lay on top of the compartment curtains. Dan, under the curtains, was not moving. Not quite sure he was awake, not absorbing exactly what was happening, he tried to push the mattress up and off of him, to no avail.

"Col, man, hold still." Dan's voice was little more than a groan. "You're on top of my legs. It hurts like hell every time you move."

"Oh, okay. Sorry." Collier held very still. "What happened?"

"Not sure, I was asleep. I think Shara screamed, and then it was black…and now this."

"How long have we been here?" Collier found it difficult to think of a situation where Shara Brandt Jacobs would scream.

"No clue. I heard some sirens a little bit ago."

"Have you heard anyone coming to help?"

"I haven't heard much…" Dan's voice drifted.

"Dan?" Fear gripped Collier. "Dan? Stay with me, okay? We're going to get out of here."

There was no response from below him. As his eyes adjusted to the darkness, he could see a sliver of light just above him. He knew any movement on his part could cause Dan more injury. "Help!" He called. "Help!"

"Kenosha fire department! Call out!"

The male voice was unfamiliar, but comforting in its firm commanding tone.

"We're here!"

The mattress lifted aside and Collier squinted into two flashlight beams.

"Sir, can you move?"

"I can, but Dan is right below me. His legs are injured. I think he passed out."

Two hands reached for him. "Take my arms, sir. We're going to get you out."

Collier reached up and let the firemen pull him from the cramped space. They laid him on a stretcher which they slid over the seats as the bus lay on its side. Collier was unable to make sense of what he saw until the firemen removed him from the bus and carried him to a gurney. As they rolled him to a lighted tent, Collier saw Shara, flanked by the shadowy forms of Jake and Tony. "Shara?"

"Oh, good heavens! Collier!" She rushed to his side. "Are you okay?" She took his hand and held it close to her heart.

"I think so. Nothing seems to hurt."

Whether it was the look on Shara's face or a flash of conscious thought on his part, Collier wasn't sure, but he focused on the hand she held. "Shara. I don't feel any pain. I…don't feel anything!"

He blacked out to the sound of Shara calling for help.

MIRA

Feeling cleaner, but no less furious after her shower and a night's sleep, Mira stared at the plate of food in front of her. Carson was ever attendant, but there was little anyone could do to bring her out of her sour funk. She wanted, for Carson's sake, to eat the scrambled eggs and bacon, but her stomach churned at the very thought of food.

Having charged her cell fully the night before, Mira had listened to the handful of messages from Collier. Her heart hurt more to see the number of missed calls from his number that involved no message at all. Closing her eyes, she easily felt his gentle touch, heard his soft voice.

For all the good I'm doing sitting here, in Madelyn's kitchen, waiting for Dusty to get out of the hospital, I could have just stayed in Nashville and come home on the band bus. Shara would have made a stop here for me.

Once again, I did the exactly wrong thing.

She picked up the phone, and dialed Collier's number. It went right to voicemail. She ended the call without leaving a message. *What's the point? What could I possibly say to him after leaving like that…and stealing from him?*

"Aunt Mira?"

Dusty's voice shook her out of her bad mood instantly. "Dusty!" She leapt from her seat and ran to the front hall to hug him. His arm was in a bulky cast, and he had a black eye, but other than that, Dusty seemed perfectly fine. "Wow, champ, what happened to you?"

Dusty grinned. "Aw man, you should have seen the other guy!"

They laughed. Mira happily ignored Madelyn's icy glare as they returned to the kitchen. "Carson made a gigantic breakfast and I was too worried about you to eat a thing. Are you hungry?"

"He's not. I made sure he had a perfectly good breakfast already this morning."

Mira wanted to slap the arrogance out of Madelyn's mouth, but instead smiled when Dusty fell on her plate of bacon and eggs, eating with abandon.

"Hospital food is terrible, Aunt Mira. The bacon is cold and the eggs taste like rubber."

Mira stifled a victorious smile. "Eat a lot of rubber, do you, buddy?"

"Oh, yeah, all the time!" Dusty laughed, his mouth full.

"Dustin! Stop talking with your mouth full!" Madelyn tried to keep her expression imperious, but her face dropped into a scowl as she stormed out of the kitchen.

Mira and Dusty shared a conspiratorial laugh, and for a moment Mira's heart was light. She and Dusty spent a half hour eating the bacon and eggs, and talking about just how cool Dusty was now, with his arm in a sling.

For one moment she felt like someone who'd made the right decision. She felt like a mother.

COLLIER

Collier fought his return to consciousness. *Don't open your eyes. Don't open your eyes. Nothing out there is good. Stay in this black nothingness. It's less painful here.*

"Collier?"

He recognized the voice. Surprised, he opened his eyes. "Uncle Archie?"

"Yes, my boy. Let me buzz the doctor. They will want to know you're awake."

It didn't take a genius to know his uncle was very concerned. *How bad is it?*

Collier closed his eyes. *Can't I just go back to floating?*

A doctor strode in, flanked by two grim faced nurses. "Mr. James, good to see you awake. How are you feeling?"

"Like I was hit by a bus." Collier smiled weakly, but realized no one else got the humor. "What's wrong with me?"

"Let's just take a look, shall we?" The doctor pulled back the sheet, revealing Collier's feet. He ran a small wheel up and down Collier's foot. "Do you feel that?"

Collier tried to swallow back the panic that bubbled inside him. "No."

The doctor moved to a point higher up on his leg and rolled the small wheel again. "Here?"

"No."

Once more, higher up on his leg. "Here?"

"Not really. Maybe a little." Collier blinked, trying to focus on what he really felt instead of any wishful sensation his brain might concoct to keep him from panicking.

"Okay. Good." The doctor covered his feet again.

"What does this all mean?" Collier tried to sound calm, but failed.

"I'm encouraged, Mr. James. I think you may have some swelling in the lower part of your spinal cord. This isn't uncommon for the type of accident you were in. There is some paralysis, but you do seem to have feeling in parts of your legs, and you have full function in your arms, all of which is good."

Collier shot a look at his uncle, who still looked less than relieved. "Okay, and what does that mean? Should I start thinking about a wheelchair?"

"Oh, no, I wouldn't go there just yet. I'd like to start on a course of steroids to see if we can get the swelling down. Mr. James," the doctor put his hand on Collier's shoulder, "injuries like this are not necessarily permanent. You got the very best care at the accident site, which is always vital. We are going to do our very best to get you up and walking sooner rather than later." The doctor murmured instructions to the nurses. Without another word to Collier, the doctor left the room.

Once the medical professionals left, Collier reached a hand to his uncle. "I can't believe you're here."

"When Miss Shara called and told me you'd been airlifted to Froedert Medical I couldn't very well stay at home sipping tea, could I?"

"Froedert...so we're in Milwaukee?"

"Yes. The accident was just north of Kenosha."

"What happened?" Collier blinked. "I was sleeping in one of the bunks and then I woke up and we'd been in an accident."

"Well, from what I gather, it was snowing quite hard there at the Wisconsin/Illinois border. Visibility was very bad, as you can imagine, and there was a car, a small car, that sort of lost control and slid across the lane in front of your bus. Your driver managed to avoid crushing the car, thank heavens, but he couldn't keep the bus on the road. You slid off the road and the bus fell on its side."

174

Collier closed his eyes. "I was in one of the sleeping compartments...and then I was...Dan!" He gripped his uncle's hand tightly. "Dan!"

"Sh, sh." Archibald patted his hand. "Dan was airlifted with you. He's in surgery right now. That's where Shara and the others are."

"So he...he's okay?"

"Well, his legs were a mangled mess, they tell me. Very serious breaks, both legs. But, yes, he's quite alive."

"And the others?"

"Tony's got a broken arm. I believe Jake had to get stitches in his head. The driver will be here a while with a skull fracture." He paused again, and brightened, "Miss Shara, miraculously, escaped without even a little scratch."

"How did she manage that?"

Archibald shrugged and smiled. "She's one who's already suffered a lifetime of injuries. Perhaps she's not meant to have more."

"Hey Mr. James…is he awake?" Bryan stuck his head into the room. "Oh, you are! Collier, awesome to see you back in the land of the living!" He came in, followed by Jake, who sported a neat row of stitches across his forehead and down his left cheek.

"Bryan, you got down here fast." Collier shook hands with Bryan and nodded at Jake, who slumped into a nearby chair. "What's the news on Dan?"

"Still in surgery. Shara's sitting with Tony to wait for news, so we thought we'd come up and see how you're doing." Bryan stood on one side of the bed and glanced at Jake, who remained silent.

"Uncle Archie just gave me the rundown on everyone."

Bryan nodded. "Yeah, you guys are really fortunate. I mean, look at Jake. He's going to look like Frankenstein for a while. But what is it you always say, Jake?"

"Chicks dig scars." Jake spoke with no inflection, his face still and ashen.

"Right, chicks dig scars!"

Collier couldn't ignore Jake's morbid stillness, or Bryan's unusual chattiness. Bryan's whole demeanor was far too giddy. "What is up with you two?"

Archibald's cell buzzed. He answered it, muttered a few words, and ended the call. "It seems they need a bit more information about the…band's insurance." He spoke softly, giving Bryan a meaningful look Collier also couldn't ignore. "Collier, I'll be back shortly."

"Okay, Uncle Archie. See you in a bit." Collier stared at the door as it slid closed behind his uncle. "Okay, you two. What aren't you telling me? What's going on?"

"What do you mean?" Bryan seemed very interested in the buttons on the hospital bed's remote control.

"I mean, Jake looks like he's never going to voluntarily speak again and you…why aren't you glued to Shara? You're here chatting with me and apparently committing that remote to memory. What's going on?"

175

"Jake's just trying to think of ways he's going to turn those stitches into time spent with the ladies. Right, Jake?" Bryan's voice was overly cheerful.

"We had no business touring." Jake mumbled. "We overstepped."

Both Collier and Bryan stared at him. "Okay, Bryan, tell me something's not up. Go ahead. Is it Dan?"

Bryan's sunny demeanor faded and his eyes clouded. He shook his head. "No, no, they say Dan should be okay."

"Well, then what? You guys are here…you're not worried about me, are you?" Collier smiled. "The doctor says the paralysis is probably temporary."

"Oh, geez, that's awesome!" Tears welled in Bryan's eyes. Collier glanced at Jake who looked slightly less morose.

"And Shara didn't have a scratch?"

"She's got a special kind of guardian angel." Bryan nodded.

There was still something they weren't telling him. Collier studied Bryan, then looked again at Jake, who had turned a deeper shade of pale. "Hey, where's Kelly? Is he with Shara?"

Bryan's jaw tightened, but it was Jake who lowered his head and sobbed. Collier's stomach churned. "Bryan, where is Kelly?"

Bryan sighed. He put a strong hand on Collier's shoulder. "He didn't make it."

Bile bubbled in Collier's throat. "What?" He didn't recognize the choked sound that was his voice.

"The paramedics said he must've exited the bus right after the crash."

"He was sitting up front with me. We were arguing about an arrangement." Jake's voice was a low groan.

"They think he got out, and was maybe trying to flag down help." Bryan's tone was low, strained. "They found his body fifty feet away from the bus, on the other side of the interstate. They think maybe a big vehicle, a truck or something, just hit him and kept going, like they never saw him."

"The last thing I told him was that he didn't know anything about music. I told him he was an idiot." Jake wiped his sleeve across his ashen face.

Collier looked at Jake. "Is he gonna be okay?"

"He's blaming himself for most of this." Bryan lowered his voice. "I don't know what's worse…the injuries you and Dan have, or what's going on in Jake's head."

"Jake, come here." As if in a fog, Jake obeyed Collier's calm command. "Come and sit on the other side here." Collier looked at both his friends, men he hadn't known four months earlier, but men he knew were linked to him now beyond simple friendship. "Okay, listen, Jake. Kelly was a good guy, the best. You guys called each other idiots fifty times a week. He knew you didn't mean it."

"I pushed him every time to go on tour. He didn't want to, you know? He wanted to play music in Rock Harbor and be the town cop. He wanted to marry some small town girl and have kids. I'm the one who pushed him, the band, to be big time. I was greedy. This was karma."

"No, Jake, this was an accident. It was terrible weather. It was an accident. Dan is going to be okay. I am going to be okay. We are all going to get through this. You got that?"

Jake calmed and nodded.

Bryan's cell buzzed. "It's Shara. She says Dan is out of surgery." He stood and patted Collier on the shoulder. "You got this?" He nodded at Jake.

"I got this." A wordless look flashed between him and Bryan. Collier pushed aside his own concerns, and ignored the possibility of his own paralysis. He needed to be a leader for the younger guys. He needed to take charge and take care of them all, especially Jake.

It was not a position he was used to being in.

MIRA

Mira closed Dusty's bedroom door and sighed. It had been a long day of quiet activities. She told him about her travels and her performance at Chance's and the Silver Screen cinnamon rolls. She left out the night in the hospital and most of her two weeks with Collier.

They played a lot of video games. *The little snot beat me with one hand tied behind his back…literally.*

When it got late, Dusty let her read a story to him, something she'd done when he was little. Mira couldn't help remembering her short days in college when she'd thought she might want to teach kids to read. Now, staring blankly at the flames in the sitting room fireplace, she wondered if it was too late to go back and try becoming a teacher.

That would certainly make me more respectable in Madelyn's eyes. Maybe she'd stop threatening to take Dusty away from me completely.

She picked up a book and flipped through the pages, absently trying to picture herself enrolled in school and attending classes. *This time I would actually go to classes.*

"Miranda." Madelyn entered the room and sat on the sofa next to her. Mira was slightly uncomfortable with the closeness, but decided, in the interest of the newfound peace in the house, she wouldn't say anything. "I see Dustin is in bed."

"Yes."

"Good. What do you have there?"

Mira looked at the book. "I don't even know. It's something that was sitting here. You know, Madelyn, I was thinking…I might go back to school."

Madelyn's firmly powdered face cracked into a half smile. "Really?"

"Yeah. I mean, I'm good with Dusty. I like kids. I might make a good teacher, you know?"

"Well, I suppose that would be a far better career choice than where you've been lately. Do you think you'd go to the UW here in Madison, and live with us?"

Probably not a good idea.

Besides, no way am I even living in the same house as The Senator.

"No, no I couldn't put you and The Senator out like that. I thought I'd see what the UW in Green Bay has to offer. Bryan Jacobs finished his masters there a few years ago."

Madelyn thought this over. "That might not be the worst idea. You could certainly benefit from the knowledge your friends there have. Molly Hunter could be a big help."

"She could. Maybe she could get me a job at Rock Harbor Community School as an aid or something, so I could support myself."

"You'd stay at the house? Alone?"

She's worried about Otis. "Madelyn, I can honestly promise you, anything you're thinking about, it's all over."

The expression on Madelyn's face was a shadow of approval, "I must say, this trip to Nashville must not have been the magic carpet ride you thought it would be. I'm glad to see you finally understand that you need to grow up."

Mira shook her head, trying to clear the memories of her triumph at Second Chances, and the feel of Collier's kisses. *I have to focus on Dusty. He's what matters now, and if I close out everything else I will still have Dusty.*

Collier…that can never happen again. I love him, but I can't live in that world anymore. For Dusty's sake.

And I can't take Collier's dream from him.

"I learned a lot on that trip, Madelyn, no doubt. And I'm ready to…be more respectable."

"Well that's wonderful. First, I think you need to change your cell number. Perhaps get a whole new phone."

"Why?"

Madelyn rose from the couch and started walking away before looking over her shoulder. "Someone named 'Col' sent you several texts of a very…personal nature."

Mira ached to slap Madelyn for reading her texts. *My own fault for using our house number in Rock Harbor as my password.*

But she's probably not wrong. Besides, Collier was a hit in Nashville. No reason for him to come back other than to clean out the loft and then go be a star.

I'll probably never see him again. What's the point in even reading those messages?

"You're right, Madelyn. I'll work on that in the morning."

COLLIER

Collier woke the next morning to a flurry of activity, most of which involved him lying completely still.

Between an MRI and several other tests, by lunch Collier felt like a lab rat. He was glad for the diversion when Shara and Bryan paid him a visit.

"So Dan came through surgery okay, I hear."

"He did. They say he'll be in a wheelchair for a while, but after a few more surgeries, he should be fine." Shara and Bryan sat next to each other. Collier noticed Bryan never let go of Shara's hand. "Dan told me this morning that they say he won't run any marathons, but that he will walk on his own. It'll just take some time."

Collier smiled, picturing Dan's cheerfully round physique. "I don't imagine he had an issue with that, right?"

"Not at all." Shara joined Collier's laughter. "You guys have to excuse me. I told Mr. James I'd meet him in the cafeteria...band business, that sort of thing."

Bryan and Collier watched her leave before looking at each other.

"How about you? How are the legs?"

"Well, Bryan, they are pretty sure once the swelling goes down on my spinal cord, I'll be just fine and dandy. They're giving me steroids, so I guess my days as a pro athlete are over."

"Very funny."

Collier let his cheerful façade fall away. He didn't have to be the strong one around Bryan. "It might be awhile, though. They're waiting on the results of the tests they did today."

"Well, whatever you need, you know you can count on Shara and me." Bryan spoke slowly, thoughtfully. "You know, I had to do some work, as part of my masters' program, with special needs kids. I actually trained Pepper to be a therapy horse. You know, for Downs' Syndrome kids or..."

"Kids in wheelchairs?"

"Yeah. So..."

"So I've got that going for me." Collier couldn't keep a trace of bitterness from leaking into his voice. He'd managed to stay away from bitterness all day. Being strong and upbeat for the

180

rest of group proved exhausting. He was grateful Tony had taken Jake to the cafeteria for some lunch.

"It's proven treatment. But hey, you may not need it." Bryan checked his watch. "I should give the school a call. I wasn't sure if I'd be here all day, and it looks like Shara isn't going to go anyplace until she's got stuff sorted out with your uncle."

"Okay, no problem. One thing?"

"Yeah?"

Collier pointed to his cell, which was plugged in on the counter across the room. "I need to contact a couple people."

"Oh, yeah. Here." Bryan handed him the phone. "Have you heard from Mira?"

Collier checked his missed calls and texts. *Nothing.* "I have no idea where she is."

Bryan shook his head. "That girl was always a question mark, but she's resourceful. I wouldn't worry."

"Yeah. Thanks." Collier waited until Bryan was out of the room before sending another text to Mira's number. This time, he got a message back. "What does that mean, 'this number isn't a valid cell number.' Of course it's her number." This time he dialed her number, and placed a call. The only response he got was the screech of a disconnection warning, and the automated voice telling him the number he'd dialed was disconnected.

What the hell, Mira? You leave and you disconnect your number?

Collier toyed with the idea of calling Cat for some hometown comfort, but she'd been pretty frantic after he called her the first time and told her about the accident. He sent a simple text to her:

"Tests went well. I'm going to be fine. No word from Mira. Love you guys."

He then shut off his phone and turned on the television, hoping daytime TV would numb his senses for a while.

MIRA

Mira returned from the electronics store with a shiny new phone to go with her shiny new phone number, compliments of Madelyn. Mira didn't like taking things from Madelyn, but it seemed to please her older sister, and Mira was now in the game of keeping her older sister happy.

She set her purse on the kitchen counter. "Hey, Carson. What's on the news?"

Carson looked up from the lunch he was preparing for Madelyn and Dusty. "I haven't had a chance to look, Mira, but the *State Journal* is on the table."

"I wasn't really all that interested."

"There are also some fresh croissants and jam."

"Now you're talking my language!" She laughed and sat at the table. Reaching for a croissant, she picked up the newspaper. The headline caught her eye.

Members of popular local band injured in bus accident. One dead. "Weather a factor" says state patrol.

"What the…" Mira scanned the article for a moment, before dropping the croissant and covering her mouth to stifle a scream. "Carson! Did you read this?"

"No, I'm sorry." Carson looked over her shoulder. "Friends of yours?"

"Yes. I mean…" She wiped tears from her eyes. "Geez, Kelly is dead?" She took a deep breath. Kelly had always been her cheerleader, even when the others wanted to give up on her. She knew the history of Teachers' Pets. Friends since their days at Rock Harbor Community School, Jake, Kelly, Tony and Dan started playing weddings as a cover band in high school. They were about to break up when Kelly met Shara. It was Shara who convinced Dirty Dog Dave to let Teachers' Pets play at the bar, and it was Shara who convinced Jake to let the band play some of the original music Kelly had written.

And it was Kelly's songs that made Teachers' Pets the top indie band they were. Kelly and Jake shared time as lead singers, but it was Kelly who kept the band focused and moving forward.

'Teachers' Pets' didn't just lose a singer. They lost their heart.

Mira blinked and kept reading. "It says…they say two of the band members might not walk again." Sorrow welled. She stood quickly, knocking her chair over. Running to her room, she passed Madelyn in the hall, and ignored her.

Once in her room, Mira slammed the door, the newspaper a crumpled ball in her hands. Smoothing the front page she reread, with growing horror, the detailed story. *Detailed except for one thing: Was Collier on the bus? Was he hurt?*

Other than Kelly's name, no other band members were named in the article.

Blindly, Mira reached for her phone and dialed Collier's number from memory. It went instantly to voicemail. "Col…" she stopped and ended the call.

What could I possibly say?

He shouldn't have been on the bus. He was going to stay in Nashville for a while. He wanted to drive his car back to Rock Harbor later. He wasn't on the bus.

"Miranda?" Madelyn knocked on her door. "Miranda, it's time to pick Dustin up from school, and you promised you would do that."

I might have been on that bus. I could have been injured. But I'm not.

I'm supposed to be here.

She wiped tears out of her eyes.

Is this how I know I'm making the right decision between Collier or Dusty?

Madelyn knocked on the door again.

It's Dusty. It's always been about Dusty. That hasn't changed.

"I'm coming Madelyn. I'll be ready to go in a minute." She balled up the newspaper and threw it in her trashcan. Her heart was broken, but the choice was clear to her.

She wiped her face dry, squared her shoulders, and opened the door.

183

COLLIER

Christmas is not supposed to be spent in a hospital.

Collier watched snow fall outside his hospital room window. Dan came though surgery just fine. He and Collier now shared a room. Both were slated to leave the hospital before New Year's, but for now, on Christmas Eve, Dan snored lightly in the bed on the other side of the room while Collier tried to forget the one word phone message he'd gotten from an unknown number.

It had to be Mira. *But it makes no sense. Why would she change her number... and then call me?*

He wanted to dial the number. He had, almost, a couple times, only to stop after punching nine of the ten digits. He listened to the one word message time after time, unable to positively identify the voice as Mira's.

But, in his heart, he knew it was her.

Jake and Tony had been released days earlier, but neither wanted to leave Milwaukee without Dan and Collier, so Archibald housed the two. Shara and Bryan had to return to Rock Harbor, but promised to come down for a Christmas Day celebration.

184

Kelly's funeral and burial was slated for the 28th, once everyone was in Rock Harbor. Kelly would be buried under the massive oak trees surrounding Rock Harbor Community Church, saluted by the police department he loved and the town that loved him back.

Trying to focus on more cheerful things, Collier had called Nashville and talked to Cat and Benny. No one else had arrived at the coffee shop yet, so Collier exchanged a few bawdy jokes with Benny and hung up.

Collier ached from loneliness. He missed the warmth of the coffee shop, and the glorious bakery smells floating like a sugary cloud. He missed sitting around the big table, talking, laughing, playing a board game. They were his family.

He looked at the other bed, at Dan, with his legs in huge, impossible casts. Collier realized this was also his family. The guys in the band, Shara, Bryan, they were all family. Broken, battered, and heartsick with the loss of Kelly, but still, this was family as well.

He realized the feeling that the family was incomplete had less to do with Kelly, whom he mourned, and more to do with Mira, whom he missed.

Whom he loved.

I finally realize I'm in love with her, and I don't know where she is, or how to reach her.

Or why she left.

She could have told me anything, asked me for anything. I would have done whatever she needed.

Collier reached up and pulled the light cord over his head. *Way to be her hero, man. Awesome job.*

In the dark, Collier let tears spill down his face.

MIRA

"Merry Christmas, Aunt Mira!" Dusty pounded on her door, waking Mira from a restless sleep. She opened her eyes, her head foggy, as if she'd been drinking. *If only.*

Mira dressed quickly. She and Madelyn spent countless hours in the past days shopping for clothes that Madelyn deemed appropriate for her new life. Having accepted her new role, Mira didn't question the conservative, wildly uncomfortable clothing Madelyn purchased for her.

The last few days had been filled with far more than just shopping. Madelyn made sure Mira made good on her promise to enroll at the University of Wisconsin in Green Bay. Mira was scheduled to start classes in mid-January, when the winter semester began. Her few credits from her failed attempt at college transferred, and the plan was that she would graduate with a teaching degree in three years.

Madelyn decided dormitory life was not the healthiest option for Mira, so she was allowed to remain at the house in Rock Harbor. The long drive back and forth, Madelyn reasoned, would take up time when Mira might otherwise be tempted to get into trouble.

186

A month earlier, Mira would have chafed and rebelled against Madelyn's tight fisted control. But now, determined to one day tell Dusty of his true parentage, Mira wanted to be worthy of the announcement. She pushed out thoughts of Collier as best she could and replaced them with her secret dream of one day being a real mother to Dusty.

"Auntie Mira! Come on!"

Mira ran a hasty brush through her hair, which was now a very mild shade of brown thanks to Madelyn's hairdresser. She stared at herself, not recognizing the stranger who looked back. "Doesn't matter," she said resolutely to her reflection. "Dusty is all that matters." She shook her head, but her hair still fell into the perfectly manicured layers, smooth, sleek, tidy. She sighed, and walked away from the mirror.

COLLIER

"Wake up, Col!"

Collier fought to stay asleep where he could dream of a happily ever after with Mira. Dan shook his shoulder. Collier opened one eye. "Geez, what are you, seven?"

"No, but it's Christmas! My parents are coming. My girl is coming. Half of Rock Harbor is coming here to celebrate with us!" Dan grinned. "And look, I've got wheels!"

Collier grinned, unable to fight off Dan's enthusiasm for his new mobility. "Can you keep it down for five minutes? I'm calling Nashville."

He dialed Izzy's number, surprised to get voicemail. "Hey guys, just wanted to let you know I'm definitely getting out of the hospital in a couple days, so all is well. Merry Christmas! Kisses to C.C."

His other phone call was to Cat's cell. Cat, he was certain would be handing coffee and cinnamon rolls out to homeless guys. It was long her tradition on Christmas morning, to be open for Nashville's street people. Collier was surprised to hear Benny's voice on the other end of the line. "Benny, hey…did I dial the wrong number?"

"No." There was an unusual note of fear in Benny's voice. Collier instantly went on high alert.

"Benny, what is it? Is it Cat?"

"Yeah, Col, it is. She went into labor last night."

"Last night? She's not due for another month."

Benny was silent for a minute. "Yeah."

"Is she okay?"

"They say so. It was…something, Col. It was a mess."

Collier exhaled slowly, trying to ease his racing heartbeat. "Okay, tell me what happened."

"There were all kinds of complications, I don't even know what. And there was so much blood when it was all over. And the baby was blue when he came out. Blue."

"But is the baby okay?"

"They've got him in NICU. We can't see him yet. Cat's getting cleaned up. There was so much blood…"

Collier sensed Benny was losing what little control he had. "Benny, who's there with you?"

"Quinn, Izzy and Jenna. Mikayla stayed at Izzy's to take care of C.C."

"Put Izzy on."

A moment passed. "Col?"

"Tell me the truth. Is Cat going to be okay?"

There was a hint of a smile in Izzy's voice. "Cat is going to be just fine. And Thor will be fine as well. Benny's the one you need to worry about. That man has lost his mind."

"I'm sorry, did you say Thor?"

"I did. It seems calling the baby Troll-Baby irritated Cat. So, in the middle of the labor, when Benny was losing it and Cat was working pretty hard, she turned to him and said, 'If this child of yours doesn't kill me, I get to name it.' She named him Thor, because that would be the exact opposite of a troll, I guess."

"Thor Jensen. Well, I doubt anyone's going to beat him up on the playground."

"How are you doing?"

"I'm going to be fine. The swelling is going down. I've got more feeling in my legs. I'll get out of here in two days and I've already got therapy lined up, and everything's set up for me until I can walk on my own again."

188

"I wish you'd come home. We would take care of you."

Collier glanced at Dan, who showed off his wheelchair skills to Tony. "I'll be okay, I promise," he said absently.

Izzy lowered her voice. "Col, I know you're worried about her."

"Mira?" Collier tensed. "What do you know about Mira?"

"Nothing. Not really."

He knew Izzy too well. She was covering something. "Iz, please. What is it?"

"Okay, let me say this: She cares for you. But there's something she has to deal with first."

Collier closed his eyes and tried to absorb what she told him. "What do you mean?"

"How is it you write such romantic songs yet you're so clueless about women? I think Mira is in love with you."

For a moment his heart soared. Then Izzy's other comment replayed itself. "Wait, this thing she has to deal with …does it have to do with the kid, Dusty?"

There was a long pause.

"Izzy, please, tell me what you know."

Izzy sighed. "Yes, it is about Dusty."

Collier's heart beat more quickly as he thought about his conversation with Cat and Benny. "Is she Dusty's mother?"

"Col, I promised her…"

"Izzy, I don't know where she is and I have no way to reach her. I would at least like to know why she left me, especially after…" To say the words out loud would make it less real, and Collier didn't want to shatter the delicate memory of Mira's face beneath him in the moonlight. "Please, Izzy?"

"Okay. Okay fine. Yes. She is Dusty's mother. She let it slip the other day. I swore I wouldn't tell you."

"Think of it as a Christmas present to me. Now, go take care of Benny. Merry Christmas, Iz. And thank you."

"Merry Christmas, Col. Keep us posted."

He ended the call. In the midst of all this tragedy, there one was thin ray of hope. *Mira didn't just leave me for no reason, she's protecting her son from…something. And she might love me.*

Knowing this didn't put him any closer to her, but somehow it gave him something to cling to.

*

They buried Kelly three days later. Dan and Collier were both there, both in wheelchairs. Molly Hunter appointed herself Collier's caretaker, a job she did well. She insisted he stay at her house until he was able to climb the stairs in the loft. Collier, though he was eager to resume a normal life, realized healing would require time and therapy. Surrounded by his new family, he was willing to do whatever it took to get better.

The funeral service was held, of course, at Rock Harbor Community Church. Pastor King presided, with his domineering wife playing hymns few felt spirited enough to sing. Shara spoke a fine eulogy, but Jake remained stony faced next to his parents. Shara and Collier, in spite of Mrs. King's protests about proper behavior at a funeral, played Kelly's favorite song, Barry Manilow's "I am Your Child." Collier, caught up in Shara's simple, clean voice, did his best not to overwhelm her with his piano accompaniment. At the end of the song, there wasn't a person without tears.

Kelly had no family at the funeral. He was an only child and his parents were buried next to the space that would soon hold him. 'Teachers' Pets' filled the front row of the church and later, were closest to the grave as they lowered the casket. The Rock Harbor police department was there in full force. Three stoic-faced officers who served with Kelly fired a twenty-one gun salute with stoic faces.

There were murmurs of sympathy and pats on the shoulder as people passed the little group. Collier couldn't help but sense the grim aura everyone seemed to wear.

"It's like this when a young person dies," Molly whispered from behind him. "No one wants to think about 'what might have been.' When you live in a town this small, losing a young person puts a big hole in the community. Especially Kelly Fuller. He wasn't just the heart of your band. He was a big part of Rock Harbor."

"I know." In the days he shared a hospital room with Dan, Collier listened to Dan and Tony's stories about Kelly. Dan and Tony's jovial personalities never wavered, but Collier saw the tears in their eyes and knew they mourned their friend just as deeply as Jake, who seemed to move around as if unconscious.

190

Pastor King did a scripture reading graveside, and said a few more words. Shara, Jake, Tony and Dan tossed white roses onto the casket as it was lowered into the half frozen ground. Then it was over. Just like that, the assembled people walked back toward the church where a lunch waited.

Molly turned Collier's chair around to follow, but Collier noticed that the others hadn't moved. "Molly, I'd like a minute with the guys, if that's okay."

Molly nodded. "Just don't stay out here too long. This damp cold isn't good for anyone."

"Thanks, Molly."

She turned him around and he rolled a few inches to be closer to his friends. No one said anything for several long moments.

"Here's to Kelly." Tony pulled a flask from his suit coat, unscrewed the top, and took a drink. He handed the flask to Dan, who took a drink, and passed to it Collier. Collier took a drink, then handed it to Jake, who paused before drinking.

Collier wasn't sure if the shadow of anger he saw pass over Jake's face was due to his demeanor or his stitches, which were still raw and angry looking. Jake took a drink and poured the remaining contents onto the casket below them. Collier didn't need to see anyone's face to know the sorrow they felt. He felt it, too. *I haven't felt this kind of loss since Pop died.*

"Hey Col?"

Collier looked up from his reverie and realized all three men were staring at him. "Yeah?"

Tony knelt to be eye to eye with him. "Col, we've been talking it over, Jake and Dan and I. We'd like you to be in the band, full time."

Surprised, Collier looked from face to face, then returned his attention to Tony, who seemed to be the spokesman. "Are you serious? I mean, you all agree?" *I doubt Jake added much to the conversation.*

"Yeah. We…Kelly thought we should talk about it after the tour. But now, with Kelly…" Tony swallowed back emotion. "With Kelly gone, we had to decide, you know, if we were going to continue. We want to, but we need another singer. I mean, Kelly's songs are such a big part of what we do, and most of them…Jake's voice wouldn't work."

Collier nodded. "Guys, I don't know what to say."

"Man, you are our brother just as much as he was."

Everyone stared at Jake, who hadn't uttered more than a handful of words since the accident. Knowing Jake agreed to the arrangement made Collier's decision for him. He put his hand on Jake's shoulder. "I would be honored." It was the only thing he could say.

Jake said nothing. He threw his arms around Collier, surprising everyone. Collier returned Jake's embrace and looked at Dan and Tony over Jake's shoulder. Any doubts he had about whether he belonged in Rock Harbor vanished.

MIRA

"Why can't I go with you, Aunt Mira?"

Mira stared at Dusty. He was whining, a trait she found unpleasant, especially coming from him. As he got older, Mira realized that the little things she found cute in a toddler were not cute in a boy approaching his teens. Whining was at the top of the list. And living with Madelyn for almost a month, Mira realized that Dusty whined…a lot. It was his way of getting things from Madelyn, his way of being heard, since Madelyn didn't seem to listen to him unless he whined, yelled or was generally unpleasant.

It's the only way he's heard around here. It gave Mira all the more reason to be successful in her new approach to life. The sooner she got Dusty out of Madelyn's house, the better adjusted he would probably be.

Or maybe he'll just be less annoying.

She quieted her traitorous thoughts. "Dusty, sweetheart, I told you. I'm going back to school."

"So go to school here. Or I could go to school in Rock Harbor."

"No sweetie, that's not how it works. I live in Rock Harbor, you live here with your…parents. But you can come and visit me any time you want." She didn't miss Madelyn's cold look of disapproval. "Not right away, though. I'm going to be super busy for a while."

"Are you studying to be a more awesome singer?"

"No." She bit her lip. Dusty loved her rock and roll image. She realized, watching him every day, he emulated her.

"Guitar lessons? Because you already know how to be awesome on the guitar."

"No, Dusty, you remember? I'm going to school to be a teacher."

"Not a teacher!" he shouted. "I hate teachers!"

Mira squared her shoulders and glanced at Madelyn, who wore a mask of triumph. *It's up to me to break this boy's heart. I won't be his cool rock and roll aunt anymore.*

But it puts me closer to being his mother.

"Dusty, I'm going to be a teacher. It's time for me to…be something…grown up."

"Why?"

"Because it is." She hated how weak she felt. The adoration in his eyes faded and vanished.

"Whatever, then. Go be a teacher. Be a boring, stupid teacher." He left the room.

"It's not going to be easy, is it?" Mira toyed with her suitcase tag.

"No. It is not. Being a grown up never is." Madelyn sniffed. "You could make it easier for him, you know."

"How?"

"You could still live here. Attend the UW."

Oh hell no!

There was no earthly way Mira was living one more minute in The Senator's house. She'd managed to avoid him for the month. He hadn't been around for Christmas thanks to a tour of the UW campuses he needed to take, Madelyn said, to 'check out the temperature of the youth vote.' Mira had her own thoughts on what and whom, exactly, he was checking out.

Her luck was about to run out. The Senator was scheduled to return in a few hours. It was time to go. Mira glanced around the room. "I have a bus to catch. Carson said he'd drive me to the depot."

"And so he will." Madelyn moved out of the doorway, allowing Mira to walk into the hall. She made her way down the staircase to the door. She reached for the knob, but the door opened.

There was The Senator.

Face to face with him for the first time in a very long time, Mira froze. She shivered. *I once I thought I loved...that.*

"Miranda. Leaving so soon?"

She tipped her chin defiantly. "I've been here almost a month."

A shadow crossed his face. "I see. And you're returning to Rock Harbor?"

"I've enrolled at the UW in Green Bay for the winter semester."

"Yes, yes. Madelyn keeps me up to date on your progress."

"Yeah, well, I have to get going." She brushed past him.

"Well, it was...very good...seeing you again, Miranda."

Mira let the door close behind her without a word. His oily voice made her skin crawl. She got into the car and didn't say a word to Carson on the way to the bus depot.

Once I get to Rock Harbor, I'll feel more like myself. Things will be normal. I'll be good.

I'll be good enough to get Dusty back and get him away from Madelyn. And away from the The Senator, and everything that man will undoubtedly teach Dusty.

She shuddered again. Carson turned up the heat.

COLLIER

Bryan stayed true to his word. Between the therapy schedule Molly controlled, and his frequent work with Bryan and Pepper, Collier's recovery progressed well. He still experienced weakness in his legs, but all his doctors were encouraged with his progress.

By the end of January Collier felt strong enough to drive so Archibald had Collier's car delivered from Nashville. Somehow, having his own vehicle in Rock Harbor made the transition from Nashville complete. While he wasn't yet ready for long road trips, his doctors were confident that in time, with continued therapy, any lingering weakness would fade

The one thing that didn't fade was his ache for Mira. He kept the mysterious one word phone message and listened to it frequently. He fought the urge to dial the number, fearing it wasn't hers, or worse, that it was but that she truly didn't want to talk to him. That, he knew, would crush him. He wasn't quite ready for that.

The rumor at Dave's was that she was back and living at the old house. But it had to be just a rumor because the few times Collier drove by the place, it was dark and lifeless. Besides, the first place Mira would have visited would be Dave's. Collier spent enough hours at the place to know she hadn't been there.

It was as if she never existed. Except, late at night, when Collier woke and moonlight poured over his bed, he knew all too well that she had. She existed, and he loved her.

The rest of his life fell into a fairly strict routine. Between therapy sessions he spent time familiarizing himself with 'Teachers' Pets'' songs, and the parts that Kelly sang. He was eager to get back into the studio and take a stab at them.

On the way home from therapy one afternoon, Collier and Shara fell into a companionable silence. Watching the gray horizon meet the gray farmland, Collier marveled at how many shades there were to gray and how a color he'd always thought of as drab seemed, in this setting, to be as vibrant and dynamic as the red and yellow neon in Nashville.

"You are deep in thought."

He turned his head from the window and smiled at Shara. "I guess."

195

"Anything in particular?"

"Just sort of comparing this place to Nashville."

"It doesn't stack up, does it?"

"Oh, no, nothing like that. I love it here. It's…home." He shook his head. "I don't think I've said that out loud before."

"Well, I'm glad to hear it. And I know how you feel. I…well, I guess I can't say I moved up here, but I wound up here. Going back was never an option because this was home."

Collier rolled this around in his mind, and was therefore unprepared for Shara's next question.

"Have you heard from Mira?"

"I…haven't."

Shara shook her head. "She never told you where she was going?"

"No." Collier tried, unsuccessfully, to push out the image of Mira as he saw her last: her skin and hair gleaming blue-black in the moonlight.

"I've heard she's back in town."

"I've gone past the house a few times. If she's there, she's not using any lights or heat because there isn't a sign of life in the place. Plus, I haven't seen much in the way of tracks in the snow."

"You've studied the place a bit, haven't you?"

Collier blushed. "Yes, ma'am, I guess I have."

"I always thought there was something between you two." Shara's words were light, vague, as if just random thoughts.

"I did, too. But, I guess, maybe not."

"Don't be too sure."

"I think just up and leaving, changing her phone number, not sending a word to anyone for months, that's pretty much a sign that there is nothing between us. And maybe," he paused, unwilling to admit to his one fear.

"Maybe what?"

"Maybe it's for the best. I mean, I am what, ten, twelve years older than she is? She's young…"

"Oh, yes." Shara's voice held more than a little humor. "And you're so ancient. Collier, you're not even forty! Do you know the age difference between Bryan and me? It's nearly twelve years. I was barely twenty-two when we met."

"Yeah, but you guys are…"

"We guys are what, Collier? And I swear if you say 'a love story for the ages' I'm going to stop this car and make you walk all the way home."

"My physical therapist might not like that."

"Your physical therapist lives in fear of Molly Hunter, and if I tell Molly why I left you on the road, your physical therapist would find this approach very appropriate."

"Okay, fine. But, come on, you and Bryan were clearly meant to be together."

"What makes you think you and Mira aren't?"

"We can start with her vanishing into thin air. Sort of hard to conduct a proper romance when half the couple is nowhere to be found."

"How's the writing coming along?"

Collier stared at Shara. "Do you understand how conversations work? Have you ever made a smooth segue while speaking?"

"It's a perfectly logical segue. You have been through a lot of stuff recently. As your employer and a member of the band, I have to know, are you putting any of this to music?"

"How many hit singles do you know about physical therapy?"

Shara punched his shoulder. "Very funny. You can walk now, right? Climbing stairs?"

Collier nodded. "Still some weakness, but yeah, I'm definitely almost there."

"Good. Tomorrow you move back into the loft."

Collier knew she was right. It was time for him focus on work.

It was time to put his thoughts to paper. Only then would he be able to completely recover.

MIRA

She unlocked the back door and shivered. It was late, and all Mira wanted to do was crawl in bed and sleep for the next four days. Six weeks into the semester and she was exhausted. Madelyn had been right about the drive back and forth. Mira had little time and even less energy to think of anything other than school and sleep.

She drove the wild, unused roads to the back entrance of her property and used the back door so the front of the house looked abandoned. She drove her new pick up, a gift from Madelyn, carefully along the little-used roads and locked it in the shed behind the house instead of the garage, where tire tracks might announce her presence As remote as the Pierce place was, Mira didn't care to be the subject of prying eyes, or well-meaning neighbors. She especially didn't care to have Shara or anyone from 'Teacher's Pets' show up on her doorstep.

Better to just let them all think I vanished into thin air. Especially Collier.

Still convinced that Collier had stayed in Nashville, Mira knew if he thought she was in Rock Harbor, he'd come back. As it was, she liked to picture him, when she allowed herself to think about him, playing the piano at Second Chances, thousands of adoring fans screaming his name. *That's how it's supposed to be for him.*

Mira told herself they were living the lives they were supposed to. She was buried in classes and he was buried in women.

She also told herself she was happy.

She rounded the corner from the shed to the house. Otis sat on the back porch. She froze. Otis represented everything she needed to avoid for herself and for Dusty. "Otis. What the hell are you doing here?"

"I heard a rumor that you were back in town." Otis chuckled. "I was starting to wonder why you were too busy for me."

She brushed past him to unlock the door. "I've been busy with school."

"School?"

"Yes. I went back to college."

"So that music thing didn't pan out, hey?" Uninvited, he followed her into the kitchen.

Mira wanted to scream. The urge to kick him out was strong, but not as strong as her sense of isolation. She was painfully lonely. "No. It didn't."

"Bummer. Anyway, I thought I'd come out here and see if the rumors were true. So, hey, as long as I'm here, ya wanna smoke or something?"

"No, Otis, I don't. I never want to smoke, and you know it!" she shouted at him.

She thought about her chemistry test, the one she had no time or energy to prepare for. Mira closed her eyes, fighting back the warning voice in her head. "I'm sorry. I shouldn't yell at you."

"No, you shouldn't. All I ever do is try to help."
His help landed me in the hospital last time.
Mira shook her head. *I could control it this time.*

"You look like you could use a little pick me up or something." Otis held up a hand to ward off the protests she didn't make. "I mean, maybe we could have coffee or a beer or something." He studied her. "Unless you're in need of something a bit stronger?"

Mira bit her lip, then spoke before she lost the nerve. "Yeah, actually. I have a huge chemistry test coming up and I could use a little energy."

"Now we are talkin'!"

"Don't get too excited. Just a couple to get me to the end of the week. And when you go, can you be sure to leave by the back road the same way you came?"

Otis' throaty chortle made her skin crawl. "I love a chick who likes keeping secrets."

Otis went to his car. Mira strode into the sitting room and started a fire. As the sparks danced from kindling to wood, she justified the pills.

This is just to get me past that test. That's all this is.

An hour later, Otis left, having convinced her to buy a full bottle of Ritalin at his 'special friends discount.' She crawled into her bed, exhausted and broke, now that she'd used her weekly allowance from Madelyn for the Ritalin. She fell asleep staunchly refusing to admit she was lying to herself.

COLLIER

"Okay guys, I think we can wrap it for today. Good work everyone. Collier, you've really picked up the vocals nicely."

Shara moved from the studio to the sound booth, leaving the guys alone.

"Hey, I think Mira Pierce's house got sold," Jake said, without preamble. He hadn't regained his confident swagger since Kelly's funeral. Collier doubted he ever would. So every word Jake spoke sounded more like a quiet statement of fact rather than the start of conversation.

All eyes turned to Collier.

"Not a chance, Jake. I ride past that place every day. There was never a for sale sign out front." Dan tucked his drumsticks into a bag at the side of his wheelchair. His casts were long gone, but physical therapy had not progressed quite as well for him as it had for Collier. There was fear that some of the nerves were damaged. He would walk, he could walk now, but very slowly, and painfully. Dan remained cheerful and determined. He could still drum, and he insisted that's all he needed.

"You know how places with land go. They're not always advertised. Sometimes people looking for farm land walk up to someone's door and then bam…the place is sold."

"Tony, really. Name me one person in the history of forever that happened to." Dan needled his brother.

"All I'm sayin' is that there was a shiny new pick up tucked behind the house yesterday." Jake's expression remained blank, as if he were sharing a cookie recipe.

Collier frowned. It never occurred to him that Mira would sell the place. He needed to find out if there were new owners, or if Mira was there with a new car. He leaned his guitar case against the wall and picked up his cane. "Guys, I gotta go."

Collier zipped his coat and headed out the door while the others shared a knowing smile.

The drive to Mira's house was less than two miles, but the longest two miles of his life. As he crested the small hill between Bryan's land and Pierce land he rubbed his eyes. *Yes! There's light in the window!*

He pulled up to the front of the house, his heart racing. Grabbing his cane, he made his way, at a frustratingly slow pace, up the snow covered walk. He knocked on the door several times, with no answer.

Collier stepped back to the walk and looked again at the lit window. There was no light there now. He blinked. *That light was on when I got here. And now it's off. Someone is hiding from me.*

"Mira!" He called up toward the dark windows on the second floor. "Mira!"

He thought he saw a curtain flicker. "Mira!"

There was no response and cold washed over him.

Collier turned and, leaning heavily on his cane made his way back to the car. Getting in and closing the door he paused before jamming the key into the ignition.

He'd never felt so old, so hopeless.

MIRA

She watched him pull out of the driveway before running down the stairs. *That was Collier! He's here, in Rock Harbor!*

Mira bit her lip. In her excitement at seeing him again, she'd forgotten one thing: There was no way she would see Collier, or any of the guys from 'Teacher's Pets'. That part of her life was put on hold, maybe forever. Her excitement crumbled and she sank into a chair, a cloud over her head.

He had a cane. *So he was one of the guys injured in that accident.*

Mira wrapped her arms around her stomach, and doubled over in her chair. *I can't bear this. What am I supposed to do?*

What do I want to do?

I want to run over the snow, over the fields, to the loft where I know Collier is and kiss him until I stop hurting.

"No," she said firmly to the empty room. "My life is very clear. I go to school, clean up my life, and I get to be part of Dusty's life. Maybe Madelyn will let me tell Dusty I'm really his mother."

Just how likely is it that will happen?

I have to believe it will happen. She stared at the door. "Look at what I've given up, what I've sacrificed. Madelyn has to see how good I'm being. She has to give me time with Dusty."

A car pulled up the drive.

Collier? Collier coming back?

She raced to the window, but disappointment deflated her. It was Madelyn's car, driven by Carson. The car came to a halt in front of the house. Madelyn got out, followed by The Senator.

"Oh, shit. He came along?"

Mira raced up the stairs. "I don't want to talk to her. And I sure as hell don't want him near me."

She went to her room and locked her door.

*

A quick check out her window the next morning confirmed she hadn't been dreaming. Madelyn's car remained in front of the house. Mira dressed herself fully before descending to the kitchen for breakfast.

"Oh, Madelyn, good morning." She took a seat across from her sister. "Is Dusty here?"

"No, of course not, Miranda. He's in school."

"But…" Mira nodded to Carson, who set a plate of toast and butter in front of her. "But you're here. Carson's here. He's here." She glanced at The Senator who read a newspaper in the sitting room. "Who is with Dusty?"

"Oh," Madelyn buttered her toast. "Didn't I mention it? We sent Dustin to a very good prep school, a very strict prep school. In Delafield. You've heard of it, I'm sure: St. John's Military Academy."

"Why?" Mira's stomach churned. "Why did you do that?"

"For a number of reasons, none of which concern you."

Mira tried to bite back the anger that bubbled inside her. "I beg to differ, Madelyn. I think what happens to Dusty concerns me tremendously, since I'm his mother."

Mira kept her voice low enough so The Senator didn't hear, but Madelyn's stare was icy. "I thought we'd addressed that already, Miranda. You forget yourself."

"No, you forget yourself. You said I could be part of Dusty's life if I changed my ways. I have. And you've shipped him off to some…some military school? Why?"

"He was starting to act out at school. And besides, this is the best education our state has to offer a young man, outside the UW system, of course."

"Madelyn, Dusty's only twelve!"

"He's nearly thirteen, he's in seventh grade, and this is a tremendous opportunity for him, Miranda. I should think you'd be thrilled." Madelyn studied her with an air of amusement. "Did you think I'd let him move up here and attend that dumpy little school in town?"

Mira dashed an angry tear from her eye. "No, of course not."

"That's exactly what you thought! Oh Miranda, you are funny."

"Why would that be such a funny thing? You and I went to Rock Harbor Community School."

"Well, it's simple mathematics."

"I don't follow."

Madelyn returned to buttering her toast. "We already have enough votes from Rock Harbor to win this county. But the connections Dustin can make through St. John's will serve us immeasurably come election time."

"You have got to be kidding me! You pulled Dusty out of school and put him someplace so he can campaign for you? You are a monster, Madelyn!" Mira shoved herself away from the table and stormed out of the kitchen.

"I'm not a monster, Miranda." Madelyn's arrogant voice floated up the stairs behind her. "I'm Dustin's mother."

Mira slammed her bedroom door and threw herself on her bed. Rage choked her, and the only thing she could think of was the hopeless expression on Collier's face the night before.

Have I given up everything…for nothing?

No. I have to hope. I have to cling to the fact that I am Dusty's mother and one day I will be able to tell him that.

One day I will tell Madelyn who Dusty's father is. And that will be the best vengeance.

Making the promise to herself, Mira was slightly less furious. But only slightly.

204

COLLIER

Collier paced the short floor space of the loft until he was certain he wore a groove in the wooden planks. *I don't care what happened last night. Mira is there. She's at the house.*

Why is she hiding? What is going on?

He wasn't sure why he was so convinced that Mira was there, but having decided she was, Collier also decided, without any real reason, that she was in some kind of trouble. That, he told himself, wasn't such a stretch given her past.

He tried lying on the bed, tried to close his eyes, but all he could see was Mira, as he'd first seen her, standing in the doorway, all thorny, demanding he give up the bed. *Had that been just September?*

Collier looked out the window. It was mid February, and he knew, mostly because Izzy told him during their last phone call, that spring was popping up all over Tennessee. Meanwhile, the scene outside his window was one of the deepest, most endless winters. Dirty snow piles were everywhere; bits of gravel and dirt and corn stalks turned everything a watery gray color. The skies hung low, promising yet more snow. Collier wondered if he'd ever see the sun again.

Across the yard, the warm glow of light shone through the cabin windows. Collier knew Bryan, Shara, and the twins were in the middle of some beautiful domestic activity. A few months earlier, the very idea of a happy couple and a happy family would have made him gag. But now, focusing on the soft yellow glow of the light calmed him, and, in a strange way, made him less lonely.

He glanced at the wall, where he'd pinned the simple wedding invitation. Once Thor was born, Benny had lost no time getting the wedding together.

"I'm going to lock her to me for life," Benny told him. "That way, when anyone asks me why on earth we named that boy Thor, I can just point to her. For the rest of our lives."

Collier grinned, still looking at the invitation. Benny had admitted, privately, he did like the baby's name, but he'd never give Cat the satisfaction of knowing that.

Collier had sent his regrets for the wedding. His physical therapist didn't recommend that long of a trip, yet.

That was just an excuse, though, wasn't it? I could have told the doctors to stuff it. There are ways around that sort of thing.

But I just couldn't…I just can't…stand the thought of leaving Rock Harbor. What if Mira's truly back?

He rolled onto his back and closed his eyes. He pictured her as he remembered her the last time he saw her, her hair a silvery blue-black in the street light, a soft smile on her face. Too well he remembered the feel of her, her scent, her taste.

And then she was gone and, in his quiet moments, Collier had little to fill his thoughts other than finding her and telling her that he loved her.

Collier sat up. "This is ridiculous," he said to the walls. "I need to do something constructive."

He got off the bed and reached for his coat. "I could go work in the studio…no…" He grabbed the heavy pair of leather mittens and the impossible wool hat with the earflaps. When Kelly presented those to Collier, Collier thought he was joking. Having worked his way through a winter in Rock Harbor, Collier realized he needed both, and wasn't likely to go outside without them until June, at the rate he was going.

206

"I'm going to Dave's." He switched off the lights and headed out of the barn. Climbing into his car, he honked the horn to let Shara and Bryan know he was leaving as he forced his car over the frozen, rutted ground.

MIRA

Mira huddled under a pile of quilts and squeezed her eyes tight shut. She shivered, she sweat. She cried.

On the other side of the door, touching the brass knob and rattling it slightly, was The Senator.

Why on earth does he think he can just come in here, after all these years? What made him think I'd let him in?

She made sure her door was locked when she was in her room. Tomorrow, Madelyn promised, tomorrow they were leaving. To keep herself focused and steady, to put on a good show for Madelyn, Mira had all but exhausted her supply of Ritalin. It was too much in too short a time span and she knew it. She felt less like a focused adult and more like a shivering, nervous dog, jumping at every sound. And the only sound she heard now was the rattle of her doorknob. He hadn't so much as looked in her direction in the last two days.

But tonight, he's decided he's going to come knocking.

There was another rattle of the knob and then a silence. Mira let out a shallow breath, not daring to hope he'd given up.

How did I ever think he was anything but evil?

Shortly after Madelyn and The Senator married, Mira, then fourteen, developed a crush on her brother-in-law. She thought she'd buried her feelings well until, shortly after her fifteenth birthday when The Senator brushed his hand across her shoulders as he passed her at the dinner table. It was summer, she remembered, and she'd been wearing a halter-top. The feel of his hands against her bare shoulders was liquor to her inexperienced brain.

The idea that her sister's husband might like her gave Mira a perverse thrill. To say Madelyn had not been a loving surrogate parent was a gross understatement. Mira hated her, and this little flirtation, an innocent touch, a sweet smile, maybe a kiss on the cheek, gave Mira a sense of revenge.

The first night he came to her room, Mira had been shocked, but curious, and more than a little swept away by the attention. He'd only stayed a moment, but it was long enough to share a real kiss, one full of sensuality and promise like Mira had never experienced.

She was convinced they were in love.

She fantasized about Madelyn dying in a fiery wreck and The Senator making her his new wife.

She felt no guilt about those short, tender moments in the darkness far from Madelyn's suite. She felt no guilt when The Senator whispered loving words to her as he kissed her shoulders.

She felt no guilt, until the night he forced himself on her.

I was so stupid. I was so stupid, I let him do it and no one would ever think, by that time that I didn't want it.

Mira couldn't think of that night without a shiver of fear. The Senator hadn't come in with tender words of love and soft kisses. No, that night, he locked her door, and said in a deep, heavy voice, "It's time for you to prove you love me."

Thanks to her sheltered childhood, Mira had little idea of what he truly meant until he peeled her pink sweat pants off her and ripped her half apart. When it was over, he looked at her and smiled.

The smile she'd once thought was so charming became twisted and evil.

He returned, not every night, but enough. She kept telling herself that she loved him, that he would one day take her away from Madelyn's icy control. She told herself it was fine, because this was what people in love did. She told herself she'd learn to like it.

They were all lies.

A year later, she was pregnant, but hopeful The Senator would leave Madelyn for her. She waited until Madelyn was out of the house to tell him.

"What are you going to do about it?" He never looked up from his newspaper.

"I don't know. What are we going to do about it?"

Still focused on the newspaper, he smiled. "Not my problem."

"It's your child."

"It's your problem."

Defiant as only a teen ager can be, Mira didn't back down. "Look, this is your child. It's your responsibility."

He snapped the paper away from his face and rose from the chair, towering over her. "Listen to me, because I'm going to say this one time: this is not my problem. Have the baby, get an abortion, I don't care. But keep my name out of it."

"Or what?" She spoke with a courage she did not feel.

"I'm a powerful man, Mira."

"I'll tell Madelyn."

The smile she'd once thought charming snaked across his face. "Go ahead. Madelyn hates you more than I do. See what happens when you tell her you're carrying my bastard."

Finally realizing The Senator was no ally, Mira had no one else to turn to but Madelyn. Fearful of The Senator in light of his threat, Mira did not admit the affair to her sister. Madelyn pulled her out of school and they went to the cabin where Mira had been born. Madelyn had a private nurse and a midwife, both sworn to secrecy, to help with the birth. Mira never spoke The Senator's name, even when, with Dusty in her arms for the first time, the nurse asked her about the father. Madelyn brushed the question away and no one else asked.

She got her G.E.D. Thanks to Madelyn pulling more than a few strings, she got into UW Madison, where she floundered for two years until she dropped out. With few goals and less drive, she drifted between the old house in Rock Harbor and Madelyn's house in Madison.

Huddled beneath her quilts now, she admitted to herself that in those early days she still hoped The Senator would come around, claim Dusty as his son, dump Madelyn, and marry her. *It was a dream. A stupid, childish, pointless, ridiculous dream.*

After years of cold indifference, he was at her door. Mira wanted to melt into the bed and vanish so he could never find her.

Mira poked her head out of the covers and looked around the dark room. She suddenly felt suffocated. *I need to get out of here. I need to get out of here now.*

She crawled off the bed silently, slipped into her clothes, opened her window and shimmied down the trellis. Staggering across the half frozen, snow-covered yard, she reached her truck. Jamming the key into the ignition, Mira breathed sharp, foggy breaths of cold air, as if breathing life into the engine. A moment, a click, the roar of life, and she swung the truck around the circle drive and onto the deserted highway.

COLLIER

Collier pulled into the parking spot closest to the door at Dave's. He realized, as he hobbled over the frozen ruts, that he hadn't been to the bar since the night of Kelly's funeral. After the funeral, the guys had thought it was a good idea to go to Dave's have a few beers, talk about Kelly. Collier shook his head at the foggy memory. *Most of my worst hangovers always seem like good ideas at the start.*

He opened the door and let his eyes adjust to the dim light. "Hey Chanel."

Chanel smiled. "Well, Collier James. We've missed you." She hugged him. "You want something to eat?"

"Maybe later. Is Dave around?"

"He's in the back, probably sound asleep. It's been dead, I was just thinking about closing early."

"Do you mind if I just play around on the piano a bit?"

"What, did Shara kick you out of the studio?"

Collier grinned. "Nothing like that. Just sometimes I like the feel of a good old greasy honky-tonk piano."

Chanel shook her head and laughed. "Boy, don't you let Dave hear you call this place a 'honky-tonk.' He's been trying to get people to call it that for a long time. I won't let him."

"Why not?"

"I have my illusions. I like to pretend I work someplace classy, like a nice club in Vegas or something. I can't be an old woman slinging burgers at a greasy honky-tonk in Wisconsin." She grinned.

Collier looked Chanel up and down, giving her his best appreciative grin. "You are no old woman, Chanel. You might just be the most beautiful lady I've ever seen in real life."

"And just for that, you get chili on your cheese fries."

"Thank you ma'am." Collier laughed as she swatted his butt with her order pad.

He crossed the dance floor to the stage. Climbing the few stairs he sat at the scarred piano and started rolling his fingers up and down the chipped, yellowing keys. He closed his eyes as images of Mira came to mind. Mira in her moods rolled through his brain like a movie with almost no plot, but a photogenic leading lady. A song, a bit of a melody, and some lyrics started to form as he watched those pictures and concentrated.

He'd brought a note pad and a pen, but he knew he really didn't need it. There was suddenly something very real about what was coming to him. Suddenly he was able to say, within the framework of this song, what he'd wanted to say to Mira. He wanted to comfort her, to protect her, to take her away and make her feel safe and warm and happy.

He stared at the piano keys, amazed. He'd never felt a song so completely before. *No way can I remember it, though.*

He played it again, and this time, as he played, he heard the arrangement, the guitar, the bass, the drums. He finished to Chanel's solo applause.

"Col, baby, that was good! That was exactly the kind of thing Shara and the boys are looking for!"

Collier smiled. "Thanks, Chanel. I…"

He stopped as a blast of cold air announced Mira's arrival. She wore no coat, just a sweatshirt and jeans. Her face was rosy from the cold, but her eyes, even from across the bar, Collier could see were red-rimmed.

"Hey, Chanel. Wow, it's cold out!"

"Mira, girl, how have you been? You want a beer?"

Mira paused, as if, in Collier's mind, she was trying to decide something.

"Get her a cup of tea and a cheeseburger, Chanel. Thanks." He stepped off the stage and walked toward them, leaving his cane at the piano.

Mira looked surprised. "Collier. I…I thought you stayed in Nashville."

He knew she was lying. He knew, in that one look, that she'd been in the house, and she'd seen him. "How have you been?"

"Good." She nodded, too quickly. "Good. Busy. I'm…I'm back in school."

"You are? That's good." He stopped walking. He didn't need to get any closer to recognize the intense light in her eyes. *She's gone back on the Ritalin.* The space between them felt too wide to cross.

"And you…are you working here?"

Collier shook his head. "Not for a while. Not since the accident."

"Oh, right. I read about that."

She read about it? She read about it and never tried to make contact with anyone? The space between them grew. He felt as if he viewed her from across a canyon.

"I came in to work on something I thought up."

"Oh. Not working at Shara's?"

"Not yet ready for that stage."

"I'd love to hear what you have."

"Really?" He studied her face and realized that in this one moment she was sincere. "Okay, sure. Why not?"

"I hope you're not using that blazing confidence to sell yourself to Shara."

"Actually," Collier shuffled his feet on the dusty floor, "Shara and the guys asked me to join 'Teacher's Pets'."

"Oh, Collier!" She jumped off the stool and hugged him quickly. She hopped back as if having the same awkward reaction he was. "That's great! When did that happen?"

"Well." Collier stared at his feet. It was still hard to talk about Kelly much with those who hadn't been in the accident.

"Oh, yeah. Kelly. Col, I'm so sorry. Kelly was…he was a good guy. Everyone loved him. He was…kind to me."

"Yeah. Yeah, he was a good guy. And a hell of a singer. I've been trying to learn his vocals in the songs."

She stared at him, her face smooth. "How's that working?"

Every word between them was stilted. "Slow going."

"Here you go, hon. Cheeseburger," Chanel set the plate in front of Mira. "I threw an extra side of cheese fries in there because you look like you haven't had a decent meal in a while. I'm going to have to work on that cup of tea, though. Not too many people order tea around here. Just your uncle, Collier."

Collier studied Mira again, certain he was right about the Ritalin. "You're not eating?"

Mira took a big bite of the burger, then set it down as she chewed. "Oh, no. No, Collier, I swear. I've been going to school in Green Bay. It's a long day then a long drive home. I go to class, do homework, drive, and sleep."

"And you aren't getting…super focused?" He hated to ask the question, hated the sad light in her eyes.

Hated that she was lying and both of them knew it.

"No, nothing like that," she murmured. "How about if you lay that new song on me while I do justice to this burger?"

Sensing any further discussion on Ritalin would be fruitless, Collier returned to the piano and started playing. As he sang the lyrics, he kept his eyes on Mira, as she sat in the shadowy corner, tapping her feet and moving in time with the music. Her lips moved, as if she sang along.

When he finished, she didn't move, she opened her eyes and stared at him. "Oh, my gosh, Col, that is amazing."

"You think so?"

She crossed the bar and hopped onto the stage. "Oh, yeah. It's so…" She leaned on the piano and tapped her lips.

Collier recognized the expression. "You think something is missing."

"I don't know about missing, but here's what I hear. Shove over." She slid onto the piano bench. "Now, you do the melody." He started singing and she added a bluesy, sorrowful harmony line above his refrain. He continued to the verse, and this time she followed his vocals, a heartbreaking echo to the already painful lyrics.

213

They finished, their voices still echoing in the cavernous room. From the bar Chanel applauded. "Guys, that is a serious, not-even-kidding hit. You two are perfect together!"

Collier ignored Chanel's cheers and took Mira's icy hand in his. "Mira, that's what I've been feeling for you all these months."

"It's a really good song, Col." Her voice was distant, cool.

"I just…I just felt like there was something…and if you could tell me, maybe I could help or…" He took a deep breath, unable to get out the words he'd practiced for so long.

"No, there's nothing. I'm fine. The song is good and I'm fine." She balled her hand into a fist within his.

"Mira, I really wish you'd talk to me. I mean, you have to know how I feel about you."

For the first time she looked directly at him. Her eyes widened. She jumped up, startling him. "I…I have to go." She hopped off the stage and strode quickly to the door.

"Mira! Wait!" Collier followed her, but his progress across the room and onto the uneven parking lot was hampered by weakness in his legs. He finally caught up with her at her truck, where she'd dropped the keys in the snow. "Mira, what is it? What are you afraid of?"

"Collier, leave me alone."

"Mira." He turned her and lifted her chin to face him. "Tell me what it is and I will help you. Whatever it is, I will face it with you. Just, please tell me."

A tear glistened in her eye like one shining star. "Collier, it would be better if you just went back inside and forgot all about me."

"I can't do that, Mira."

"Why not?"

He brushed a strand of hair from her face. "I've fallen in love with you."

She blinked, and the star was gone. "Well, you're going to have to try. I can't...I just can't..." She pushed him away, knocking him to the cold, hard earth. Without looking back, she got in her truck and peeled away.

"Collier!" Chanel tripped across the lot, unsteady in her high heels and helped him to his feet. "What happened?"

"There is something wrong, Chanel. Something really wrong with her." He tried to take a step and sank to his knees.

"There's something wrong with you!"

"Chanel, don't worry about me. I have to go after her!"

"No, you have to get looked at. A fall like that might have aggravated things. Come on. We'll get to the hospital."

"No!" Collier let her help him up again and leaned on her heavily. "No more hospitals. I'm done with hospitals."

They hobbled back to the warmth of the bar and Chanel eased him into a booth and helped him get both legs onto the seat. "Col, you clearly need medical attention. "

Collier leaned against the wall, closed his eyes, an d focused on how his legs felt. *Numb, tingling, but I still feel them.* "Just get me a beer. I'll be fine in a minute."

"I guess pig headed men aren't born in just this part of the country. I guess they grow down in Tennessee." Chanel frowned. "You are determined to be pig-headed, then I'm going to at least make sure I don't have to answer for anything. I'm calling Molly Hunter."

"Don't call Molly. She'll just yell at me."

Chanel shook her head. "Boy, I think that girl did more than just push you down. Did she hit you in the head? Molly Hunter was an emergency nurse in Milwaukee before she ever hit this burg. Plus, she's been at your side for just about all your therapy. And besides," Chanel went behind the bar and poured a beer, "she's also knows everything about everyone in this town. She might know what's going on with Mira."

Collier accepted the beer with a nod. He knew Molly was going to yell at him, whether tonight or tomorrow. "Go ahead. Call her. And throw two of your best cheeseburgers on the grill. Maybe if I feed her, she won't yell as much."

"Oh, she'll yell. But not until after she's eaten. She won't yell with her mouth full."

*
—

Molly showed up ten minutes later, wearing her heaviest winter gear and a dark frown. "What did you do to yourself?"

215

"I'm going to be fine. I…tripped in the parking lot and felt a little weak and numb."

Molly knelt in front of him, pulling off his boots and socks so quickly Collier didn't even realize she'd moved until she poked the arch of his foot with a pen. He yelped in surprised pain. "Okay, you'll be fine I think, but what do I know about this kind of injury?"

Chanel set a burger in front of each of them and Molly's frown darkened. "You're bribing me. Why are you bribing me, Collier James? What aren't you telling me?"

"No, I figured you'd be hungry after…driving out here in the middle of the night."

"Chanel," Molly looked over her shoulder, "would you care to tell me what happened here?"

"Be happy to," Chanel told Molly everything. Molly listened closely, then turned her attention back to Collier.

"Okay, I'm not going to yell at you right now. But we're going to the hospital."

"No more hospitals!"

Molly let out a sharp bark of sarcastic laughter. "Oh, Chanel, isn't he adorable? He thinks he has a choice."

"Just like every pig-headed fool. I'll help you get him to the car."

"Come on, Collier. Lean on us." Molly got up and helped Collier stand.

"I feel fine. I'm sure this is nothing."

"Collier James, you go out on a night like this and get into a tussle with that girl, that's your business. But the minute I get word of it, then it becomes my business and now that it is my business you don't have a vote in the matter." Molly and Chanel eased Collier out the door and into the back seat of Molly's car.

The ride to the hospital was short, but bumpy. Collier brooded in the back seat. "Are you driving through a cornfield?"

"Be thankful you can feel the bumps. That's a good sign."

"Molly, I want to talk to you about Mira."

Molly glanced over her shoulder then turned her attention back to the road. "I told you what I know for fact, and the rest is rumor."

"Then I want to know the rumors."

Molly pulled the car into a parking space in front of the hospital and looked over the seat at him. "Why do you think people trust me? Because unlike most people around here I know how to keep a secret and I don't repeat rumors. Now, we're here." She got out and helped him slide out of the car.

He leaned on Molly's shoulder until she was able to ease him into a wheelchair. The waiting area in the ER was empty, except for an old lady sitting in the far corner.

Molly wheeled him toward the old woman.

"Molly, what are you doing?"

"I'm parking your chair while I go get you registered."

"Yes, but why are you parking me close to that old woman."

"Oh, what, you can't be social with an old woman while you're waiting?"

Has she lost her mind? It's almost midnight. I don't want to be socializing with some strange old woman.

"Well who have we here?" The old woman raised cloudy eyes to them.

"Gertie, this is my friend, Collier James." Molly patted Collier on the shoulder and set the break on the wheelchair. "Collier, this is Gertie McCall. She used to be a nurse here and when her son, Dr. McCall, is working the ER, she likes to keep company with the people in the waiting room."

"Oh, you're Mr. Archibald James' nephew, right? You're the one who was in the accident with those other nice boys from town."

"Yes, ma'am."

"Oh, Molly, what nice manners!"

"You two get acquainted while I see if we can't get a doctor to look at Collier."

Gertie waited until Molly was out of earshot. "Tell me, Collier James, what seems to be the problem? And don't be nervous, dear. I was a nurse for many years. I've seen it all."

"Well, ma'am, I tripped in the parking lot at Dave's."

"You haven't been drinking have you?"

Collier shook his head. "No ma'am, just one beer, and that was after I fell."

"Why on earth were you out in Dave's parking lot in this weather?"

"I was…" Collier looked at Gertie and realized he didn't want to lie. "I was trying to talk to Mira. But she knocked me down and drove away."

Gertie looked puzzled. "Mira?"

"Gertie you know, Miranda Pierce?" Molly walked up behind Collier, startling him.

"Oh, yes. Miranda. She's a sweet girl. I don't know that I like her tattoos, and she always looks like she needs a meal and a shower."

"That would be her," Collier murmured.

"And tell me, how is her mother?"

Molly cleared her throat. "Gertie, Ellen's been passed since Miranda was very young. Remember? She died while they were away right after Miranda was born."

"No, dear, I know Ellen is gone. I went to the memorial service." Gertie leaned in to Collier. "Molly thinks just because I'm old, I'm losing my marbles."

Collier decided he loved Gertie.

"Then I'm confused." Molly's face was smooth, blank, but Collier sensed she knew something.

"I mean Madelyn, of course."

Collier noticed that Molly didn't look quite as surprised as he felt. "I'm sorry, Miss Gertie. Madelyn raised Mira, but they're sisters."

Gertie frowned. "Well I don't see how that's possible. Molly, you remember Doc Granger?"

"I do."

"I was his nurse for years, and I recall, very clearly, having Madelyn Pierce in the office. She couldn't have been more than fifteen or sixteen. She was a cold one, that girl."

Collier shot a look at Molly, who seemed determined not to acknowledge that he wanted her to speak. Swallowing hard, Collier spoke instead. "Miss Gertie, I don't mean to be rude, but a lot of girls go to…women doctors when they're teens."

"Well, of course they do. But I remember Madelyn very clearly because I recall thinking that she was too young."

"Too young?"

Gertie smiled. "Too young to be pregnant. Oh look, there's Scottie's nurse. It's your turn."

Collier waited until they were out of Gertie's earshot. "You brought me here just to talk to her?"

"No, you're seeing a doctor. Gertie was just a happy coincidence."

She rolled him into the exam room. "Here he is, Dr. McCall. I'm hoping you can put the fear of God into him."

Dr. McCall grinned. "Molly, if you can't, then no one will be able to." He looked at Collier's chart. "So, we haven't been taking it easy, have we?"

"I don't know about you, Doc, but I've got stuff I have to do."

"Right now the only stuff you have to do is x-rays. Then we'll just see what stuff you'll be allowed to do."

An hour later, after a stern admonishing from Dr. McCall, Collier was released, his x-rays showing some increased swelling, but no further damage to his spine.

Still confused about the conversation with Gertie, Collier let Molly roll him to the doors before standing and walking to the car. "What the devil was this all about? With Gertie?"

"I told you. I don't repeat rumors."

Collier settled into the seat and rubbed his eyes. "So Madelyn's her mother, not her sister? Why does that make Mira run away from me every time I try to get close?"

Molly started the car and drove in silence for a few minutes. "I think history might be repeating itself."

"Dusty." Collier closed his eyes and recalled what Izzy told him. "He might be Mira's son, not her nephew."

Molly looked impressed. "You've been paying attention."

Collier shook his head. "No. I have friends who do."

"Well, whatever. If you want to get to Mira's heart, you need to think about Mira. What's most important to her? I wouldn't be putting it past Madelyn to threaten her, and use Dusty in the process."

"What does Madelyn have against me, or against Shara and the band?"

"I doubt Madelyn gives two thoughts about anything Mira does, other than to keep her under her thumb. What's Mira been doing since Nashville?"

Collier shrugged. "I'm not sure. She vanished from Nashville and I didn't see her again until tonight. She said she was going to school."

"Prior to tonight, has Mira ever mentioned going to school?"

"No. Music is her passion."

Molly arched an eyebrow. "You think you know her well enough to know her passions?"

Collier stared at the moonlit fields and recalled, too clearly, Mira in his bed. "I do."

"So she cares about music, and I'll bet she cares about you. She's kept herself away from you and away from music. But she's stayed close to that boy." She pulled her car up Shara's drive and stopped. "I never liked Madelyn. Too cold for my taste. But I like Mira. And I like you." She patted his shoulder.

"Thanks." He opened the car door and got out.

"Collier?"

"Yeah?"

"I'll tell you this. Madelyn…she's a very powerful woman. A dangerous one. Whatever is going on with Mira, I'm certain Madelyn's behind it and it might not be wise to get in Madelyn's way."

"Haven't you heard, Molly?" Collier grinned. "I only go for the women who are the worst choice for me."

Molly smiled. "Good."

He watched her back down the drive and, when her headlights vanished around the bend of the drive, he pulled his cell out of his pocket, dialed the mystery number, and listened to it ring.

MIRA

Driving home, Mira tried unsuccessfully to clear her head. She ignored the buzz of her cell. *What was I thinking, going over to Dave's and seeing Collier? Of course he was there, working. Of course I wanted to be near him, to sit next to him.*

To...

She stopped the thought. *I can't think about that. I have to get home and get back into my house before Madelyn realizes I'm gone. I can't risk her thinking I've slipped.*

I can't risk Dusty. He's all I have.

She cut the lights on her truck and eased it silently back into its spot behind the house. She shimmied up the trellis and crept into the window she'd left open. Stripping down to her t-shirt and underwear, she shivered as she crawled back under the covers.

Sometime later, there was a knock at her door. Mira rubbed her eyes and squinted at the clock. *The Senator's trying again? It must be after midnight and he's giving it another shot?*

Another knock. "Miranda, wake up and open this door please."

Mira sat up, startled by Madelyn's voice. She grabbed her jeans and zipped up while unlocking and opening her door. "Madelyn? Is something wrong? Is it Dusty?"

"No, everything with Dustin is just as it should be." She shivered. "Is your window open?"

"It was earlier." Mira slid into a sweater and hugged it tight to her. "I'm not home often, you know, so I don't keep the heat turned on all that high, even at night. I've gotten used to sleeping in the cold."

"The Senator left for Madison an hour ago and I'm leaving shortly." Madelyn's eyes were black and hard. "You and I have some things to go over. Please come downstairs."

Without a word, but with plenty of worry, Mira followed her into the study where Madelyn sat behind the desk and shoved Mira's school books and papers aside. "Please, Miranda, have a seat."

A cold shiver ran through Mira. She searched her memory to find something she'd done wrong in the last several weeks that could have displeased Madelyn, and came up with nothing, other than sneaking out tonight, something Madelyn didn't know. Yet, there her sister was, looking very stern. "Is there something wrong, Madelyn?"

"Wrong? No," Madelyn forced a smile, which made her look creepy and foreboding. "No. As I said, I think everything is just as it should be."

"Okay." Mira sat down, her stomach churning. "This isn't about school, is it? Because I did turn in that paper. It was just a day late." She felt ridiculous. *I'm twenty-eight and I sound like a child. What is wrong with me?*

"No, this isn't about school." Madelyn pulled some papers from her briefcase. "I'd like you to sign these." She pushed the folder across the desk toward Mira.

"What are they?"

"Parental termination papers. The Senator and I are going to officially adopt Dustin, so you need to sign those now. I have a meeting with our lawyers in the morning back in Madison, so I have no time to dilly dally."

Mira felt as though someone punched her in the gut. "I'm sorry, what did you say?"

Madelyn pursed her lips. "The Senator and I feel you will never be a fit mother for Dusty. I've had these papers drawn up for you to sever any future claims you might think you have on the boy."

Mira blinked, trying to absorb exactly what Madelyn was saying. Her stomach churned. "And just what are you going to do with Dusty?"

Madelyn smiled, the greedy glint in her eyes so familiar to Mira. "I will continue to raise him as my own, of course. Having a child keeps a woman young."

"Dusty's not that young anymore."

"Another bonus to having him at St. John's. We can tell people he's there without ever having to have his unpleasant personality around. And, when he's out of college and married, he'll have a child and then I'll be the youthful grandmother."

Madelyn's description of Dusty's personality grated on Mira. "This has nothing to do with whether or not I'm fit for Dusty to live with." Mira grit her teeth. "You just want something, anything to make you look younger and since you've done about as much plastic surgery as you can without your eyes meeting at the back of your head, you're now going to try and take away my son."

Madelyn closed her eyes and inhaled. "I don't know why you're so ungrateful, Miranda. What's really going to change in your life? All I'm asking is that you make legal what we agreed on years ago."

You're calling me ungrateful? You're terminating my rights to my son and you're calling me ungrateful?

"I can see you're wrestling with this, so let me make something clear." Madelyn's eyes narrowed. "I did everything for you when Daddy died. I've always done everything for you. This is how you're going to repay me. You're going to sign your son over to me, like you should have done when he was born, and you're going to stay out of our lives. It's not too much to ask when you consider all the sacrifices I made for you."

That made Mira wince. The old guilt. "I don't see why we have to change anything, Madelyn."

"Your feelings aside, the fact remains: We feel you are not a good influence on Dustin."

"Why not?"

"Well, for one, you don't have a job."

Mira jumped up. "I had a job. I had a really good job. You told me I had to quit that job and go to school full time if I wanted to keep my rights to my son."

"I never said anything such thing."

"You did, Madelyn, you know you did."

"Then where is the document to prove it? I have insurance forms and receipts that prove I've not only been raising and caring for Dustin since the day he was born, but I've been paying your way through life since the day you turned five. You are twenty-eight, Miranda, it's time to get on your own. To that end..." Madelyn pulled out another folder. "Here is a check."

"A check for what?"

Madelyn blinked as if surprised by the question. "I'm buying your half of this house. We don't see the need for it. This county barely has enough votes to make anything worthwhile. We're going to sell the property, after we level the house. Farmland is worth quite a bit up here. We're going to buy a house in Waukesha County which is far more populated, and, of course, far closer to Dustin's school. Now we do pretty much have a buyer, so you needn't worry about anything. Just take your half and be out of the house by the time the bulldozers show up at the end of the week."

"Is this about tonight?" Mira wanted to bite back the words before they were completely out of her mouth.

No surprise registered on Madelyn's face. No reaction at all registered. "I'm very aware of the fact that you left earlier this evening and I doubt I have to think too hard about where you went."

"Do you know why I left the house?"

Madelyn again showed no emotion. "Miranda, whatever you did, and why you did it tonight has no bearing on the fact that you are going to sign those papers. This was a decision I made some time ago."

"Madelyn you can't do this."

"Oh, Miranda, I assure you, I can."

"You're taking away my son, and my home." Mira barely choked out the words. "After I've done everything you told me to do, I gave up everything to stay in my son's life. You're taking it all away?"

"Other than half ownership of this house, there was nothing to take away. We are tired of supporting you. So, as long as we are making a clean sweep of things, once the semester is over, we will no longer be paying for your schooling. It's long past time you supported yourself."

Impotent rage flowed through Mira. "I was supporting myself," she said slowly through gritted teeth. "And you told me if I kept supporting myself with my music, you would take away my rights to Dusty. So I gave it up. I gave up a very important shot at what could have been a very good thing for me and I followed your rules. I stayed here, and I shut myself away from everyone and everything that was important to me because you told me if I did, I would get to stay in Dusty's life. You told me to go to school, and I did. You told me to go full time, and I am. You said it was okay if I went to Green Bay, and probably a good idea NOT to stay in the dorms, so here I am, an hour drive one way, going to school five days a week, working my butt off with a double class load so I can graduate sooner rather than later, and now, now you're telling me, no matter what I do, no matter how well I behave, I'm still going to lose Dusty?"

For the first time since Mira could remember, Madelyn smiled. It was a real smile, though one completely devoid of any cheer or heart, something that made Madelyn's face look like an unnatural mask. It wasn't a smile of shared joy, but instead, a smile of realized victory. "Why yes, Miranda, I suppose that is a very good way of putting it."

Mira stood up and paced the width of the room a couple times. *Now. Now is the time to lay this on her. Now is the time to break her down with the truth.* "Well, if that's the case, I'll save you even more time. The Senator won't need to sign the adoption papers."

"Why is that?" Madelyn's strange smile never waivered.

"Because he's Dusty's father."

"Why are you telling me this?" Madelyn's face was again smooth, undisturbed.

"You and I had an agreement, Madelyn, when Dusty was born. I promised you I would never tell Dusty I was his mother until he was twenty-five. You promised to never ask me about Dusty's real father. And, based on those two promises, you and I had a truce. But since you are hell bent on taking what little right I do have to my son, and you're doing it because I played by your rules and put myself in a corner where I have no way to fight out, I figure I should probably just let you know that it was your beloved husband who fathered my son." She took a breath, and seeing Madelyn had nothing to say, Mira continued. "I had a crush on him. I was fifteen. He was handsome and he was sort of nice to me, which is more than I can say for you. One night he showed up in my room and took advantage of that, and he forced himself on me. But he made me promises, Madelyn. He promised me more than just a college education. He promised me things I'd never had before, things like affection, comfort, love."

Madelyn started laughing.

"What's so funny?"

"You thought you'd somehow shock me." Madelyn stopped laughing, but the smile remained. "That strikes me as funny."

Mira studied her sister with a growing sense of horror. "You think this is funny?"

"I find it amusing that you thought I didn't know this."

225

Madelyn's words stopped Mira dead in her tracks. "You knew?"

"Oh, Miranda...maybe you are mentally deficient. I always thought you were, but you know Daddy refused to have your I.Q. tested. And by the time he died, well, we were all just so used to you being...not very quick."

"You knew. You knew he was raping me."

"That's hardly the word I would use for what happened."

"Well." Mira sat down. "I guess that explains a lot. I mean, growing up, I thought you were so mean to me because I had a crush on him. I guess, if you knew he was sleeping with me, well, that would explain why you've been such a bitch to me my entire life."

Madelyn pursed her lips. "Miranda, there's no need to use foul language."

Mira frowned. "No, but see, I think there is. I think this is the perfect time for foul language. Your husband, from the time I turned fifteen until the day I told him I was pregnant, your husband took advantage of my feelings and seduced me and then raped me several times. And you knew about it and didn't stop it. So yeah, I think it's time for a little foul language."

"Why would I have stopped it?" Madelyn seemed sincerely puzzled.

"Why would you...Madelyn, do you hear yourself? Why would you have stopped it? Because I was a child! Because he was your husband! Because...why didn't you stop it?"

Madelyn leaned back in the leather wingback chair and tapped a pen to lips. "Miranda, be reasonable. What happened that was so horrible? I think I negotiated a very nice arrangement all the way around. You got to live out a teen fantasy. The Senator got to dally with some forbidden fruit. I got to live a life I very much like."

The room started spinning. Mira gasped for air. "You negotiated this? What the hell are you talking about?"

"Do you remember what you looked like at fifteen? At fourteen? We Pierce girls, we grow up far too fast. Father always said that. You looked...a lot like me, when you were fourteen. Far older than your years." Madelyn's voice drifted a little, as if she were remembering something.

"What has that got to do with anything?" Mira stood in front of the desk, leaning forward, staring at Madelyn.

"Miranda, The Senator took a liking to you almost instantly. I knew it. By the time we met, I had just crossed into my thirties, and I was saddled with you. You caught The Senator's eye. I managed to negotiate an arrangement with him that was mutually beneficial."

"You negotiated your sister's rape? What gave you that right?"

A fire heated within Madelyn's eyes. She stood, and leaned on the desk, her fists braced on the polished mahogany. Face to face the women stood, glaring at each other. "You were mine," Madelyn hissed. "You were mine and you were all I had."

"I was not yours!" Mira tensed and leaned in.

"You were mine in the way of the most natural of laws. You. Are. My. Daughter."

All sound sucked from the room. Mira felt a tremendous pressure on her chest, as if she couldn't get enough air. She wasn't sure how she was able to stay upright. "I'm what?"

Madelyn didn't blink. She leaned closer, close enough for Mira to see the deep lines in her face that no amount of make-up would be able to cover. "My daughter. You are my daughter."

227

"Then who…who is my father?"

"Daddy."

The word was more than a physical pain. Mira crumbled into the nearest chair. "That's not…"

Madelyn sat back in the chair, relaxed as if saying the words out loud released her from some very restrictive clothing. "Not possible? I suppose, you only knew the old man, the dear, doddering old man who died of a 'broken heart'." Madelyn waggled her fingers with air quotes.

"He did. He died after Mother…"

"What? After Mother died birthing you? Please. Mother had no time for Daddy. She couldn't stand him one bit. She hated the farm. She hated Rock Harbor. But she liked Daddy's money, the power he had, even if it was in this stupid little town. She liked that very much."

"But…"

"Oh, just shut up, will you?" Madelyn opened the lower drawer of the desk and pulled out a bottle of whiskey and a pair of crystal tumblers.

"Want some?"

Mira shook her head, numb.

"Suit yourself. Where was I? Oh, right. Well, Mother had no trouble accepting that her husband had an affair. After twenty years of giving her no peace, she was happy he was bothering someone else. She was not, however, happy that I was the one."

"But Madelyn…"

"You may as well know everything." Madelyn drained the first glass of whiskey and poured herself a second. "It docs feel good to get this all out in the open. See, you think I'm a monster, but I'm not. I have a great clarity of vision. I know exactly where power and money come from and I know how to secure them. Mother wanted nothing to do with him, but even at a young age, I knew Daddy was the most powerful man in this town. Seducing him wasn't all that hard when I think about it."

Mira stared at Madelyn. "You…you?"

"One thing you must know by now." Madelyn filled a glass with whiskey and pushed it toward Mira. "I will always do what I must to get to my goal. And my goal, Miranda dear, will always, always be about getting as much power and as much money as I can put my hands on. And if that means I have to seduce a sweaty farmer and birth his bastard then that's what that means."

"But, Madelyn, he was our father!" Mira's voice was a thin wail, a primal howl to her ears.

Madelyn's expression melded into a shadow of surprise. "Wait, you think…oh, yes, of course. You would think that, wouldn't you? I suppose everyone thinks that. Let me put one thing to rest. Your father was not my father."

Mira reached for the whiskey, her hands trembling as she closed her fingers around the cut glass. "What?"

"Mother met him shortly after she got pregnant with me. The way Mother told it, they met in Madison when he was at some farming association meeting or something and she was working as a waitress in a diner at the airport." Madelyn held her glass to the light and studied the amber liquid. "I suppose that's why I have no respect for waitresses. God knows I had no respect for her."

Mira set her glass down and hugged her knees to her chest, feeling like a small child in the oversized leather wing back chair. "So who was your father?"

"Who knows?" Madelyn shrugged. "Doesn't matter. Daddy fell in love with Mother for some reason and they got married quietly after I was born. He inherited this farm from his father and moved us all up here. I suppose everyone just assumed I was his daughter."

"Still, he raised you. How could you…" Mira's mouth burned with words she could not say out loud.

"It was really quite easy when you think about it. Mother had locked her door to him for more than a decade by the time I was old enough to know what I wanted and how I was going to go about it. All it really took was enough double entendres and feigned innocence and one cold evening of brandy and quiet talk. He drank the brandy, I talked. Oh it didn't matter what I said, the fact that I was female and paying attention to him, that's what mattered. He had a few, then a few more, and I helped him to bed. And I gave him an innocent kiss on the cheek, just like a good daughter." Madelyn's smile was soft, almost gentle. "You know, I was fond of him. And you'll be happy to know, if you must know, that he did try to resist. But, after a while, I've found, a man simply cannot resist certain primal urges."

Mira wiped her face on her jeans and glared at Madelyn over her knees. "I'm not going to listen to any more. Stop talking."

"Well I don't see why we should stop here. I may as well tell you what happened after I wound up pregnant."

"You got pregnant that one time?"

Madelyn's smiled softened even more, and she shook her head. "Oh, no. There were other evenings. Not many, of course, Daddy never was completely comfortable with our arrangement. But there were other evenings. We probably could have been very happy that way for a long time. I suppose my mistake was not getting you aborted before I told him. I did think he'd be happy. After all, Daddy longed to have a child of his own."

More tears welled in Mira's eyes. "He wasn't though. He couldn't have been. Not like that."

229

Madelyn nodded, her whimsical smile turning melancholy. "That's true. He was…ashamed. He was so ashamed, he told Mother, who was going to throw him out."

"But she didn't?"

"Of course not." Madelyn's voice dripped with derision. "She had no real skills. What was she going to do, go back to waiting tables? All she had she'd gotten from Daddy. I convinced them both to pass you off as their child."

"You planned that?"

"Pretty sad when the fifteen-year-old is the smartest person in the room." Madelyn sighed. "Daddy packed the family truck and we headed out to this dismal hunting cabin he had in Canada. And there, about two days after you screamed and heaved your way into the world, Mom shot herself in the head. I will say this…" Madelyn held the brandy up to the light. "She didn't make a mess. She shot herself at the edge of the pier and fell right into the water. No muss, no fuss."

Mira rubbed her temples. *It's too much. None of it's true.* "Mother died in California and is buried in California."

"Okay, you keep believing that if you want." Madelyn set the glass on the desk. "Would you like to know the rest?"

"Hell, no."

"Well I'm going to tell you anyway. After that, we came back, only now, I had this baby to take care of. I could have run away. I probably should have. But I knew Daddy had money and by all that was holy I was going to benefit from this whole mess. So I stayed with him. I raised you, squalling brat that you were. He doted on you. You would have thought the sun rose and set with you. In fact," Madelyn poured herself more brandy, "I found out he was going to change his will and instead of leaving us both equal shares, he was going to leave everything to you, since you were his actual child and I was the reminder of his weak nature. Naturally I had to make certain that didn't happen."

There was something cold, sinister in Madelyn's voice. Mira looked up, her face sticky with hot tears. "What? What did you do, Madelyn? What did you do to Daddy?"

Madelyn smiled and drained the glass. "I don't see the point in telling you. There's no possible way you can prove it, and it doesn't matter anyway. I left you with Molly Hunter and traveled a bit, but it turns out Daddy didn't have quite as much money as everyone thought he did, so I had to get creative. Except, how creative can one get when one is saddled with you?"

Mira shook her head. "I don't want to hear any more of this! It's all lies!" She didn't recognize the defeated, moaning voice in her own head.

"Oh, no, you're going to listen. Besides we're just getting to the good stuff. I packed up what little we had and we went to Madison to learn a thing or two about politics. I never had any real power…and power is what I craved. So I moved to Madison, told everyone I was going to school. I hung around the State Capitol and learned a thing or two. Got a job as a secretary, then a better job as an aid to The Senator. I worked hard and I swore I would never, ever let anyone have any power over me." She smiled. "I found out early on how The Senator felt about women. I was in my twenties, already too old for him. But you, you were just like me, you matured quickly. By the time you were twelve, I knew I had just the right bait. That's when he and I started the early stages of a negotiation. His end of the bargain was that he married me, gave me everything. In return…well, he got my skills for campaigning, which turned out to be stellar, and you."

"I was a child." Mira swallowed. "Your child."

"Yes, so be thankful he didn't get to you when you were younger. He waited until you were fifteen. Why? I made him wait. And he stopped when you got pregnant. Why? Because he has no interest at all in mothers, in women who have given birth. It's why he never had any real interest in me. He didn't want to go near you after that."

Mira looked up and frowned. "But…he did."

Madelyn gave her a grim look. "Yes, I know. It took all the powers of persuasion I had to convince him that you were still his ideal, that it was almost like you hadn't birthed Dustin, that I was the one who gave birth." Madelyn shook her head. "And then you refused him. Suddenly your door was locked. So he finally stopped trying. And because he stopped going to you, he went elsewhere."

Mira stared at her. "Are you mad at me for that?"

"Of course I am!" Madelyn slammed the glass down. The base of the heavy tumbler cracked beneath the force of her anger, and a thin line of brandy leaked through the crack as she poured herself yet another drink. "Do you have any idea how hard it is to

231

cover up his indiscretions? And you were right there, and yet I managed, even though you got older and had a baby, to make sure he never lost interest in you, but oh no, you couldn't just go along with the plan. You liked him well enough for a while, but then suddenly you had no interest."

"Madelyn…"

"You had no gratitude! You were an ungrateful little bitch from the moment you were born and you've done nothing but make my life miserable!" Madelyn flung the tumbler at the wall, shattering it. She inhaled and exhaled slowly, as if regaining herself after some out of body experience. "I even gave you a chance tonight, to make things right. I convinced The Senator to give it one more try. But you didn't open the door. No, instead you chose to return to that dive of a bar and spend the evening with your filthy friends. That's your choice, Miranda, and you've made it. Which is why now, I have Dustin." She tidied up the desk. "And you are going to sign those papers." She smoothed the files at the edge of the desk and looked at Mira expectantly.

Mira ran her hands through her hair, shaken and unable to understand anything Madelyn was telling her. "Madelyn, I…I can't. I won't. Not after what you've told me."

232

Madelyn sighed and picked up her briefcase. "Well, that is unfortunate, but I understand. You've had a little overload of family history, and you never have been very mentally strong. Go back to bed. And in the morning, you sign these papers and fax them to me, I will then give you this check." She waved the folder with the check in front of her. "And you can go off to do whatever it is you do with the underworld and I'll raise Dustin to be an upstanding citizen, which is something you simply do not have the skill to do."

"And what if I don't?"

Madelyn's creepy smiled returned. "Mira, you think I've done horrible things to you? You think I'm a horrible person?"

"Yes!" Mira leapt to her feet and spat out the word. "That is exactly what I think!"

"My dear, you have no idea just how horrible I can be. Sign those papers, or you will find out. You, and everyone you care about will find out."

Mira was unable to respond. She slumped in her chair and stared at the floor, unwilling to even look up as Madelyn walked out of the room, put on her coat, retrieved her purse, and left the house. Only after Mira heard the car engine fade down the long drive did she stand up, run to the door, and whip it open. Falling to her knees, Mira screamed her primal, all-encompassing pain to the dark, heavy winter sky.

COLLIER

Collier woke in a cold sweat. Something was very wrong, the feeling overwhelmed him. Searching the shadowy corners of the loft, he half hoped to see Mira, though he knew she wasn't there. He'd left a message on the mystery phone number, but there was no way of knowing if she got it.

He sat up and shivered in the chilled air. He couldn't shake the look on her face as she pushed him away. Closing his eyes, he saw her again, sitting in the corner at Dave's, listening to him, then next to him, creating magic with her voice. She was peaceful and happy. And then...

And then she shoved me away and drove off.

He'd wanted to drive to her house then, after they'd left the hospital. But Molly was driving and Molly didn't even want him to go to the loft. The only way she agreed to leave him was if he swore to her he would stay put, at least for the rest of the night. Collier found that a difficult promise to keep.

More than anything he wanted to break his promise to Molly and storm over to Mira's house. But climbing the stairs to the loft had exhausted him. He'd barely given Gertie's revelation a thought before he fell into an uneasy sleep.

234

Now, however, he was wide awake, and unable to pinpoint the source of his disquiet. He glanced out the window. Everything in the cabin was dark and still, just as it should be. Pulling on his jeans and flannel shirt, he made his way, down the stairs. The horses stirred in their stalls, but made little noise as he opened the back door and looked at the orange-streaked sky.

He glanced at his watch. *It's just after four.* Too early for sunrise. Nothing else, however seemed amiss. He went back upstairs and closed the door.

Collier tensed at the sound of the barn door opening and closing. He moved to the front window: the cabin was dark. It was unlikely Bryan or Shara would be in the barn. And yet, there was the unmistakable sound of a person moving around below him. The horses stirred and whinnied.

Someone is in the barn.

He crossed the loft again and opened the door quietly as possible. Other than leaving the lights off, the person made no attempt to hide their presence. His legs starting to burn and weaken, Collier took a couple shaky steps down the stairs and peered over the railing.

Mira.

She sat on a bale of hay, huddled into a tight ball. She stared at nothing as she rocked back and forth muttering something.

Struggling to remain calm, he eased himself down the stairs, ignoring the pain shooting up his spine. "Mira?" He kept his voice low, approaching her as he would a wounded animal. "Mira? What's going on?"

There was no sign that she was aware of him. She remained tightly balled, her thin arms stretched around her knees. She continued to murmur something he couldn't decipher.

Collier took a few more steps, and turned on the overhead lights. Seeing her in the brighter light did nothing to assuage his concern. Her eyes were wild, and streaks of black marred her arms and face. "Mira, what is this?"

"It's burning. It's all burning." Louder now, Collier realized she wasn't answering him so much as chanting.

"What's burning, Mira?" He moved closer to her, now standing in front of her. Her body trembled, but, though she wore nothing but a thin T-shirt and sweats, she seemed more angry than cold.

She lifted her head and met his gaze. She spoke, though Collier doubted she actually saw him. "It's burning. It has to. Everything has to burn."

The image of orange streaks in the sky came back to him. *That's not the sunrise. It's on the west side of the building. That's a fire.*

Collier moved as quickly as he could to the door. Jerking it open, he staggered across the yard to the cabin. "Bryan!" He pounded on the door and shouted at the dark door. "Bryan!"

The porch light blinded him for a split second as the door creaked open. "What's going on?"

Collier hobbled past Bryan and into the cabin. "Mira...in the barn. I'm pretty sure her house is on fire."

"What?" Bryan stared at him.

Collier nodded to Shara as she walked up the hall, wrapped in a pink quilt. "Mira is sitting in the barn right now, mumbling something about burning and she's got these black marks on her arms and face, like soot. And look." He pointed out the picture window. The orange light was unmistakable. "I'm pretty sure there's a fire at her house…and she might have set it."

Bryan grabbed his coat from the peg on the wall. "Shara, call the fire department. I'll meet them there."

"I'm coming with you." Collier took a step toward the door and paused, his legs dangerously close to failing him.

Shara muttered a few words into her phone and ended the emergency call. "You'll do no such thing, Collier James." Shara put her hands on his shoulder and guided him to the couch. "You sit down. Bryan, be careful," Shara gave her husband a quick kiss. "Now, Collier, I'm going to go get Mira."

"No, Shara. Let me help." He stood to prove he was able. "Please?"

Shara studied him for a moment and nodded. "Fine, come on. Let's go see what's going on with her."

Mira startled as Shara rolled the door open, but other than that, she gave no indication she was aware she was no longer alone.

Shara and Collier sat on either side of her. "Mira?" Shara brushed a strand of hair away from Mira's face. "Mira, honey, what's going on?"

Stony silence. Collier looked at Shara over Mira's hunched shoulders. "I don't think she hears us, Shara. I don't think she's quite…with us."

Shara nodded. "You might be right. We need to get her someplace warm." She stood. "Let's see if she won't at least walk to the cabin for us."

Collier helped Mira to her feet. She weighed less than he remembered. They moved her across the yard to the cabin. Collier settled Mira onto the couch, and wrapped her in a quilt while Shara called Molly.

Molly arrived less than half an hour later, her face a study in concern. "Has she said anything?"

"Not a word. Not since I first saw her in the barn." Collier moved from Mira's side to allow Molly room. "She won't drink or eat anything either."

Molly stared at Mira's skeletal frame. "What's she on, Collier?"

Collier shook his head. "Nothing…"

Molly glared at him. "Collier James, there's one thing I can't abide and that's a liar. I haven't seen this girl close up in months, but it's obvious to me that she didn't just lose a couple pounds. Look at her. What has she been taking?"

Collier sighed and sank into the nearby armchair. "Okay." He told Molly about Nashville and Ritalin. Shara nodded, having witnessed much of the story, but Molly's expression grew darker with each sentence. Collier told them everything, including his futile visit to her house, leaving out only the detail of their one night together.

"You didn't think to tell me about any of this?"

"Look, I haven't seen her since she left my apartment before Christmas. She changed her cell number. She hasn't called me. If I hadn't seen her at Dave's tonight I still wouldn't know for sure she was in town."

"Okay, well, it's clear that she is still taking Ritalin." Molly frowned. "I don't have to think too hard to figure out where she's getting it."

"Otis Drumm."

Molly nodded at Shara. "The local source of every problem like this. We need to get her to the hospital."

Shara and Molly loaded Mira into Molly's car. Shara sat next to Mira, a protective arm around her. Collier, reluctantly, got into the front passenger seat. He tried to avoid Molly's stern glare as they raced to the hospital. Once there, the women moved forward, but Collier felt as if he were trapped in a horrible dream. Slowly he followed them into the brightly lit emergency room. He sat silently, speaking only when spoken to directly. Shara gave the nurse most of Mira's story while Collier sat frozen, unable to say anything that would help Mira come back to them.

They took Mira away, Molly and Shara following. Collier, left alone in the waiting area, sat motionless as if moving would shatter what frail hold he had on Mira and what frail hold Mira had on life.

"Collier?"

He startled as he looked up into Bryan's soot-streaked face. "Wow, you're a mess."

Bryan coughed and sat next to him. "Not my first go round with a fire. But they got it out okay. The house is gone, but no one got hurt. Dan showed up with Tony."

"Really?"

"Yeah. He really wants to help, but those legs of his…" Bryan nodded at Collier. "You definitely got the better end of that."

"Not feeling that way right now."

"I know. But at least you can walk. Dan…he's still in a wheelchair most of the time, isn't he?"

"Yeah." Collier picked at the armrest. "So the fire's out?"

"Yeah. I figured you guys were here when I got home and no one was there. It's a good thing we live in a small town. I mean, the kids were still in bed, no adult in sight."

"Sorry."

Bryan grinned and slapped him on the shoulder. "I got our neighbor, Marva, to come over and get them up and ready for school. It's not the first time they've gotten up in the morning and we've been called out someplace."

"Part of being kids of super heroes," Collier muttered.

"I can see you're in a great frame of mind, so I'm just going to go find Shara and see what's going on."

Bryan left Collier to his thoughts, and Collier wallowed in pity for another half hour before dozing off into a troubled sleep.

He woke when Molly tapped his shoulder. "You can go in and see her."

"Is she…okay?"

"She's unconscious right now. She fainted, probably because she's dehydrated."

"Just like in Nashville."

Molly reached her hand to him. "Come on. You can go in for a few minutes."

He followed Molly up the long hallway to a dimly lit room where Mira lay in a hospital bed.

"What's that on her wrists?"

Molly frowned. "Restraints. She put up a fight before she fainted. It's not unusual in cases like this. Don't worry. Go sit next to her. Go on."

Collier pushed a nearby chair next to the hospital bed and sat. He said nothing until he heard the soft swoosh of the door closing. Turning to Mira, he patted her cold, pale hand. "Mira, what did you do? Why did you do this to yourself again?"

She stirred but made no sound. Collier stroked her hand and hummed tunelessly. He had so many questions he wanted to ask her, but what he really wanted to do, what he ached to do, was to crawl into the bed and wrap himself around her tiny frame. He longed to shield her from whatever it was in the outside world that put her in this position.

Instead, he spent the better part of the early morning hours humming and singing softly to her, hoping she heard him and hoping it soothed the pain in her heart.

*

He wasn't sure what time it was, or how long he'd been asleep, when the door snapped open. Collier sat up and rubbed his eyes. Before him stood as frosty a woman as he ever hoped to see. Behind her stood an older man.

The woman took two short steps toward him. "Who are you and what are you doing in my...sister's room?"

Madelyn. Collier stood. "Miz Anderson, pleased to meet you, ma'am. My name is Collier James. I'm a friend of your...sister's." He watched Madelyn's face for any reaction to his mirrored pause of the word, 'sister.' If there was one, he missed it.

"Yes, well, you can leave now. Only family is allowed and the last I checked, you're not family."

"No ma'am, I'm not. But I'm the one who found her and I'm the one who took care of her before, so I guess I'm going to stay until someone from the hospital staff tells me to leave, if that's all right with you." Collier amplified his Southern accent, and his sarcasrm.

"Well, I can assure you, this will be the last of this nonsense. Do you know what she did to my house?"

That would be the thing to focus on. "I heard about the fire. She got out, though, thank goodness. Now she needs a little tending after her shock." Collier studied Madelyn's face, looking for any trace of humanity. He found none. "I can understand your concern for Miss Mira, but right now she needs peace and quiet. And beggin' your pardon ma'am, but those there," he pointed to the line of photographers just outside the door, "don't exactly lend themselves to peace and quiet."

Madelyn took a step closer and lowered her voice. "You can be certain, Mr. James, Miranda will get the medical and psychiatric care she needs."

Cold ran through him. "I don't believe she needs all that, ma'am. She needs to be loved. She deserves to be heard."

"Oh, yes, I see what your kind of love has done for her. No, your ilk has done enough damage. Now it's time for her family to take over her care. I'll make sure she gets exactly what she deserves."

"She'll make sure I never see my son again."

Collier and Madelyn stared at Mira. She was sitting up, her green eyes flashing furiously as cameras clicked and whirred.

MIRA

Once she'd made it to the barn, nothing felt real to Mira. The heat from the fire, the smell of burning, even the feel of hay against her skin all seemed like a far away dream. What was real was Collier's hand on hers and his soft voice gently drowning the sound of screaming inside her head. At the hospital, though she was unconscious, she was aware of Collier singing to her. His voice and touch gave her peace.

It was Madelyn's voice that shattered her peace. Mira heard Madelyn's voice before she could absorb the words, and struggled to open her eyes. She heard Collier's defense and knew nothing he said would be strong enough to stand up against Madelyn and her ever-present photographers.

I have to speak. I have to say something.

"If she commits me, I'll never see my son again."

Mira wasn't positive she'd said the words out loud until Collier looked at her. "Your son."

Mira nodded, surprised that Collier didn't seem shocked. "Dusty Anderson is my son." She spoke as loudly and as firmly as she could, so that every one of the members of press standing outside her room could hear.

241

Madelyn's eyes popped with rage. She put her hands on Collier's shoulders and pushed him out of the room. "Get out!" She managed to push him into the hall, into the throng of cameras. "You are the one responsible for my sister's condition and I am going to take her someplace safe right now and make sure you never get your filthy hands on her again!"

She slammed the door. "Carson! Make sure no one comes through that door!" Satisfied he'd obeyed her command, Madelyn walked over to the bed. "Now, Miranda, let me explain to you how this is going to work. You have burned down my house. You have consorted with a known drug dealer. These two facts no one can refute. And now I will have no trouble proving you are mentally unstable and certainly too dangerous to be around an impressionable child like Dustin."

Mira struggled against the restraints. "You can't do this, Madelyn. You can't! I'll tell everyone about you!"

"Do you honestly think anyone is going to believe you once you've been committed to a mental hospital?" Madelyn adjusted the collar on her suit. "My dear, that's the whole reason I came here this morning. I knew those cameras would follow me, and they'd get this," she looked Mira up and down, "lovely image on film. There's no family court in this state that will believe a word you have to say once this all plays out in the media."

"You didn't come here this morning for any reason other than to destroy any hope I have of ever truly being Dusty's mother?" Mira leaned forward, the last flicker of hope dying within her.

"Miranda, honestly. When I left last night I had absolutely no intention of making direct contact with you ever again. I was going to get the forms from you and then let you rot in whatever hole you decided to dig for yourself. Setting fire to the house was nothing more than an annoyance, until I saw exactly how this might play out in my favor." Madelyn smiled, an expression that made Mira nauseous. "The beauty of it all is, the thing I was really dreading the most, you know, how I could destroy Dustin's devotion to you. Well, you made that so easy, didn't you?"

"How?"

"Do you think he's going to want anything to do with a pill popping lunatic who set fire to the family home? His feelings for you were weak enough once you gave up music, but you dealt yourself the final blow. I didn't have to do a thing." She stood in front of the closed door and glared expectantly at Carson.

"How can you do this, Madelyn?" Mira's voice was thin. "How can you turn your back on me, your...daughter?"

Madelyn glanced over her shoulder. "Clearly you don't understand, so I'll spell it out. From this moment forward, you are dead to me. You are dead to me, dead to The Senator, and yes, you are dead to Dustin. I am going to put you someplace where you will never, ever see the light of day. I'm going to put you someplace where your dirty little friends will never find you."

"Madelyn..." Mira's voice was a strangled whisper.

"As for how I am able to do this, that's simple. You are not good for my plan any more. I don't need you. I have Dusty. I can't have you cluttering up the picture." She gave Carson a nod, and he opened the door.

Mira fell against the pillows as she listened to Madelyn coo to the photographers.

"Carson?" Mira said, uncertain he heard her, until he paused in the doorway.

"Miss?"

"Can you…will you help me?" Her voice sounded pathetic, and she hated that she couldn't muster any stronger a tone.

Carson glanced warily down the hall. "You know I'll always do what I can for you. But this time I don't know what I can do."

Mira closed her eyes, tears streaming down her cheeks. "Carson, you have been kind to me. I appreciate it." She took a deep breath. "Please look after my boy."

Carson nodded. "That I will do as best I can." He took a step into the hall and paused. "There is one other thing I can do."

"What's that?"

Carson kept his gaze fixed at a point down the hallway Mira couldn't see. "Is there someone I can contact once I find out when and where you'll be moved? Get me a phone number." With that, he vanished down the hall.

243

Mira glanced wildly around the room. *Oh sure. Give you a phone number. I haven't a clue where my phone is. It's probably burned up with everything else at the house.*

Besides, whose number could I give you?

Collier's voice echoed in the back of her mind. The memory of his touch on her hand warmed her skin. *He was here. He sat with me. That means something.*

But I abandoned him after the bus crash. I left him in Nashville and I stole from him.

He was here because I dragged myself into his life. There's no point in getting him more involved in my mess.

She closed her eyes and let her hands fall limp in her lap. *It's hopeless.*

COLLIER

Collier sweet-talked one of the day nurses into dropping him off at his car in Dave's parking lot. He got into the car and, without much thought, drove to the loft. As if on automatic pilot, he climbed the loft stairs, grabbed his guitar, went back down the loft stairs and crossed the yard to the studio. The studio was empty, though it didn't matter. He was not moving by conscious thought. He followed blind instinct.

Closing the door behind him, Collier turned on a single overhead light and, in the shadows, he started to write.

*

He wasn't aware of anything. Time, hunger, day, night, it was all the same to Collier as he played and sang and scribbled on notepaper. He worked feverishly, as if racing some dark entity, something he could not see or touch, but something he knew was there, just beyond the feeble reaches of the light.

He did not work as if his life depended on it. He worked as if hers did. Foremost in his mind, with every note, every word he wrote, was Mira's image and the last words he heard her speak.

"Dusty Anderson is my son."

The rumor was confirmed. *It all makes sense. Mira must have been sixteen, seventeen when he was born. Madelyn is raising him as hers. Izzy was right.*

Collier paused long enough to drain the bottle of water sitting on the music stand.

Madelyn could be trying to control Mira by withholding time with Dusty. That would explain why Mira left Nashville without a word, and why she didn't try to contact any of us after the accident.

Another refrain poured out of Collier's fingers. He pictured Mira in Nashville, fragile, sick and driven. Driven by forces he couldn't see. Every thought he had about Mira went back to Madelyn.

If she's Dusty's mother, why doesn't she just take Dusty and go away? She doesn't need Madelyn's support. What else is there to tie Dusty to Madelyn?

244

A cold, jagged thought slashed through him.

The Senator.

The idea was so startling, so sickening, Collier dropped his pencil. He stared at the music in front of him, and everything became as clear as the notes on the page.

Having Madelyn as an enemy is one thing. But The Senator is a powerful man, someone who could make threats, and keep them. Madelyn can threaten to take Dusty away from Mira, but The Senator can threaten to take away even more.

He bent and picked up his pencil, but the fever was over. He'd completed the song. He'd completed the song and the puzzle to Mira.

But what can I do to help her?

Footsteps behind him broke Collier out of his reverie. "Miss Shara?"

Shara set a handful of music stands in the corner and smiled at him. "You must be deep in thought, calling me 'Miss'," She patted his shoulder. "How's Mira?"

Collier pushed the image of Mira's pale face and sunken, desperate eyes from his mind. "She was conscious when I left the hospital. Her sister kicked me out."

A shadow crossed Shara's face. "Yes, I suppose Madelyn would be there, wouldn't she?"

Collier was surprised to hear the edge in Shara's voice. "You don't like Madelyn?"

"Bryan knows her better than I do, but I never cared for her." Shara shook her head. "But never mind that. What are you doing here so early?"

Collier stared at the music, and realized the notes weren't quite as clear on paper as they were in his head. "I have a song…I was hoping you could listen to it."

"It's not going to suck, is it?" Jake asked as he dragged a stool close to the piano.

"Jake!" Tony, following Jake, was horrified. "How about some manners? So not cool, man!"

"Manners slow things down." Jake waved Tony off and turned his attention to Collier. "Well?"

"No, I don't think it sucks."

Jake crossed his arms. "You didn't think the last one sucked."

Collier stretched his arms over his head. While he appreciated Jake's recent return to his old self, Collier was exhausted and had little patience for Jake's banter. "How about if I play it and you decide?"

A silence fell over the room. Collier smiled, feeling an unfamiliar surge of confidence. For the first time in recent memory, he said something and people heard him. Shara and the guys filed into the booth, giving him space to perform.

He settled his guitar on his lap. He didn't bother tuning it. He knew he was ready. Any weakness in his legs, any physical pain vanished. As he played, he felt the tightly controlled anger and faint sense of hopelessness that led him to this song pour through his voice.

Collier didn't look at the group behind the glass. He channeled his energy into the story he told. When he was finished, he set his guitar back on its stand and waited as Shara, Tony, and Jake filed in and leaned on the piano.

"Holy shit. That was brilliant."

Three shocked sets of eyes glared at Tony, who had clearly embraced his new role as spokesperson for the group, but who rarely used salty language.

"Tony!" Shara scolded.

Collier smiled. "He's not wrong."

The tension broke and everyone chuckled.

"Man, that's what I'm talking about!" Jake crossed to his guitar stand. "You could rock it out a little if you did this with the lead guitar."

He started playing a harmony Collier liked. Collier picked up a harmony with his guitar and sang the melody, but stopped when Shara put a hand on his shoulder.

"Guys, I hear this as a duet."

"Shara, no offence. You hear everything as a duet." Tony shook his head.

"I'm serious. I hear a female voice doing this." Shara slid onto the piano bench and played the first verse, singing in a perfect, throaty alto. When she finished the verse, she said, "I hear two voices do something with the refrain."

Collier nodded. "Go ahead, you do the melody."

Shara did, and Collier worked his own bluesy harmony around hers. Tony and Jake stared at them.

"Okay, 'fess up, Shara. You knew he had this song before we came in this morning. He gave you a copy of it last night or something." Tony picked up Collier's scribbled notes and frowned. "What is this? Did flying monkeys write these notes?"

Shara grinned. "That is the only score for this song. Collier's been working on that for days and this is first time anyone's seen it."

"You've never seen this, and it's unreadable." Tony put down the music. "Then how can you add to it so perfectly?"

Shara shrugged. "You guys refuse to respect my genius." She waved at Tony and Jake. They recognized the dismissal, but both grumbled on the way out. She waited until they closed the door. "How long have you been in love with her?"

There was no lying to Shara. Collier shook his head. "Probably longer than I'm willing to admit," he shrugged. "First I had to realize I wasn't in love with someone else, so I lost time. And now it might be too late."

"It's never too late." Shara patted his shoulder. She cleared her throat. "Put the final touches on this one. I want to see what the fine music lovers of Rock Harbor think of this song, tonight, at Dave's. I'll sing the female part, but just tonight." Shara straightened and smiled. "Then, the next time you sing it, you'll have a different partner."

247

MIRA

Mira stared out the window. How many days had she been strapped to this bed. *One? Two? A week?*

It didn't matter. As long as she was still in Rock Harbor, she wasn't locked away for good.

From what she'd been able to squeeze out of the nurses, Madelyn spent quite a bit of time wrangling with Mira's psychiatrist. Madelyn wanted Mira moved immediately. The psychiatrist wasn't sure there was a need to commit Mira.

The idea that anyone pleaded her case gave Mira a tiny bit of hope. No one had been to visit her, not even Collier, since the first morning.

Not that I blame him. After all, what am I really? A junkie. I'm a Ritalin junkie who can't do anything worth doing without pills.

What about Otis? Maybe Carson could contact Otis?

The thought made her laugh.

"I don't see what you have to laugh about."

Madelyn's voice silenced Mira. "What are you doing here?"

248

Madelyn shot her a sickly sweet smile. "Today is a marvelous day. Today I finally convinced that provincial wad they call a psychiatrist that you are a danger to yourself and to others and that you need to be moved to a secure facility for no less than thirty days."

Mira absorbed the stomach punch in silence.

"I'm disappointed. No snarky comment? No whining complaint?"

Mira blinked. "How did you manage it?"

"Oh, I'm so glad you asked." Madelyn's smile widened into something twisted, macabre. "I got a bigger, better known, more respected psychiatrist to examine you."

"When did this happen?"

"Does it matter?"

"It sure as hell does to me."

"Miranda! Language!"

"Oh, no, Mommy, I think I get to use as much language as I please if it means someone listens!" Mira struggled against the restraints.

"Fine, since you asked, I'll tell you this. It doesn't matter what my psychiatrist said, his word is respected. What he says, goes. Actually…" She checked her lipstick in the mirror. "What I tell him to say goes."

"That's not how doctors work."

Madelyn looked at Mira's reflection in the mirror. "Poor, innocent, Miranda. Don't you get it yet? Money and power are the only truths in this world. I have money and the power. You have wrist restraints and an order to be put in a secure facility. Therefore, as far as anyone is concerned, I'm the one telling the truth."

Furious, Mira raged against the restraints. "You can't do this, Madelyn! You can't!"

Madelyn paused at the door. "Keep ranting like that. I won't have to say one more word. Between the scars on your arms and legs, and your temper, you look insane enough. They'll want to transport you right away instead of waiting until tomorrow morning."

Madelyn left the room. Tears streamed down Mira's face as she gave her restraints a final furious yank. Depleted, she fell against the bed and wept.

COLLIER

"Ladies and gents," Collier exhaled into the microphone. His hands trembled as he touched his guitar strings. "Thank y'all for coming out tonight." He glanced at Dave, who wore a fiery expression of disapproval. When Shara told Dave 'Teachers' Pets' was doing an impromptu performance he was delighted. When she informed him the finale was a song written and performed by Collier, he was less than enthusiastic.

"New songs and new singers don't fill the tip jar."

"Collier's played here before," Shara laughed at the big man. "Besides, I have made you wads of money. So tonight we're going to lay a new song on your crowd."

He pointed at Collier, "My dishwasher wrote this song and you're telling me it's worth putting on my stage?"

"That's exactly what I'm saying, Dave."

Dave seemed to give up the battle, until Shara left the office. "You." He growled at Collier.

"Yes?"

"This song best not suck, boy. Shara and I go way back, but if you're misleading her…"

"I doubt anyone could mislead Shara." Collier spoke with a confidence he didn't feel during that conversation, and he certainly didn't feel now, looking at a sea of expectant faces.

Shara cleared her throat, breaking Collier's concentration. He locked eyes with her, returning her smile. He felt better. "I'm honored to be sharing the stage tonight with 'Teacher's Pets'. Haven't they been great tonight?"

The crowd roared and Collier's nerves steadied. "Some time ago I came here to Rock Harbor to see if Shara could help my music career. One of the first things she told me was that winter comes early around here and lasts forever, but that it would help my writing because there wouldn't be much else to do. Being from the South, I had no clue just how long your winters are."

An appreciative chuckle rose from those at the tables.

"I've had a chance to experience winter for the first time. I can't believe y'all act like it's nothing to be outside chatting when a blizzard roars around you."

Even Dave had to laugh at that.

"In spite of the weather, Rock Harbor has become home to me, and you have become my family. So tonight I'm sharing a song I wrote about someone maybe you know. She's had more than her share of troubles and tonight she's in trouble. She doesn't even know she pulled me out of a dark place not long ago. I hope I can return the favor soon."

There was a smattering of confused murmurs as people shifted in their seats to look around for the mystery woman. Dave's icy glare reached the stage and heated Collier's face.

"Okay, anyway, I hope you enjoy it." Collier closed his eyes, and pictured Mira lying in the hospital bed, mired in dark secrets. He counted out a measure, feeling the weight of his guitar turn into her weight in his arms, the smell of beer and grilled burgers replaced with the smoky cold smell of her hair after the fire. As he started to play. Shara's voice floated through the first verse. He met her with his harmonies without conscious thought. Where he would have normally tried to make eye contact with one or more audience member, tonight all he saw was Mira's empty chair at the end of the bar.

He wasn't positive he'd actually played the song until he glanced at Shara who, along with the rest of the band, gave him a standing ovation. Blinking, he looked beyond the stage lights to the crowd who was also on its feet. At the back of the house, Dave looked pleased.

"That's your hit!" Jake shouted at him as they left the stage. "That's the song that's going to make your name immortal among the rock gods!"

"A little over the top, Jake," Tony shook his head as he helped Dan maneuver his wheelchair backstage. "But hey, it is awesome."

Shara hugged Collier and beamed. "Tell me you've got more songs."

"I do. I have several." Collier smiled. "But Shara's right. They're all duets."

The group calmed and looked at each other.

"Boy, I do know how to bring down a room, don't I?" Collier laughed, awash with optimism and humor. *It's all going to work out. Somehow Mira is going to make it back to this place and we are going to make the best music together.*

Collier's phone buzzed. He looked at the number, and realized it was Mira's. "Mira?" He had to shout over the cheers in the bar.

"Is this Mr. Collier James?"

Disappointment overwhelmed him at the sound of a male voice. "Yes. Who is this?"

"Mr. James, this is Carson."

"Carson…why do you have Mira's phone?"

"Sir, I have Miss Miranda's old phone. The one she supposedly disposed of some time ago. Fortunately, she did not. That's how I'm able to contact you."

A cold hand gripped Collier's heart. "What do you need to tell me?"

Collier listened with growing horror as Carson told him Madelyn's plan to commit Mira the next day. He motioned to Shara for a pen and paper and wrote down times and directions. "Okay, I think I have it. Thank you so much, Carson."

"I must stress something."

"What's that?"

"I will have to destroy this phone. If you are not able to keep Mira from being committed I must protect Dustin as best as I can. I can't do that if I'm fired."

"I understand, Carson. Thank you." He ended the call and stared at the floor, the euphoria of the evening evaporated.

"What is it, Col?" Shara put a hand on his arm.

"Mira's sister is having her committed to a secure facility for at least a month, probably more. They're leaving tomorrow afternoon. They're going to put her in the Waukesha County Mental Health Facility."

"Since when can they put anyone in Waukesha County? Don't they have to reside there?"

"They do. Carson just told me they moved to a place in Delafield three weeks ago, so they are residents of Waukesha County. After the Waukesha facility they are lining up a long term-place, somewhere with high security. They're making a case that Mira is a danger to those around her because of her addictions and violent behavior."

"Because of the Ritalin episode in Nashville?" Shara asked.

"No, they don't even know about that. They're pointing to her long time friendship with this Otis Drumm and the house fire." Collier paused. "And the cutting she's done to herself." He looked from face to face, waiting for someone to express surprise. No one did. "They did a tox screen on her this morning…that'll probably come back positive for Ritalin." Collier took a deep breath, ignoring the darkening expressions around him. "Madelyn's got her big time psychiatrist saying that the trip to Nashville is proof that Mira is a flight risk and might wander away at a moment's notice."

"Wander away at a moment's notice my ass," Jake growled. "We had that trip planned for months and she was slated to be on it for weeks before we left."

"And the hospital is buying this? What about the psychiatrist at our hospital?" Dan spoke quietly.

"Apparently big money wins." Collier said.

"Not always." Shara tapped her chin. "If I know one thing I know there isn't much that can't be slowed down with legal action. Collier, call your uncle. Get him up here now."

"It's awful late…"

Shara put a hand on Collier's shoulder. "Call him."

*

Archibald James arrived at Dirty Dog Dave's four hours later. Dave and Chanel poured endless cups of coffee and fried up mountains of eggs and bacon as the aged lawyer listened to Collier's story.

At the end of the litany, he sat in silence. He sipped coffee while every eye was on him. His watery blue eyes sparkled with mischief as he kept them waiting.

"I believe we're missing the real point of this case," he said softly.

"That Mira's really Dusty's mother?"

"No. That sort of thing happens all the time, Daniel."

"That Madelyn is really Mira's mother?" All eyes shot to Collier as he spoke. He shrugged. "Don't look at me. The other night, when I…fell, Molly introduced me to a nice lady named Gertie. She had a pretty strong memory about Madelyn being a pregnant teen."

Mr. James made a few notes, but shook his head. "I agree, that's very interesting, but that's not the bullseye that's going to stop Madelyn Anderson in her tracks."

"What, then, Mr. James?" Shara patted his hand.

Mr. James smiled. "The question no one seems to be asking is, who is Dustin's father? But, as I look around the table, my guess is at least one of you has giving the concept some fleeting thought?"

Collier nodded. "I have."

"Then perhaps we won't need these." Mr. James pulled several charts from his brief case.

"What are those?" Tony picked one up.

"One of my pastimes in my old age has been politics. Oh, I admit I've always been fascinated by the only profession more reviled than my own. In the last twenty years or so, however, I've really focused on rising politicians, these new 'young guns' some people call them."

"Senator Anderson is at the head of that pack."

"Just so, Miss Shara. I've been watching his career since he won his first election almost twenty years ago. If you look at these charts," he pointed to the pieces of paper they all held, "you'll notice Senator Anderson's always polled very, very high with the young voters. College students love him. College women, especially, love him."

"That's what it looks like on these first charts. But what's the second chart?" Tony pointed to the lower half of the sheet he held.

"Good catch, Anthony. The second chart on each page indicates his poll numbers immediately after he visited the college in each voting district."

"His numbers really die. Guess he's not as impressive in person." Jake chuckled.

"More importantly, his number really 'die' as you say, Jacob, among young women voters." Mr. James handed out a second set of papers. "Now, these charts I made shortly after Senator Anderson was married to Madelyn Pierce, who was, at that time, thirty. I believe Miss Miranda would then have been fourteen?"

Collier glanced at Shara, who nodded assent.

"Good. Well, you see in the first two years of the marriage, the pattern continues. But then, in the third year…look."

"There's no change in the polls. His numbers with young women stays the same or gets better."

Dan looked confused. "What am I looking at here?"

"Dude, he was banging college co-eds while on tour!" Jake clapped his hands. Everyone at the table glared at him. "Oh, what, I can't crack a joke? Come on, everyone says politics is showbiz for ugly people. So this guy is good looking. He gets out on the campaign trail and he gets plenty while he's out there." No one stopped him. "So then he gets married to Madelyn Pierce who, if you grew up in this town, you know is a royal ballbuster."

"Delicately put as always, Jake." Tony put his face in his hands.

"But he's married to her for a couple years, and nothing changes. His college booty palooza continues. And then it stops. It stops for maybe just over a year."

"That's correct, Jacob."

"So that means either The Senator stopped touring, which is not likely, or Madelyn Anderson found some sexy trick to keep him at home, which is also not likely."

Dan and Tony groaned at the mental image.

"But maybe he's got the best of it all right there in his house. Maybe he's got his tasty little sister-in-law…"

"Step-daughter," Collier corrected.

"Yeah, but doubtful he knows that. So maybe she's got a teenybopper crush on him. That just makes it easy for him. And why should he work so hard out in the field when it's right there at home?"

Tony shoved Jake off his chair. Both he and Dan scolded Jake loudly.

"Stop you guys," Collier said softly. "He's not completely wrong." Collier turned to his uncle. "Would these…hold up, in court?"

"Oh, my, no. These are just the scribbling of an old man. But I do have a document that will hold up." Mr. James pulled yet another piece of paper from his briefcase and handed it to Shara.

"What's this?"

"This is a copy of a parental termination. According to public records, Madelyn *Pierce*, not Madelyn Anderson, had begun the process of parental termination a few months ago. I can only surmise why there's been a delay, but I can tell you that if she is filling out this form it means that at the time of Dustin's birth Miranda Pierce never gave up her parental rights. Not legally, anyway."

There was a general cheer around the table, Collier remained somber. "How do we prove any of this? I mean, I thought about it, but with DNA testing, if The Senator is Dusty's father, then won't Madelyn win? Madelyn and Mira have the same DNA."

"The same. Not identical." Mr. James looked smug. "Let them test. Mira will, without a doubt, be named the biological mother. And, if Jake's theory is correct, and I believe it to be, The Senator will be named as the father. Which means..."

"Which means the man who wants to be our next governor had sex with a minor child in his care," Shara smiled. "That won't be good for Madelyn's ambition."

"They are going to attempt to move her later today?"

"Yes, Mr. James. That gives us a few hours to get some sleep before we go to the hospital." Shara helped Mr. James out of his chair. "You're welcome to stay at Molly's house again if you'd like."

"That sounds lovely." Mr. James waved to the guys. "Gentlemen, I'll see you all tomorrow."

Collier waited until everyone else left. Sitting alone at the bar, staring at the cold grounds in his coffee cup, he felt stronger, more determined than he ever had about anything.

Nothing is standing in my way. This time tomorrow, Mira will be safe, and where she belongs.

With me.

256

MIRA

Mira wrestled against sleep. A childish logic deep within her kept her awake, staving off the daylight. *I can't fall asleep. I can't fall asleep and let Madelyn take me away from Dusty forever.*

There had been weak moments, throughout the years, when she thought Madelyn might be the better parent, the more stable home. Paging through her memories like an old photo album, Mira realized that those were the moments when she felt alone and lost herself. *What did I have to offer him? What do I have to offer him now?*

Lying in a hospital bed, restraints on her wrists, her body and hair sweaty and unwashed, she realized she had one thing to give her son that Madelyn did not: Love.

I am his mother. I love him. I am the one who will provide for him because I love him. Nothing else matters.

I will battle Madelyn tomorrow and the next day and the next.

Feeling strong, she pushed the buzzer and asked the nurse for some food and water.

COLLIER

Shara and Collier pulled into the drive at the cabin as the first light of dawn broke across the sky. Shara exited the car, but Collier stayed in his seat.

"Col? Are you okay?"

"Yeah. I just…" He got out slowly and met Shara at the back of the bug., "Is there any chance I can drive over to the hospital?"

"I don't know, Col. You really should get some rest."

"I know, I know. I just…I want to be as close as I can to her."

"They won't let you in to see her."

"I know. I'll go and sleep in the waiting area. I promise, I'll get rest."

Shara sighed and smiled. "Molly will probably scold me, but I know exactly how you feel. Go ahead. We'll see you later in the morning."

*

He made his way through the hospital quietly, attracting no attention to himself. The early morning shift change on all floors provided Collier enough cover to get to the fourth floor. Settling onto a couch in a small room near the nurses' station, he let himself relax. *It's almost over, Mira. It's almost over and you and I are going to win.*

*

The elevator bell woke him. Sunlight streamed across his body. *How long have I been asleep?* He checked his phone. *Not that long. It's only eight in the morning.*

"We are here to move my sister. I have an ambulance downstairs."

Madelyn Anderson's sharp tone broke through the last of Collier's morning drowse.

What's she doing here so soon? Carson said they weren't moving her until late this afternoon.

"I'm sorry. We aren't releasing Miranda Pierce until four today. Dr. Dorian has to sign her out."

"Yes, well I'm a very busy woman and I'm here now. So you can call your Dr. Dorian and get him out of bed because I want this over as soon as possible."

Collier fumbled with his phone as he sent a mass text to everyone. *Madelyn here. Now. Trying to take Mira.*

The nurse paged Dr. Dorian, who arrived by elevator a few moments later. "Mrs. Anderson, you are early."

"Dr. Dorian, I want to be done with this business as soon as possible. I'm sure you understand."

"No, ma'am. I do not. I want to again say that I don't see any need for any of this."

"Then you're an idiot. So thank goodness I brought a real doctor. And he'll be here shortly, so I suggest you prepare my sister for transport. Now."

Collier knew Dr. Dorian was no match for Madelyn. He waited until Madelyn had moved to the far side of the nurses' station to make a phone call before moving down the hall to Mira's room. His lower back ached and his legs weakened with each step. *I should have grabbed my cane.*

He entered her room. She was still asleep, sunlight brightening her damp, greasy hair. "Mira," he whispered. He took a step into the room, wary now that he couldn't see down the hall. "Mira!"

She stirred awake. "Collier?"

The welcomed gratitude in her eyes was more than he could stand. He raced to her side and wrapped his arms around her. "Mira." He murmured her name over and over as he kissed her face and head.

"I can't believe you came."

"Mira, listen. We don't have a lot of time. They are coming for you. They are going to take you away."

"Now? I thought it wasn't until this afternoon…" Tears welled in her eyes.

"Your…Madelyn is here. Mira, I have to leave, but we have a plan to help you."

"You do?"

He pulled himself from her with great effort. Making his way to the door, he glanced out. The hall was still clear. "Yes. We have a plan. But you need to stall. You need to do whatever you can to make things difficult for them."

"What can I…" Her voice drifted.

"Mira," He was at her side again, his hands on her shoulders. "You can't fade on me. You need to make things as difficult for them as you possibly can." He grinned. "Just pretend they're me."

She grinned. "I know what you meant, Col, I was trying to think of the best way to make things difficult for good old Mumsy." She studied his face. "You don't seem shocked."

Collier shook his head. "Someday I'll introduce you to Gertie."

"I can't wait. But right now, don't you have to go?"

He held her face in his hands and groaned. "I love you, Mira." He kissed her lips softly, so he wouldn't frighten her with the overwhelming emotion he felt.

"Collier…" she whispered. "I love you, too."

He ached to stay with her. The idea of being separated now was more painful than he wanted to consider. The sound of footsteps closing in on her room sounded an alarm. He kissed the top of Mira's head one more time and moved as quickly as he could to the doorway. Peering out, he saw an army approaching. Nurses, doctors, even a police officer and at the back of it all, wearing an unabashed smile of victory, was Madelyn, flanked by two assistants.

Collier checked his cell. Nothing from anyone. He resent the urgent text and made a break for the stairwell door, right across the hall. Forcing the door closed, he was able to watch the parade enter Mira's room. He listened to her protests and knew she was fighting as hard as she could to delay any action.

I have to get outside, to the ambulance.

His path to the elevator was blocked. There was no way he'd be able to sneak through the throng in the hall without attracting attention.

The stairs, then.

Collier looked down the winding stairwell, counting the stairs, and trying not to think about what sort of pain and weakness would come from the jarring of each step. Gritting his teeth, he started down.

MIRA

"You can't move me yet. I'm not supposed to be moved until this afternoon." Mira stiffened.

"Miranda, really, what does it matter? The sooner we get you to a real hospital with real doctors who can take care of a person with your…problems, the sooner you will be well and you'll be able to return to our little family."

Mira did not miss the sour expressions of the hospital staff as Madelyn spoke. *I might have allies.* "I don't have any problems. Dr. Dorian is a real doctor and he thinks I'm just fine."

Madelyn offered everyone an exaggerated expression of patience. "Yes, you're just fine, you just need a rest in a proper facility closer to family."

"You want to lock me away. You want to lock me away because I'm an embarrassment to you and to The Senator. I dropped out of high school. I couldn't finish college. No matter what I did with my music, it wasn't good enough for you because it didn't involve your upper crust University people." Mira bit her lip, weighing the pros and cons of continuing her rant and revealing the dark family secrets. *I can't tell them the story. They'll all think I really am insane. I have to just focus on the embarrassment.*

"Mira, you have problems. That's why you couldn't finish school. We should have gotten you help, but you kept running away. And this last time, you ran all the way to Nashville, with such an unsavory set of people."

"You mean the music tour I did with Shara Brandt Jacobs and her band?" Mira glanced around the room, aware the effect her words had. Everyone in Rock Harbor had been touched in some way by Shara's generosity. *It might be something Madelyn doesn't know, but I do. No one in this town disrespects Shara and no one will take kindly to anyone who does.*

"I'm talking about when you ran off at Christmas to Nashville."

"Yes. That was our tour. Shara's band planned it months before and I'd been added to the schedule six weeks before we left." Mira paused for effect. "That wasn't running away, Madelyn. That was my job."

Madelyn looked like she'd choked on her own tongue. The psychiatrist she'd brought murmured a few words, then waved at Dr. Dorian. The doctors and Madelyn left the room.

"At least you made them stop and think," one of the nurses said and smiled at Mira.

But will it be for long enough?

COLLIER

Collier's legs threatened to fail him at the bottom of the last flight of stairs. He leaned against the door to catch his breath. With a push that took the last of his strength, he stumbled into the mid morning sun and crumpled to the ground. EMTs standing near the entry ran to him.

"I'm okay, I'm okay," he panted.

"I think we need to get a doctor to look at you."

If they take me back into the hospital I won't find my way back out. "No, no. I just need to sit down for a minute."

"Okay, here." They helped him to their ambulance where he sat on the back bumper.

"Can we call someone?"

"Molly Hunter…she's sort of my private nurse."

"Who?" The men looked confused.

So you boys aren't from around here. Which means this is the ambulance that'll take Mira.

"Never mind. Just let me find my phone…" He dialed Molly's number. "Hey, Molly? Yeah, I'm at the hospital. Yeah, it got bad a lot sooner than I thought. Can you come and bring Uncle Archie? Thanks." He put his phone back in his pocket. "I'll just sit here a minute, if you don't mind."

"Well we're here on a pick up and they're supposed to be down really soon."

Collier waved a dismissive hand. "Molly will be here long before you need to move."

He hoped he was right.

MIRA

The debate didn't last long and, given the look on Madelyn's face, Mira knew the result. She listened as the doctor gave orders to the nurse and attendants to load her onto another gurney, restrain her, and to move her to the ambulance downstairs.

"Wait!" she cried as the nurse unbuckled her wrists.

"What now?" Madelyn muttered.

"I haven't had a proper bath in days, just sponge baths. I still smell like smoke from the fire. I'd like to at least get cleaned up, maybe wash my hair?"

"I really don't have this kind of time. We have a long drive ahead of us. Miranda, I assure you, they will bathe you all you want once you get to where you're going."

"Ma'am, I could at least wash her hair properly." A young nurse patted Mira's shoulder. "No lady likes to travel with dirty hair."

Madelyn let out an exasperated growl. "You have fifteen minutes."

The room cleared again. The nurse peered out the door and whispered. "They've left a guard. I was hoping they wouldn't."

Mira gave her a grateful smile as the nurse unbuckled the restraints. "It's okay. We just need to stall. I have friends who are working on something."

"Well let's see how long we can stretch this fifteen minutes." The nurse grinned and handed her a towel.

Mira stayed in the shower until she heard Madelyn's enraged voice in the outer room. Turning off the water, she dried herself and slipped into the clean scrubs the nurse left for her. Feeling a bit more human, she emerged from the bathroom and climbed onto the gurney.

I did my best, Col. I hope it was enough.

Mira gripped the edges of her restraints and closed her eyes.

COLLIER

"They're coming down? Okay, we'll be ready for transport." One of the EMT's looked at Collier. "Okay, sir, I'm sorry, but our patient is coming down now and we have to be ready to load her. So I can help you inside if you want to wait for your nurse."

Collier waved his hand and tried to look more pathetic than he felt. *This whole not being able to walk thing would be great...if it wasn't true.*

He tried to ball his toes and make himself feel his feet. "I'll be fine, I will. I can wait over there on that very nice bench. Molly will be here soon."

"Okay sir, if you're sure?"

Collier nodded and stood. He tried to hide his surprise at his ability to do that much. With careful, measured steps he managed to make it to the side of the ambulance and out of the sight of the EMT's. He leaned against the ambulance, grateful for the balance it offered him.

Time is running out. They're going to load Mira and take her away and God only knows when or if we'll be able to find her then. Plus, if she's committed, it's going to make her battle for her son so much harder.

I have to buy her more time.

He groped his way along the side of the ambulance, the numbness increasing with each step. Unable to feel his legs, Collier tumbled forward, landing in front of the ambulance. He looked around and realized no one had seen his fall.

Okay, not the most heroic method of stopping them, but it'll work.

He dragged himself forward a few more feet so he was positioned directly in the path of the driver's side tire. He glanced over his shoulder to the parking lot. *No sign of Molly yet. What is taking her so long?*

265

MIRA

The elevator ride to the lobby was fast, too fast. Mira searched the faces of those in the elevator with her, all were blank. This was clearly a distasteful task for everyone involved and they were doing it with as much efficient detachment as possible.

Once in the lobby, she strained to see beyond the doors, hoping against hope that someone, anyone, was truly coming. Everything was a blur as they got closer to the doors.

Just as the doors opened, she caught sight of Molly Hunter crossing the parking lot. "Molly!" She screamed and strained against the restraints. "Molly!"

Molly broke into a run, leading an old man.

"Molly!" Mira flung her weight from side to side. The attendants pushing the gurney stopped.

Molly headed right for her, but suddenly changed direction. Mira couldn't see her because she was behind the ambulance, but Mira heard Molly's screams.

Everyone left Mira's side and raced to the source of the screaming. Only the old man continued toward Mira. There was a flurry of activity before he reached her as nurses and attendants ran back into the ER waiting room to get another gurney. A moment later, they rushed the gurney past Mira.

She caught a glimpse of the patient. "Collier?" She strained backward against the restraints. "COLLIER?"

As they rushed him down the hall, Madelyn exited the elevator. Seeing Mira unattended, Madelyn's eyes narrowed as she started toward her sister.

The old man beat Madelyn to Mira's side. "I'm Collier's uncle. I am your lawyer. Tell her I am your lawyer."

"What are you saying to her? Get away from my sister!" Madelyn grabbed the gurney rails and tried to pull it.

Rattled, and worried about Collier, Mira fought to focus. "He's...he's my lawyer." She pointed at Archibald.

"He's your what?" Madelyn stared blankly as if hearing a foreign language. "You're being ridiculous, Miranda. You are getting into that ambulance if I have to push you there myself."

"He's. My. Lawyer." Mira said loudly enough for the nurses in the hall to stop and take note.

"He is not your lawyer. You don't have a lawyer and we are getting out of this ridiculous town right now."

"I'm sorry, Mrs. Anderson, I cannot let that happen." The lawyer gripped the rails on the other side of the gurney.

Madelyn inhaled. It was a habit, Mira recognized, as Madelyn's last attempt at control. "And just who are you?"

"I am Archibald James, and I am Miranda Pierce's lawyer."

"The hell you are."

"I was enlisted for Miss Pierce yesterday."

"Who hired you?"

"Miss Pierce's employer."

"That filthy fat man who owns the bar where she sometimes sings?" Madelyn's lip curled in derision. "That fool doesn't have two nickels to rub together."

"As point of fact, the gentleman in question is one of the wealthiest men in the state. But that is neither here nor there. I was retained by Miss Pierce's employer, Shara Brandt Jacobs who owns 'Orphans and Runaways' recording studio. Perhaps you're acquainted with Mrs. Jacobs?"

Mira stifled a smile as the sound of Madelyn grinding her teeth filled the small space between their three faces.

"Very well, I'll play your game. What is it, exactly, Shara Jacobs wants with my sister?"

Mr. James leaned closer to Madelyn and lowered his voice. "Mrs. Anderson, you and I both know Miss Pierce is not your sister."

Madelyn blanched and stumbled back a step. "She told you? You can't believe a word she says. She's been an addict most of her life. Just ask the local drug pusher, Otis...something. He'll tell you."

Mr. James patted Mira's hand, but kept his gaze steady on Madelyn. "I assure you, Mrs. Anderson, my source of this information is unimpeachable."

Madelyn exhaled and gathered herself. "What of it?"

"I should think you'd understand this, Mrs. Anderson. But since I have to spell things out, perhaps you'd like to go someplace that's a bit more private?"

"I would not."

Mira did not miss the twinkle in Mr. James' eye. "Very well. Mrs. Anderson, I know Miss Pierce is not your sister, just as I know Dustin Anderson is not your son." He held up a finger to silence Madelyn's protest. "I also know that any DNA test we take of Dustin will show that your husband is, indeed, his father, and that Miss Pierce here is his mother. And any judge who can do math is going to be able to see that Miss Pierce was not of legal age when Senator Anderson…availed himself of her."

The color drained from Madelyn's face. She looked as if she were calculating a very difficult algebra equation. "What is it you want?"

"Our requests are very simple." Mr. James handed Madelyn a blue folder. "You will cease your attempt to adopt Dustin. You will drop your petition to have Miss Pierce committed."

"I will not. I can prove she's an addict. I can prove she's not a fit mother."

"And I can prove that while your daughter was in your care, your husband raped her and produced this child. Of course, if that's not enough I'm sure I don't have to search too many college towns to find young women willing to corroborate the theory I have regarding Senator Anderson's…extracurricular activities." Mr. James' expression held the faintest hint of a smile. Mira liked it.

268

"You can't prove the…second part." Madelyn turned a strange shade of gray and for a brief second Mira was certain she'd faint.

"That might be true. And in my line of business, not having proof is troubling. In your husband's line of work, however, unsubstantiated rumor, especially that of a salacious nature, might prove just as damaging in light of what we are able to prove about The Senator."

Madelyn straightened, cleared her throat, and handed the folder back to Mr. James. "If that's what you want, fine. She's all yours. And Dustin is all yours. You think this matters? You win, Mira. Happy?"

"Please direct any comments you have to me."

Madelyn glared at Mr. James for a beat before storming toward the door.

"Oh, and Mrs. Anderson?"

"What?" She did not look at them.

Mr. James cleared his throat. "Just one small thing, hardly anything in light of what we've managed to compromise on today. These activities of your husband's? They are certainly not indicative of the kind of behavior we expect in our next governor."

Madelyn whirled on her heel, her eyes red with rage. "You. Cannot. Be. Serious."

"I'm not saying this is the sort of thing that will completely destroy his political career, of course. This sort of thing rarely does. I'm just suggesting that someone with such…nontraditional hobbies might want to be less visible."

Mira wanted to laugh at Madelyn's expression. *She looks like she's choking on several marbles.*

Madelyn stormed through the doors of the hospital and out of their lives.

"Oh, Mr. James! Thank you!" Mira strained to hug him. He fumbled with the restraints for a moment, then freed her. She wrapped her arms around his neck. "Thank you so much!"

"My dear girl, thank me in a few hours when I have your son here at your side."

269

Tears welled. "You can do that?"

Mr. James nodded. "I have a very good friend in the administration office at St. John's. Dustin is quite eager to transfer to Rock Harbor Community School and live with his mother. He will be here later this afternoon."

Mira hugged Mr. James and wept on his shoulder. "I don't know how I'll ever thank you enough!"

"You should be thanking Collier. He's the one who figured out much of this on his own."

"Collier!" She sat up and glanced around the waiting room. "Where did they take him?"

"He's down the hall." Molly walked into the waiting room. "He'll be okay, but he really did a number on himself."

"What did he do?"

"Well." Molly wheeled the gurney around and started pushing it down the hall. "It seems he maneuvered himself down eight flights of stairs to make sure he could delay the ambulance until we got here. He even managed to lay himself out in front of the ambulance wheels, just so they couldn't drive. He's set his recovery back a very long time."

"His recovery?"

Molly stopped the gurney. "You don't know."

Mira blushed. "He and I haven't...we haven't spoken in several months. I mean, we were both at Dave's..." She brushed a tear from her eye. "I was so cruel to him."

"More than you know."

"What do you mean?"

"Miss Molly, I don't think we need to put this girl..."

Molly stared at Mr. James. "Mr. James this girl needs to know what's going on before I let her go barreling in that hospital room." She turned her attention back to Mira. "Collier was injured in that bus accident. He bruised his spinal cord. He was recently able to walk again because the swelling in his spine decreased and he worked at therapy. But the other night, when you pushed him to the ground, he landed on his back, aggravating the injury. Today he crawled down several flights of stairs and walked too much without his cane."

Mira closed her eyes and saw his face again, the night he came to her house. "He needs a cane. Oh Molly! I didn't know!" Tears streamed down Mira's face. She felt helpless and stupid. She felt like the person Madelyn said she was.

"Now, stop." Molly's tone softened. "It's not like Collier would listen to reason where you're concerned. He will move heaven and earth to protect you" Molly helped Mira off the gurney and walked her to Collier's room.

"He's been my hero more than once."

"He would never think of himself that way."

Collier was so still and pale, Mira thought for a wretched heartbeat he was dead. Then he turned his head and opened his eyes. There was a soft, joyful light glowing in his steel gray eyes. "Hey there," he whispered, "I knew you'd do a great job making things difficult for them."

"Oh, Col! What did you do?" She crossed the room to his bed. She took his hand in hers and wept.

"Shh..shh...hey, it's okay." He kissed her fingers and smoothed her hair. "Why the tears?"

"You...your legs...Molly said..." Mira couldn't control her sobs.

"Okay, okay, calm down. It's not as bad as all that. Really." He put an arm around her shoulders. "Come on, climb in here with me and calm down."

Mira sat on the edge of the bed. She wiped her eyes. "Col, I know what you did for me, and I want you to know…" she bit her lip, unsure of what to say next. "I want you to know I love you so much it won't ever matter to me if you can't…" She stopped and gulped air too quickly. She instantly hiccupped.

"Darlin', I love you too, and it's great that we're finally saying it out loud, but why do I feel like you're making some grand sacrifice?"

Dr. Scottie McCall entered the room, chart in hand. "Collier, I told you the other night you need to be more careful. You've definitely aggravated the injury and right now the swelling in your spine is severe."

Mira stilled, listening carefully

"What are you telling me?"

"It may be quite some time before you're able to walk without aid."

"So it's a good thing I can do my work sitting down." Collier grinned. "See? So I'll be okay."

"I recommend strict bed rest for at least a week."

Collier relaxed and pulled Mira closer to him. "Bed rest, you hear that? And Doc, would some sort of, oh I don't know, therapy…maybe massage therapy…would that be recommended?"

Dr. McCall snapped his chart closed and shook his head. "Musicians." He left and let the door close behind him.

"Yeah, musicians. You should probably run away now, while I can't catch you."

"I'm not running anyplace."

Collier grinned. "In that case, you owe me eighty bucks."

She pulled away from him and shook her head. "What, the money I took from your wallet? You owed me that."

"How do you figure?"

"The first night you showed up at Dave's. You distracted me. I told you, I was short eighty bucks."

"You've gotta be kidding me!"

271

"I am not kidding. When they put restraints on you, there isn't much to do but think. And I figured it out. I don't owe you a dime."

"We're really going to argue now?" He pulled her back to his chest.

"Of course not." Mira snuggled against his chest and closed her eyes. "But let's talk a little more about this massage therapy you're going to need." She giggled and met him halfway in a kiss.

SIXTEEN MONTHS LATER
<u>COLLIER</u>

Collier sat in the rocking chair enjoying the view. It wasn't the first time he was glad they'd completely torn down the charred remains of Mira's childhood home. "I'm not opening a music studio, I don't need a burned out house on the property," he'd told Shara.

Now, sitting on the porch of the wide, stairless ranch home they'd built with the royalties from their first album, he felt completely at home. With warm weather finally reaching Rock Harbor, Collier shed layers of clothing along with the rest of the town and enjoyed the short months of summer.

There was a new path worn through the tall grasses between the Jacobs' place and theirs. Dusty, now fourteen, loved horses almost as much as he loved playing bass guitar. He was a regular at the studio when he wasn't shadowing Bryan. *The kid is quick and he's talented. He's going to go places in the business.*

Accepting Mira as his mother had been easier for Dusty than anyone expected. The rest of the twisted family history was more difficult for him to handle. Collier knew Mira held back the worst of it. There would be time enough, when Dusty was older, to share everything. For now, Dusty's transition to life in Rock Harbor had been smooth and everyone was thankful for that.

Collier accepted his role in Dusty's life. He wasn't a father, he wasn't an older brother, and Dusty didn't call him 'uncle' like he addressed the other guys in the studio. There was an ease between the two of them and Collier was happy with that. It could have been so much more difficult, he knew.

As for difficult, the hardest thing Collier had to do each day was to hold his tongue every time a story about the now disgraced Senator Anderson or his ex-wife Madelyn popped up in the newspaper. Some woman with a child showed up one day with a positive paternity test. The Senator's proclivity for young women was uncovered. His political career ended bit by bit as women from all across the state went public. Finally, when his bid for reelection failed, Madelyn left him. Where either of them wound up, Collier didn't care.

"Turn on your computer!" Mira strode up the long drive to the porch. "I just checked the computer at the studio. Izzy sent an email to our shared account."

Collier reached for the laptop. Izzy wrote the best emails. He often felt like he was still there at the coffee shop, sitting in a circle with everyone, solving problems and eating cinnamon rolls.

"What does Izzy have to say?" Mira spoke with no trace of tension or jealously.

"It looks like that student of hers is going to make it to the junior nationals this year. They're headed to the Twin Cities. She's wondering if we want to meet them at a layover in Chicago for dinner."

"Hmmm. Will Quinn be there?"

Collier play punched her arm and Mira's laughter filled the air. "I imagine, but if we go you're just going to have to behave yourself."

"I can't promise anything." Mira moved her chair closer to him. "What else does she say? How's Cat?"

" 'Cat's tongue gets sharper every day.' I can imagine."

"Yeah, with Thor and Thorina, and Benny, she's got her hands full of poop."

Collier laughed. "Mira, they did not name that girl Thorina. They named her…" He scratched his head. "Okay, I haven't a clue what they named that baby. Who can keep it straight with those two having babies thirteen months apart?"

"Does it surprise you?"

"Nope. And neither does this. 'Benny has been keeping an eye on your apartment quite a bit lately. We're all convinced that he's spending time there with his *thoughts* and when you guys come into town you should probably disinfect the sofa.'"

"I miss that sofa." Mira patted his arm. "I have too many fond memories of that sofa."

"We'll get to relive those memories soon enough. We are on for the Bridgestone Center in September."

Mira clapped her hands. "That's awesome!"

Their album debuted at number one on two very different charts earlier in the year. They were number one on the country charts and number one on the independent/alternative chart. The cross appeal of Collier's blues and country harmonies mixed with

Mira's free, unfettered melodies was undeniable and their four month tour, starting in July, proved to be a hot ticket.

Shara was right about almost everything. Teachers' Pets will not open for us. Collier smiled at the thought. *They'll be our 'special guests.'*

It was a fair enough concession on the part of the band. With Collier working on material with Mira and Dan enduring multiple leg surgeries, there had been no touring. But now that the band had a tour bus equipped to handle wheelchairs, neither "Teacher's Pets" nor Collier and Mira could see a reason to stay off the road.

"I was thinking," Collier paused. He wasn't sure how Mira would react to his suggestion. It was a topic they'd discussed frequently, but never with any seriousness. "I was thinking maybe Dusty could play bass for us. You know, since I'll be playing piano. I think it would be a kick for the kid, and he's more than got the skills."

"Dusty? I don't know, Col."

"Oh, come on. You're going to get all 'conservative mom' on him now?"

"No, of course not. But it's a four month tour."

"And?"

"And he'll miss Homecoming in September. He was thinking about asking that cute Emma Shepaski, you know, the grade school principal's daughter. It's his first Homecoming, Col."

Collier shook his head. "So let him make the choice."

"Of course. After dinner."

"Lordy, I married a housewife from the 50's!"

"Lordy, I married a man who says 'Lordy.'" She bent to kiss him on her way into the house. "Hey, isn't that Dan's truck?"

Collier squinted down the drive. "It is. He said he had something to show me."

"No more playing chicken with the wheelchairs! I can't repaint the hall again. I just can't!"

"I can't promise anything." Collier grinned as she play punched his shoulder.

"Hey Col!" Dan parked his truck in front of the house. "Wait until you see what I got!"

Tony hopped out of the passenger's side and opened the
bed of the truck. "Just got this from the doc today. Talk about
sleek!"

Tony pulled a motorized scooter from the back of the
truck and pushed it to the driver's side of the truck. Dan slid
himself sideways onto the seat. "See? Slick!"

"That is cool! And it's a good sign, right?"

Dan wheeled the scooter up the ramp to the porch. It was
a ramp Collier no longer needed, but they left it for Dan. "It is.
I've got steel rods in both legs now. Docs say it'll take some
time, but I'll be able to walk before the year is out."

"Awesome!" Collier clapped Dan on the back. "Mira's
making dinner. How about if you guys join us?"

"Lead the way," Tony bounded up the ramp and stood
next to Dan.

Collier stood and opened the door. "Guests first." He
waved them in and then paused a moment, waiting for Dusty
who ran across the field to the house. "Hey Dusty. You made it
for dinner.

"Collier, can I talk to you a minute?"

"Sure, man. What do you need?"

"Do you...I mean, do you need to sit?"

Collier arched an eyebrow. "Should I?"

"I don't know. Maybe."

"Tell you what. How about if you tell me what's on your
mind and while we both sit?"

"Okay." Dusty sat next to Collier's rocking chair and
waited. Collier tried to put an authoritative look on his face.

"Do you...do you think you could be my dad?"

The question came like a blinding lightning bolt. A shiver
ran through Collier as he studied the boy, looking for any sign of
mockery. He found none. "What brought this on?"

"I dunno. It seems like now I'm in high school,
everyone's dad is involved. Even the ones who are dirt bags.
Their dads all come to stuff, unless they're in jail or something. I
never had a dad. I think I'd like you to be my dad."

A tear welled in Collier's eye, but he ignored it. "I would
love nothing more than that, Dusty. Do you want to...make it
official?" Collier hated his stilted tone.

"You and Mom got married, that's official. So, yeah."

Collier nodded. "I understand. Tell you what, I'll check with Uncle Archie and see what we need to do. It might take some time, but we'll get it done."

Dusty's smile was a study in relief, but there was obviously something else troubling him. "Col?"

"Yeah?'

"Maybe, you know, could I call you 'Dad?' Like starting now?"

Collier trembled as he stood. Dusty followed suit. "I would love nothing more than that." He embraced the lanky boy for a moment, awash in gratitude and joy.

Dusty grinned as they broke the embrace, his problem solved. "Great. Do I smell hamburgers?" He ran into the house, the screen door snapping closed behind him.

Collier paused on the porch, looking across the budding fields. He smiled.

Who knew this would ever happen to me?
I am Captain Freakin' America.

ACKNOWLEDGEMENTS

Thank you to my fantastic critique partners, Authors Linda Schmalz and Kelly Moran. You are both wonderful and I am a better writer for knowing you. (Find their brilliant work anyplace digital books are sold.)

Thank you to Carolyn Schultz for all your hard editing work. Welcome to the team, Carolyn!

Thank you to everyone who read "Fresh Ice" and demanded that Collier get his own novel.

Every author has a soundtrack when they write, and I have to acknowledge a few musicians/bands because without you, Collier and Mira probably wouldn't have their voices:

James Durbin, *New Minstrel Revue*, Little Big Town, *Barry Manilow*, Rick Springfield, *Delta Rae*, Sleeping with Sirens, *Ben Moody*, Corey Hart, *and of course*, **Toto**.

A Word about the Author:

Sarah J. Bradley is a lifelong Upper Midwest girl who lives in Wisconsin with her husband, two children, and four rescue cats. When not writing, Sarah loves finding restaurants offering great coffee and soup. She dreams of living next door to a Waffle House.

*

Thank you for purchasing this SJB Books publication. For other wonderful stories of romance, suspense, and humor, or to find out what's coming next, like us on Face Book:

www.facebook.com/sjbbooks

Also by Sarah J. Bradley

Dream in Color

Lies in Chance (Rock Harbor Chronicles #1)

Fresh Ice (Rock Harbor Chronicles #2)

Love is… (Rock Harbor Novellas)

Also from SJB Books

Not While I'm Chewing: Elsie W's FIRST Book
Sarah Jayne Brewster

Unsafe at Any Speed: Elsie W's OTHER Book
Sarah Jayne Brewster

 Missing in Manitowoc: A Nora Hill Mystery
S. J. Bradley

Superhero in Superior: A Nora Hill Mystery
S. J. Bradley

Made in the USA
Monee, IL
05 September 2023

42159527R00155